The Librarian

SALLEY VICKERS

PENGUIN BOOKS

PENGUIN BOOKS

UK | USA | Canada | Ireland | Australia
India | New Zealand | South Africa

Penguin Books is part of the Penguin Random House group of companies
whose addresses can be found at global.penguinrandomhouse.com.

First published by Viking 2018
Published in Penguin Books 2018
004

Typeset by Jouve (UK), Milton Keynes
Printed and bound in Great Britain by Clays Ltd, Elcograf S.p.A.

A CIP catalogue record for this book is available from the British Library

ISBN: 978–0–241–33023–4

www.greenpenguin.co.uk

Penguin Random House is committed to a
sustainable future for our business, our readers
and our planet. This book is made from Forest
Stewardship Council® certified paper.

For Philip Pullman and Jacqueline Wilson – two great storytellers –
and for Rowan Brown, who understands the importance of stories

'People can lose their lives in libraries. They ought to be warned.'

– Saul Bellow

I

Sylvia Blackwell was just twenty-four when in 1958 she took up the post of Children's Librarian in East Mole.

It was only her second real job. After a spell helping out at her local Boots lending library, she took a position as Assistant Librarian in Swindon. There, as an enthusiastic graduate from one of Britain's new library schools, she introduced some of her own favourite authors and was dispirited when *The Treasure Seekers* and *Comet in Moominland* remained on the shelves, their covers as pristine as the day she had unpacked them.

'I could have told you,' Clive Henderson, the Senior Librarian, said. He had worked at Swindon Library for years and considered that this experience had granted him a knowledge of Swindon's cultural tastes which the new Children's Librarian had been uppity in ignoring.

Sylvia stuck it out in Swindon for eighteen months before successfully applying for the post at East Mole. She moved from a bedsit in Swindon to a cottage in Field Row on the outer skirts of East Mole, a redbrick terrace which sat oddly amid the green of the surrounding meadows and petered out at number 5.

The rent for the cottage was low – almost alarmingly so, though on a librarian's salary Sylvia didn't feel inclined to argue with her landlady, Mrs Bird, on that score.

'It was my grandma's originally,' Mrs Bird had explained. 'Lived and died there. No inside WC, no bathroom or running hot water then and brought up five kiddies single-handed, more or less.' Mrs Bird's diminutive stature together with her jaunty little black-feathered hat made for a quite uncanny fit with her name.

Sylvia said that it sounded just what she was looking for and Mrs Bird gave her directions and said she would meet her at the address to take her round and show her the ropes. She arrived slightly late for their appointment, briskly shoved open the garden gate and ducked under a branch that overhung the path. 'Blessed tree. Next door won't see to it. Here you are then. This is number 5.'

The cottage's tiled roof was shaded by a tall ash tree and greened over with moss, which made it all the more appealing to Sylvia's innocent eye. Inside, the kitchen walls bore orange stains of damp but the window over-looked the garden and the sweating flagstones and the flaking distemper seemed to Sylvia, born and bred in Ruislip, rustic and picturesque. The sitting room, only slightly larger than the kitchen, was heated by an open fire. Up a steep flight of stairs, unlikely to be passed by modern building regs, were the two bedrooms.

Her landlady indicated the smaller of the two rooms. 'This is where my mum, bless her soul, and her sisters slept. They only had the one boy. He was sickly, poor lad. Died of pleurisy. Probably for the best.'

The bathroom, painted a patchy pale primrose, was fitted with a crazed water-stained basin. A chipped bath had been jammed in awkwardly at a partial angle beside it.

'The WC's downstairs by the kitchen. There wasn't a bath here before but we squeezed one in when we decided to let. If you need to go in the night you can always use that.' Mrs Bird pointed out a white china chamber pot. 'You're young and your bladder'll still be in good nick. You unmarried ones don't know your luck.'

Sylvia, whose mother had never openly referred to menstruation and had divulged the facts of life so obliquely that for years Sylvia had believed babies were conceived through a painful hospital operation, blushed.

Number 5's garden abutted a thistle-filled field in which two decrepit donkeys had been pensioned off to see out their latter days. The garden itself was overrun with impenetrable clumps of brambles and rampant nettles but Mrs Bird assured Sylvia that it would 'come back in no time'. She indicated an ancient plum tree. 'The fruit's all right for stewing but I wouldn't touch it uncooked – we used to eat them raw as kiddies and we got a belting when they gave us the runs.'

She stopped to survey a particularly dense patch of nettles. 'That's where my grandad grew rhubarb. He only grew it to spite the rabbits. One thing they won't eat. I don't s'pose you're handy with a gun? My grandma made a grand rabbit pie.'

Sylvia considered mentioning that Peter Rabbit's father

had been put in a pie by Mr McGregor but thought better of it.

'There's no phone. But next door but one'll let you use theirs if there's an emergency.'

Mrs Bird handed over a bunch of assorted keys and, having established that the rent was to be paid on the first of the month, hurried away to collect a grandchild from school.

Sylvia's possessions were easily accommodated in the cottage's limited space. A good deal of what looked like discarded furniture had been crammed into the tiny rooms. A lumpy-looking sofa, propped up on a brick where a leg was missing, was covered in a pink chenille bedspread and two chairs upholstered in shiny red chintz dominated the sitting room. An ashtray in the form of a scallop shell bore the legend 'Welcome to Cromer'. Sylvia, whose family holidays had been spent on the chilly Norfolk beaches, on the whole found this welcoming.

The larger bedroom was mostly taken up by a heavy wooden bedstead on which reposed a dauntingly high mattress. On the wall opposite the bedhead a text in coloured Gothic script announced uncertainly *'Surely goodness and mercy shall follow me all the days of my life.'*

There were no bookshelves on which to house Sylvia's principal possessions and after packing out the window-sills she stacked as many as she could on to the slanting shelves of the cupboard in the smaller bedroom. The rest of the books had to stay for the time being in the cardboard boxes from Swindon Library, Clive Henderson's parting gift.

But for all its apparent inadequacies, her new quarters offered promise.

Sylvia's life had hitherto been ordinary, insofar as any life can be called that. Her father held a minor managerial position in a firm based on London's Great West Road that sold soft drinks. Her mother was the daughter of one of the firm's salesmen, which is how the couple had met. Her mother had given up her job as a receptionist with the arrival of Sylvia. There were no other children. Sylvia had never liked to enquire, even inwardly, into the reasons for this but from the time her father came home from the war there had been separate bedrooms, which supplied an answer of a sort.

Sylvia's school reports were middling. 'Sylvia must learn to buckle down to her studies' and 'Inclined to dream' were typical assessments. Only Miss Jessica Jenkins, the Children's Librarian at her local library, had a sense that there was more to the girl than met the eye.

Long hours spent alone in her bedroom had encouraged in Sylvia the habit of reading, often by torchlight under the bedclothes far into the night. On Saturday mornings, while her father read the papers and her mother made a martyr of herself over the household chores, Sylvia got in the way of walking down to the library, unescorted – for with the recent perils of German bombs no longer a threat no other possible dangers to a child were envisaged – where Miss Jenkins had set aside books she thought the young girl might enjoy.

Librarians are not alone in having favourites among their clientele but a shared love of reading is an especially powerful bond. It was through Jessica Jenkins that Sylvia met those versions of reality, the characters in fiction, who if not larger than life can become a shaping influence and an inner guide.

Early practice in negotiating her mother's moods had made her, superficially, easy-going and she was not without friends. But in this way, books became her silent allies and sometimes her more-than-friends.

For all the dreaminess that vexed her teachers Sylvia did well enough to gain a place at the new London library school, near enough for her to continue to live cheaply at home. 'A job with a proper future,' her mother said approvingly when her daughter revealed her career plan. Hilda Blackwell was privately relieved that her daughter's surprising success as Bottom in the school production of *A Midsummer Night's Dream* had not, as she had for a time feared, led to a demand to go to drama school.

Apart from reading, the only other notable passion in the Blackwell family was chess.

Sylvia's father had been taught the game by a young Czech officer for whom he had crewed during his war years in the RAF. The officer had been part of the attack on Bremen and had not returned from the raid. Norman Blackwell, who had injured his arm, had been stood down for the flight and he felt the inevitable guilt of the survivor. The death of the young officer who had lost his family to the Nazis affected his tail gunner in a way for which he had no conscious words. The dead man had revealed in Norman Blackwell an unexpected flair for chess and when Pavel Prager was reported killed in action there were no living relatives to whom his few possessions could be conveyed.

'You might as well have this, Blackwell,' the mess sergeant had said, handing Norman the chess set with which he had learned the game.

Perhaps out of respect for his dead commanding officer, or perhaps in default of anything else to give her, Norman Blackwell had attempted to pass on this interest to his only child. In the evenings, when Sylvia had finished her homework, while her mother listened to the Light Programme on the wireless, Sylvia and her father would sit opposite each other over the kitchen table and play with the inherited chess set.

Sylvia was not a natural at chess but she was a sensitive child who divined an unmet need in her father and out of loyalty did her best to master the game. Chess players, however pacific in other areas of their lives, are ruthless when it comes to chess, and in spite of his best efforts for years it was impossible for her father not to beat his protégée. It was a defining moment for them both, one Sylvia never forgot, when she contrived one evening to checkmate her father.

'You might as well have this,' her father had said, unconsciously repeating the words with which he had been given the modest wooden box on which the scratched initials of his lost colleague were still visible. 'With you gone, I shan't have anyone to play with.'

2

East Mole – if there ever was a West Mole it had long vanished into obscurity – was one of those small middle-English country towns whose reputation rests on an understanding that it has known better days. Back in the late nineteenth century the town had been blessed by the patronage of the Tillotson sisters, teetotal spinsters from a branch of a local family who had made their fortune in gin. The sisters had chosen to purge any alcoholic taint in the family blood with a substantial legacy to East Mole, a charitable act which had produced the Town Hall, the Assembly Rooms and the library.

These buildings, redbrick, unashamedly ugly, with little towers serving no apparent purpose and displaying florid plaques announcing the dates on which they were ceremonially opened by long-gone local dignitaries, were trenchant examples of late-Victorian civic taste. Funds had also been left by the sisters for the buildings' upkeep. But over time, two world wars, a series of incompetent investments, together with an increase in running costs had reduced the financial management of the buildings to a source of recurring headache for the council. The frugal Tillotson sisters, who had passed a lifetime of self-imposed thrift, would have been appalled at the speed with which the family money had apparently leaked away.

The cottages that made up Field Row also had a connection with the Tillotson sisters. Their brother had set up a foundry by the canal to make a winnowing machine that he had designed and patented in the expectation of a handsome return and the cottages had been intended for the foundry workers. Neville Tillotson was not as shrewd as his sisters; agricultural machinery took a different turn and the foundry failed. By the time Sylvia moved to East Mole the foundry's crumbling remains had become the dangerous playground of the local children.

Sylvia was standing in number 5's overgrown garden when she first encountered one of the Field Row children. In fact three children, but two were concealed behind brambles.

'I'm Sam,' the boy said. He was wearing a knitted Fair Isle pullover of the kind Prince Charles could be seen wearing in newspaper photographs and he looked about ten, the young prince's age. Unlike the prince, at least in the press photos, this boy's knees were muddy and copiously scabbed. But his tone had something of the House of Windsor's self-possession.

'Hello, Sam, I'm Sylvia,' Sylvia said.

'We're from number 3,' the boy explained. 'My mum did this out when it was let.'

His proprietorial manner became clearer. Mrs Bird had confided that they couldn't make a go of it as a holiday business.

'Your mother cleaned the house when it was a holiday home?' Sylvia enquired.

'We were let play here.' The grey eyes scrutinised her steadily.

A movement among the brambles alerted Sylvia. 'Are there more of you?'

'Jem and Pam's in there. They're hiding.'

'Tell them they can come out. There's no need to hide.'

The boy addressed the brambles. 'You two, come on out!'

A pair of smaller girls, identical and dressed in matching gingham frocks, appeared. The only distinguishing marks that Sylvia could detect were the coloured hair ribbons that adorned their bunchies.

The boy followed the direction of Sylvia's gaze. 'Jem's the red, Pam's is green. Only they swap to muddle us so you can't tell mostly.' Their brother had something of the air of a ringmaster in charge of a couple of temperamental circus animals.

'Which is which today?' Sylvia asked.

It seemed that if they were to be believed on this occasion the twins were sticking to their assigned colours. 'She's Pamela. She's Jemima.'

'Like Jemima Puddleduck?' Sylvia asked, and regretted this when the boy scowled. 'She's in a book,' she explained. 'I'm the new librarian for the Children's Library.'

'We don't go there – much,' Sam said. It was apparent that the 'much' was added for reasons of tact.

'Well, perhaps you'd like to come and visit me there. What do you like to read?'

The boy considered. 'I like the *Beano* and the *Dandy*. The *Topper*'s all right. What I don't like is that sissy Dan Dare.'

The twins unbent sufficiently to say that they liked *Playbox*.

'They can't read it,' their brother said. 'They just look at it in wet playtime.'

'We CAN read,' one of the little girls shouted. 'We just don't say.'

It appeared that the children at number 3 were not obviously acquainted with any actual books. Sylvia, hoping that this was not to be Swindon all over again, suggested, 'How about Enid Blyton?'

'Noddy's only for the Infants,' Sam said scornfully. 'Stupid little twit.'

'Mrs Stewart reads it us,' Jem offered. 'I liked it when he was got by the goblins and they took off all his clothes.'

Setting off on her bike the next morning, Sylvia encountered the children's mother hanging out washing on a rotary clothes line.

'Our kids any trouble, you send them straight back here. They got used to playing in number 5 when I was doing the change-over.'

Sylvia said it was fine and maybe the children would like to earn some pocket money helping to clear the brambles.

'They'll help you for nothing or they'll get what for. I'm June, my husband's Ray – Ray and June Hedges. Anything you need, phone or anything, you pop round to ours. Next door's funny. You'll see.'

June explained that numbers 1 and 2 in Field Row were empty and the properties had been boarded up. So far Sylvia had had no sighting of any inhabitants of number 4, though, other than the aged apple tree whose boughs hung untidily over her garden path, the regimented beds in next door's front garden suggested fussiness. She cycled along the potholed tarmac which fronted Field Row, speculating on her neighbours.

It was over a mile into town along the towpath which ran by the canal that had served Neville Tillotson's ill-fated foundry. She passed a lock, with a lock-keeper's house, and on the outskirts of the town the biscuit factory where much of East Mole's female population was employed. The main road took her past the cottage hospital and the swimming baths. She arrived at the steps of the library half an hour before opening time.

Her boss, Mr Booth, the Senior Librarian, met her in the hall. 'Welcome to East Mole. I hope you'll be as happy here as I am.'

Ashley Booth had been a part of the interviewing panel when Sylvia applied for the job. A heavy-jowled man, wearing a bow tie and with liberally Brylcreemed hair, he had not given an impression then of any great content-ment with his lot.

'Miss Blackwell, what characteristic would you say is most important in a children's librarian?' he had asked her.

Sylvia had said that she thought it was maybe imagination. Mr Booth's response to this had not promised well. 'Imagin-ation is as imagination does, Miss Blackwell,' which, when you thought about it, Sylvia said to herself, made no sense.

Anxious to put any bad feeling behind them, she smiled

now and said she was sure she would be happy in East Mole. Mr Booth's expression suggested that might be doubtful. He escorted her to a chilly little L-shaped room furnished with a couple of scruffy armchairs and a Formica-topped table on which stood a bottle of Camp coffee, some assorted cups and saucers and an ashtray advertising Bass beer.

'This is the staff room. There's a gas ring down the hall for tea or coffee. I don't know if you smoke but if so here's the place. Obviously we don't allow it in the library.'

Years of concealment from her parents had sapped Sylvia's natural candour. 'Oh, I don't smoke.'

Mr Booth's expression suggested he was not to be taken in by this. 'Our part-timer does. Like a chimney.'

'Part-timer?'

'Mrs Harris,' Mr Booth said darkly.

The Tillotson legacy had allowed for substantial premises and the Children's Library, down the corridor and past the Reading Room, had a large room to itself.

Sylvia's brief inspection on the day of her interview had revealed an outdated collection, much of which would hardly pass for children's reading in the twentieth century. Sir Walter Scott, for example, occupied several shelves; also Dickens, Shakespeare and John Ruskin, including a number of copies of his three-volume *The Stones of Venice*, a work which few of even the most enthusiastic adult readers manage to complete. Charles Kingsley, Mrs Molesworth and other once-fashionable Victorian writers known for their concern for the higher morality were also heavily represented.

The rest of the books, she saw now, were well-known

favourites: *Little Women*, *Heidi*, Biggles, *Just William*, Billy Bunter, several copies of *The Swiss Family Robinson* muddled in with a popular series about a girls' chalet school in Switzerland and quantities of Enid Blyton.

That the Children's Library was allotted a much larger budget than she had had at her disposal in Swindon had made the position especially appealing to Sylvia; but first the books already there needed to be got into better order. Whatever system of cataloguing had been in place appeared to have been long abandoned. Apart from the solid rows of Dickens and Walter Scott and the lofty Victorian moralists, the other authors had apparently been put back on the shelves anyhow.

At lunchtime, Mr Booth appeared in the staff room, where Sylvia was eating sandwiches. 'How was your first morning? I trust you got on all right.'

'I think we maybe need to re-catalogue the whole library, Mr Booth – I mean, the children's part only, of course.' Her boss's expression indicated that if she chose to act like a madwoman it was her own affair. 'I was wondering if maybe the part-timer, Mrs Harris, you mentioned, could help?'

'Do I hear my name being taken in vain?'

A stocky middle-aged woman was standing at the doorway. Her scent, gardenia, or something equally pungent, filled the room.

'Dee Harris at your service. Diana by birth but my friends know me as Dee.'

Mr Booth frowned. 'Good afternoon, Mrs Harris.' He made no introduction so Sylvia introduced herself.

'Brave girl coming here. They couldn't get anyone else.

He won't like me telling you that' – Mr Booth's frown deepened – 'but all's fair in love and war.'

Sylvia, who had read some Freud, sensed a history beneath this apparent irrelevance. But at least the part-timer seemed well disposed towards her.

'I was wondering if you might help me to reorganise the children's section?'

This apparently struck Mrs Harris as hilarious. 'That'll take a month of Sundays and no mistake. Hasn't been seen to since God knows when.'

She directed a look at Mr Booth, who returned a furious stare and left the room.

Mrs Harris laughed again. 'No love lost between yours truly and His Lordship.'

3

Sylvia was a little puzzled to learn that in Dee's case 'part-timer' meant volunteer.

'You mean you're not paid?'

'Doesn't bother me. It means His Lordship can't sack me.'

'But why would he want to sack you? Surely extra help should be welcome.'

'You've a lot to learn about Ashley Booth!'

The work of reorganising the books in the Children's Library was, as Dee had intimated, a major undertaking and she offered to come in some evenings to help out.

'It gets me out of the house when he's off with his boys.' Her husband, she explained, ran a club called the Woodlanders for the male youth of East Mole.

To aid the task, Dee had brought in some cardboard boxes from the local grocer's. 'Osborne's deliver Tuesdays and Thursdays,' she explained. 'Means I can walk home with nothing heavier to carry than a packet of Senior

Service. God knows who we can palm some of this lot off on.'

Sylvia had suggested that maybe to gain space Sir Walter Scott and Ruskin could be sold off. 'They're not exactly children's reading. And the one book by Ruskin you could say is suitable, *The King of the Golden River*, isn't here.'

'I think you'll find they're all Tillotson legacies which under the Trust we have to house.'

Sylvia had heard mention of a Trustee at her interview. 'Who is this Trustee exactly?'

Dee shrugged. 'Some old relative of the Tillotsons. His Lordship trots her out when he wants to get his way.'

Sylvia had turned her attention to Charles Kingsley. 'I suppose people do still read *The Water Babies* but I'm not sure about Mrs Molesworth.'

The flyleaves of Mrs Molesworth and her fellow moralists were inscribed with uplifting messages in faded ink.

Sylvia opened *A Child's Illustrated History of Palestine* and read out, '"To dear little Edith, May you walk for ever in the Paths of Righteousness. From her Loving Cousin Win." Oh dear! But *The Trail of the Sandhill Stag*, and all the old Ernest Thompson Seton animal books can certainly stay.'

Dee was on a chair, inspecting an upper shelf. 'We could quietly ditch most of these – they've not been taken out for donkey's years. *Stories of the Patriarchs, Jesus at Play*, I ask you!' She took out *Stories of the Patriarchs* and opened it. A dead moth fell out. 'Christ Almighty! I wonder how long that's been there. *Caring for Your Guinea Pig*. How about this one? *The Joys of Obedience*. I can see that going down a treat with today's kids, I don't think!'

'Maybe not *The Joys of Obedience*,' Sylvia conceded, 'but someone might be very glad of a book about guinea pigs. What about your husband's Woodlanders?'

Dee guffawed. 'All they're interested in is tits and we're not talking the feathered variety.'

With the books somewhat better organised, Sylvia felt it was time to tackle the borrowers' details. Their cards were lodged in a solid-looking oak filing cabinet but when she tried it none of the drawers could be opened.

Mr Booth looked irritated when she asked what she should do about this. 'I'm sure I don't know, Miss Blackwell.'

'But how do we keep track of the books? To be frank, Mr Booth, it isn't at all clear exactly who has what.'

'I really can't answer for how it was managed. Miss Smith was in charge of all that.'

Miss Smith, Dee had confided, had left her employment after rumours of a nervous collapse.

That evening Sylvia called round at the Hedges'.

Mr Hedges was fixing the gate in the front garden. 'Evening. Our twins swing on this and it comes off its hinges. You're our new neighbour.'

Sylvia agreed that this was the case.

'Go in, do. The door's open if you don't mind dogs. The wife's inside.'

'Actually, Mr Hedges, it's you I'm hoping can help me.'

She explained about the filing cabinet. 'I was wondering if I could maybe borrow some tools.'

Mr Hedges said to call him Ray and that if she went in he would join her once he had seen to the blasted gate.

Hysterical barking met Sylvia as she opened the door

and a pair of excited Scotties rushed at her ankles. A voice from the kitchen shouted, 'Melanie, Misty, get down.'

With Melanie and Misty still yapping at her feet, Sylvia found her way to a kitchen, where June Harris was hanging washing on a wooden airer.

'Sorry about them. D'you like dogs?'

Sylvia, who had vainly pestered her mother for a pet, said that she did.

'I'm not a dog fan myself but he's always had dogs and the kids like them.'

The Hedges children summoned for supper reintroduced themselves. Or rather Sam did. 'That's Jam and that's Pem.' The little girls looked solemn as their brother collapsed on to the floor in a fit of laughter. 'Bet you can't tell which is which now.'

'Samuel, behave yourself,' his mother said indulgently.

Sylvia explained why she had come. For all her children's apparent ignorance of books, June Hedges seemed abreast of the goings-on in the library.

'Miss Smith, the one before you, left very sudden. Funny little soul. They say your boss and her were – you know.' June made a suggestive face.

Although Sylvia was familiar with adultery in literature, she had so far had no knowing encounter with it in life. 'Mr Booth? But isn't he married?'

'No one's hardly seen the wife. He keeps her locked away, unless he's done her in.'

'Like Bluebeard?' Sylvia wondered. She found Mr Booth's appearance and manner repellent and wasn't sure whether to be alarmed or intrigued by this glimpse of a shady side to her boss's character.

Ray came in and requested tea. He kicked out Melanie and Misty, who had been masturbating frenziedly against Sylvia's shins. 'Blimming dogs. Now, what exactly d'you need these tools for?'

Ray, his wife had explained, being an electrician, was handy. It was agreed that he would go down to the library to see what he could do about the filing cabinet.

'Can I come?' Sam was lying under the table, kicking the underside. The twins had disappeared into their bedroom.

'Miss Blackwell doesn't want you bothering her, Samuel.'

But Sylvia was delighted at the chance of a new recruit. 'I'd be glad to show Sam the library. And it's Sylvia, please.'

'Not when Miss Blackwell's working, mind,' June ruled.

Ray biked over to the library with Sam on the handlebars the following evening. Sylvia was sitting outside on the steps waiting for them.

'Lovely evening. Makes you glad to be alive.' Ray, it appeared, had the happy knack of ready enjoyment.

A company of birds with raggedy wings were performing swooping ellipses in a near-cloudless sky. Sylvia pointed to them. 'The birds look as if they think so too.'

Ray had taken off his cap as if out of respect for the wheeling birds. 'Rooks. My old dad, God rest his soul, used to shoot them for rook pie. But I'd rather see them like this.'

Sam said, 'Rook pie! Grandad made us eat it when we went round Saturdays.' He made a retching sound.

'Now, now,' said his father.

The filing cabinet turned out not to be locked at all but merely jammed with great wodges of cards. Ray prised the drawers open with his screwdriver.

It looked as if at some point a mouse had got in: most of the cards were fretted at the edges. Somehow, water must have penetrated, leaving them stuck together in inseparable clumps. Sylvia spread them out on the library table.

'You could try drying them out in the sun,' Ray suggested.

Sam was looking at the shelves of books. 'Are there any comic annuals?'

'No,' Sylvia said. 'But there's other books you might like.'

She tried to interest him in Biggles but he waved that aside contemptuously and picked out a copy of *Coral Island*. 'What's this about?'

'He's been to the Isle of Wight,' his father explained.

'I don't honestly know, Sam. It's supposed to be a classic but to tell you the truth I've never read it.'

Sam opened the book, skimmed a page and put it back. 'You got anything about pirates?'

'There's this.' Sylvia took *Treasure Island* from the box Dee had labelled 'Give Away'. 'We seem to have several copies so you can have this one if you like.'

'What do you say?' Ray looked meaningfully at his son who was flicking through the pages.

'Does anyone get put to death in it?' Sam asked.

Sylvia carted the library cards back to number 5, where she peeled apart as many as she could before deciding to abandon them. It was a fine evening so she took her supper of biscuits and cheese outside. One of the donkeys in the field ambled over to the fence and stood observing her with its large brown eyes.

The closest Sylvia had come to a donkey was in the school production of *A Midsummer Night's Dream* when, wearing a papier-mâché ass's head, she had been wooed by Rita Shepherd as Titania. Slightly nervous, she offered the living creature a cream cracker. The black whiskery lips rolled back to reveal gleaming spotted gums and a set of long yellow teeth. But the donkey snaffled up the offering most delicately from her palm.

'That one's Doris. She's safe enough. You want to watch Boris, though. He can bite.'

A man, perhaps in his late sixties, was looking into her garden. The evening sun, shining through a fuzz of hair around a pink freckled scalp, gave him a gingery aura.

'Jeremy Collins, from number 4, your immediate neighbour.'

'I'm Sylvia Blackwell,' Sylvia said, noting the 'immediate'.

'I'm the chair of the Library Committee,' her neighbour announced. 'I read your references.'

'Oh,' Sylvia said, wondering if she should thank him for his support, though it was by no means clear from his expression that he had given it. 'I was very pleased to get the job.'

Her neighbour ignored this. He gazed past her at the savage-looking nettles which marked Mrs Bird's grandfather's rhubarb patch. 'You're going to have your work cut out with that garden.'

'To be honest I feel a bit overwhelmed.'

Mr Collins' pale eyes swivelled round to a leggy shrub

growing out of the kitchen wall. 'That buddleia wants seeing to or it will pull down the brickwork.'

'Oh dear.'

'They spread like nobody's business.' His little mouth, a petulant pink rosebud, reminded her of a portrait she'd once seen of Henry VIII.

'I'm afraid I'm not much of a gardener,' Sylvia confessed. Perhaps this could be a bond with her 'immediate' neighbour. 'Maybe you could advise me, Mr Collins, what to do with it.'

'Poison,' said her neighbour and turned back towards his own buddleia-free garden.

Boris, Doris's supposedly more aggressive mate, wandered to the fence and stood there, stockily expectant. Ignoring her neighbour's warnings, Sylvia offered him a cream cracker. The donkey stared at her placidly then softly hoovered up the biscuit from her hand.

Sylvia laid her hand against the donkey's warm shaggy neck. 'You're not a danger, are you, Boris? You're as gentle as a lamb.'

She had taken a book outside with her supper but now she set it aside to watch the small birds threading deftly through the maze of brambles, occasionally daring, not too near her feet, to flit down to peck up crumbs. One tiny bird, perched sentinel on a high-flung bramble, began to throw its thin voice out into the yellowing sky. It was not, she thought, an especially tuneful sound; it was more like the syncopated syllables of some old language – possibly an ancient Eastern one, whose script would be hieroglyphic – that with diligent study she too might be able to acquire.

Across the fields she heard the East Mole Town Hall clock chime. The shade of a moon had risen and was hanging in the light sky like a tissue-paper globe lantern. Peace seemed to drop around her with the dew as she sat planning her new life and all she meant to accomplish at the library.

4

'Can you suggest where I might put up notices, Dee? I want to try to attract more children to the library.' It was one of Dee's days for coming in.

'You could try the Co-op Guild or the WI.'

Next to the stationery cupboard was a Roneo machine, which worked by laboriously turning a cumbersome rolling drum to make copies in purple ink. Impossible to use, Sylvia found, without badly staining one's fingers.

She had prepared what she hoped was an all-purpose announcement:

EAST MOLE CHILDREN'S LIBRARY
MONDAY–FRIDAY 9 A.M.–5.30 P.M.
SATURDAY 9 A.M.–12.45 P.M.
NEW READERS AND OLD
ANY AGE ALL WELCOME
Sylvia Blackwell
Children's Librarian (by appointment)

The 'by appointment' was an afterthought and possibly rash.

She was busy duplicating copies of this when Mr Booth found her. Dee had counselled against advising him of this step.

'He'll only find a reason to object.'

'How can he object to my raising the library's profile?'

'He'll find one, you'll see, or you can cut my legs off and call me Shorty.'

Mr Booth picked up one of the notices and clicked his teeth. 'Where do you propose displaying these, Miss Blackwell?' So there was to be no threat to Dee's legs.

Sylvia explained her plan to approach the Co-op Guild and the WI.

'I suppose the Co-op was Mrs Harris's idea?'

'I've talked this over, naturally, with Mrs Harris, Mr Booth. She's been very helpful writing out the names for the new borrowers' cards.'

'I don't believe we can say that "all' are "welcome". There are, for instance, gypsies.'

Gypsies sounded romantic. 'Goodness, are there gypsies in East Mole?'

'There have been. Some of our valuable Ruskins disappeared. And, I believe, a first-edition Carlyle.'

'Surely not from the Children's Library, Mr Booth?'

The plum-coloured veins on Mr Booth's cheeks deepened. 'In our benefactors' day Carlyle was read by children. We had a number of handsome volumes.'

'Gypsies, my eye! More likely he sold them,' Dee said, when Sylvia reported this conversation. 'He sells them off to a chappie in Salisbury who deals in antiques. He'll have cooked up that story about gypsies to explain their disappearance.'

'Really, Dee?' Even Clive Henderson at Swindon would have had more respect for the books.

'Like I said, you've a lot to learn about Ashley Booth.'

Sylvia was sitting in the garden enjoying the last of the sun and the sound of birdsong, when June Hedges called round with a trug of wallflowers.

'I thought you might like these to drown out the smell of damp indoors.'

It was true: number 5 did smell dank. Sylvia inhaled the scent of the velvety gold and tawny flowers. 'Thank you, June. These are gorgeous.'

'Ray grows them between his bean rows. I'll bring some of them round when they come on. We have runners coming out of our ears.'

June stayed for a cup of tea.

'Do you know anyone in the Co-op Guild or the WI, June? I'm trying to get more children to use the library and Dee suggested I might recruit their support.'

'The WI's easy. My mum's a member, though she's poorly and not been able to get there lately. The Co-op Guild I think you have to be Labour to join.'

'Are you not Labour?' Sylvia was surprised.

'Ray votes Tory. He says Macmillan was educated to know how to run the country. Mind you, next door's a Tory councillor and Ray can't stand him. My dad's a Labour councillor – he grew up in the East End. I don't really bother.'

'You don't vote?'

'What's one vote going to do?'

Sylvia, whose twenty-first birthday had fallen just before the last General Election and who had met her first chance to vote with excitement, felt slightly put in her place. 'I suppose if everybody thought that . . .'

'I know what you're thinking. "People better than you went to prison for you to get the vote." Dad says that.'

June stretched and smiled comfortably at her own short-comings. With the sun on her big bare arms, she looked for a moment like a pagan goddess. I don't know anything, Sylvia thought. All this carry-on about the library just makes me sound silly.

'Sam's really taken to that book you gave him,' June said suddenly. 'I've never known him read a book before. He made us die laughing last night, tapping round the table with my umbrella, playing some blind fellow. Ray was in fits.'

The following day, as Sylvia was wheeling her bicycle past number 3, June called out to her to say her mother had had a word with the chairwoman and Sylvia was welcome to attend the next meeting of the WI which was to be held that evening.

To fill in time after work, before her assignation, Sylvia decided to treat herself to supper. Eating out on her salary was a luxury so she explored the possibilities with care. She ruled out Patsy's Tea Shoppe, too many dark beams, and settled on the ABC, which was brightly lit and promised value for money.

The only other diner was a large elderly woman sitting by herself save for a whippet arranged in graceful lines at her feet. The woman looked up as Sylvia came in and nodded.

Sylvia, forbidden a live dog, had had for years an imaginary whippet called Malt. She stopped now to stroke this real live whippet's pale flank. 'Hello, you.' The whippet looked up with mild hazel eyes at this new friend. 'What's her, or his, name?'

The whippet's owner was eating a scone and took some moments chewing it before she spoke. 'She is Sylvia.'

'Oh, but that's my name. Sylvia Blackwell.'

The woman nodded. 'Yes, I supposed you were she.'

The large woman seemed disinclined to further conversation so Sylvia found a table and ordered tomato soup and a roll.

The WI met in the Assembly Rooms around the corner from the library. Refreshments were under way when Sylvia arrived. She accepted a cup of instant coffee and a Rich Tea biscuit from a tiny woman who introduced herself as the Membership Secretary.

'I was detailed to look out for you. I'm Ivy, Ivy Roberts, you'll soon pick up the other names, though' – her voice dropped – 'the chairwoman, Mrs Brent, likes to keep things formal.' She shepherded Sylvia to the front of the rows of chairs. 'We're thrilled to have such a young potential new member. You're down to speak in Other Business.'

The items on the agenda were the branch contributions to World Refugee Year and an invitation to the new General Secretary, a Miss Alison King, to visit East Mole.

Ivy nudged Sylvia. 'The previous Gen. Sec., Dame Frances, resigned. We never managed to entice her here but we have high hopes of Miss King.'

The motion that the branch should collect for World

Refugee Year was passed without objection but tempers were more taxed over the proposal that the new General Secretary should be invited to visit the branch.

Competition for a stake in this event was heated. One member claimed a connection to Miss King's family. 'Not a blood relation, no,' she conceded on being closely interrogated, 'but a friend of my cousin's was at school with her cousin during the war.'

Another member in a stylish hat and a good deal of costume jewellery, made a new bid. 'My husband will be delighted to drive the General Secretary up from town.'

'Her husband drives a Packard,' Ivy confided to Sylvia.

The chairwoman put an end to growing discord by announcing that the matter would be postponed till the next meeting in order to 'allow time for Miss Blackwell, our new Children's Librarian, who has kindly come to address us tonight'. She afforded Sylvia a regal smile and indicated that she should come forward to address the meeting.

The WI members, thwarted in their hostility towards each other, prepared to turn it instead upon this interloper. Armed with suspicion, they were all set to dismiss anything she proposed which, if her age and appearance were anything to go by, was bound to be some modern nonsense.

Sylvia, recalling her father's advice when teaching her chess – 'Remember, a pawn is worth sacrificing for a chance at a queen' – set aside her prepared speech.

'To be honest, Mrs Brent, I'm really here to ask your advice.' The mood of the room palpably relaxed. 'I'd like to encourage more children to join the library and it would be such a help if your members could kindly spread the word among your children or grandchildren.'

'That went down well,' Ivy said as the meeting was disbanding. 'You must come to tea some time,' she added, getting in hastily before Mrs 'Packard', who was hovering.

Mrs 'Packard' took a card from her handbag. 'Do telephone us. Geoffrey and I would love to see you at one of our soirees.' She smiled at Ivy and moved away.

'Thinks she's God All Bloody Mighty with her blessed soirees,' Ivy said. 'Excuse my language.'

Sylvia's instinctive sympathy was always with the underdog. 'Actually, Ivy, I can't telephone her. I haven't got a phone.'

With the WI seemingly supportive, Sylvia decided that the local school should be her next target. The Hedges children attended East Mole's primary school so she went round to number 3 to consult.

'What's the best way of approaching the school, would you say, June?'

'Mr Arnold's the head. You're welcome to use our phone.'

'I think I'd maybe better write.'

'Sam'll take a letter for you. You'll take a letter for Miss Blackwell to Mr Arnold, won't you, Sam?'

'She said I could call her Sylvia.'

'Not at school, Samuel, please, or Miss Blackwell won't lend you any more books out of her library.'

Sylvia had been disappointed to learn that the early success of *Treasure Island* had not lasted. Sam looked sheepish when she asked how he was getting on with it.

'Did you not like it, Sam?'

'That Blind Pew was all right. I didn't like the boy, what's his face.'

'Jim Hawkins?'

'Him. He's sissy.'

'What about Long John Silver?' Silver had been one of Sylvia's childhood favourites.

'I didn't get all that thingy with Squire what's his name.'

'I'll have a think about another book you might get on with better,' Sylvia promised.

But if Sam was, at least at present, a reluctant reader, he was more than happy to be the bearer of a letter about the library to his headmaster. Mr Arnold, he confided, was respected by the boys at the school for his handiness with the cane.

Sylvia had attended a genteel girls' school which her parents had scrimped to afford. Its academic attainments were at best modest but it prided itself on not using corporal punishment. Sylvia, who had frequently been slapped by her mother on the back of her calves for minor misdemeanours, was dimly aware that children were punished with beatings but she was slightly disconcerted to hear of it first hand.

'My friend Micky O'Malley had it for spitting,' Sam told her proudly.

Nevertheless, Sylvia bought Basildon Bond notepaper and matching envelopes in order to write to Mr Arnold. She composed the letter carefully.

Dear Mr Arnold,

As the new librarian at the Children's Library, I want to encourage the local children to use it more freely. I would be

delighted if any of your teachers would like to bring their class
along so I can acquaint them with our collection of books.

Yours sincerely,
Sylvia Blackwell
Children's Librarian

She read the letter through and added:

PS I enclose an sae for ease of reply.

On Dee's advice, Sylvia had said nothing to her boss about her meeting with the WI but she could hardly keep quiet about possible parties of schoolchildren arriving at the library. This time she was braced for disapproval.

'I don't know about this, Miss Blackwell. I did request that you run any future arrangements past me first. We shall have to keep a *very* sharp eye on the books.'

'Why is that, Mr Booth?'

'Naturally, they will steal them or rip out the pages. A whole class let loose in the library is simply asking for trouble. I shall have to refer this to the Library Committee.'

With the exception of Sylvia's neighbour Mr Collins, the Library Committee was composed of those among the elected District Councillors of East Mole who could be cajoled into spending their evenings discussing the library's resources rather than snoozing before the fire or playing darts at the pub. In terms of status, it was well down the Council Committee list, falling below even Sewerage and Waste Disposal. But if Mr Booth had lodged any objections with the Committee they could not have percolated through to the school. Two days later the postman delivered an envelope addressed to Sylvia in her own hand.

Dear Miss Blackwell,

I should be very glad to meet to talk to you about your proposal for the children.

Yours sincerely,
Keith Arnold

5

Mr Arnold had included a number to ring for Sylvia to make an appointment to visit the school and when she called round to ask if she could use the Hedges' phone she showed his letter to June.

'Nice writing. He's a one for good handwriting. Sam comes home with his shirt cuffs stained in blue-black.'

Sylvia was relieved that she'd taken the trouble to write with her fountain pen. 'What's he like, the headmaster, June?'

'Strict but fair, I'd say. He was in the Navy during the war. Runs a tight ship.'

Sylvia made no mention of Sam's respect for the beatings. Instead, she offered to take the three Hedges children to see the library after her meeting with the headmaster, which had been arranged to take place just before the twins' coming-home time.

When Sylvia arrived at the school a group of girls in vests or liberty bodices and knickers were playing netball in the playground. One of the teachers was coaching them with the aid of a whistle. 'Mark, Sheila, mark!' Sylvia heard her shout, and then a sharp blast of the whistle: 'Gaynor Richards, you're offside!'

She climbed noisy stone stairs to the Headmaster's office, where his secretary offered her tea. 'He shouldn't be long. He's talking to the Education Officer about the 11+ timetables.'

Mr Arnold finished on the phone and came through to usher Sylvia into his room.

He doesn't look like a flogger, Sylvia thought. Aloud, she said, 'Thank you for asking me in. I'd really like to encourage the children to use the library more.'

'I'm with you on that front. It's a question of how best to organise it. Since the war even here in East Mole the classes are large. We have over forty in both 4A and 4B.'

Sylvia had read of the shortage of qualified teachers to match class numbers. The British had celebrated the end of the war with serious procreation. 'Perhaps we could organise the children to come in groups? I have had a preliminary word with my boss, Mr Booth.'

'To be frank with you, Miss Blackwell, we have tried in the past to enlist the help of the library in encouraging the children to read – very few of them have books at home – but we were informed that the Library Committee had expressed reservations.'

He showed her to a classroom that was used as the school library.

'As you see, our cupboard here is pretty bare. So if there's anything you can do to involve the children with the library you have my full support.'

When the bell rang to mark the Infants' going-home time Sylvia was outside waiting for the twins. They rushed at her delightedly. Neither was wearing a ribbon.

'I can't tell which of you is which.'

One of the girls pointed to a red star that had been gummed on to her frock. 'I'm Jem.'

The other twin giggled. 'She's *not*, I'm Jem.' She pointed to an identical red star on her collar.

'Why have you both got red stars?'

'Mrs Stewart got muddled,' one of the twins said, and doubled over with mirth.

Sylvia, who remembered her own childhood, said, 'Well, see if I care which of you is which,' at which they stopped giggling and looked surprised.

The twins were habitually overseen to school each morning by their brother, who was also charged with collecting them. The Juniors got out at four o'clock, half an hour later than the Infants. 'Twins, what do you normally do after school while you wait for Sam?' Sylvia asked.

'We go to the caretaker's office,' one explained.

'He gives us Rolos if we sit in his lap,' the other confided.

While they waited for Sam the twins climbed on to the railings outside the Juniors' and poked their sandalled feet through the rails.

'Don't get your feet stuck, girls,' Sylvia urged, and then saw her mistake when they began to stick their feet through with more enthusiasm.

She was about to caution them again when Sam appeared. 'They playing you up?'

'Not really. But I'm glad to see you, Sam.'

Sam and Sylvia sauntered along to the library while the twins skipped ahead, flapping their cardigans like fairy wings.

Thursdays were Mr Booth's afternoons off. Mindful of his request to be forewarned of any new venture, Sylvia had left a note on his desk explaining about her meeting with Mr Arnold. So she felt caught out when they met him in the hall.

He tutted at the twins, who were hopping round the tiles that ornamented the hallway floor.

'I'm introducing some of the schoolchildren to the library, Mr Booth. Mrs Harris is kindly minding the fort.'

'So I see.'

'It's a pilot scheme,' Sylvia improvised. 'I've been discussing it with the Headmaster.'

Her boss flushed slightly. 'I think I said, Miss Blackwell, I would be grateful if in future you ran these meetings past me first. I can't stop now, I have an appointment with the Trustee.' He hurried out, knocking into one of the twins.

'Hey!' Sam shouted after him. 'Watch where you're going, Mister.'

The twin on the floor began to wail.

'Get up! You're not hurt.' Sam took hold of her shoulders and shook her.

The twin stopped crying and began to look around. 'Is this a palace?'

'In a way,' Sylvia told her. 'It's a palace full of stories.'

The twins scampered down the corridor and seemed genuinely impressed when they were shown into the Children's Library. They stood quite still, taking the 'palace' in.

The library was now in much better order. Sections were marked with handwritten notices according to age and there were special shelves devoted to Sport, Nature, Science, History and a section that Dee had just labelled General.

'It's for the books we couldn't think where to put,' she explained. 'I'll be off then, if you don't need me. Good luck with those two.'

'What is all they books for?' one of the twins asked, looking amazed.

'They're for reading,' their brother informed them. 'If you behave, Miss Blackwell will let you take some books home.'

'She said we could call her SYLVIA!' the other twin yelled.

'You be quiet now!' her brother said. 'Or you'll go outside.'

Sylvia took the twins over to the shelves marked three–five where they began to pull out the books on the bottom shelf to build a house.

'Stop it! They're not for mucking about with.' Sam shoved a picture book into the hands of each twin. They seemed quite content with this treatment and sat on the floor sucking their thumbs and flicking over the pages.

'Would you like to see if there's something you might like better than *Treasure Island*?' Sylvia asked. 'How about this?' She took down a Dr Dolittle from the nine–twelve shelves but Sam was examining the books in General.

'What's this about?' It was a book that Sylvia recognised at once from the jacket, *Chess for Beginners*, the first book she could remember her father giving her after he came home from the war.

'It's about chess, Sam. It's a game.'

'I know that!'

'I don't really know what else to tell you,' Sylvia said. 'I started to learn to play it about your age.'

'Did you like it?'

Sylvia considered this. 'I was mostly fascinated by the way the pieces looked. I can show you if you like. I've got a set at home.'

Sam put the book back at once and pulled out one on sailing knots. He drifted about the library pulling books out from the shelves and putting them back again. Sylvia looked over to the twins, who seemed utterly absorbed.

'Would you like to take your books home?' she asked, kneeling down beside them.

But the interruption only caused difficulties. 'I want what she's reading!' one twin demanded.

'It's mine!'

'They can't read,' their brother called from the other side of the room.

The twin with the desirable book got up, shouted, 'I CAN READ!' and ran out of the room, at which the other twin threw herself lengthwise on the floor and began to howl.

'Sam, can you go after her?' Sylvia begged. 'What was it your sister was reading?' she enquired.

'I DON'T KNOW!' the deprived twin roared. 'I CAN'T READ. I DON'T KNOW WHAT SHE WAS READING.'

'I tell you what,' said Sylvia. 'Let's find another book for you.'

She looked along the bottom shelf and pulled out a

large illustrated *Cinderella*. 'Here, look at this. There's the fairy godmother with her wand, and the mice and the pumpkin coach.'

The twin sat up, still shaking with sobs, and eyed the illustration suspiciously. 'Maureen Allan says fairies aren't true.'

'Maureen Allan doesn't know what she's talking about,' said Sylvia firmly.

The absconding twin was carted back struggling in Sam's arms. Sylvia wrote out envelopes with the children's names and address on them and showed them how the library card had to be inserted inside. 'That's to show us who has got the books.'

'Can we keep them?' The *Cinderella* twin was clutching her book to her chest, guarding it from her sister.

''Course, not, stupid,' Sam said.

Fearing another outburst of tears, Sylvia said, 'You can keep it for three weeks. And then if you want to keep it longer you can come back to the library and have it stamped again.'

She allowed Sam, who was borrowing a volume entitled *Basic Morse Code*, to stamp all three books.

'Are you sure that's what you want to take home? You can take out three books at a time, all of you.' But the children had had enough.

They walked home along the towpath, passing the lock, where the twins made as if to dart across the lock gate.

'*No!*' Sylvia cried.

They stopped and looked reproachful. 'Our mum lets us.'

Sylvia turned a querying look on Sam.

'Don't listen to them,' Sam advised. 'They'll say anything.' He raised his voice at his sisters. 'Don't you play Miss Blackwell up now!'

But the girls were ready for this. 'She said we could call her SYLVIA!' they bellowed in return.

6

A clement April passed into a warm May and the children of East Mole Primary due to move on to secondary school began to feel nervous or defiant about the impending 11+ exams.

Sylvia's suggestion that the schoolchildren be allowed to visit the library had yet to be put to the Library Committee but the WI had done its work. One Saturday morning Mrs Bird appeared, pushing before her a basket on wheels and a child.

'I wasn't able to come to the WI meeting where you spoke but I heard good reports. This is my Dawn's Lizzie.' She shoved forward a round-faced bespectacled girl wearing over-large shorts.

'Hello, Lizzie.'

Mrs Bird smacked the girl's shoulder. 'What do you say?'

The girl's voice was so muted that Sylvia guessed rather than heard the reply. ''lo.'

'She's a bag of nerves over these blessed exams. I told

her mother, Miss Blackwell might be able to help. I hope all's well at number 5.' Mrs Bird levelled a look at Sylvia as if to remind her that exam coaching was included in her rental contract.

Sylvia said, 'Yes, thank you. Though I've not really had time to see to the garden.'

'My husband'll give you a hand. I'll leave Lizzie here, then, while I get the shopping.'

'I suppose that's all right. But I will have to see to the other borrowers.'

'Lizzie'll be no trouble. You won't be any trouble, will you, Lizzie?' Not waiting to see if her granddaughter had plans to make trouble, Mrs Bird hurried away, expertly manoeuvring her basket.

Sylvia directed Lizzie to the nine–twelve shelf and continued looking through a publisher's catalogue. After quite a bit of prevarication, Mr Booth had finally revealed the precise budget for the Children's Library.

'It seems an awful lot of money,' Sylvia had said to Dee.

'Poor little Smithy never touched the budget so I reckon it's mounted up.'

As a result of Miss Smith's negligence Sylvia was able to indulge herself with a long list of additions to the library. Post-war publishing was under way and any number of new children's books were coming on to the market. She had already ordered her own childhood favourites: Beatrix Potter, Mary Plain, Moomintroll, *The Just So Stories*, *Puck of Pook's Hill*, *Huckleberry Finn*, *The Princess and Curdie*, *At the Back of the North Wind*, *Emil and the Detectives*, *The Wind on the Moon*, all E. Nesbit, and, in addition, *Ferdinand*, the Blue, Brown, Olive and Lilac Fairy Books, *Swallows and Amazons*, all the Borrowers and Mary Poppins, *The Magic Pudding*, *The Incredible Adventures of Professor Branestawm*, *Trust Chunky*, *Little Pete Stories*, *The Minnow on the Say*, the Katy books and the collected Narnia.

This last choice was vindicated when she looked across to see Lizzie sitting cross-legged, engrossed in *The Lion, the Witch and the Wardrobe*.

Thanks to Sylvia's prompting, Mrs Bird was not the only one who had taken a renewed interest in the Children's Library. Saturdays were a half-day and now the library's busiest, so it was not until nearly closing time that Sylvia had time to talk to Lizzie. Mrs Bird had 'popped in' then 'popped out' again on some unspecified errand.

'Are you enjoying that?' Sylvia asked.

Lizzie lowered the book. Her blue eyes behind her round spectacles were large with wonder. 'It's smashing!'

'You've met the White Witch?'

'And the faun, Mr Tumnus. But the White Witch's got him. Is he going to be all right?'

Sylvia hesitated. She herself always enjoyed a book more if she knew how it would end. 'Do you want me to tell you or would you rather find out for yourself?'

'Please, Miss, I want to know.'

'He's all right in the end. It's that sort of book.'

Reassured, Lizzie took up the book again, unwilling to suffer further distractions.

The Saturday borrowers had chosen their reading and had gone home to lunch. Looking at her watch, Sylvia saw it was twelve thirty, only a quarter of an hour till closing time. She hoped that Lizzie's grandmother would be back in time. There was something unreliable about Mrs Bird.

She had tidied all the books and filed all the borrowers' envelopes when the door was pushed open and a man came in with a child. A girl perhaps around Lizzie's age, taller than Lizzie and with none of Lizzie's abjectness.

On the contrary, this girl carried herself unusually upright and was visibly assessing the shelves of books. In her prim floral frock and with two gleaming plaits she looked to Sylvia for all the world like a child in a book illustration.

The man began to apologise. 'I hope we're not too late. We've come to register Marigold.'

'You're just in time.' Sylvia got out a form to take down the girl's name and the contact details for her parents.

'It's Dr and Mrs Bell. I'm the new GP.'

'I'm comparatively new, too,' Sylvia said.

He smiled down at her, a tall, dark-haired man wearing glasses. 'We newcomers must stick together. I'm told East Mole is a close community.'

'I've found it very friendly, so far,' Sylvia said.

'Well, you're in the right place to meet its most vital members.' He looked fondly across at his daughter.

It was apparent that Marigold had none of Lizzie or Sam's unfamiliarity with books. She had gone straight to the twelve–fourteen section and was exploring the shelves.

'She's only ten,' her father said, 'but her reading is quite advanced.' He shrugged slightly to indicate that he took no credit for this.

'What does she like to read?'

'Pretty much everything. She read my *Grey's Anatomy* when she was down with bronchitis last winter. I think she's probably consumed more of it than I have.'

'I'm in the lucky position of having a generous budget to buy new stock with,' Sylvia volunteered. 'So if there's anything she'd especially like to read do let me know.'

Marigold came over to the desk with *White Fang*, *Ballet Shoes* and T. H. White's *The Sword in the Stone*. She stood a moment, apparently considering, then returned *Ballet Shoes* to the shelf and came back with *White Boots*.

'I see your game, scamp.' Dr Bell patted his daughter's copper-coloured hair and she grinned up at him.

'It's as good a way of choosing as any,' Sylvia said, unaware that she was made a little jealous by this example of family concord.

It was past twelve forty-five when Mrs Bird reappeared, full of excuses about someone who had stopped her on her way back and wouldn't let her go.

Lizzie had presented three Narnia books for stamping. 'I've read more than half of this one already, Miss.'

'Don't worry, you can bring it back the moment you've finished it and take out more books,' Sylvia reassured her.

Mrs Bird, about to march her granddaughter away, suddenly remembered why she had come. 'We came to ask you about the exam. I'll forget my own head next. But Lizzie can come round to number 5 next Saturday. You can go round to Miss Blackwell's, can't you, Lizzie?'

'I'd like to help, of course, Mrs Bird,' Sylvia said cautiously. She was not yet immune to the common tendency to placate the practised tyrant. 'But you see I never sat the 11+.'

Mrs Bird's method with dissent was to choose simply not to register it. 'There's too many in her class and they only help the ones in the A stream they reckon'll get to the Grammar.'

Lizzie looked mutely at the floor and Sylvia, noting the child's worn plimsolls and odd socks, unconsciously made an inner decision. 'Perhaps Lizzie could come round next Saturday after I've finished up here?'

'I told my Dawn you'd help,' Mrs Bird declared. '"Miss Blackwell's the girl to help our Lizzie," I said. You can ask my husband when he comes over to see to the garden.'

Mr Bird brought Lizzie round the following Saturday while Sylvia was sitting outside finishing her lunch in the garden. He parked his van by the donkeys and ducked under Mr Collins' apple tree.

'Nearly had my eye out on that branch.' He stared at Sylvia's plate. 'The wife said to say she couldn't ring when you've no phone,' as if, Sylvia noted with amusement, the lack of a telephone was the result of her own negligence.

It had in fact slipped her mind that she'd been inveigled into bargaining away her Saturday afternoons in return for Mr Bird's help with the garden and her first reaction was resentment. But the sight of Lizzie's ardent little face melted her.

'Miss, I'm on to *Prince Caspian*. They come back to Narnia, Lucy and the others.'

'Do you know, Lizzie,' Sylvia said, 'I've only read the first one. You'll have to tell me what happens next. And you can call me Sylvia. You don't have to call me "Miss".'

She brought out lemon-barley water in the glass jug she'd discovered at the back of a kitchen cupboard and offered Lizzie a biscuit.

'My nan said I wasn't to take anything.'

'She could hardly mind you having a biscuit, Lizzie.'

Lizzie gingerly extracted a broken Digestive from the package and a small bird with a slate-blue head flew down to peck at the spilt crumbs.

'That's a chaffinch,' Sylvia said. She had borrowed one of the library's books and had been teaching herself to recognise the garden birds.

But Lizzie merely looked alarmed at this sudden exposure to new information. She rummaged in her shorts pocket and produced a crumpled sheet of paper. 'This is what I don't understand, Miss. Our teacher said they had it for Comprehension in last year's exams.'

Sylvia read the purple ink. A poem, one very familiar to her, though it had been set out very badly so that all the verses ran into each other.

'They've got the last line wrong anyway,' she said.

Lizzie perked up. 'How have they?'

Sylvia read a verse aloud.

"'In my youth," said the sage, as he shook his grey locks,
"I kept all my limbs very supple
By the use of this ointment – one shilling the box –
*Allow me to **send** you a couple?"*

'It should be "allow me to *sell* you a couple". That's not half so funny. The point is Father William is offering to *sell* his son this ointment, which isn't what you'd expect between a father and son.'

Lizzie looked bewildered so Sylvia went on. 'They don't seem to have given you the whole poem. It's from *Alice*. You know Lewis Carroll's *Alice*?'

Lizzie said that she thought she had maybe heard of it but she still didn't understand the questions.

'I don't blame you, Lizzie. They're pretty banal – silly, I mean. *Father William seems to be a queer old fellow. What are the queer things he gets up to?* How patronising! You could answer that, though, couldn't you? What are the odd things we are told he does?'

Lizzie looked blank and fiddled with a gold cross that hung round her neck. 'I can't remember.'

'Try reading it out aloud.'

Lizzie, looking even more alarmed, began to read, faltered and dried up.

'They haven't helped by running all the verses together in that annoying way,' Sylvia said kindly. 'Listen.'

She knew the poem by heart and recited it through, throwing in the missing verses.

> '"You are old, Father William," the young man said,
> "And your hair has become very white;
> And yet you incessantly stand on your head –
> Do you think, at your age, it is right?"
>
> "In my youth," Father William replied to his son,
> "I feared it would injure the brain;
> But now that I'm perfectly sure I have none,
> Why, I do it again and again."
>
> "You are old," said the youth, "as I mentioned before,
> And have grown most uncommonly fat;
> Yet you turned a back-somersault in at the door –
> Pray, what is the reason of that?"

"In my youth," said the sage, as he shook his grey locks,
"I kept all my limbs very supple
By the use of this ointment — one shilling the box —
Allow me to sell you a couple."

"You are old," said the youth, "and your jaws are too weak
For anything tougher than suet;
Yet you finished the goose, with the bones and the beak —
Pray, how did you manage to do it?"

"In my youth," said his father, "I took to the law,
And argued each case with my wife;
And the muscular strength which it gave to my jaw
Has lasted the rest of my life."

"You are old," said the youth, "one would hardly suppose
That your eye was as steady as ever;
Yet you balanced an eel on the end of your nose —
What made you so awfully clever?"

"I have answered three questions, and that is enough,"
Said his father; "don't give yourself airs!
Do you think I can listen all day to such stuff?
Be off, or I'll kick you down-stairs!"'

Explosive laughter signalled the arrival of Sam. '"Be off, or
I'll kick you down-stairs,"' he carolled ecstatically.

'I expect you two know each other,' Sylvia said,
relieved that she didn't have to continue with the Comprehension.

'She's in 4B. They go to the Secondary Modern.' Sam

swung on the gate with the nonchalance of one who belongs to an elite.

'Well,' said Sylvia, 'that's what you think. Lizzie and I are practising for the exam. I except she'll pass with flying colours.'

Sam jumped off the gate and came over to inspect the poem.

'What's it about?'

'You can read it for yourself.'

He did so and then, wrinkling up his eyes, said, 'It's about an old geezer and his son.'

'And . . .?'

'The old geezer gets one over on his son. The son sounds like a twit. I liked the bit you said about his dad kicking him downstairs.'

'I agree, the last verses are the funniest. I can't see why they left those out.' Sylvia recited the final two verses again and was gratified when Lizzie laughed.

'I like the bit about the eel, Miss.'

Sylvia was close enough to her own childhood to be aware that any educational venture is less daunting if tackled collegiately. 'Shall we see if we can answer the questions together?' She read out the other questions appended to the poem.

b) What prank did Father William think might do him harm when he was young and why did he change his mind?

c) What does "incessantly" mean? What is a back-somersault?

d) How does Father William keep supple? And do you keep supple in the same way?

e) What signs of age does Father William show?

It was agreed among the three of them that once you knew what 'prank' meant question b) was easy-peasy.

'Why do they want to use words we don't use?' Sam asked.

'I think that's part of the test. It's why it's a good idea to read,' Sylvia said cunningly. Then, seeing the children looking downcast, repented. The last thing she wanted was for reading to be perceived as the means to passing dull exams. 'You can nearly always work out the meaning of words you don't recognise from the context – from the rest of the sentence. For example, "incessantly" means . . .?'

'All the time?' Lizzie suggested.

'Over and over,' Sam said hastily, not to be outdone.

'Exactly,' Sylvia said. 'You see, it's not so difficult. A lot of this exam business is guesswork.'

They were unanimous that the question about the back somersault was just plain daft. Sam was especially indignant.

'How we s'posed to explain this?' He crouched down, executed a back somersault and sprang up again, throwing out his hands in a theatrical gesture.

Lizzie appeared transfixed and Sylvia said admiringly, 'That was very neat, Sam. I agree. It's a ridiculous question. The trick is not to get stuck on questions like this. Just bung down "a somersault backwards" or something.'

'That's daft,' Sam said again.

Sylvia said, 'I suspect quite a lot of the questions will seem daft. Adults set these questions and children are generally too sensible to grasp the point of the nonsense they're being asked.' She felt indignant for Lewis Carroll having his wry, humorous parody turned into a clumsy educational hurdle.

'*Do you keep supple in the same way?*' Sam bent double, poked his face through his legs, leered up at them hideously and blew a loud farting noise on his forearm. He collapsed on the ground, overcome with mirth at his own wit.

Mr Bird, who had been hard at it hacking down the brambles, stepped over Sam's prone form announcing that he had a terrible thirst on him and was there maybe something he could drown it with. Eyeing the cut-glass jug, he said, 'That belonged to my Auntie Val when she was still with us.'

'Oh, you must take it then,' Sylvia said hastily. 'I found it in the kitchen cupboard.'

Mr Bird said that his wife was in charge of number 5 and it was as much as his life was worth to meddle. He knocked back a glass of barley water and took a judicious look at Mr Collins' apple tree.

'Want me to take off that branch? You could do yourself a mischief on that.' Sylvia looked at the tree, alight with pale pink buds and blooms. A clutch of mistletoe was visible in the cleft of the rogue branch which overhung her path. 'The law says you can take it off if it overhangs your property,' Mr Bird said, wiping his forehead. 'The wife's been down the Town Hall asking about it.'

'It's pretty,' Sylvia declared. 'Maybe we could leave it for now, Mr Bird?'

Mr Bird said she must please herself and there was a fox's litter down the back end of the garden so he'd not touched the brambles there.

Father William was abandoned while they all hurried down through the cleared garden to inspect the cubs. But only a glimpse of the vixen's ruddy coat and black prick ears could be seen through the remaining tangle of brambles.

Lizzie said she'd like to have one of the cubs as a pet.

'Your nan'd have something to say about that!' Her grandfather winked at Sylvia.

'It'd just be killed when hunting starts,' Sam said.

Sylvia saw Lizzie's eyes well with tears at this piece of equivocal comfort. 'The hunt doesn't get them all, Sam. You can come up here, Lizzie, and watch the cubs grow up.'

'Can I, Miss?'

'Of course you can, Lizzie. And if you like we can maybe have a go at some more Comprehensions.'

'I'll watch them too,' Sam said. He was concerned to protect his status with the new librarian and wasn't having a B streamer colonise her on his home ground.

7

Although Sylvia had greeted Mr Collins when she passed him working in his front garden, so far they had had no further conversation. She was sitting one evening by the upturned barrel, observing the fox cubs cavort on what – since Mr Bird's hard work – passed for a lawn when the gingery figure of her 'immediate neighbour' appeared at the gate. The cubs, with incremental boldness, had dared further and further towards the house and she had been flattered by their trust and enchanted by the little tawny creatures' lively games. So she was put out when at Mr Collins' arrival they turned tail and raced back to the bottom of the garden.

She met him with what she hoped was a neighbourly smile. 'Mr Collins?'

'Miss Blackwell.' His tone was hardly neighbourly.

'Can I offer you tea? Or there's barley water. I'm afraid I haven't anything stronger.'

'That won't be necessary.' His pale eyes raked over the

garden and then turned on the house. 'I see the buddleia is still with us.'

Sylvia had looked up buddleia in the library and had learned that it was a favourite with butterflies. 'It seemed a shame to pull it out.'

But the buddleia was for the moment spared. 'It's those foxes I've come about.'

'Oh.'

'Vermin.'

Sylvia was surprised into indignation. 'Surely not. They aren't rats.'

'I think you'll find they are categorised as vermin.' The pink rosebud mouth puckered tight.

I shall check that, Sylvia resolved. Aloud, she said, 'I'm not sure what I can really do about them, Mr Collins.'

In reply, her neighbour placed a packet on the upturned barrel. 'You dissolve it in water and then soak a piece of meat.'

It took a moment for Sylvia to understand. 'The trouble is, Mr Collins,' she said, inspired by an adrenaline shot of rage, 'the foxes are part of a project I'm participating in with the school. The children are making observations and recording them with the help of our reference books from the library. I think if anything happened to the foxes there would be an outcry.'

'Does Ashley Booth know about this scheme?'

I'm not surprised he and Mr Booth are thick, Sylvia thought. Thick as thieves – they even talk in the same way. She produced a fickle smile and her neighbour withdrew, leaving the package by her teacup on the upturned barrel.

'CAUTION: POISON. Eliminates mice, rats and other vermin. Handle with care,' the package read. She tipped away the remainder of her tea.

Number 3's door was permanently ajar and Sylvia found Ray and June in the sitting room watching the news. Sam was on his stomach on the floor with a copy of the *East Mole Echo*. He rolled on to his side and looked up at Sylvia. 'Who was the next President of the USA after Abraham Lincoln?'

'He's done the crossword already,' his mother said proudly.

'I'm not sure, Sam. Ulysses S. Grant?'

'*Wrong! Andrew Johnson!* And he never *ever* went to school.'

'He doesn't have to look it up. He's got it all up here.' Ray tapped his forehead.

'Who was Prime Minister before Mr Churchill?' Sam demanded.

'I know that one. Neville Chamberlain.'

Sam looked disappointed and began, 'Who –'

'Miss Blackwell hasn't come round for you to show off,' June interceded.

'She's SYLVIA!' shouted one of the twins. They were each sporting, Sylvia noticed, one red and one green ribbon.

'You must be Jam and Pem,' she said, at which both twins began to giggle delightedly.

Sylvia explained why she had come. 'I was so livid I made up the school project on the spot. But now he'll check up on me and he's the Chair of the Library Committee, apparently – though heaven knows why, he doesn't strike me as a reader – and very in with my boss.'

'It's not just the Library Committee,' Ray said. 'Word is him and your boss are' – he pulled up one trouser leg and winked and when Sylvia looked puzzled said – 'Freemasons, the pair of them.'

'Grown men prancing around making secret signs and pulling up their trousers, for heaven's sake,' June said. 'I wouldn't worry about him. Samuel, didn't you say your class was doing the countryside?'

'The Wiltshire Countryside – Our Heritage.'

'Can't you suggest to your teacher you're watching Miss Blackwell's foxes for that?'

'She's SYLVIA!' shouted the twins, not quite in unison.

Their mother ignored them. 'How about you go round to' – she hesitated – 'to Sylvia's now and see what you can do about the little foxes for her?'

'D'you want to hear all my answers to the quiz?'

'I'd love to. Why don't you bring the paper round to mine, Sam?'

Sylvia was genuinely impressed by Sam's answers to the *Echo*'s quiz. 'How on earth do you know which mountain in Europe is the highest? And I haven't a clue which the longest river in Africa is. I couldn't have answered half of these.'

'My grandpa's got the *Encyclopaedia Britannica*. I read it when we're round his.'

'Your grandpa who shoots rooks?'

'That was my dad's dad. He died. Grandpa's my mum's. He doesn't believe in shooting.'

'I'm glad to hear it. And Sam, listen, I really need you if we're going to protect the foxes. Do you think your teacher might help? What's her name?'

'Miss Williams.'

'How old is Miss Williams?'

Sam looked vague and then said his teacher was maybe fifty, he wasn't sure.

Sylvia had been hoping for a younger person, more likely to be an ally. 'Do you think she'll help about the foxes?'

Sam said they had a nature table in their classroom with tadpoles and Micky O'Malley had brought in a jar of sticklebacks for it so she might.

'It would be fun, wouldn't it, to observe them? We could ask Lizzie to join in too.' But at this Sam looked dubious. 'Have you something against that, Sam?'

'She's a girl.'

'I'm a girl too. You like me, don't you?'

'That's different. You're grown up. Anyway, she's Catholic.'

'Whatever's that got to do with the price of eggs?'

'What's that mean?'

'It's a saying. But come on, Sam. Catholic? What does that matter, for goodness' sake?'

Sylvia herself was a little surprised to learn of Lizzie's Catholicism. But Sam's objection to Lizzie, Sylvia surmised after more careful probing, had less to do with religious prejudice than what an association with her might do to his reputation in the playground.

'She's in 4B,' he explained.

'You know,' Sylvia said, 'I can't help feeling that all this streaming business is a mistake.'

'We don't mix with the B's.'

'Perhaps you should. You might learn something.'

This piety got short shrift. 'Yeah, I might learn what it's like being dragged into the girls' toilets.'

'Is that what happens?'

'If you don't watch it, it does.'

'You mean if you palled up with Lizzie Bird you'd risk getting dragged into the girls' toilets?'

'She's not Bird. She's Smith.'

'If you palled up with Lizzie Smith, then?'

'Yeah. If I don't watch it.'

'How childish,' Sylvia decreed, and then laughed at herself. 'I suppose you are only children.'

But this sting to Sam's pride effected a surprising volte-face.

'I'm just saying. But if you like she can watch the foxes with me when she comes round yours.'

8

A loose arrangement between Sylvia and the Hedges children had developed so that on Thursdays Sylvia left her bike behind and went on foot with the three of them on their way to school. The following morning, when they parted at the library, Sam took with him a note for Miss Williams.

When Sylvia got in Dee was up a stepladder dusting some plaster busts on the top shelves. 'That's going beyond the call of duty, Dee.'

'There's a package come for you from the publisher's. It's shocking, the dirt up here. These old boys, whoever they are, could do with a wash and brush-up.'

'That one's Gladstone,' Sylvia said. 'I wonder what he's doing there. But who's the other? He looks very stern.'

'Lord only knows but whoever he is he needs a good clean.'

Dee had begun to lug down the plaster bust when the doors were pushed open and Mr Booth came in. He stood staring and then rapped out, 'May I ask what you are doing with Alderman Coot?'

'Is that who it is?' Dee looked arch and then addressed the bust. 'Pleased to make your acquaintance, Your Worship.'

Mr Booth looked up at her coldly. 'Alderman Coot was a patron of the library.'

Dee began to mouth kisses at the plaster effigy, swayed, screeched and slid down the steps of the ladder. The bust met the parquet floor and fell into two neat halves.

'Dee, are you all right?' Sylvia ran over to her colleague, who was on her back, making protesting noises.

Mr Booth snatched up the fractured pieces and marched out.

'Jesus bloody Christ,' Dee said. She attempted to rise, yelped and slumped back down again. 'I've done something lethal to my back.'

'Oh dear,' Sylvia said. 'Shall I get somebody?'

'You'd better. You're not strong enough to haul me up and I'm not going to humble myself and have you ask His Lordship.'

'I think you should have a doctor,' Sylvia said.

Dee said her GP was a Dr Monk and the number was in the book. Sylvia rang and got an elderly woman who said she would put Dee down on the doctor's visiting list.

'It's quite urgent,' Sylvia said. 'Mrs Harris has fallen and she can't get up.'

'I'm not drunk, tell her,' Dee shouted from the floor. 'The old bat'll go telling everyone I'm drunk,' she explained when Sylvia had rung off.

'Who was she? His wife?'

'Mrs Eames, his housekeeper. He hasn't got a wife, or not one we've heard of. She doubles as his receptionist.

63

She's a gossip. I've heard on good authority she reads the medical notes.'

Sylvia, who had registered with Dr Monk, vowed to stay healthy.

Luckily, the library did very little business in the mornings. A couple of mothers with toddlers came in, which was a distraction for Dee since it allowed her to reprimand the children. One of the mothers supplied some junior aspirin from her handbag. And Mad Mary, the local simpleton, who by general unspoken agreement had licence to go pretty much where she wanted in East Mole, drifted in and shared a jam doughnut with Dee, who said later that it had done her more good than the aspirin.

Just after eleven the doors swung open and a man carrying a doctor's bag came in. It was not Dr Monk but the new GP who had recently registered his daughter at the library.

He nodded at Sylvia and squatted down beside Dee. 'I'm Dr Bell and you must be Mrs Harris, the wounded soldier.'

Dee, who had been lying legs sprawled, adjusted her skirt. 'Fell down those ruddy steps.'

Dr Bell made a sympathetic face. 'Bad luck. Are you in pain?'

Dee said, frankly, she could do with a treble scotch.

Dr Bell laughed. 'I know how you feel. Now, I'm going to examine you.' He looked at Sylvia. 'I might need your help to move Mrs Harris – if that's all right with you, Mrs Harris?'

'Oh, don't mind me!'

'We'll do our level best to mind you. I'm sorry,' he said to Sylvia, 'I've a bad memory for names.'

'Sylvia,' Sylvia said, and blushed. 'Sylvia Blackwell.'

Dr Bell raised his eyebrows and said, 'Blackwell? That's a fitting name for a bookish sort. Now, we need to roll Mrs Harris very gently over so I can examine her back. If you could just lend a hand so that I don't jolt her and add to her suffering . . .'

Together they began to roll Dee over, who said, 'I feel like a blimming beached whale,' and gave a snort of laughter, which made Sylvia laugh too.

'Cow!' Dee said. And, as they laid her on her side, 'I hope you're having fun, you two!' so that Dr Bell also smiled.

He pressed his fingers down Dee's spine. 'Are you playing the piano on me?' she asked coquettishly.

Dr Bell appeared not to hear this. He made Dee move her legs and finally pronounced that he was going to send her to the cottage hospital for an X-ray.

'I don't like the idea of them,' Dee said, in a childish voice. 'Do I have to?'

For a moment both Sylvia and the doctor assumed she was joking. Then Dr Bell said, 'Best to see that nothing is broken,' just as Sylvia was saying, 'They don't hurt . . .'

Dee looked unconvinced. 'It's radiation, isn't it? I don't like the idea of those rays going right through you after what you read about Hiroshima.'

Dr Bell, who had stood up, squatted down again beside her. 'I know,' he said. 'Those bombs were most regrettable. And worrying.' He took off his glasses and polished them, looking thoughtful. Then he said, 'But X-rays, though a form of radiation, are truly quite a different matter.'

'It's still radiation, though, isn't it? I saw the pictures.'

There was a telling silence. They had all had seen the

newsreels of the aftermath of the two great atrocities done in the name of world peace.

'Dee,' Sylvia said. 'Dr Bell is trained. He wouldn't recommend anything harmful for you.'

'Tell you what,' Dr Bell said, patting Dee on the shoulder. 'I'll call an ambulance and hop in with you and take you to X-ray myself. I took you over from Dr Monk because his call-out list was full. So you're my only call out this morning. Might that help?'

He unfolded his long frame again and went over to the phone to call an ambulance.

'It's almost worth crocking my back for,' Dee whispered to Sylvia. 'I'm smitten.'

Once Dee had been carried off on a stretcher, attended by Dr Bell, Sylvia began to unpack the books she had ordered. But her thoughts lingered on the tall doctor with the sensitive hands. Although his smile was warm, his expression in repose had a melancholy look about it.

Once, on the Tube to Ruislip, travelling home in a heat wave, she had put her hot face to the open window at the carriage end and met a man's face, oddly familiar yet not in fact known to her, at the open window of the adjacent carriage. For some minutes, as the train rattled along, they had looked into each other's eyes and she had fancied she had seen in his a reciprocal light of recognition. She had hovered by the Tube doors at the next stop, hoping he might alight there, ready to jump off to join him. But if he had indeed left the train she had missed him and when she went back to the window the face was gone.

Sometimes, not too often, Sylvia thought about that

man. She found herself recalling him again as she unpacked *The Eagle of the Ninth*.

It was a book that had failed dismally at Swindon but she hoped to have more influence in East Mole. Her own dry-as-dust school history lessons had left her so bored that more than once after a night-time's reading, she had fallen asleep and been set many detentions accordingly. Rosemary Sutcliff's characters fell in love. History was much more convincing somehow when there was love involved.

When June came round to number 5 that evening Sylvia was outside, reading *Warrior Scarlet*.

'Do you have to read all the books then?'

'I don't "have to" read any of them. But I like to keep up with the new ones coming out.'

'What's that one about?'

'A boy in the Bronze Age with a withered arm.'

'Nasty!' June made a face.

'Especially as he has to kill a wolf single-handed to become a member of his tribe.'

June made another face. 'Makes you glad you're not living then, doesn't it? There's a boy had polio in Samuel's year. Timmy Sutcliff, poor little mite. He has to peg along in a leg iron.'

'Oh, but this book is written by a writer called Rosemary Sutcliff. She spent most of her life in a wheelchair. Timmy might be interested.'

June looked sceptical. 'He's in the C stream. I don't think they can hardly read. Here, Sam's Miss Williams sent you back a note. And I've brought you some of Ray's greens.'

'Are you sure, June? There's a lot there.'

'To be honest, you'll be doing us a favour. The twins won't touch them and Ray's not that keen. Mind you, I was the same, till I fell pregnant with Samuel and then I forced myself.'

'I expect that's why he's so brainy,' Sylvia said. She told June about Dee's tumble.

'Nasty! She's heavy too. Has she broken anything?'

'I don't know. I spoke to her husband but he wasn't very forthcoming.'

June became confiding. 'There's rumours about him,' she said. 'And those boys he has in his club.'

'I hope they aren't true.'

'You don't know, do you?' June said. 'People love to talk. All I know is Samuel wasn't keen to join.'

Miss Williams' note suggested that Sylvia should call by the staff room during the dinner break. When Sylvia arrived at the school the following day, it was playtime. Children were chalking squares for hopscotch, turning skipping ropes, kicking balls, tossing jacks and shrieking cheerfully. She spotted Sam and waved at him but either he didn't see her or the playground conventions prevented him from returning her greeting. Lizzie, however, called out 'Hello, Miss!' and waved vigorously back in answer to Sylvia's wave.

She knocked at the staff-room door and waited. Someone inside could be heard saying, 'I give the new maths till the end of the year,' and an answering voice said, 'It'll be all change again if they kick out Macmillan's government.'

The door was opened by a pretty full-bosomed woman. 'You must be Sylvia. I'm Gwen Williams.'

'Oh, hello.' For a moment Sylvia was taken aback. From Sam's account, she had put his teacher's age at past forty.

'Pleased to meet you at last. I've heard plenty about you.' Sylvia's thoughts flew anxiously to Mr Booth. 'Nothing to worry about. Glowing reports, in fact. You've quite won young Sam Hedges' heart.'

'I haven't done anything . . .'

'He's bright as ninepence but I've been at my wits' end trying to motivate him and you've somehow captured his interest in a matter of weeks.'

Gwen suggested they nip outside. 'It's a fug in the staff room. I smoke so I can't complain but by the end of the day your clothes reek.'

Sylvia accepted a cigarette, saying she hoped they wouldn't run into Mr Booth. Sam's teacher appeared to know all about Sylvia's boss and was greatly amused when Sylvia explained about the foxes and her neighbour's threat.

'That Mr Collins thinks he's somebody because he's a councillor and used to work up in Birmingham before he retired.'

'What did he do? I can't understand why he's Chair of the Library Committee.'

'Search me. My guess is he was the only one they could get to do it and he and your boss are pals. Don't they play bowls together?'

Sylvia reported the Hedges' remark about Freemasons.

'Could be that. They're all bonkers, aren't they? Anyway, it's a smashing plan to involve our children in your foxes – they love anything like that – but are you sure you want hordes descending on you?'

'If it protects the foxes. And it's a chance to meet my potential clientele.'

Gwen patted her on the back and called her 'a sport'. 'I owe you a drink for this. You must come down the Troubadour one evening.'

It was agreed with Gwen that the fox-watching project should be restricted to the pupils of class 3A, but Lizzie was excepted. She came round to number 5, unaccompanied, the following Saturday afternoon with a Brownie 127.

'I had it for my birthday from my grandad. I'm going to take photos of the little foxes for my album.'

Sam, who had joined them, stared enviously at the camera. 'Can I have a go?'

'My nan says I mustn't let anyone else handle it in case it breaks.'

Sam made a dismissive face. 'My grandad had a Leica he got off a German in the war.'

The little foxes obligingly posed in winning combinations about the lawn while Lizzie snapped them with her Brownie. Sylvia went inside to make the children drinks. When she came out voices from the bottom of the garden told her the children had decamped there so she settled to read some examples of the 11+ papers that Gwen had loaned her.

Complete the following well-known phrases and sayings:
A rolling stone . . .
A stitch in time . . .
There's many a slip . . .

She turned the page to the passage set for Comprehension: a dreary account of some convicts being shipped off to Australia.

'What crimes had the convicts committed to be sent away? What do you think it would feel like to be put in chains?' Very probably not unlike a child required to sit the 11+.

The children did not reappear so she walked down to the bottom of the garden.

Lizzie was sitting cross-legged, drawing in her exercise book. Sam was making critical observations over her shoulder.

Sylvia looked and saw a sketch of the vixen lying in the sun.

'That's really good, Lizzie.'

'She hasn't got the size quite right,' Sam said.

'But the face and the prick ears are perfect.'

Sam had had enough of this. 'I thought we were going to do Comprehensions.'

Sylvia decided to leave the convicts to their fate and try the children out on the proverbs.

'"A rolling stone . . .'"?'

Lizzie looked stricken.

'Might hit someone on the bonce,' Sam said, and laughed loudly.

'That's very probably true, Sam, but unfortunately it's not the answer they want.' She recited the proverb for them.

'What does it mean?' Sam said. 'I don't get it.'

'It means that if you flit about and don't settle down, you . . .' But here her powers of explanation failed. What did it mean, really? And were stones helpful similes for human beings in all their complexity?

'What's moss got to do with it?'

'You know, Sam, I don't really know either. It's what's called an image.'

Lizzie had gone over to the back-door step and was examining the large stone under which, Mrs Bird had explained, the spare key was kept. 'This has got moss on it.'

'Yes. So, you see, that stone stays put. It's not, for example' – Sylvia had a happy inspiration – 'like the stones you kick into the canal, Sam.'

'So what?'

Sylvia capitulated. 'So maybe it's best just to learn them by heart.'

Sam said that if Lizzie liked she could come round to his and watch the football. The pair of them went off, chanting, 'Too many cooks spoil school din dins – There's many a slip on to your B T M!'

A mellow sun was still high in the sky and Sylvia decided to stretch her legs. Other claims had so far prevented her from exploring the deserted foundry but now she took the path to its remains.

A profusion of flowers, pink, white and blue, embroidered the long grasses by the rutted track and she stopped and picked some, wishing she knew their names. She passed a field where cows were grazing and in another field a single white horse stood, staring philosophically into the distance.

'Good luck to you, good luck to me, good luck to that white horse I see.' She spoke the words aloud, touching her collar as she did so.

The foundry gates were fastened with a rusty padlock. She climbed over and jumped down.

Swallows were swooping after insects and chittering around the ruins and she stood watching them, shading her eyes against the sun, enjoying the warmth on her shoulders and bare arms.

A man in khaki army shorts with a gold-brown spaniel appeared from behind the foundry ruin. 'Miss Blackwell?'

'Dr Bell!' She had not recognised him at first.

'Marigold and I are here on a recce.'

His daughter appeared, carrying a piece of rusted iron. 'What's this, Daddy?'

Her father examined it. 'I'm not sure, poppet. Looks as if it could be a part from the ill-fated winnower.'

'You're the librarian,' Marigold pronounced. The spaniel looked up expectantly. 'This is Plush.'

The three of them, with Plush sniffing at water-rat holes, strolled along the canal bank, where Marigold picked flowers and taught Sylvia their names.

'This is red campion and that's white. This purply-bluey one is a kind of vetch, I'm not sure which exactly, there are tons of different ones, and that's viper's bugloss.'

'She's terrifically well informed,' Sylvia remarked to her father.

'Fiendishly so.'

He was too polite to express obvious pride but it is almost impossible, Sylvia thought, for people to conceal their feelings about their children. 'Does Marigold have any brothers or sisters?' she enquired.

A hint of a shadow crossed Dr Bell's face. 'No, she's our one and only. I try not to spoil her . . .'

'I expect spoiling is better than neglect.' This was not quite a true expression of Sylvia's feelings but she felt an impulse to reassure him. 'What school does she go to?'

'She's at the local primary but we're moving her to a private school in the autumn. She's already a year above her age group and way ahead of the others in her class.'

He looked so apologetic that Sylvia felt bound to ask, 'Isn't that a matter for rejoicing?'

'I'd prefer that she mixed with all sorts. The girls at St Catherine's are a certain type, if you know what I mean.'

Marigold ran up to point out to Sylvia some tall purple flowers growing on the bank on the far side of the canal. 'That over there's loosestrife. It's in *Hamlet*. The queen says it – "long purples" – and that there that looks like a kind of cow parsley is hemlock. Socrates drank that when he was put to death. He was –'

'Yes, I know who Socrates was,' Sylvia interrupted, feeling a need to keep her end up. 'Oh, look.'

A streak of azure blue had caught her eye. She bent down and detached a feather caught on a sticky burr. 'What is it?'

Dr Bell took it from her. 'A jay's feather.' He examined it, twirling it round in his long fingers, and then placed the feather carefully on her outstretched palm.

She stood with her other hand cupped around the miniature work of nature's art. 'It's beautiful.'

Looking up, she saw he was smiling at her. 'Yes. Beautiful.'

They had reached the towpath and it had begun to rain. Large spots dropped down on to their heads. Marigold stuck out her tongue to catch the drops.

'I'll leave you here,' Sylvia said. 'But Marigold, if you

need any books on' – she tried to think what might tempt the girl – 'ancient Greece or anything, do come and ask'.

Walking back past the white horse, she touched her collar again. 'Good luck to you, good luck to me, good luck to that white horse I see.' Who knows, it might bring luck whether or not you believed it.

9

There had been no news of Dee since her accident and after some days of hearing nothing Sylvia decided to call at her colleague's house after work.

Dee answered the door in her dressing gown. Her face, without its customary patina of face powder, looked strangely vulnerable.

'Sorry, I look a fright but I haven't got the energy to put on my war paint.' She showed Sylvia into a room, where many china ornaments were on display.

'I'd offer you tea but I can hardly lift the kettle.'

Sylvia said she could make tea for them both. 'How are you, Dee?'

'It's a disc. I've been flat on my back here. I'm bored out of my mind.'

Sylvia said that Dee mustn't think of coming back to the library till she was recovered. 'What does the doctor say?' She felt an inhibition at referring to Dr Bell by name.

'Him! He's bloody useless.'

'He seemed very efficient.' Sylvia felt indignation on behalf of the tall doctor who had dealt with Dee so kindly.

'Not Dr Bell. He's all right. A bit of all-right too.' Dee laughed coarsely. 'I got returned to Dr Bloody Useless. He diagnosed my neighbour with a boil when she'd broken her arm. How's His Lordship?'

'Oh, much as usual.'

'He'll be pleased as punch to have me off sick.'

'Why has he got it in for you, Dee?'

'He's like that.'

This was true enough. Sylvia went through to the kitchen to boil a kettle. When she came back with a tea tray Dee was stretched out on the sofa. She struggled to sit back up to take a cup.

'This is nice. Cyril does his best but the truth is he can't wait for me to get back to work.'

Dee's accident seemed somehow to have produced an increased intimacy. Sylvia said, 'I am very grateful for all your help, Dee, but I can't help wondering why you bother, given how Mr Booth behaves.'

Dee put down her cup. 'It's like this. When he first started here at the library I was his assistant. In fact, I ran the Children's Library.'

'Oh.'

'I'm not trained but I like books and I like to get out of the house so I applied for the job and he took me on.'

'What happened?'

'There was this weekend conference in Birmingham. He suggested I come, to give me more idea about "the workings of librarianship", as he called it. Anyway, we had a bit to drink one night and well, one thing led to another.'

Sylvia, too astounded to speak, said nothing.

'So we had a bit of a carry-on,' Dee said.

'Goodness!'

'Goodness hadn't much to do with it. Anyway, his wife found out and he told her I'd thrown myself at his head. The cheek of it. As if I would!'

'I see.'

'No, you don't. I was going to leave Cyril for him. His idea, not mine. Cyril and I, well, we've separate beds, always have had – his idea, not mine – and Ashley said it was the same for him and his other half.'

'And he just dropped you?'

'He sacked me. He got the Library Committee to say it was because I wasn't trained – and he hasn't had a good word for me since. I only took on volunteering to embarrass him. He can't refuse because he's got Len Salmon – who's a bit, you know, odd in the head, and can't get paid work – to help him for nothing when he's off on one of his sprees. Bloody exploitation.'

'But it must hurt you,' Sylvia said, who had observed her boss bullying a bowed man in too-short trousers, 'him being like that.' She was indignant at this tale of loss and treachery. 'And it must be horrid for you seeing me in your job.'

'Oh, bless your heart, I'm long over that – and His Lordship. What I like nowadays is being a thorn in his side. He tried it on with your predecessor too, poor little Smithy. I found her crying her eyes out in the cloakroom so I told her what happened to me. It's why she left.'

June had hinted as much. This confirmation of Mr Booth as a latter-day Lothario was disquieting.

'Don't worry, he won't try anything on you,' Dee said,

reading her mind. 'You're too young and too pretty. Poor Smithy was a scrawny little body and even in my heyday I was no oil painting.'

When Sylvia got back to number 5 she found Sam in the garden with a group of strange children.

'They've come to look at the foxes,' he announced. 'But they haven't got their notebooks.' He was enjoying his classmates' ignorance of the proper forms.

'I've got plenty of paper. I'll fetch you some,' Sylvia offered. 'What are your names?'

'She's Miss Blackwell,' Sam explained to the other children. 'But I'm allowed to call her Sylvia.'

Sam's classmates had studiously copied down what Sam told them to write on Sylvia's Basildon Bond and had been given lemon barley and Digestive biscuits and been packed off back home. Sam, however, lingered, swinging on the gate.

'D'you want to test me on mental arithmetic?'

'Not really just now, Sam.'

'Go on.'

'All right. Multiply 7,296 by 479.'

Sam screwed up his eyes for a moment. 'Easy. 3,494,784.'

'Goodness, Sam. If that's right then you're a genius.'

'I've been top at arithmetic three years running.'

'Well done. I was always near the bottom.'

Sam looked pitying. 'Girls are no good at arithmetic. There's five of us boys top of the end-of-year tests – me, Micky O'Malley and three others – before you get to a girl.'

'I expect the girls do better at reading, don't they?'

Sam climbed to the top bar of the gate, balanced there a moment, then leapt down. 'Reading's not hard. It's just boring.'

IO

For all his protestations about reading being 'boring', Sylvia had observed Sam covertly consulting some of the battered old Ernest Thompson Seton books at the library. Perhaps this was prompted by his unofficial role as keeper of the foxes. Certainly he was punctilious in marshalling his classmates when they arrived at number 5, issuing diktats about the proper behaviour for animal observation and correcting misapprehensions about the fox cubs' habits.

Lizzie, too, came faithfully for 11+ coaching. She had improved considerably in her ability to grasp the Comprehension questions and she and Sam, who had elected to join in the sessions, could now be heard chanting the 'well-known phrases and sayings' in a litany.

'Too many cooks?' Lizzie would begin.

'*Spoil the broth!*' Sam would declaim.

'A stitch in time?'

'*Saves nine!*'

Sam coached them both in arithmetic. He explained how to do long division, a skill that Sylvia had never fully mastered, and begged them to pose him complex multiplication sums, which he solved in his head.

It was decided by Mrs Bird that to steady her nerves Lizzie should come over to number 5 for a final run-through before the first 11+ exam. Lizzie was deposited at the library and Sam joined them and steered them to Osborne's, where, in view of Lizzie's coming ordeal, Sylvia had promised the children could choose whatever they wanted for a special pre-exam tea.

'Cherryade's her favourite.' Sam gestured at a mute Lizzie.

'Are you sure this is what you want, Lizzie? It's a horrible colour.'

'She likes it. I like Tizer but I can live with Cherryade.'

The three of them walked up the towpath together. Passing the lock-keeper's house, Lizzie said, 'My cousin lives there.'

'Really?' Sylvia was intrigued. 'I've always rather fancied being a lock-keeper.'

'He's not her proper cousin,' Sam said. 'Her grandmother's his great-aunt. Miss Williams says it's important to be accurate.'

Lizzie looked crushed and Sylvia said, 'It's also important not to be a know-all, Sam!'

Sam ran off ahead and Sylvia and Lizzie walked on more slowly behind. Sylvia was in the middle of what she hoped was an encouraging pep talk when Sam came belting back along the path.

'Miss!'

Fright appeared to have banished informality. 'What, Sam? What's happened?'

But for once Sam was speechless. He grabbed her hand and began to tug. They ran the rest of the way to number 5.

'There!' Sam pointed.

The vixen was lying motionless on the lawn. It was apparent to Sylvia that she was dead.

Lizzie began to whimper and, white-faced, Sam shouted, 'We have to take her to the vet.'

Sylvia went over to where the animal lay and knelt down. Flies were already busying themselves about the corpse. 'I'm afraid it's too late for that, Sam.'

She laid her hand on the stiff little body. Behind her, Lizzie set up a great howl.

Sam, stricken, shouted again. 'It's *not* too late. Hurry, we have to take her to the vet.'

'See, Sam.' She laid his hand on the fox's flank. 'She isn't breathing.'

Tears welled in Sam's eyes and ran unhindered down his cheeks. He flung himself on the ground. Unsure whom to comfort first, or how, Sylvia knelt there.

After a while she said, 'These things happen. We must give her a proper burial.'

'Where are the cubs?' The two children rushed to the bottom of the garden. The den was empty. 'What's happened to the cubs?' Sam yelled.

'I expect they're hiding,' Sylvia said. 'They were almost grown.' She didn't expect this to be any solace.

She was grateful when, having returned after escorting a tearful Lizzie home, there was a tap at her door and she opened it to Ray.

'June said I was to bury the poor creature for you.'

'Oh, Ray, would you mind?'

Ray carried the vixen to the bottom of the garden, dug a trench and laid her out in it. The two of them stood looking down at the body, which looked pathetically slight in the clayey grave.

Sylvia had said nothing in front of the two children but she was convinced that this was the work of her 'immediate neighbour', Mr Collins. 'The awful thing is, Ray, I think this is next door's doing.'

Ray nodded. 'That's what June said. He's a blighter.'

'He suggested I poison them. Is Sam still very upset?'

Ray nodded. 'He's like me, the lad, takes things hard. When we lost my dad's black lab he was heartbroken.'

'Do you think he'll guess about next door?'

'We'll say nothing but he's smart and he'll work it out.'

It was clear that Sam had worked it out by the following morning. He arrived while Sylvia was still eating breakfast.

'I've tipped him the Black Spot.'

'What?'

'The Black Spot. Like Blind Pew.'

'Who have you tipped the Black Spot?' Sylvia asked, knowing perfectly well.

'Him next door. He'd just better watch out, that's all.'

On the day of Lizzie's arithmetic exam Sam brought her round to the library after school. 'I've had a look at her paper and I'd say she's got about 75 per cent. She's got the Comprehension tomorrow so she's coming back with us when you finish work.'

Sylvia was flattered. 'You'll do all right tomorrow, Lizzie. Just keep your head.'

'And keep your hair on,' Sam advised.

Mr Booth was off on one of his mysterious errands and Len had been left in charge, so Sylvia sent him off early and locked up. She and the children walked back to number 5, reciting 'Old Father William'.

'You seem to know it, Lizzie.' Sylvia was agreeably surprised.

'She learned it for the exam,' Sam explained. 'She thinks she'll get it again.'

Lizzie blushed and said, 'I never. I learned it 'cos I liked it, Miss.'

They drank Cherryade and Tizer and ate chocolate fingers and swapped dirty rhymes, of which Lizzie had a surprising store.

They were swinging on the gate, intoning, 'Yum, yum, bubble gum, stick it up your mother's BUM,' when Sylvia held up her hand.

'Shhh! Look.'

A black nose was peeping through the hawthorn brake. The children froze.

Sylvia stole inside and came out with a slice of corned beef. She tossed it on to the part of the lawn nearest the hedge. After a few minutes a wary cub emerged. He stood on the lawn, his black-tipped ears pricked, golden eyes narrowing. Then he sprang at the scrap of meat.

'Oh Miss!' Lizzie couldn't contain her delight.

The cub started, looked towards the gate for a second and then bolted down the garden.

'He knew us.' Sam was certain.

'D'you think he did?' Lizzie's eyes were full of appeal.

'I'm sure he did,' Sylvia said. 'He came to wish you luck, Lizzie.'

'He did, didn't he, Miss?'

'None of the other children will have had a fox's blessing,' Sylvia assured her. 'So you are going to be fine.'

'So long as that pig next door doesn't get his bloody hands on him,' Sam said.

'He won't,' Lizzie said. She was smiling. 'Not now.'

11

With the 11+ out of the way the whole school could begin to wind down. Gwen Williams sent a note with Sam. He presented it to Sylvia, who was reading in the garden.

'It's to ask if our class can come to the library to find out about Stonehenge.'

'You didn't open the envelope, I hope, Sam.'

Sam looked hurt. 'It was my idea for us to come to the library in the first place. We're going to Stonehenge for the end-of-year outing.'

'Well done,' Gwen congratulated Sylvia when she arrived with a crocodile of excitedly chattering 3A pupils. 'You've managed to move the mountain. It's been like getting into Fort Knox getting the kids in here. It's going to make their lessons a whole lot more fun.'

Sam, as Sylvia's neighbour, assumed with her a collegiate manner. He conducted his classmates round the library, pointing out where books on ancient Britain and archaeology were shelved and offering advice on how to read a map and use an index.

Gwen watched him with amusement. 'I'm fond of that lad. He'll go far. I wanted to ask, any chance you could come with us to Stonehenge? Sue Bunce, who teaches 4A, gets car sick so she asked if I could find someone else to act as watchdog with me. None of the other staff can leave their classes.'

'It's during my working hours,' Sylvia explained.

'Couldn't you say it's one of your library projects?'

'I'd love to,' Sylvia said. 'I've never seen Stonehenge. But we'd have to close the Children's Library. There's no one to take over.'

But after encountering Dee at the Co-op, Sylvia decided to take a chance. She tracked Mr Booth to the Reading Room.

'Would you have any objection if I took next Wednesday off, Mr Booth? Only the school have asked for my help with a trip to Stonehenge. Mrs Harris is recovered from her slipped disc. I was wondering, perhaps she could be persuaded to come in for a day?' She knew better than to ask for the loan of Len.

Her boss blew out his cheeks in what looked like a preparation for refusal but only said, 'There's someone taking the *Listener*.'

'At least, whoever the thief is, they're cultivated.'

This was a risk but to her surprise her boss only adjusted his bow tie and said, quite mildly, 'If Mrs Harris is willing. It will naturally have to come out of your contractual holiday time.'

And when Sylvia said, 'Naturally, Mr Booth. I wouldn't

expect otherwise,' he didn't even look suspicious and walked off, whistling.

Lizzie's anxiety over the 11+ had been contagious. Sylvia was conscious of a relaxation in her own mood as the coach set off for Stonehenge. She and Gwen sat together in the front by the driver. The children, free from adult scrutiny, pinched and tickled each other, boasted about their packed lunches, identified passing cars and ignored the sights of nature which Gwen occasionally pointed out from her seat in the front.

'I can't blame them. They've grown up with the countryside. I was raised on a Welsh farm and at their age couldn't wait to get away to the city smog.'

'I'm the other way round,' Sylvia said. 'I came from a London suburb and I'm loving discovering birds and flowers.'

Sam could be heard further down the coach, instructing the others about the various theories of who had built the henge. Someone mentioned Druids but Sam was scornful. 'That's just a made-up story.'

Whoever it was who had designed and built Stonehenge, it was undeniably impressive. The children, when they arrived, stood almost silent in admiration at the sight of the vast obelisks encircling the smaller inner rings of standing stones.

'How did they get those whopping ones up there?' one boy asked, pointing up at a massive stone that bridged two mighty supporting pillars.

'It's a trilithon,' Sam informed him. 'It weighs about fifty tons. They did it with pulleys and ropes.'

After a rather one-sided group discussion about ancient technology, in which Sam held the floor ('To be honest,' Gwen confided to Sylvia, 'I didn't really take in myself how they were supposed to have done all this'), the children wandered about, playing at being ancient Britons and inspecting modern graffiti on some of the standing stones. Gwen asked Sylvia to help her keep an eye on them. 'I don't trust some of them not to have brought penknives.'

They ate their packed lunches, cracking hard-boiled eggs on the ancient sacred surfaces. Sam abandoned his pedagogic role and lay spread-eagled on the great central horizontal stone. 'Look, Miss, I'm a human sacrifice.' He was being careful, Sylvia noticed, to avoid using her Christian name.

Gwen and Sylvia leant against one of the sarsen pillars, smoking and relishing the heat of the July sun.

'Nice to see the little blighters enjoying themselves,' Gwen said. 'Only sports day and the school play to get through now. What are you doing for the summer holidays?'

Sylvia had been in a quandary about the summer. Each week she received a letter from her parents detailing an account of their activities but lately the letters had included probing hints about the holidays.

'My parents go to Cromer and I always go with them.'

'I know. Mine are the same. But you have to be cruel to be kind sometimes.'

Sylvia, who doubted the truth of this, said that she supposed so.

'You don't fancy coming to France? I'm going camping with a friend but there's room for one more.'

'Are you sure?'

'My friend's got an old Morris Traveller, plenty of space, and we could do with one more to share the petrol so you'd be welcome.'

'I've never been abroad.'

'Nothing venture, nothing win!' Gwen had perhaps unconsciously picked up the 11+ fixation with well-known phrases and sayings.

Sylvia had forgotten that Marigold, Dr Bell's daughter, would be among the 4A pupils but now she saw her talking to Sam. Sam was gesticulating and looking heated, so Sylvia strolled over to see what was up.

It seemed that Sam had met with resistance to his account of the Druids.

'They did exist,' Marigold was assuring him. 'It was just that the Victorians spread a lot of make-believe.'

Sam was having none of this. 'My grandpa says that's all baloney.'

'Some of it may be. But that doesn't mean Druids didn't exist.' Marigold smiled and Sam looked more belligerent.

'I think you're both probably right.' Sylvia tried to smooth things over. But Sam muttered something incomprehensible and flounced off.

Marigold grinned at Sylvia. 'Boys don't like being wrong.'

'I don't think anyone does, much,' Sylvia suggested.

After lunch Sylvia and Gwen took the children on a nature walk up the slope of the escarpment. Larks hovered trilling above them and chalkhill blue butterflies and brown fritillaries, identified for them by Marigold, danced over the warm turf, settling lightly on flowers. Marigold also named the flowers. 'That's a spotted orchid and that's a bee orchid because it looks like a bee. These little yellow flowers are bird's-foot trefoil – some people call them Bacon and Eggs – those pale blue ones are harebells, in Scotland they're called Scotch bluebells.'

'If she wasn't really quite a nice kid you'd want to scrag her,' Gwen remarked.

Marigold's father was waiting when the coach arrived back at the school. He greeted Sylvia as she descended. 'Good trip?'

'Everyone seemed to enjoy themselves,' Sylvia said. Her voice sounded in her ears unnaturally shrill.

'I hope my daughter behaved?'

'I explained to them about Druids,' Marigold leapt from the coach step into her father's arms.

'I hope you weren't a pain, poppet?'

'She was a pain too,' Sam said as he and Sylvia walked to the library together. 'A right pain in the bum! Thinks just because she's in the fourth year she can bloody swank.'

Sylvia, who had forgotten that Marigold was young for her year, said, 'She is older than you.'

'She's not,' Sam said indignantly. 'She's the same age as me. Just 'cos her dad's a doctor and her mum made a right fuss she got put up.'

When they got back to the library they found Dee unpacking a fresh consignment of books. Sylvia picked one out. 'You might like this, Sam, it's new – about a boy called Tom.'

Sam opened the book and flicked through it. 'It's about a girl!' He pointed to an illustration of a young girl in Edwardian dress.

'It's about a boy and a girl. But there's this – about two boys.' She handed him a Geoffrey Trease.

'That's history.' Sam's spat with Marigold had put him in a bad mood.

He took down from the General shelf a tome about falconry, which Sylvia had considered relocating to the Adults' Library, and went and sat in a corner.

'How was your day?' Sylvia asked Dee.

'Pretty quiet, as it goes.'

'Any trouble with –'

'*Cue for Treason* – what's this about?' Dee had picked up the book Sam had rejected and seemed to be examining it.

'It's about some boys who get to know Shakespeare and prevent a plot against Elizabeth I's life,' Sylvia said, a little surprised. She had not thought of Dee as especially taken with historical fiction. Indeed, Dee's taste seemed mainly to be for sensational thrillers or popular romances of a suggestive kind.

Dee put the book down. 'I'll finish up here. You get off home.'

'Are you all right locking up? Only you know how fussy –'

'Yes, yes. I know the drill.'

On the towpath home Sam remarked, 'You know that man with the bow tie?'

'Mr Booth, you mean?'

'He was hiding from us in the hall. He thought I didn't see him.'

'Really, Sam? Hiding?'

'Yep.' Sam kicked a stone neatly into the canal. 'He's an arsehole. Did you know a peregrine falcon dives at 180 miles per hour? That's faster than Stirling Moss.'

12

The week after the Stonehenge trip was the last week of term and June invited Sylvia to the end-of-year primary-school show. The twins were appearing as the children who lived in Mother Hubbard's shoe. They skipped about on the way to the performance, chanting, 'She baked them some BROTH without any BREAD and writ them all soundly –'

'It's "whipped",' Sam corrected them but to the twins the very idea of their being whipped was an absurdity.

Sam had already disclosed to Sylvia that he was being made to play one of King Arthur's Knights of the Round Table.

'Which one?' Sylvia had asked.

'I dunno.'

'Galahad?'

'Nah. He's a sissy.'

'Parsifal?'

'Nah, he's a twit.'

'Kay?'

'Yeah.'

'What's the matter with Kay? He's Arthur's adopted brother.'

'He's got a girl's name.'

Perhaps it was the indignity of this but Sam's performance as Sir Kay was wooden. When it was 3A's turn to perform he swung his cardboard sword in a lacklustre manner and mumbled his few lines.

The twins had shown no such inhibitions. They had scrambled nimbly around the cardboard silhouette of a huge shoe and squealed delightedly when they were whipped by one of their classmates dressed in a sun bonnet and brandishing the school caretaker's broom.

The Infants were permitted to come and join the audience after their performance. The twins sat between Sylvia and June, whispering and sucking Spangles, which they displayed to each other on their tongues.

Class 4A were to perform the show's finale. As the top class, about to make the crucial crossing to secondary school, they commanded respect and even the twins quietened as the audience waited for curtain-up. A slight bulge in the faded velvet heralded the appearance of a small girl wearing red, white and blue ribbons on her plaits.

'Class 4A present *The Coronation of Queen Elizabeth II*,' she announced in an attempt at a BBC accent and bowed and then retreated back through the curtains.

Sylvia had been woken early by her parents on that damp June morning of the Coronation. She had stood amid the heaving, cheering crowd, valiantly trying to wave the little

Union Jack flag that her father had bought, trembling with excitement at the spectacle she was too small to see. Some time later she had watched on a newsreel at the cinema the new Queen caped in gold, sitting on the ancient throne, her expression grave, her head on its slender neck erect to receive the crown, a slight, lonely-looking figure, not much older than the age she, Sylvia, was now – surely too young to bear the endless duties that lay before her.

By contrast, Marigold Bell looked supremely up to the job. The picture of self-confidence on a chair draped with a curtain and wearing a fancy lace petticoat, she held her cardboard sceptre magisterially aloft.

A boy in a dressing gown placed on her head a painted crown. He spoke words copied from the actual ceremony, at which the new-crowned monarch rose from her throne.

'My subjects,' she began, bestowing a radiant smile upon the assembled cast and audience.

There followed a lengthy speech, during which the young Queen repealed a number of Acts of Parliament and instated a new Act reducing the age of suffrage to twelve. There was to be a special endowment for those who had pets, and books, the monarch announced in conclusion, were henceforth to be free for children.

The cast adjusted their socks and whispered to each other while this revamping of the laws of the land was being delivered. Some of the audience looked disapproving and one brave soul laughed, which earned him a glare from the Queen.

'That went on a bit,' June said to Sylvia. 'I was getting worried the twins mightn't be able to hold on and might wet themselves.'

'We DIDN'T wet ourselves,' the girls shouted, furious at this aspersion.

'You'd best go now or you will,' their mother said, propelling them towards the toilets.

Outside the hall Marigold was being congratulated. 'I wrote it all myself,' she was explaining to her admirers. To Sylvia's surprise Sam seemed to have joined these. He caught sight of Sylvia and said in respectful tones, 'Did you hear what she said about abolishing fox hunting?'

'I did.'

'And about suffrage – that means when you can vote.'

'Yes, I know.'

'Can I ask her round to yours?'

'Wouldn't you prefer to ask her to your own house?'

Sam frowned. 'The twins'll act up if she comes round ours.'

Gwen stopped her on her way out of the school. 'Wasn't the coronation killing? Fancy coming down to the Troubadour Saturday lunchtime?'

The Troubadour, by the canal, was the more social of the two East Mole pubs, boasting a beer garden, hung about in summer with strings of coloured lights. Inside, cases containing varnished catches, supposedly from local rivers, were displayed about the walls.

'"What a mercy that was not a pike!"' Sylvia remarked, noting a long fish with spiky teeth.

'I think it *is* a pike,' Gwen corrected her. 'What'll you have?'

Sylvia said she would have a lemonade shandy. They went outside to sit by the canal.

'Have you thought any more about the holiday?' Gwen asked.

'I wasn't sure you were serious.'

'I wouldn't have asked if I wasn't. Like I said, we need help with the petrol so you'll be doing us a favour.'

Sylvia had, in fact, written in her head several tactful letters to her parents but had not found the courage to translate into pen and ink her excuses for missing their customary family holiday. For years now she had been frankly depressed by the chilly Norfolk beaches, the dreary boarding house with pallid food, swirl-patterned carpets and candlewick bedspreads. But she was aware how important her presence was to her father.

When she got home, fuelled by the lunchtime drink, she took the pad of Basildon Bond outside.

Dear Mother and Dad,

Thank you for your letter with all your news. I am so glad you have finally solved the problem with the twin tub. I have spent most evenings in the garden as no doubt you have too (if Mother's hay fever has permitted).

This was dreadful. She screwed up this attempt and, with the intention of clearing her head, decided to take a walk.

She passed her immediate neighbour aggressively mowing his front lawn and the twins swinging on number 3's gate.

'Hello, Jam, hello, Pem.'

'We AREN'T Jam and Pem.'

She stopped to look at the white horse, recalling how on her previous walk to the foundry she had met Marigold and her father. So she was not altogether surprised to see Dr Bell as she climbed over the gate.

'I was just thinking about you – and Marigold.'

'Were you? Well, as I say to Marigold, thought is real.'

The gold-brown spaniel appeared and rubbed herself against Sylvia's legs.

'Hello, Plush. She's a King Charles, isn't she?'

'They're sweet-natured but very dim. She's Marigold's really but I tend to end up walking her.'

'I was never allowed a dog. How is Marigold?'

'Relieved the exams are over.'

'I don't imagine she had much cause to worry.'

'No.'

Sylvia tried and failed to think of something more to say. Looking around him, Dr Bell said, 'I rather like it here.'

'Yes?'

'I like these industrial ruins.'

'Me too.'

'It reminds me of a song by Ewan MacColl, the folk singer. Do you know him?'

'No.'

All of a sudden he began to sing.

> *'I found my love where the gaslight falls,*
> *Dreamed a dream by the old canal,*
> *Kissed my girl by the factory wall*
> *Dirty old town, dirty old town.'*

Sylvia felt something happening to her bones.

'MacColl does it much better.'

'No. It sounded beautiful.'

'I've got the record. I can lend it to you if you like.'

Sylvia, who had no record player, said, 'Thank you. I'd like that.'

The spaniel ran up, panting, and stood there, alert by his side. 'Mrs Harris's back holding up all right?'

'I think so, yes.'

'You should mind yours, lifting all those boxes.'

'It's an occupational hazard. I'm quite strong.'

'Yes,' he said. 'Yes, I remember.'

A shyness fell suddenly and wrapped them around in its shady nets.

She began to say, 'If Marigold –' but he was already speaking. 'I suppose I'd better be getting along.'

'Me too.'

They stood there. The sun glinting on his glasses obscured the expression in his eyes.

'Well,' he said, 'I dare say I'll see you at the library when Marigold comes to change her books.'

Sylvia tried again to think of something intelligent to say. 'I expect so, yes, if it's Saturday. Well, I'm there all the time if you . . . but you're only free on Saturdays, of course.'

'I'm afraid so. No rest for the wicked.'

Sylvia attempted a bright laugh. 'I don't think you can call what you do wicked.'

'No,' he said. 'No. Or not if I can help it.'

'I'm sure not,' she said, wishing she could take back her last remark. How gauche he must think her.

'Well, so long, then,' he said finally. 'Nice meeting you again.'

'Yes, it was. Thank you for the song.'

'I've got a lousy voice.'

'Oh no,' she said, and blushed. This was awful. Desperately, she blurted out, 'Marigold was very good as the Queen, Dr Bell.'

He smiled the ruefully proud parental smile. 'She's born to rule, I'm afraid, my daughter. And it's Hugh, please.'

> *'Dear Mother and Dad* [Sylvia's father read aloud over breakfast two days later], *I realise that this may come as a bit of a surprise but I hope you will forgive me. A new friend I've made, a teacher at the local school, has invited me to go to France with her and another friend over the summer. They have a Morris Traveller and plan to camp in Brittany or the Dordogne. As you know, I've never been abroad and would like to take her up on the invitation. But it would be grand if you'd maybe come and visit me here.*

'I suppose it had to happen.' He put the letter down and began buttering his toast.

'Norman – butter knife! We'd better cancel her room at Mrs Banham's.'

'We might try somewhere abroad ourselves, Hilda, what d'you say?'

'Mrs Banham would be dreadfully offended.'

Since the end of the war, Norman Blackwell had nursed a desire to visit the country he had helped to liberate. 'I've a fancy to see Paris.'

But Mrs Banham's position was inviolable. 'Another year, Norman, when we've had more time to plan.'

13

'How were the froggies?' her father asked before he was through the gate and Sylvia had had time to greet her parents. *'Parlez-vous français?'*

Sylvia, who loved and pitied her father and was aware that he was putting a brave face on her having missed their usual holiday, tried not to mind this.

Her mother made a dab at her daughter's cheek. 'We had a very pleasant stay with Mrs Banham. She sent you her regards.'

'Did you get the deposit back?' Sylvia couldn't resist asking. The matter of a 'deposit' for the room she no longer required had been referred to in her mother's letters.

Her father began to make reassuring noises but her mother interrupted. 'We got your postcard. Just the one.'

'I only sent one, Mother. I'm sorry.'

'I expect you girls were too busy enjoying *la belle France*. Were there any *grands amours*?' Her father twirled an imaginary moustache.

'Don't be daft, Dad,' Sylvia said, managing affection. 'There was nothing like that.'

(The holiday in France had not, in fact, been entirely satisfactory. Gwen and her friend Chris, though amiable enough, tended to stick together, leaving Sylvia feeling something of a gooseberry. The pair of them shared a tent, where she could hear them chattering and laughing at night, while she couldn't help feeling left out in a tiny narrow tent that Chris had used as a Girl Guide.)

Her father took in their luggage while her mother surveyed the garden. 'Better get your father on to those weeds.'

Inside, she turned her criticisms to the sitting room. 'Smells damp. I hope she's not charging much, your landlady.'

'The rent is very reasonable, Mother. It's bound to be a bit damp. It's the country. Let me show you upstairs.'

'Those stairs look a liability.' Breathing hard, her mother laboriously climbed the stairs to Sylvia's bedroom. 'That bed's not big enough for two.'

'That's all right, old girl.' Her father winked very dreadfully, at her mother. 'Nice and cosy!'

Her mother closed her eyes.

'Dad can have the other room and I can sleep downstairs on the sofa,' Sylvia hurriedly offered. How could she have forgotten the separate bedrooms? 'I'm sorry, I should have –'

'No, no,' her father began to protest as her mother said, 'If you don't mind, dear, it might be best . . .'

Sylvia had prepared supper with garden produce donated for the occasion by the Hedges. Her mother had found their radishes 'indigestible' and the ham 'fatty' and Sylvia had run out of topics for conversation. The evening was fine and, slightly out of desperation, she suggested a walk.

'I've no shoes to walk in. Your father will go with you.'

'I'm game,' Norman Blackwell said, and he and Sylvia were about to set off when Sam appeared at the garden gate.

Sylvia welcomed him enthusiastically. 'Sam, these are my parents. I've told them all about you.'

Sam eyed Norman Blackwell. 'Did you fight in the war?'

An acute observer might have noted Norman Blackwell's shoulders slightly broaden. 'I was a tail gunner in the RAF.'

Hilda Blackwell had long ago heard all her husband's wartime reminiscences. 'Is it me or is it getting chilly?'

'My dad was in the army. Did you shoot down many Nazis?'

'You bet we did. Best time of my life.'

Hilda Blackwell sighed. 'I'll need my cardigan. Norman?'

'I hate the Nazis,' Sam said, turning on her blazing eyes.

'I think we all do, dear.'

'My grandpa's a Jew,' Sam said. 'I'm not because my mum's not. Her mum wasn't. You're only Jewish if your mother is,' he explained to Hilda Blackwell, who blinked nervously and said, 'Well, I never knew that.'

'The officer I flew with was Jewish,' Norman Blackwell said. 'Great chap. He taught me how to play chess.'

'A bomber pilot playing chess?'

'He was a demon at it.'

'What happened to him?'

'Norman!' Hilda Blackwell warned. 'Sam doesn't want to hear all this.'

'Shot down,' Sylvia's father said, avoiding his wife's stare. 'One of the best, old Prager. He taught me to swear in Czech too. *Jdi do piči!*'

'What does that mean?' Sam's interest was now firmly captured.

Sylvia's father looked shifty and said that it meant buzz off.

'You and Sam could maybe have a game of chess, Dad,' Sylvia suggested. Her father was in the habit of airing this expression at moments of exasperation and research had revealed to her that the literal translation was 'go into a cunt'.

'D'you fancy having a go, old chap?' Her father sounded eager.

Sam thought about it. 'Don't mind.'

Sylvia fetched out the wooden box and her father set up the chessboard on the upturned barrel. Sylvia's mother was pacified with an old copy of *Woman's Own* that had been lining the chest of drawers until June came round, ostensibly to make sure that Sam wasn't 'being any bother' but in fact, Sylvia guessed, to get a look at her parents.

Sylvia's mother complimented June on her garden produce, making a special point of commending the radishes. She was persuaded to go round to the Hedges' to watch their TV.

'See, Norman, the Hedges have a TV,' Hilda Blackwell said.

'It's only one my dad rescued from being chucked out,' June apologised. 'He's an electrician so he got it to work for us.'

'It still goes hazy sometimes,' Sam said.

Norman Blackwell settled down to instructing Sam in various chess moves so Sylvia went inside to wash up and turned on the wireless.

'And now we have folk song's famed couple, Peggy Seeger and Ewan MacColl, with the song that Ewan Mac-Coll wrote at the end of the war.'

And from the radio issued two voices . . .

I found my love where the gaslight falls,
Dreamed a dream by the old canal . . .

It was as if, she reflected later, lying on the lumpy sofa listening to her parents' reverberating snores in the rooms above, Hugh Bell had sent her a coded message through the ether.

The week of her parents' stay went by with surprising ease. They visited her at the library, where they met Mr Booth, who surprised Sylvia with unusually cordial behaviour.

Hilda Blackwell was very taken with him. 'He's good-looking, isn't he, your boss?'

Sylvia, who was baffled by Mr Booth's reputed success with women and found his ageing-matinee-idol looks repulsive, nodded.

She treated her parents to a cream tea at Patsy's Tea Shoppe, where her mother greatly admired the warming pans and her father flirted with the elderly waitress. And with June taking her mother under her wing and her father coaching Sam in chess the time passed so smoothly she was almost sad when it was time for them to leave.

'You and I, young man,' Sylvia overheard her father say to Sam, 'have to stick together with all these womenfolk around.'

Before he left he shyly handed Sam a book.

'It was hers.' Sylvia's father nodded towards his daughter. '*Chess for Beginners*. I brought it from home for her but it strikes me you have more use for it now.'

'But I'm not a beginner any more,' Sam protested, and was ticked off by June.

'Thank Mr Blackwell properly, Samuel, or he'll take his book back. We'll see you here again very soon, I hope.' She handed Hilda Blackwell a newspaper parcel of earthy radishes.

'Keep this one out of mischief for me, won't you?' Sylvia's father said to June, thumping his daughter's shoulder.

A taxi had been ordered to take the Blackwells to the station and as it pulled away and Sylvia was waving her parents off Mrs Bird appeared. She ducked under the apple tree and settled herself by the upturned barrel.

'It's come back nicely, the garden.'

'That's thanks to your husband. Tea, Mrs Bird?'

Sylvia made tea, wondering what her landlady's visit boded. It was apparent that she had a surprise up her sleeve. She drank her tea and sat with a sphinx-like smile before ceremonially handing Sylvia a paper bag.

'Black Magic. I prefer Milk Tray myself but I said to myself, "Miss Blackwell is a Black Magic girl."'

'Thank you,' Sylvia said, puzzled by this gift.

Mrs Bird inclined her head and smiled still more. 'Our Lizzie's got into the Grammar.'

'That's terrific!' Sylvia said, thrilled. 'Good for Lizzie.'

'Like I said to my Dawn, "Miss Blackwell'll get her in."
We left school at fourteen but education's important if
you want to get on. That school! Our Lizzie's quiet as a
mouse so they didn't bother about her but I knew she had
it in her. A dark horse, is Liz.'

'You were quite right, Mrs Bird,' Sylvia said. 'And I
agree with you. Would you ask Lizzie to come and see
me? We must celebrate.'

Sam, when told of Lizzie's triumph, said, 'I helped her
with her Arithmetic. And her Verbal Reasoning.'

'You did, Sam. She'd never have passed without you.'

He seemed genuinely pleased at Lizzie's success and
when she appeared, looking shy in a skirt and clean T-
shirt, he whacked her on the back and said, 'Well done,
old girl,' in a perfect imitation of Sylvia's father.

Sam supervised the shopping for Lizzie's celebration
tea. The children gorged themselves on Twiglets, Wagon
Wheels and Playbox biscuits while Sam outlined to Lizzie
what she could expect at her new school.

'You might get some prejudice.'

Lizzie looked scared. 'What do you mean?'

'You're Catholic. The Grammar's Church of England.
Girl Catholics mostly go to Our Lady of Sion.'

'I'm sure that won't be the case,' Sylvia said. 'How will
anyone know?'

Sam looked at her witheringly. 'Catholics don't eat meat on
Fridays. I know about prejudice because my grandpa's a Jew.
And she's from the B stream,' he added, relentlessly heaping
coals of fire, 'so they'll think she's not as good as them.'

'Sam,' Sylvia said, 'shut up. I have every confidence in
Lizzie. She's done extremely well in the exam and she's

going to show them all what's she's made of, aren't you, Lizzie?'

'I was just saying,' Sam said. 'I think you'll be all right too, Liz.'

They fed the donkeys cream crackers. Lizzie was nervous at first and Sylvia reassured her that she too had been nervous of them and described how at school she had acted the part of a donkey in *A Midsummer Night's Dream.*

'It's a play by Shakespeare. I expect you'll be studying it at your new school. Bottom, one of the characters, is turned into a donkey by a naughty fairy called Puck and the fairy queen falls in love with him.'

'Bottom!' Sam didn't know whether to be scornful or amused. 'Like bum?'

But Lizzie's interest was caught. 'Why does she fall in love with a donkey?'

'Because her husband, the fairy king, has put a spell on her to make her fall in love with the first ugly-seeming creature she sets eyes on.'

Lizzie looked puzzled. 'Why does he do that?'

'To get his own back because the fairy queen won't give him what he wants. But, you see, Shakespeare believed that the donkey was worth falling in love with, even if he seemed ugly, and that in the end it did the fairy queen good.'

'Sounds stupid,' Sam said. 'Fairies and bums.'

The tea with Lizzie had reminded Sam of Sylvia's promise that he could invite Marigold round. He pestered her about this.

'Sam, of course Marigold can come but you will have to invite her.'

'I don't know where she lives.'

'I don't either.'

'You do,' Sam said. 'It's on her library card.'

Sylvia knew, in fact, that the Bells were away in Cornwall for a fortnight because before she left Marigold had requested a double ration of library books and told her the date that they would be back.

June caught Sylvia about to set off for work that Saturday morning.

'I came to ask if you'd mind having the twins this afternoon. Only Ray's at football and my mum's poorly again so I said I'd pop over.'

'Of course,' Sylvia said, anxious to be on her way.

'You look nice,' June called after her as she biked away.

'Everything all right?' Dee asked, as Sylvia came back from the lavatory for the third time. She looked Sylvia over. 'Nice lipstick. What's that you're wearing?'

Sylvia blushed. 'Coty L'Aimant.'

'Meeting someone after work?'

'It's no one, really.'

'Go on with you. You're young, you should be enjoying yourself. Make hay while the sun shines.'

Marigold and her father arrived just before closing time. He looked harassed and Marigold looked sulky. She banged down the books she was returning and went off wordlessly to examine the shelves.

Her father raised his eyebrows. 'Sorry about that. She's up in arms about our decision to send her to St Catherine's next term.'

'Oh?'

'She wants to go to the Grammar School.'

'Ah.'

'I'm actually with Marigold on this but Jeanette's very keen and we've paid the fees for the first term. They're not refundable so . . .'

Marigold appeared with some books. 'My happiness is of lesser importance to my parents than the state of their bank balance.'

Hugh Bell sighed and Sylvia asked, 'Why do you prefer to go to the Grammar School, Marigold?'

'The St Catherine's girls are all goody-goodies.'

'I'm sure you'll make new friends there,' her father suggested.

Marigold stuck out her tongue at him and slammed down three books with ancient bindings. The books she had chosen were all boarding-school stories written for readers of an earlier era.

Her father read out the titles. '*The Youngest Girl in the Fifth, The Madcap of the School*. I take it this is some sort of protest.'

'If you propose sending me to that sort of school then I shall need to be adequately prepared.' Marigold opened *The Jolliest School of All*. A smell of fungus rose from the brown spotted pages. '"I say, Megsie, old chum. Wouldn't it be a tremendous jape if we could snaffle old Greenie's tuck box? She has some simply scrumptious buns stowed away there."'

Sylvia couldn't suppress a snort of laughter and her father asked, 'Does it really say that?'

His daughter banged the book shut. Dust flew from the pages and Sylvia sneezed. 'I shall have to practise my vocabulary,' Marigold announced. 'Come on, Daddsie, old thing. Let's roll home to jolly old Mummsie and see what simply super tuck she has got for our jolly old tea.'

She gathered up the books and pushed open the swing doors, rather as if they were the doors of a saloon and she was the hero in a Western.

Her father hovered a moment. 'Might see you at the foundry this evening. Plush has been in kennels and she'll be keen to resume her walks.'

'There's a little madam for you and no mistake.' Dee was examining the books that Marigold had returned. 'College-trained doctor and that slip of a girl's got him twisted round her little finger. Mind you, it's the wife wears the trousers in that household.'

Sylvia tried not to look interested. 'Really?'

'She's not too popular, the doctor's wife.'

'Oh dear. Why not?'

'Snobbish,' Dee decreed. 'Thinks she's a cut above.'

With her mind on Marigold and her father, Sylvia had forgotten that she had agreed to look after the twins, who were waiting for her when she arrived back at Field Row.

'Sylvia, Sylvia!' they yelled, flinging their arms round her legs.

'Girls, be careful of Miss Blackwell's nice dress.'

'She's SYLVIA!' they bellowed. 'SYLVIA, WE LOVE YOU.'

Impossible not to feel warmed by such enthusiasm. 'It's all right, June. You go off to your mother's.'

'They've had their dinner.'

'It was yucky!' the twins chorused. 'Yucky, yucky, YUCKY.' They pranced about the lawn, lifting up their skirts and showing off frilly knickers.

'I don't know what to do with them,' June said. 'They won't touch their greens.'

'They seem very healthy without. You get off to your mother's, June.'

Sylvia had been banking on help with the twins from Sam but the twins informed her he was at the football with their dad. 'What we going to do?' they asked, plumping down on the grass.

'What would you like to do?'

'Cooking.'

The little girls skittered about, gathering dandelion and daisy heads and a variety of leaves, which they mashed through a sieve with wooden spoons into one of Mrs Bird's saucepans. Sylvia had to stop them adding some dubious-looking berries to the mix.

'I wouldn't put those in, girls.'

'Why?'

'They might be poisonous.'

'They's currants,' one of the twins insisted.

'I don't think so.'

'Our dad grows them.'

Sylvia inspected their crop of translucent scarlet berries. 'I'm afraid they're some sort of nightshade.'

'Is they poisonous?'

'Very.'

'If we eat them will we die?'

'You'd certainly be very poorly.'

'Would we have to go to hospital?'

Sylvia sensed that she was being led into some trap. 'All I know is that you would feel very, *very* sick and have very bad tummy ache and you would never ever be allowed to play here again.'

'We won't eat them,' Pam decided. 'We like playing with you.'

Sylvia consented to being fed a banquet of wild flowers until the twins grew bored.

'Would you like me to read to you?'

'Is it Noddy?'

Sylvia was learning that candour with children was an ally. 'Actually, Twins, I don't like Noddy.'

'Noddy hasn't got a willy,' Jem confided. 'We saw when the goblins took all his clothes off.'

'How about Mary Plain?' Sylvia suggested. She had read the little girls one of the books about the small bear with twin sisters and her bespectacled friend, the Owl Man.

'No, we're dressing up,' Pam corrected her.

Sylvia brought down some scarfs that her mother had passed on to her and attached them with safety pins to their dresses for wings.

'I am Queen of the Fairies,' Jem announced.

'No, I am.'

'NO.'

Sylvia intervened. 'How about one of you is Titania and one Queen Mab?'

'Who is they?' The twins looked suspicious.

'Both very important fairy queens in very important plays.'

'"Plays" like we do?'

'Plays by Shakespeare. He was what's called a playwright.'

'We know that,' Pam said scornfully. 'Sam said.'

The twins zipped about the garden, casting spells and releasing prisoners taken by 'old Gingernut' next door.

Sylvia tried to quieten them. 'Shhh, Twins, please. Mr Collins might hear.'

'Our brother's going to get him,' they assured her.

'He tipped him the Black Spot,' Jem said. ''Cos of what he did to the foxes.'

'Means he's going to die,' Pam said, with satisfaction.

The Town Hall clock had chimed five. The twins had set to racing snails but at half past five Sylvia made a decision.

'Now then, you two. We're going for a walk.'

'Why?'

'To see the foundry,' Sylvia asserted.

'Our mum says we mustn't go there 'cos a boy drowned.'

'You'll be all right with me.'

'We won't drown?'

'Oh yes, I think so,' Sylvia said. 'I'm going to put you in a sack, weigh it down with stones and chuck you in.'

The twins looked doubtful and then Pam began to shout with laughter.

'You aren't really, are you?'

'Not really. But there are some very pretty flowers on the way. You can pick Mummy a bunch.'

The twins danced along the lane, grabbing at flowers and dropping them when they encountered any flying insect. They insisted on struggling over the rusty gate unaided and clambered about on the crumbling brickwork.

Sylvia sat on a wall, with a lift going up and down in her stomach, dreading and longing for the appearance of Hugh Bell.

He appeared at last with Plush and raised eyebrows at the sight of the twins.

'I see you have companions. Mine's deserted me. She's still sulking about her new school.'

Side by side, they sat on the wall, their arms not quite touching.

'I was wondering something,' Hugh said at last. 'I was wondering – but you must promise to say no if it's inconvenient – I was wondering if I could ask you to look after Marigold for an afternoon. Not look after,' he corrected himself, 'if she could maybe wait in the library with you. Only I have surgery and her mother's off to see her sister and we're so new here that we don't really know anyone well enough yet to ask if Marigold could go there. It's a problem in the holidays.'

Sylvia tried to sound business-like. 'When would that be exactly?'

'Next Thursday.'

'That's fine. It's my boss's afternoon off.'

'If you're sure?'

'Honestly, it's no trouble.' She looked away to conceal her pleasure. 'Twins, where are you? Don't go anywhere near the canal, please!'

'We wasn't.' One small head poked out from a large earthenware pipe. 'We was hiding to spy on you.'

'I think you'd better come out of there,' Sylvia said. 'That looks like some sort of old sewerage pipe. Your nice frocks will get filthy.'

Jem stared at Hugh Bell. 'Are you the Owl Man?'

'He's in a book about a bear. The Owl Man's her friend,' Sylvia told him. She felt admiring of Jem's conversational courage.

'A good friend, I hope?'

'Can we take your dog walkies?' Pam asked.

'I'm afraid Plush and I have to go,' Hugh said. 'If you're sure about next Thursday, Miss Blackwell . . .?'

'She's SYLVIA!' Pam yelled delightedly.

'"Who is Sylvia? what is she,"' Hugh said, apparently to no one.

They watched him walk away.

'Why did that man say that?' Pam asked.

'Say what?'

'Why did he say Sylvia what is you?'

'It's from a song,' Sylvia said.

'Can we sing it?'

'I'm afraid I don't know the rest of the words. It's a song from a play by Shakespeare, you know, who wrote about Titania and Queen Mab.'

'We sing sometimes,' Jem said. 'When we're in the mood.'

They sang, 'Here we go gathering NUTS in May, NUTS in May, NUTS in May,' tunelessly all the way down the track from the foundry, as if, Sylvia thought, they had in their childish wisdom somehow caught a sense of her own disoriented mind.

14

Sylvia, in general a sound sleeper, slept fitfully the night before Marigold was to be entrusted to her care. She woke before five, tried on each of her three summer dresses and then discarded them all in favour of a skirt and blouse. As an afterthought she put on the pearls her mother had given her for her twenty-first birthday.

Sam was hanging on the gate when she stepped outside.

'You look like the Queen. I seen her picture in the papers. Can I come to the library with you?'

'I'm in a hurry, Sam.'

'I can ride on your handlebars.'

Sam behaved beautifully all morning, replacing the water in the flower vases, fetching the steps for Dee. 'You can dust up high for me, Sam,' she said. 'I can't risk another undignified tumble.'

Sylvia was too nervous to eat lunch so Sam ate her sandwiches for her. They sat outside on the library steps until Sam got bored and went to climb on the railings. She was just screwing back the top of her Thermos when father and daughter appeared, hand in hand.

'Here we are. I'm delivering the cargo.' Hugh Bell's voice sounded suddenly hearty.

'Sam Hedges is here too,' Sylvia said, to have something to say. She gestured over to the strip of grass by the ornamental cherries, where Sam could be seen swinging along the railings.

Marigold ran over to him and her father looked down at Sylvia, who, numb with nerves, seemed to be fixed to the stone steps. 'This is really very kind of you, Sylvia.'

'It's honestly no trouble.' She couldn't say his name.

'She's fairly well trained.' Marigold's father sat down beside her on the steps. She could smell the tweed of his jacket in the sun. Looking over to where Marigold and Sam were chatting, he said, 'It's a responsibility, isn't it, children?'

'I wouldn't know.'

'But you obviously like them. And they pretty clearly like you.'

'Probably because I'm hardly out of nappies myself,' said Sylvia, deliberately trying to wound herself. She sprang up and began smoothing down her skirt. 'I'd better get on.'

He rose more slowly. 'I'll make sure the surgery finishes in good time to collect her.'

She was wondering if she could suggest bringing Marigold round to the surgery when Sam bounded up. 'Can Marigold come back to yours after you finish up here?'

'If her father says she can.'

'Oh but –' Hugh Bell began but Marigold interrupted. '*Please*, Daddy?'

'If Miss Blackwell really doesn't mind.'

'Sylvia won't mind,' Sam said. He smiled reassuringly at Hugh.

It seemed to Sylvia, later that day, that perhaps she was not the only one who had fallen in love. Sam showed Marigold solemnly round the garden, pointing out various points of interest: the best place to feed the donkeys, the hedge sparrows' abandoned nest containing the fragile fragments of azure shell, and the remains of the den where the fox cubs were reared.

Marigold, who was ignorant of the foxes' history, listened to his account of Mr Collins' villainy. 'That's absolutely disgusting. You should've called in the RSPCA.'

Observing his slight frown of puzzlement, Sylvia came to Sam's aid. 'I'm not sure the Royal Society for the Prevention of Cruelty to Animals would be able to prove anything.'

'Don't need proof,' Sam said darkly. 'We know who did it.'

'He sounds like a bastard, that Mr Collins,' Marigold remarked.

Sam looked at her with increased respect. 'A right royal bastard.'

Sensing that she was an intruder in some modern version of courtship, Sylvia retired to the kitchen to make up a jug of lemon barley.

When she came out again Marigold was showing off her handstands. Her long legs flashed up against the cottage wall as, with her skirt over her face, she gave chapter and verse on how long she could remain there. Sam, not to be outdone, was balancing on one leg on one of the fence posts that separated the garden from the donkeys' field. He leapt down from there to demonstrate how he could stand on his head. The two of them vied with each other over their various acrobatic accomplishments and then decided to explore the shed. They went off down to the end of the garden to make a den with some old beer crates and a tarpaulin they had found there.

Sylvia was reading when a grey Hillman car pulled up in the lane. She buried herself deeper in her book and assumed a look of surprise when Hugh Bell called out, 'Hello there. Everything all right?'

'Yes, thank you. Marigold and Sam are at the bottom of the garden making a den.'

He came through the gate, shading his eyes against the sun. 'A den? Well, it's a fine evening for it.'

Sylvia summoned her social courage. 'Can I offer you a drink?' Before he had left, her father had presented her with a bottle of Harvey's Bristol Cream sherry.

'A drink would be grand.'

Sylvia brought out the still-unopened bottle and two of Mrs Bird's smaller pub glasses. They sat by the upturned barrel as swallows performed against a harebell sky.

'The swallows will be off back to Africa before we know it,' Hugh Bell said. 'I always feel sorry when it's time for them to leave.'

'Marigold's been teaching us the difference between swallows and swifts.'

'She's good at identification.'

'She strikes me as good at everything.'

'It's being an only child. It has its drawbacks.'

Tiny flies zizzed round the tangle of honeysuckle and high above the swooping swallows a lone bird hovered in the sky.

'Kestrel,' Hugh Bell observed.

Sylvia looked obediently upward while her heart, which seemed to have acquired a life of its own, knocked manically against her ribs.

'Can we get out your dad's chess set?' Sam asked, arriving breathless from the bottom of the garden. 'Marigold wants to learn.'

Thrilled to discover an area of superior expertise, Sam drilled Marigold over the various chess moves until June came to summon him for supper.

'Marigold is welcome to come and have some too. It's only bangers and beans . . .'

'Can I?' Marigold asked. 'They've got a TV.'

Her father said she could of course have supper at the Hedges' and it was very kind of Mrs Hedges but he would be eating later. He sat by Sylvia in the garden as the sun began a regal descent towards the far hills.

Sylvia began to slap at her forearm. 'Here.' He offered her a cigarette. 'Keeps the biters at bay.'

'I still feel guilty doing this,' she said, hoping to account for her hand shaking as he lit her cigarette. 'My parents still don't know I smoke. It sounds absurd but I found myself smoking surreptitiously when they were staying recently.'

'I take it they do themselves? We expect one law for us and another for our children. I'd be horrified if Marigold started and yet she sees me puffing away like a chimney.'

'Perhaps she won't smoke. She seems very independent-minded.'

'Sometimes too much so, her mother says.'

They sat and smoked and Sylvia felt grateful for the cigarette with which to manage the silence.

'My wife's gone to her sister's because we can't agree about Marigold,' Hugh Bell said suddenly.

'Oh.'

'I've often thought couples should be required to take a test before marrying to see in advance where the future incompatibilities are likely to be.'

Not knowing how she should handle this confidence, Sylvia suggested, 'Like the 11+?'

'Rather more discerning than the 11+, one would hope. Speaking of which, your name is being vaunted through town by a woman who claims you got her granddaughter through the exam.'

'That's my landlady. I wish she wouldn't. Lizzie, that's her granddaughter, should have the credit. And Sam. He was the one who helped her with her arithmetic.'

'He seems a nice boy.'

'The whole family's nice. I'm glad Marigold's taken up with him.'

'I'm glad too. I worry that she's not really palled up with anyone in her class.'

Sylvia could guess why. His daughter would seem to other children a know-all. But Sam was too, in his way.

'Sam's exceptionally bright and they're of an age.'

'She's quite a tomboy so he suits her. She could do with some sibling substitutes.'

Fearful of trespassing, Sylvia said, 'I'm an only child.'

'You seem to have turned out all right.'

'I was lonely,' she volunteered.

He seemed to study her face and she willed herself not to colour. 'How did you cope with that?'

'I read. The local library was at the end of my street and I used to go there every Saturday morning and read till they closed. I'd come home with three books and by the next Saturday I'd read them all and couldn't wait to go back to the library to take out new ones. In the end the librarian let me have double rations.'

'That explains why' – he was polishing his glasses and paused a fraction – 'why you are as you are. Why you became a librarian, I mean.'

'Really, it was she, Miss Jenkins, that was the librarian, who educated me – or the books she recommended. I wasn't much cop at school.'

'Cop enough to become a librarian yourself.' He glanced down at the book she had been reading. 'You didn't want to work with adult books?'

'I like children's books.' She spoke a little defensively. 'And poetry,' she added. Poetry sounded more sophisticated. 'I still read children's books, mostly. I, I suppose I just prefer them.'

'Why? I mean, why do you prefer them?'

Never having articulated this to anyone, Sylvia looked down at the book she had been reading. It was a strange book, one Miss Jenkins had introduced her to, but it was a strangeness that had spoken to something deep inside her and it had become an old friend.

'Maybe,' she said hesitantly, 'maybe it's because children's authors can write about magic, other worlds, and be taken seriously. I mean, suggest that somewhere, even if hidden, there's another reality as real as the everyday world we take for granted that enlarges our sense of ordinary reality, gives it more meaning, if you see what I mean?' It was the longest speech she had ever made to anyone.

'I'd never have thought of that. But boys aren't encouraged to read about magic. Or I wasn't. I had a pretty public-school kind of an education.'

'Wasn't that . . .?' but she didn't want to presume.

'It got me to Oxford and then to medical school. And the music was first rate; that I am grateful for. But it was a culture I disliked. I was seemingly very reserved but underneath I suppose you could say I was sensitive, if that doesn't sound too absurdly self-absorbed and mealy-mouthed. Hence my reservations about Marigold's schooling.'

Another silence enveloped them. Sylvia tried hopelessly to think of something else intelligent to say. She was about to say, 'At least Marigold has a dog,' but Hugh spoke again.

'What children's book, then, would you recommend?'

'For Marigold? She hardly needs my recommendations.'

'I meant for me. What children's book would you suggest I read now?'

'You don't really want me to?'

'I do, yes. How about that one?' looking down at her book.

'*At the Back of the North Wind?* Not that one, no,' Sylvia said.

'Why not?' He looked amused and began a half-laugh.

But she was serious. 'Books have to be a fit. That one isn't right for you.'

15

As August petered out the East Mole parents began to make preparations for a new school year. Sylvia met Mrs Bird with Lizzie walking to the bus stop. Her landlady was wearing her hat with the feathers, which meant business.

'Say good morning to Miss Blackwell, Lizzie. We're off to Salisbury to buy her uniform. There's a list as long as your arm, right down to green gym knickers.'

Sam was to begin his final year at the primary. Sylvia dropped by the Hedges' one evening and found him lying on the living-room floor on his stomach.

'What are you reading, Sam?'

'*A Tale of Two Cities.*'

'Heavens!'

'It's by Charles Dickens,' Sam explained. 'Marigold said to read it.'

June and Ray were watching the news. Crowds of angry youths with greased-back hair and snarling expressions could be seen throwing bottles and cans at windows and kicking down doors while lines of helmeted policemen struggled to haul them back.

'Terrible, these race riots,' Ray said. 'I've nothing against coloureds but if they come over here and there's our own people can't get housing, it's asking for trouble.'

'I don't know, it reminds me of Cable Street,' June said. She saw Sylvia looking uncertain. 'The big fight in the East End. I was only a tiddler but I remember how scared we all were. Fascist hooligans! It was why Dad had us move here.'

'He's a Socialist, June's dad,' Ray said. 'All fine and good, I say to him, but you have to keep law and order.'

The twins emerged in pyjamas. 'SYLVIA!' They rushed at her, clamping her round the knees.

'Get back to bed, you two,' June said. 'You've school starting next week and you don't want Mrs Tate seeing you with black rings under your eyes.'

'We can't sleep. It's too light.'

'There's a poem about that,' Sylvia said.

> *'In winter I get up at night*
> *And dress by yellow candle-light*
> *In summer quite the other way*
> *I have to go to bed by day.'*

'It's NOT FAIR!' they shouted. 'We have to go to bed BY DAY!'

Sylvia had called at the Hedges' on her way to the Troubadour to meet Gwen and some of her colleagues before the start of the new school year. She found when she got there that she had become a quite a celebrity.

'I'd never have predicted Lizzie Smith would pass,' a

weary-looking middle-aged man who introduced himself as 4B's teacher told her. He looked into his head of beer as if it might reveal the secret of Lizzie's success. 'Not in a month of wet Sundays, I wouldn't.'

'It's all wrong, isn't it?' Gwen suggested. 'Sorting them out at this age. But what can you do?'

'There might have been any number of Lizzie Smiths in 4B,' a young woman who had introduced herself as in her probationary year volunteered.

4B's teacher began to look defensive and Sylvia said, 'What about the C stream? Mightn't they have undisclosed talents too?'

The others rolled their eyes and a woman who had so far not spoken said, 'You can forget that. 4C are animals!'

Sylvia's success with Lizzie had fostered a feeling of camaraderie among the East Mole primary staff and they became quite passionate over her plans to start an after-school reading group.

'My impression,' Sylvia said, bucked by this show of support, 'is that the children, some of them, anyway, enjoy quite adult books. Sam Hedges, for example, has taken *A Tale of Two Cities* out of the library. I saw him only this evening reading it.' She was aware that this development had more to do with Marigold than any influence of hers, or the library's, but it seemed a good card to play.

'My God,' Sue Bunce said. 'I haven't read that myself. What's it about? Sam's in my class next year and he's bound to test me.'

'It's about the French Revolution,' 4B's teacher explained. After his failure with Lizzie he was anxious to recover his intellectual credentials.

'It's really about loyalty and friendship and being noble,' Sylvia said, and then, seeing 4B's teacher's face, added hastily, 'but it's true that it's set in the time of the French Revolution.'

'I'm not sure I want to encourage any revolutions,' Sue Bunce said. 'Not till the 11+ is out of the way.'

Sylvia went to bed that night feeling well satisfied. Her plans were working out better than she could have wished. The WI was on board and now the schoolteachers seemed to be allies and Sam, 'her' Sam, as she privately thought of him (for unlike parents, unmarried young women are allowed favourites), was reading Dickens. Just as well she and Dee had not thrown them out. She lay back contentedly on the hard mattress. Above her, Mrs Bird's coloured text promised, '*Surely goodness and mercy shall follow me all the days of my life.*'

Sylvia was waiting on the station platform for Mrs Bird when an express train rushed through, blowing her backwards into an ice-cream vendor's cart. She was struggling out of her coat, with ice cream dripping down her neck, when the train began to scream. Unable to put her hands over her ears to block out the sound, she awoke in a freezing draught.

There was a sound of something untoward. Water. Somewhere, surely, water was dripping loudly, and the bedside light was refusing to respond. Trying to recollect where she had seen a supply of candles, she sprang out of bed, stubbed her toe on the pile of books and made her way gingerly towards the stairs.

She went carefully down the steep flight to the kitchen. No luck with the lights there either.

Outside, she could hear branches of the ash tree being thrashed about and crashing on to the roof, and the wind was screaming like a trapped animal. There was a mighty clap of thunder and almost at once lightning flashed so brightly she could see that the downstairs windows had been blown in and water was gushing through the ceiling.

There was a knocking and she opened the door to Ray holding a bicycle lamp. 'Looks as if your roof's gone.'

'The windows seem to have blown in too.'

'You'd best put on your wellies and get round to ours. I'll sort out some buckets from the shed here to catch the worst of it.'

As she picked her way through the wet darkness, another sheet of lightning revealed the figure of Sam, torch in hand, signalling her up the Hedges' garden path. Behind him, wild screeches could be heard. She went through to a kitchen lit by candles, where she found June with a pair of excited twins.

'It's raining, it's pouring, the old man's snoring,' they chanted, capering round the kitchen in their pyjamas.

'Has your roof held up?' Sylvia asked. 'Mine seems to have been blown off.'

'Be quiet, Twins, you're upsetting the dogs. Ray got ours seen to last year. Yours hasn't been touched since Mrs Bird's grandparents passed on.'

Ray returned to report that he'd placed strategic buckets to catch the rain in number 5 but there was no way Sylvia could spend a night there. The dogs were shepherded into the linen cupboard and bedded down with biscuits. The humans drank cocoa, discussing where Sylvia should sleep. Finally, Sam was relegated to the floor of the twins' tiny room and Sylvia was allocated his bed-room, where the floor was mostly taken up by a railway track.

'That's my Hornby,' Sam said. 'I'll show you how it works in the morning.'

'It's morning now,' June said. 'Off to bed, the lot of you!'

No one got much sleep and the following day there was a move from the children to be allowed off school.

'We is tired,' the twins wailed.

'They're tired! What about me kept awake all night by their bloody natter?'

'Samuel, language! You're none of you poorly and every-one else at school'll likely be tired too.'

Before breakfast Sylvia and Ray went to inspect number 5.

'That ash's dropped half its branches on your roof — looks like most of the tiles are gone. And if those timbers aren't rotten my name's not Raymond Hedges.'

'Oh no, the plum!' Sylvia was looking at the splintered trunk.

Ray examined it. 'That'll have to come down. Pity. It's been there since I was a lad.'

'Did you live here as a child, Ray?'

'Three generations of Hedges there've been now, living at number 3.'

Mr Collins' roof had also suffered, though not as badly as Sylvia's. His aged apple tree, however, unlike the plum, had survived. There was no sign of their neighbour.

'Since the fox's death I've hardly seen him,' Sylvia said. 'Do you think he's gone for good?'

'Good riddance, if he has. But he goes to his sister's in Hungerford. Likely he's there.'

Sylvia walked into town with the Hedges children, navigating fallen branches along the towpath. People were out surveying the storm's devastations and gloomily predicting the cost of repairs. The children peeled off to the school and Sylvia reached the library to find the ornamental cherries flattened along the grass, which was littered with debris and broken tiles.

Mr Booth met her with a long face. 'I'm afraid the damage is very severe. Water has penetrated the Adults' Library and much of the plaster has come away. The Children's has suffered no obvious damage.' His tone seemed to suggest that Sylvia should apologise for this.

It was decided that as much of the Adults' Library as could be housed there should be moved to the Children's. Sylvia went round to the Birds' house, bone-weary after a day of pushing trolley-loads of books, to ask what was to be done about number 5.

She met Mrs Bird on her doorstep, about to set out in her little feathered hat. Her landlady was keen to relay details of damage inflicted by the storm.

'Mrs Brent's greenhouse is in bits. Glass everywhere. They've had to close the swimming baths and half the tiles came off the roof of the biscuit factory.'

'I'm afraid it looks as if the roof's completely gone on number 5, Mrs Bird, and most of the windows on the west side are blown in.'

'Don't you worry, I'll get Joe down the lane to come round. We must thank the Lord no one was killed.'

She hurried away to see to one of her daughters whose chimney had fallen in.

Nothing was said about where Sylvia was to sleep while

Joe saw to the roof. Sylvia felt she could hardly impose upon Sam's bedroom for more than a night. But in the Co-op, where she had gone to buy shortbread as a thank-you to the Hedges, she met Dee.

Dee was looking extra smart in a new suit and patent heels. She had had her hair permed and her formerly bushy eyebrows had been plucked to thin semicircles.

'I could have done with you today, Dee. Mr Booth had me moving books till I thought my arms would drop off.'

Dee looked awkward. 'I'm sorry, I had to stay home. I was having the locks changed.'

'Oh?'

'I've kicked out my husband and I didn't want him wangling himself in behind my back. He only left yesterday so I had to get the locks seen to pronto.'

Unsure how to greet this news, Sylvia said nothing.

Dee hesitated and then said, 'It's been on the cards for some time – long story,' and went on hurriedly to say that from what she had heard on the wireless the damage over the whole of the south of England was severe. 'How did your cottage hold up?' she asked.

Sylvia, concerned to spare Dee's feelings, launched into a detailed account of the damage to number 5. 'I'm not sure where I am going to go. Mrs Bird rather shut down any conversation about that.'

'Thelma Bird's a chancer. By rights she should be putting you up at her expense but, look, you're welcome to come and stay at mine.'

'Dee, are you sure? That would be marvellous.'

'You'll be company. There's a spare room and there's

his room now too. It goes without saying I'll change the bedding.'

Over supper that evening, after Ray had helped transport her few things from number 5, Dee enlarged on the history of her marriage.

'There were separate bedrooms from the word go. His idea. I was too green to read between the lines.'

'How long have you been married, Dee?'

'Twenty years it'll be in October. God knows how I stuck it out. Mind you, when Cyril proposed, I was so grateful I accepted without thinking twice. I thought no one else would have me.'

Sylvia's bike had been a casualty in the storm. Walking to work from Dee's one morning, she heard footsteps behind her.

'Well, you're fit,' Hugh Bell said, catching her up, a little out of breath. 'I've been racing after you. What are you doing here?'

Sylvia, whose heart seemed to be trying to escape her body, managed to explain about the storm. 'Mrs Harris is very kindly putting me up.'

'I hope the damage to your cottage isn't too serious.'

'It's far worse at the library. We've had to move the Adults' section into the Children's.'

'We were in Caernarfon, visiting the castle – it was Marigold's last days of holiday. The storm passed clean over Wales so we knew nothing about it until we got back.'

Sylvia racked her brains for something intelligent to say. 'Has Marigold started at her new school?' Marigold, she had divined, was a subject her father was always happy to default to.

'We've said she must give it a go. I asked her what the other girls were like and she described them as "mostly wet". I'm hanging on to the "mostly" in the hope that there are at least a few saving souls among the benighted pupils of St Catherine's.'

'Sam will miss her,' Sylvia said. She hoped she was betraying nothing personal with this remark.

'Yes, they hit it off, those two. We're hoping she might make some new friends now. Not that . . .'

He looked embarrassed and Sylvia said, 'Of course she needs to make other friends.'

They parted at the High Road, where he left her, saying that while she stayed with Dee they were 'practically neighbours' and he would hope to 'enjoy' her 'company again'.

Sylvia walked the rest of the way to the library mulling over these few conversational fragments. It was apparent to her that Sam was not considered a suitable friend for Mrs Bell's daughter. It was even less likely that she would be considered a fit person to mix with the Bells. And yet there was something, she was almost sure she hadn't imagined it – Hugh Bell seemed to like, even to want, her company.

In the process of exploring the havoc caused by the storm, years of deterioration in the whole fabric of the library building had been revealed.

'The survey found extensive dry rot,' Mr Booth divulged. 'There may even be deathwatch beetle.' He sighed as one who shouldered great responsibilities. 'We are having to convene an Extraordinary Meeting of the Library Committee. I'm afraid your school Reading Project will have to be postponed, Miss Blackwell.'

For the time being, as Dee said, they had to muddle along. Moveable shelves on castors were brought in and as many as possible of the adult books were allocated a place on those in the Children's Library. With Dee's help Sylvia managed both the libraries while Mr Booth was in long discussion with the various firms who had been approached to give estimates for the repairs.

The truce between Dee and her boss gave every sign of holding. On more than one occasion Sylvia spotted the two of them in close conversation. Though not incurious, she was not the sort to ask nosy questions. But Dee brought the subject up one evening over supper.

'I dare say you've been wondering about me and Ashley Booth.'

Sylvia, feeling that, as a guest, diplomacy was called for, said untruthfully, 'Not especially.'

'It's what led to me showing Cyril the door, if you want to know.'

Sylvia, who didn't much want to know, said nothing.

'Ashley and I buried the hatchet – if that's what you'd call it.' Dee gave a yelp of laughter. 'As I said, there's been precious little how's your father between me and Cyril since the day we got married. You wouldn't guess it but Ashley's a bull in bed.'

At this unwelcome image, Sylvia blushed deeply.

'Anyway, I thought, what the hell. That's why I gave Cyril the boot. He can't complain, he knows fine well I've grounds.'

'I'm sure,' Sylvia agreed. 'Shall I clear away?'

But Dee was tasting the peculiar pleasure of confession. 'I used to cover for him when questions were asked. "It's not having a son of his own," I'd say, when people started to wonder why he was always so keen on those boys. "He's just being affectionate." People'll believe anything.'

'Shall I make us some Nescafé?' Sylvia asked, anxious to escape further revelations.

'To my way of thinking, he didn't do the kids any real harm,' Dee said. She had kicked off her shoes, as if they represented past restraints. 'I'd never have let it go too far.'

Sylvia, who was beginning to discover that concern and indifference were not the antitheses she had hitherto supposed but could go hand in hand within the breast of the same apparently decent person, wondered how Dee would know if things had gone 'too far'. Her train of thought was interrupted by Dee saying suddenly, 'Just so you know, Ashley might drop round the odd evening. I thought I'd better warn you.'

'He's not planning to come when I'm here?' Sylvia was now thoroughly alarmed.

'I was more hoping you'd understand if I asked you to spend the odd night away. It won't be too often. He has to find an excuse to put his wife off the scent. How's your love life?'

To Sylvia's dismay she began to colour again. 'I haven't got a love life.'

Dee raised her new-plucked eyebrows. 'You could've fooled me!'

*

As days passed into weeks, Sylvia began to miss number 5 badly. Dee's hospitality scarcely made up for her garrulous late-night confiding, the stuffy bedroom and the terror of possibly encountering a naked Mr Booth. Nor was the proximity of Hugh Bell any compensation. If anything, she had come to dread meeting him in the mornings, when he appeared so friendly and affable while she became so tongue-tied. She found too that however much she practised when alone and for all he had urged it she was unable to address him aloud by name. 'Hugh' seemed too frighteningly intimate; 'Dr Bell' no longer quite fitting.

He had enquired during one of their morning encounters about the children's book he had asked her to recommend. 'Have you had thoughts on my book yet? I'm in need of re-education.'

'Oh, I'm still thinking.' As if she had not spent half her waking moments on this question.

'I hadn't intended it to be a burden, Sylvia.'

The mere sound of her Christian name from his lips made her want to bend double, hooped with desire.

One morning when she caught sight of his angular frame striding ahead of her faster than usual she sensed that something about him was different. Perhaps it was the set of his shoulders. Slightly steeling herself, because she was still in fear of seeming foolish, she quickened her pace and caught up with him as he was about to cross a road.

He glanced down at her and nodded acknowledgement.

They crossed the road together in silence. Holding on to her fraying nerve, she suggested, 'It's a nice morning.'

It was already October and the East Mole weather prophets, noting the profusion of berries in the hedge-rows, were predicting a cold winter to come. But now it seemed an Indian summer had set in. Sylvia had abandoned her coat.

Hugh Bell met this remark with a blank look, then said, 'Yes, I suppose so.'

Abashed, Sylvia made as if to go on, but he stopped her with a hand on her arm. 'I'm sorry. I've, we've had ructions at home.'

'Oh,' Sylvia said, and waited.

'The mother of one of Marigold's classmates rang us last night to rescind an invitation for Marigold to have tea at the girl's house. It's all some petty schoolgirl quarrel but we, I, anyway, challenged her about it and she screamed at me and rushed out of the house. Jeanette thinks the other girl's to blame but I felt we should try to get to the bottom of it.' He frowned and said, 'She seems to rub her peers up the wrong way.'

'Sam likes her,' Sylvia said. 'He likes her a lot.'

'Yes, yes, I know.'

'When number 5 is finally fixed,' Sylvia said stoutly, 'if it ever is, Marigold must come round again.'

The repairs to the library were also hanging fire and, while the Reading Room had been converted to house some of the overflow, which Len was occasionally summoned to oversee, it looked as if the amalgamation of the Adults' and Children's Libraries would have to be continued for some months.

'Months? Years more like,' was Dee's view.

She arrived one morning pushing a trolley on which a

long cabinet rested. 'The Restricted Access collection. Where shall I put it? We don't want the kids getting to these.'

The Restricted Access section of the library consisted of those books which while not banned outright by the Censor were nonetheless considered unsuitable for the open stacks and for which readers had to put in a written request. The books could only be read under surveillance at the library, which in the case of East Mole meant exposing your reading tastes to Mr Booth.

'What are the books anyway?' Sylvia couldn't help being intrigued.

'Your guess is as good as mine. The only one I caught a glimpse of was *The World of Susie Wong*.' Dee manoeuvred the cupboard into a niche beside Hobbies. 'It should be safe enough there. The kids never borrow those.'

'Yes, I've noticed. I wonder why not.'

'Have you looked at them lately? Kids nowadays don't want to make model trains out of tin cans or knit pincushions. They want rock 'n' roll.' Dee swung her hips. '"Rock around the Clock", Bill Hayley and His Comets.'

'Would you like me to ask June's dad to take a look at your roof?' Ray asked Sylvia when on yet another visit to Field Row it was evident that the repairs to number 5 had still not got under way. 'It could be next Christmas before Thelma Bird's Joe gets round to it.'

'Dad's had to replace half of those timbers,' June said over a cup of tea in number 3's kitchen the next time Sylvia called to survey her home. 'Rotten through and through. Just as well there was the storm, if you ask me. The roof could have fallen in on you any time.'

Finally, on the Friday before the autumn half-term, Sam came by after school to say that number 5's roof was fixed and that his mum had said he was to ask if Sylvia wanted help moving back.

'That's wonderful news, Sam. I'll ask Mr Booth if I can leave early.'

But Dee said there was no need to bother him. 'I'll stay and man the boats. You get off and fetch your things. You can leave the door key on the kitchen table when you go.'

Sylvia was surprised by the upsurge of warmth she felt for number 5 when, with Sam manfully lugging her suitcase, she caught sight of the redbrick. Unlocking the front door, she was met with an even bigger surprise. The kitchen and sitting room were freshly painted. The threadbare rugs on the sitting-room floor and the pink chenille on the sofa had disappeared and the musty odour had been replaced by a pleasing smell of distemper.

'Goodness, who has done all this, Sam?'

'Me, with my grandpa. Mum slung the rugs and that out – she said they stank to high heaven. Grandpa's mended your bike too.'

'How kind you all are.' For a moment Sylvia felt overwhelmed. 'It's such a treat to be back, Sam. I hadn't realised how much I'd missed it – and all of you next door.'

'Next door but one,' Sam corrected her, but he looked pleased.

June came to the door to invite her for supper. 'It's Friday, so it's fish and chips. Rock or hake? Ray's about to go off for them.' She stepped inside and looked round the sitting room. 'Looks a lot better without those old rugs.'

'I can't thank you enough, June. And I must thank your

father too, it's . . .' For a moment she struggled but, seeing June look tactfully away, managed, 'I only hope Mrs Bird pays your father.'

'She won't dare not. Dad's on the Housing Committee and Thelma Bird's eldest's applied for council housing.'

'It's a pity your father's not on the Library Committee.'

June said if there was anything Sylvia needed to know then he would find out for her.

'I was wondering about the timetable for the library repairs. Mr Booth seems to want to keep us in the dark.'

'I'd have thought your Mrs Harris could find that out,' June suggested. 'She's been seen around enough with him since she gave that husband of hers his marching orders.'

16

Autumn was in full flush: the trees were glorious in copper, ruby and gold and the East Mole children were sent out with enamel basins to gather blackberries to be baked into pies and windfalls for apple crumble. Sam filched sweet chestnuts from boarded-up number 2's tree and he and the twins went blackberrying with Sylvia and gathered hawthorn for its crimson berries and sprays of dog rose for the scarlet-and-orange hips.

'My mum made those into rosehip syrup,' June told her. 'We were dosed with it every winter against the cold after we moved here. But you get it now on the National Health.'

A mild autumn melted into a foggy November. Sam and the twins wheeled round a guy dressed in a pair of Ray's discarded pyjamas, in the twins' old pram, asking for pennies. Sylvia was invited to number 3 while they burned the guy on a bonfire from which satisfying machine-gun volley of loud retorts issued from bangers strategically placed amid the newspaper stuffing.

After one particularly loud explosion, Mr Collins poked his head over the fence and June offered him a shovel of chestnuts roasted in the embers, which he refused.

'Shirty!' June said, a little too loudly.

'SHIRTY SHIRTY SHIRTY,' the twins yelled.

'Shhh, you two. That's rude.'

'But you said it!'

'It's him on the fire,' Sam confided in a whisper to Sylvia.

The days crawled towards December. In the mornings, frost spangled the skeletons of trees, the hours of daylight grew shorter and the skies grew whiter and then darker. The East Mole children were sent to school in woolly hats and scarfs, and mittens threaded on elastic through their coat sleeves, their chapped knees and lips gleaming with Vaseline. Sylvia developed chilblains. And still nothing was said or done about the library repairs.

With her return to number 5, Sylvia's week had become more of a pattern. Nerves on edge, she waited, along with Sam, who had taken to accompanying her to the library on Saturday mornings, for the regular appearance of Hugh and Marigold Bell.

One Saturday Marigold presented a book for date-stamping with a picture of a castle on the cover.

'I love this,' Sylvia said. 'I'm not sure it shouldn't really be in the Adult section.'

'What is it?' Hugh Bell picked up the book and read the title. '*I Capture the Castle*. Is it an adventure story?'

'No. Not at all. Except maybe in a certain sense. It's about a girl growing up. A rather unusual girl in rather odd circumstances. She lives in the castle with her eccentric family. You remember you asked me to recommend a book . . .?'

'I've been waiting with exemplary patience.'

'Maybe this one, then?'

He scanned the first pages. 'Right you are. I shall read this and deliver my verdict.'

'You don't have to like it,' Sylvia said, feeling self-conscious now. 'It's more of a girls' book.'

'"Girls' book"? You can read it first if you like, Dad.' Marigold went over to talk to Sam.

Hugh winked at Sylvia. 'Don't take that personally. It's part of her current anti-St Cat's, anti-girly-stuff campaign. I shall read it and give you an honest report. And I wanted to say we are having some people for Christmas drinks in a couple of weeks if you're free.'

'When exactly?' Sylvia asked, as if her diary might be full of competing delights. She was taken aback at being included among the Bells' social circle.

'Saturday the thirteenth.'

Hoping she sounded poised, Sylvia said, 'May I let you know?'

'Sure. But do come. Jeanette has invited some crashing bores and we're in need of yeast to leaven the mix. Come along, madcap. Miss Blackwell will be wanting to close up.'

'Can I go back with Sylvia and Sam, Dad?'

'"Miss Blackwell", please, and you can't simply invite yourself round like that.'

Sam looked pleadingly at Sylvia, who said at once, 'Marigold is most welcome and, honestly, Sylvia's fine by me.'

144

'Only when she's not at work, mind,' Sam said. Even Marigold must be drilled in the proper forms.

Marigold's father said he would collect her around four, if that was all right by Sylvia, and the children ran off ahead along the towpath. By the time she reached number 5 they were swinging on her gate discussing the mistletoe on Mr Collins' apple tree.

'It's a parasite,' Sam was pronouncing.

'I know that. Did you know that mistle thrushes are called that because they eat mistletoe?' Marigold retorted.

Sylvia, who guessed from Sam's expression that he was ignorant of this ornithological nicety, said, 'Honestly, Marigold, I wouldn't recognise a mistle thrush if I saw one.'

'They're bigger than song thrushes,' Marigold explained. 'With darker speckles on their breasts. Did you know that, for the Druids, mistletoe was sacred?'

Sam began to retort and, fearing a revival of the children's squabble at Stonehenge, Sylvia said, 'All I know about mistletoe is that you're supposed to kiss under it. Now what about food for the two of you?'

Sam asked if they could take it down to the bottom of the garden to their den.

'Yes, but tell your parents that you're round here first.'

He came back from number 3 with some jelly cubes on an enamel plate and two jam jars of milk. 'Dad said OK by him. I got us some jelly.'

'I've never had it like that.' Marigold sounded impressed.

'We have it when there's no pudding. Can we take your chess set, Sylvia?'

*

'I haven't seen them all afternoon,' Sylvia said when Hugh arrived in the Hillman just after four. 'They must be getting cold by now.'

But other than two empty jam jars and Pavel Prager's chess set, the den was empty.

June had taken the twins to see her mother and Ray was watching *Grandstand* when Sylvia and Hugh Bell went round. Ray hadn't seen the children all afternoon either.

Sylvia began to become distraught. 'I am *so* sorry. I feel dreadful. I thought they were playing chess or just playing.'

Hugh said reassuringly, 'I shouldn't worry. They've probably gone to the foundry.'

Ray looked grim. 'It's out of bounds for ours without an adult since a young lad drowned. Come on. I'll take a torch. It's getting dark.'

But there was no one at the foundry either. Hugh and Sylvia combed the ruins and Ray explored the canal with his torch. They yelled till they were hoarse and Sylvia succumbed to tears.

'I am *so* sorry,' she kept repeating.

Hugh touched her shoulder. 'Don't work yourself up. I think I'd know in my bones if anything bad had happened to Marigold.'

'What's going to happen to my son when we find him is a damn good hiding,' Ray said.

'Oh no, please,' Sylvia begged. 'This is my fault. I should have kept a proper eye on them.'

But at that moment they heard running steps and two figures shot past them at the bottom of the track.

'Samuel!' Ray bellowed.

The figures stopped. 'Dad?'

'Samuel, come here this minute!'

'We just went into town,' Sam said. In the louring light he looked scared.

Marigold said in a simpering tone, 'It was *all* my fault, Mr Hedges. Honestly. I persuaded Sam. We wanted to get something for Sylvia – for Miss Blackwell – so we didn't want to tell her. We thought we'd be back before Dad came.' Marigold's bright, confident face shone in the torchlight.

'Samuel knows better than to go into town without saying anything,' Ray said, but he sounded relieved.

'There wasn't any need to get me anything,' Sylvia said. She was touched by the children's gesture.

'We didn't,' Marigold said. 'We couldn't find anything nice enough, could we, Sam?'

Sam said that no they couldn't. He sounded sulky.

'I'm sorry my madcap daughter gave you such a fright,' Hugh Bell said, after stowing Marigold into the Hillman. 'She's a bit inclined to go AWOL. I'll tick her off.'

'Oh, please don't,' Sylvia said. She could still feel the touch of his hand on her shoulder.

The following Saturday Marigold and her father didn't make their usual appearance at the library. Sylvia lingered over the process of locking up in case they were simply late. Sam had not come either. She worried that the events of the week before had caused some trouble – especially in the Bell household.

She had planned to go into Salisbury after work to buy something to wear for the drinks party – nothing she had already would do. Waiting for the bus, she saw a grey car approaching. It pulled up by the bus stop and Hugh Bell wound down his window. 'Where are you off to?'

'Salisbury.'

'Hop in. I'm off there too.'

She sat tongue-tied until he said, 'We were sorry not to see you today. Marigold's ill.'

Relief made her fluent. 'Oh dear, I hope it's nothing serious.'

'She's come down with a nasty cough. Her chest's her weak spot, so she's been banished to bed.'

'I hope she recovers soon.'

The road into Salisbury was winding and the mid-afternoon light poor. A low mist hung across the road. For some miles he said nothing more than 'Are you warm enough?' and 'Not too draughty for you?' but, turning on to the main road, he began to speak about *I Capture the Castle*.

'It's not a book I would ever have chosen for myself but I found it charming. And amusing. Very.'

'Yes?' She tried not to sound too pleased.

'What's the bestseller her father has written that's a mixture of philosophy and poetry? That made me laugh out loud.'

Sylvia said, 'It was called *Jacob Wrestling*. I'm glad it made you laugh.' She wondered a little if he'd finished the book. The ending, where devotion is allowed to go unrewarded, had left her melancholy.

'The girl Cassandra is enchanting. How old is she?

Seventeen? I suggested to Marigold she read it. For all her boasting, it's a touch above her age range but she's –'

Grateful that her choice had proved a success, she interrupted him. 'Oh, Marigold is quite up to it. I was fifteen when I read it, when it first came out, and I wasn't half as sophisticated a reader.'

'How old are you now, if that's not an awfully impertinent question?'

'Not at all,' Sylvia said, blushing hideously. 'I'm twenty-five in April.'

'A mere babe in arms.'

There seemed nothing to say to that.

'What are you up to in Salisbury?'

'Only some Christmas shopping.'

They were passing through a village and an elderly couple started to cross the road, hesitated and stumbled back. Hugh stopped the car so that they could cross.

'Not a good plan for a local doctor to run over the aged population of Wiltshire,' he said as the man waved a tremulous thank-you. The car moved off again and he continued, 'I don't know if this would interest you but I have tickets for a concert in the cathedral this evening. Jeanette couldn't come because of Marigold and I'm unlikely to be able to sell the ticket at this late date. It's *The Dream of Geron-tius*, Elgar, as of course you know, and a favourite of mine.'

Intending to conceal her ignorance, she said instead, 'I didn't know it was Elgar, in fact. I'm a complete novice when it comes to music but yes, please, I'd love to come.'

'That's settled then. It starts at seven fifteen so perhaps you would allow me to give you an early supper? We'll pass the George and Dragon when I drop you in the town centre. Is five thirty too early?'

For the next couple of hours Sylvia was in a frenzy. She went from shop to shop desperately seeking the right frock for the drinks party and another she could change into for the concert. Thank goodness she had drawn enough cash out to be able to just about manage both. But what to choose? Something sophisticated for the drinks party? Something arty for the concert? The choices available to her, none too desirable in the first place, were made impossible by the turbulence of her mind.

After struggling into and dragging off a medley of garments she settled on a slim green dress for the drinks party and a bolder full-skirted coral-coloured one for the concert. The latter looked all wrong with her sensible librarian's shoes so with her last ten shillings she bought a pair of black patent pumps from Freeman, Hardy and Willis.

The shop assistant was approving. 'They're all the rage in America. You off to a dance?'

Sylvia explained it was a concert and the assistant said that might be nice too. She obligingly bundled up Sylvia's old shoes with her skirt and blouse and let her retouch her lipstick in the staff cloakroom. Her serviceable navy coat now looked all wrong but, too bad, there was nothing to be done about that.

Then there was the problem of finding the George and Dragon. In the confusion of shopping she had lost all sense of direction and arrived sweating and in a panic ten minutes late.

She draped the coat over her arm and found Hugh sitting at the bar.

'Well done, you made it,' he said. 'There's no rush, it doesn't in fact start until seven thirty. I misread the time.'

He led her to a table and took her through the menu. At his suggestion Sylvia ordered steak-and-kidney pie but she refused beer.

'Honestly, I don't really like it.'

'A G and T, then?'

But she refused that too.

Over dinner, he told her he had been visiting an old army friend. 'He's not too well, poor chap. A neurological disease and not a pretty one. I try to keep up his morale. We were both in the Medical Corps during the war and landed up together as POWs towards the end.'

'You were a prisoner-of-war?'

'For four years. My friend was captured at Dunkirk. He and I escaped together in the last weeks.'

'Goodness. How?'

'Nothing glamorous. We bolted from the line we were being led off in under SS orders and we thought, frankly, we'd bought it.'

'Was it awful being a prisoner?'

His face took on the melancholy aspect she had noted when Dee had talked about Hiroshima. 'Pretty awful at times. But mostly because of what we heard about what was going on in the camps. For a time I was with some of the Jewish Brigade – the Jerrys moved us about – and these men had a fair idea of the atrocities. They were formidable.'

'Jewish POWs?'

'Oh, very much so.'

'But not put in concentration camps?'

'Not the soldiers, no. But they were conscious, of course, of all that was happening in the camps. Sure you won't have a drink?'

'I don't drink much, not alcohol anyway.'

'I think I'll have another.' He ordered a beer and when it came smiled and said, 'It had its down sides, of course, being cooped up like a ruddy chicken, but it had its up sides. We enjoyed ragging the Germans. They couldn't understand why, when we misbehaved and they doled out what they considered demeaning punishments, we all greeted them with roars of laughter. And we amused ourselves putting on plays and so forth. I made, I'm told, a passable Brutus.'

'I like Shakespeare,' Sylvia said, and wanted to sink through the floor. What an idiotic, vacuous thing to say.

He smiled at her. 'Me too. How about a brandy to warm you up before we walk to the cathedral? It's nippy out and cathedrals can be cold as sin.'

She had thought he hadn't noticed her change of dress but when the brandy came he said, 'That's a charming colour. It suits you. What would you call it? Flamingo?'

'The girl in the shop called it rose.'

'I'm hopeless about women's clothes. Jeanette always says so.'

The mention of his wife closed down her power of conversation.

It seemed to have closed down his too and they walked through the cathedral close in silence. The night was frosty and the stars behind the outlines of the soaring spire made splinters of light in the vast fabric of the sky.

Sylvia, a little tipsy after the unaccustomed brandy, skidded in her new shoes and he took her arm.

'Here. I don't want to be ferrying you to hospital with a broken limb.'

At the cathedral entrance he said, 'Wait here a mo, would you mind?' and went over to the man who was checking tickets.

Sylvia stood in the vestibule of the great Gothic structure, her heart pounding. It was as if she was standing on tiptoe on the cliff edge of some momentous discovery. Stepping outside again, she peered up at the lofty shape of the spire reaching way up into the immeasurable dark.

'You'll need your coat on,' Hugh suddenly said behind her.

The wooden chairs stood in unmarked rows and he spent some time deliberating where they should sit.

'I'll get us some programmes. With any luck they'll have printed the libretto. It's awful tosh but I confess I'm a bit of a sucker for Newman.'

She knew nothing about Cardinal Newman either and said so.

'He made a stir by leaving the Anglican Church and going over to Rome.'

He came back with two programmes and Sylvia read the opening lines:

> *Jesu, Maria – I am near to death,*
> *And Thou art calling me; I know it now.*
> *Not by the token of this faltering breath,*
> *This chill at heart, this dampness on my brow –*
> *(Jesu, have mercy! Mary, pray for me!)*

'Tis this new feeling, never felt before,
(Be with me, Lord, in my extremity!)

The brandy ran through her veins, warming her, as she sat on the hard chair by Hugh Bell in the solemn dimness of the half-lit cathedral. Unfamiliar as old Gerontius was to her, she was in sympathy with his 'feeling never felt before'. She knew what it was to have those feelings and prayed that she had adequately camouflaged them.

And then the music began.

Sylvia never forgot that evening when she first heard the dying Gerontius passing through the pains of Purgatory and meeting the priest, whose resonant bass spoke to her of surpassing wisdom, and the angel, whose fiercely sweet admonitions seemed to ravish and open her heart. When at last the old man reached the precincts of Paradise and the orchestra gathered to one glorious, inimitable chord, she turned to her companion a face wet with tears.

Silently, he passed her a handkerchief.

'I'm so sorry,' she said when it was over, and blew her nose.

'For heaven's sake, don't be. I'm glad it was such a success.'

'Success' didn't do it justice. 'Oh, yes.'

He steered her through the chattering crowd into the cold dark. 'Another brandy to settle you?'

'I'm not sure I want to be settled.'

'That's the spirit. Home, then?'

They crossed the close and he took her arm ready to

escort her over the road. Above them a fragile fingernail clipping of pale light emerged from a sailing cloud.

'Look,' she said, pointing. 'A new moon. We should wish.'

'What would you wish for, Sylvia?' But he had stooped and was gathering her body to his, so she didn't answer.

17

'I have wanted to do that since I met you in the foundry.'

They were in Hugh's car, where there had been more fervent embraces.

'I didn't know,' she said.

'Really not? I would have thought it was obvious.'

'Not to me.' She buried her face on his shoulder. The rough tweed smelled of the cold night air.

'I suppose we had better get going.' He sighed and switched on the ignition. 'If I'm back too late . . .'

Sylvia said nothing and he turned off the engine.

After a while he said, 'Jeanette and I got married before I left for France in 1940. It seemed the right thing to do. I mean, it was what she wanted. It was that sort of time – uncertain, everything up in the air, you know, well, you don't, of course.'

'I do a bit. I remember my father going off to fight.' He had had tears in his eyes when he kissed her goodbye.

'Remember me, won't you, Princess?' She was only five but she had never forgotten that.

'I was going off to fight in France,' the man in the car beside her said, 'unsure if I'd be coming back. I wanted to leave her with some sort of stability, some sort of comfort, if only the comfort of the prospect of a widow's pension. We hardly knew each other, though we kidded ourselves we did. It must have happened to thousands like us. A cliché, I'm afraid.'

'How did you meet? Was she a nurse?'

'No, a friend of my sister's from school. In fact – this is a sort of quirk of fate – I was infatuated with another girl, who was a nurse. She dropped me for a more senior colleague and one Christmas I took Jeanette out in her place, to, I don't know what, really – take some sort of revenge on this other girl, not that she'd have noticed, she was dead set on my colleague – cheer myself up – pique – God knows, I don't any longer. I'd gathered from my sister that Jeanette was keen on me and it boosted my punctured self-esteem. We, I, anyway, got plastered and, well, one thing led to another. She was a virgin. I didn't know.'

'Oh.'

'Or she said she was, I have wondered since.'

'Oh.'

'And the years as a POW rather cemented our differences. I came home hoping for the best and found we'd grown further apart. I'm sorry to unload all this sordid stuff on to you.'

'Please. It doesn't matter.'

'It does rather, you see, because I can't give you much. I can't leave her. There's Marigold.'

'It's all right. I know.'

'So if you want to slap my face or get out here and have me find you a taxi home . . .'

'I don't.'

'And this, what's happened tonight, can stop right now and I'll never touch you again.'

'Please don't.'

'I shan't, I promise.'

'No, please don't not touch me again.'

'Are you sure? I can't give you much.'

'I know. Please don't keep saying that.'

They drove back with his hand on her knee, saying little. As they approached East Mole Sylvia said, 'You can't drive me all the way home, someone will see you. Drop me at the towpath.'

He pulled up near the canal and got out to open her door. 'I can't let you walk there alone.'

'It's perfectly safe.'

'Don't be a goose. I'm coming with you, at least till we're within spitting distance of your house.'

They walked by the canal, hand in hand. Suddenly he began to sing, as he had done before

> *'I found my love where the gaslight falls,*
> *Dreamed a dream by the old canal,*
> *Kissed my girl by the factory wall.'*

My shoes, my other clothes, Sylvia suddenly remembered. I must have left them at the George and Dragon or in the cathedral. But she didn't interrupt him.

*

Although she would have sworn she had not shut her eyes all night, Sylvia was woken from a delicious dream by the sound of banging. She hurried downstairs in her dressing gown. A pink-faced Mr Collins was at the door.

Since the episode of the dead fox, exchanges with her neighbour had been perfunctory but civil. But now his pale eyes looked baleful. Instinctively, Sylvia adopted an ameliorating tone.

'Good morning, Mr Collins. Nothing wrong, I hope.'

'I am afraid there is.'

'Oh?'

'It's my apple tree. It's been damaged.'

'Oh dear.'

'I'd like you to come and see.'

'Would you mind if I dressed first, only it's a little cold?'

She dressed hurriedly and, looking about for her shoes, remembered she had left them in Salisbury. Pulling on wellingtons, she went outside, where her neighbour was standing by the fence.

'Look at this.' He pointed to where a branch of the apple tree that had overhung her path had been torn away, leaving a ragged stump.

'Yes, I see.'

'Well?'

'I can only say that it wasn't me, Mr Collins.'

'I didn't imagine it was, but those Hedges children constantly play in your garden and on your gate.'

'It must have been affected by the storm. Perhaps that branch just fell off.'

Her neighbour's expression became more truculent. 'If it "fell off", as you put it, the branch would be here. I'm not a fool, Miss Blackwell, and I know my rights. This is malicious damage. I must advise you that if you fail to supervise those children when they visit you and there is another such occurrence I shall inform the police.'

He walked out, banging the gate, and Sylvia went back inside to make tea and toast.

It was so cold in the cottage that she took her breakfast upstairs and got back into bed, trying to recover her dream. She felt that it had been of Hugh but Mr Collins' rude incursion had banished all nebulous delights to oblivion. But there were plenty of exciting real-life events to ponder.

She lay back in the bed to review what had happened.

Although she had been at an all-girls' school, she had escaped the usual crushes on older girls or the mistresses. But during a brief religious phase there had been a boy in the church choir she had once been kissed by, and for a while she had been entangled with a fellow student at library school. She and he had fumbled uncomfortably in various cinemas but these forays had not gone beyond his slipping an inexpert hand inside her bra. A suggestion that she visit him while his parents were abroad in Malta had come to nothing. Not that this was any great disappointment. She was aware enough to know that her feelings for him were the manufacture of the wish for experience rather than born of real desire.

She recalled again that uncanny experience she had had on the London Tube. The stranger in the next carriage, whose face at the open window that hot July evening she had so mysteriously seemed to recognise. From the first, Hugh had evoked in her that same feeling of familiarity. It was as if she already had a blueprint of him inscribed on her soul, merely awaiting realisation in the flesh. She had read about elective affinities. That expressed what she felt for Hugh Bell. And the wonder of it, the glorious wonder, was that he seemed to feel it too.

Before they parted he had placed his two hands on her shoulders and said gravely, 'Sylvia, this isn't something I have ever done before, I promise. Unsatisfactory as my relationship with Jeanette has been, I have, in practice anyway, been loyal to her. But I feel as if with you I have some prior loyalty. It's very odd, my dear. Odd but, I must say, marvellous.'

Odd but marvellous. The words, so exhilarating at the time, as she rehearsed them now seemed to offer fewer possibilities. What could he, what could they do? As he had made clear, there was Marigold. And he was a GP with a reputation to maintain. Any meetings they had could only be infrequent. But that did not for the moment detract from the extraordinary and astonishing and altogether unlooked-for sense that even now he was thinking as she thought, feeling as she felt.

Wanting the good that had come to her to be shared, Sylvia dressed and went round to the Hedges' to warn Sam that Mr Collins was on the war path. But their neighbour had anticipated her.

'He was round here first thing, threatening us and making his accusations.' June was livid.

Sylvia, who was pretty sure it was Sam who had torn off the branch, asked if she could have a word with him.

The twins were on the sitting-room floor, their legs outstretched, fashioning paper chains from strips of coloured paper. They had already licked off all the gum and were having to stick the chains together with paste and squabbling over the paste brush.

'Shall we make paper chains for you, Sylvia?'

'Yes, please, Twins. I'd like that very much.'

'We're not twins today,' Jem said. 'I am being Queen Elizabeth and she is being Princess Margaret.'

'Princess Margaret is the pretty one,' Pam explained.

Sylvia stepped over the paste and went through to the tiny room which served as Sam's bedroom. Sam was working his Meccano funicular.

'You heard all that, I dare say, Sam? Only, if anything like that happens again, he may well call the police.'

'See if I care!' Sam looked defiant.

'Listen,' Sylvia said. 'It's no skin off my nose. Just as long as you know the score.'

Unable to read or settle to anything, she decided to walk to the foundry. The rutted mud on the track was frozen hard, the hedges beside it beaded with scarlet hawthorn berries and wreathed in clouds of old man's beard. Pondering the fracas over Mr Collins' tree, which she guessed Sam had robbed for the mistletoe, she was reminded again of Hugh's kisses.

She had gone to the foundry half in hope of finding him to match her thoughts of their first meeting there but the only other sign of life was a lone ginger cat which only put her in mind of Mr Collins. Poor pathetic Mr Collins with his pettifogging, old-maidish concerns. In her present mood she felt benignly towards him.

As if reading her mind, the cat came and wrapped itself round her legs and she crouched down to stroke its matted fur. 'Hello, puss.' The cat inclined its head. Two limpid green pools looked steadily up at her. Then the cat shook itself and walked off with its tail in the air. 'I am the cat that walks by itself, and all places are alike to me,' she called softly after it.

Still restless, she walked along the canal to the lock. The door of the lock-keeper's house was open and a young man about her age was at the door.

He shouted across to her, 'Mind how you go. Jack Frost's been out.'

Sylvia remembered. 'You know Lizzie Smith?'

'Young Liz is here now, as it happens.'

Mrs Bird appeared in the doorway. 'It's brass-monkey weather. Tea's just brewed and I've brought Ned here some of my Christmas cake.'

Sylvia crossed the lock gate to the cottage and was shown into a tiny room, where a heavy-looking fruitcake was being passed round. Lizzie was at first struck dumb by Sylvia's arrival but she became more vocal once her grandmother had followed Ned into the kitchen.

They could hear her through the thin partition, saying, 'Don't tell me anyone's going to be going through that lock on Christmas Day or, if there is, there ought to be a law.'

Sylvia, who had refrained from asking about the Grammar School in front of Mrs Bird, risked, 'How is the new school, Lizzie?'

'The maths is hard. I'm in the bottom set. But I'm in the top set for English.'

'Good for you.'

Lizzie looked bashful and added, 'I'm going to be

Mustardseed, Miss, in the school play. I did the audition for our English teacher, and we start rehearsals next term.'

'That's terrific, Lizzie. Do you remember we talked about that when you and Sam were feeding the donkeys? I was Bottom when I was at school.'

'Janine Gates is being him. Her mum makes puppets so she's doing the donkey's head. Will you come and see it, Miss?'

'It's still "Sylvia", Lizzie, and yes, I should love to come and see you. I'll bring Sam.'

'He won't want to come.'

Freshly attuned to the sensibilities of the lovelorn, Sylvia said, 'I'm sure he will. You must come round and see us over the holidays. He'd like to see you.'

'We could practise for his 11+ together, like you did with me.'

'We could,' Sylvia agreed, privately guessing that this would be beneath Sam's dignity. Sam was expected to sail through the exam.

Mrs Bird came back from harassing Ned and began to shoo Lizzie into her coat. 'Hurry up or your grandad'll be back from the pub and expecting his roast on the table.'

'Fancy something stronger,' Ned asked, once they had left, 'now I've got Auntie Thelma out of my hair?'

This seemed a good idea. 'Thank you. I'd love one. She's your aunt, Mrs Bird?'

'Great-aunt. Her husband, Uncle Jim, and my dad's dad are brothers, but she likes "auntie", and what Thelma wants, she gets, as my mum used to say.'

'Your mum . . .?'

'She died of the flu. Complications.'

'I'm sorry.'

'Auntie Thelma helped Dad out with us lot. He wouldn't have managed without her so I let her go on at me. It doesn't hurt.'

Sylvia, not knowing what to say, said, 'She seems very kind.'

Ned laughed. He had a rather lumpen face but it lit up when he laughed. 'Not if you get on her wrong side, she isn't. A right termagant, she can be. Mum didn't get on with her too well, to be honest. What'll you have? I've Scotch, gin and tonic, sherry, beer?'

'A G and T would be grand.' Hugh had offered her that the previous evening. 'You're well stocked up.'

'I get myself one or two treats in for Christmas. It's snug here with a few drinks and the wireless.'

'You don't get lonely?'

'I like my own company. Here you are. Cheers.'

Sylvia sipped the sparkling drink, feeling grown up and excited. The sun glittered on the tracery of frost etching the windowpanes and refracted on the dancing bubbles in the glass.

'You're the new librarian,' Ned said. 'I like books, myself.'

'What do you like to read?'

'Most things. Crime, history. I'm reading this at the moment.' He held up *The Guns of Navarone*. 'I'd have served in the Navy if I'd been old enough.'

'My father was in the RAF,' Sylvia said, her mind reverting to Hugh. Four years in a prisoner-of-war camp. And then coming home to a marriage he had grown tired of.

'I wouldn't have minded that either,' Ned said. 'I'd have given anything to have served.'

'I still remember the relief when it was all over, finally.' Those awful night raids, her head under the bedclothes, worrying that her father might be killed. 'And rationing. Wasn't it extraordinary, those first bananas?'

'I do remember my first banana being a red-letter day.'

Her new friend seemed pleased for her to stay sharing recollections of the war. He had been to London, he told her, and had been horrified at seeing the devastation of the bomb sites. 'You had it hard, you Londoners, with the Blitz.'

'We lived more in a suburb,' Sylvia said. 'But it was near enough. You could hear the planes overhead at night.'

He was the only person of her own age she had met to talk to in East Mole – even Gwen was her senior by some years. There was a comfort in it. As if she could, if need be, confide in Ned Bird.

18

Sylvia had not known what to do about the shoes and clothes she had lost somewhere in Salisbury. She had tried ringing the George and Dragon from a phone box but a foreign-sounding woman answered and she couldn't make her understand. She was on tenterhooks in the hope of hearing from Hugh, but it was not until the day of the drinks party that she saw him again.

He arrived just before the library's closing time. Dee was still busily tidying the shelves so their conversation was oblique.

'I'm returning these books for Marigold. She's much better but wheezy so she's still confined to barracks.'

'I'm sorry to hear that.' The words sounded inane.

'I'm bidden to choose some books for her. She didn't, in the end, read this. I'm afraid my enthusiasm put her off.' He passed her *I Capture the Castle*, fixing her with a stare. 'You mentioned wanting to reread it yourself.'

Dee said, 'Just nipping to get some cards from the stationery cupboard and then we can pack up.'

When she had gone Sylvia whispered, fearful Dee should come back suddenly, 'Is it all right for me to come tonight?'

'You bet. That's why I came, to make sure.' He squeezed her hand. 'I'd better get back or I'll be in the doghouse.'

'Hugh' – it still felt odd saying his name aloud – 'I'm sorry to ask but, stupidly, I left some of my clothes and my shoes in Salisbury – maybe in the pub. If you are going to see your friend again, could you maybe ask there for me?'

'I'm glad I went to your head enough to make you leave your clothes behind.'

When he had gone Sylvia opened *I Capture the Castle*. There was a note inside, written on the surgery paper.

She was reading it when Dee came back through the swing doors. 'You all right? You look a bit flushed.'

'It's hot in here with the radiators on. Shall we lock up now?'

On the way out Dee remarked, 'You need stouter footwear than those in this weather.'

The problem of her shoes had occupied Sylvia. The pumps she had bought were hardly suitable for cycling or the wet and slushy towpath so she had stuck to wellingtons and changed into the pumps for work.

'My other shoes have sprung a leak,' Sylvia improvised. 'But I've got wellies for to and from work.'

'What size are you? Must be about the same as me. If you want to come back to mine, I've plenty I can spare.'

Sylvia went back to Dee's house and tried on shoes and found a pair that fitted. Dee pressed her to stay for lunch and over cauliflower cheese Sylvia mentioned the Bells' drinks party.

'I haven't been invited. Jeanette Bell wouldn't ask the likes of me. Not the right class.'

'I'm sure it isn't that, Dee.'

'Damn right it is. Himself's been invited. Not that I care.'

Before Sylvia left Dee said, 'You can come and change into your glad rags here, if you like. Save you arriving chez Bell covered in mud, and you're welcome to a berth afterwards, if that's any use to you.'

Later that afternoon, Sylvia cycled back to Dee's. Dee welcomed her and sent her off to the spare room to change.

'Very classy,' she said when Sylvia emerged, feeling self-conscious. 'They say green's unlucky but I like it on you. Your knicker line's showing, though. Haven't you got a roll on? You're skinny as a rake but, if ever a frock needed a roll on, it's that one.'

'I don't like being constricted.'

'You'd do best to take your knickers off then. They're ruining the line.'

Sylvia resisted Dee's offer to back-comb and lacquer her hair.

'No, Dee. I don't want to look tarty.'

'You need a touch of rouge or you'll look pasty.'

She was turned round, inspected and had the seams of her stockings straightened. 'You'll do.' Dee patted her bottom. 'Now go and show up Lady Muck next door with her la-di-dah ways.'

The Bells' house, a pebble-dash semi with a neat front

garden, stood at the end of a cul-de-sac. The kind of neighbourhood her mother aspired to, Sylvia thought, not really the environment she had envisaged for Hugh. She stood some minutes on the doorstep before nerving herself to ring the bell. Marigold opened the door.

'I'm reading *Gigi*. I'm half through it already.'

'Marigold, stop chattering and bring our guest through.'

A tall, statuesque woman, her copper-coloured hair – Marigold's hair – in a French pleat, came forward. 'How do you do? Jeanette Bell, Marigold's mother. And you must be our librarian. Your reputation has gone before you. Marigold hangs on your recommendations for books.'

'Marigold hardly needs my recommendations,' Sylvia said. 'She has very sophisticated tastes for a girl her age.'

'So we are told.' Hugh's wife smiled graciously and took Sylvia's coat. 'Marigold, take Miss Blackwood's coat upstairs to our bedroom.'

'She's Sylvia,' Marigold said. 'We all call her that.'

'Not here.' Jeanette Bell turned her smile back on Sylvia. 'I'd rather we kept to the formalities, if you don't mind. I gather it has become fashionable to treat children like little adults but Hugh and I prefer to preserve the forms. You've met my husband at the library?'

'Yes,' Sylvia said. 'He's very conscientious about bringing Marigold. It must be a nuisance sometimes, him bringing her every week after the surgery,' she added, discovering in herself a surprising diplomacy.

Jeanette's smile became more gracious. 'He's a very devoted father,' she observed.

Hugh appeared through a door to the kitchen. 'Can I get you a drink?' He avoided, Sylvia noticed, using her name. 'We have almost everything – Scotch, G and T, sherry, French vermouth or there's orange or tomato juice, if you'd prefer something soft.'

'I'll have a G and T, please. I've recently acquired a taste for them.'

'Pour me one too, would you, Hugh?' Jeanette Bell said. 'I'm taking Miss Blackwood through to meet the vicar.'

She escorted Sylvia into a room decorated with a large Christmas tree. Little coloured lights had been hung around the door frames.

'I like your decorations,' Sylvia attempted.

Mrs Bell ignored this. 'Father Austin, I'd like you to meet our new librarian, Miss Blackwood. Father Austin is a great reader. We think he must be related to the famous novelist.'

The Reverend Austin was a balding, genial-looking man who pumped Sylvia's hand. To her relief, he didn't enquire about her church-going but once Jeanette Bell had moved away began to deny any link with the famous author. 'It's a different spelling. I'd adore to bask in the reflected glory of the divine Jane but I'm afraid the notion is pure moonshine.'

'I'm Blackwell, actually,' Sylvia said. 'Not Blackwood. Sylvia Blackwell.'

The Reverend Austin smiled. 'In East Mole it doesn't do to kick against the pricks.'

For a second Sylvia wondered if he had winked at her but his head was turned towards a grey-haired woman nodding vigorously at a tiny woman who was saying, 'It's not as if we didn't make money on the tombola.'

'That's my wife, Audrey, talking shop with one of her

WI cronies. A far more influential body here than the church, aren't you, my dear?'

The vicar's wife was used to her husband. 'Miss Blackwell, you remember Ivy Roberts, our treasurer. Mrs Brent, our Chairwoman, sadly couldn't make it but Mrs Wynston-Jones you'll recall.'

She indicated a woman in a royal-blue cocktail dress whom Sylvia recognised as Mrs 'Packard'.

'Is my landlady, Mrs Bird, here?'

Audrey Austin looked uncomfortable and the vicar raised an eyebrow and said, 'Not quite out of the right drawer, for our hostess,' so that Sylvia forgave him the 'divine Jane'.

Over the course of the evening Sylvia was introduced to a number of East Mole notables who, she surmised, must have come from the right drawer. She swerved around Mrs 'Packard', who, luckily, seemed to have forgotten the invitation to her 'soiree', and discovered the headmaster, Mr Arnold, nibbling from a tray of cocktail biscuits.

'Do have one before I consume the lot. They're not half bad.'

Sylvia, who was feeling the effects of only the second gin and tonic she had ever drunk in her life, helped herself to cheese straws.

'I hear congratulations are in order over your success with Lizzie Smith.'

'It was Lizzie's success, not mine.'

'I'll be frank with you, it gives one pause. We don't take enough account of a certain kind of background. Marigold here is exceptional but she has, let's be honest, advantages.'

'It's not all background, though, is it?' Sylvia suggested. 'My neighbours' son Sam Hedges is bright as paint and his parents, like mine, in fact, though very bright too, aren't' – she hesitated, not wishing to be disloyal either to her parents or the Hedges – 'especially well educated. But he's a dead cert for the Grammar.'

'No, no, I see that. And the Grammar School is there to see that lads like Sam from – how shall we say? – modest backgrounds get on.'

Sylvia was wondering how she could do as his note had suggested and snatch a private moment with Hugh. To her relief his wife, after her brief introduction, seemed to be busy at the far side of their drawing room and Sylvia, who had been waiting for a moment to signal to Hugh, reckoned that it was time to make a move.

As she was deciding this there was loud rapping at the front door.

'Sorry to be tardy, dear lady,' Mr Booth said, greeting Jeanette Bell as she hurried into the hall. His hair under the hall light gleamed with an evil-smelling pomade. 'My other half' – he gestured at a depressed-looking woman in a headscarf beside him – 'kept me waiting.'

'Mrs Booth?' Jeanette proffered a manicured hand.

Mrs Booth presented their hostess with a mildewy pot plant. 'It's an African violet.'

'How kind,' Jeanette said, putting the pot down and brushing crumbs of soil from her hands.

Mr Booth was making a play of noticing a bunch of mistletoe hanging from the lampshade. 'May I?' He stepped forward as if to kiss his hostess but she swerved in time to avoid him. 'Hugh will take your coats upstairs. Hugh!'

Mr Booth, who had caught sight of Sylvia witnessing this brush-off, flushed. 'You've met our Assistant Librarian, Dr Bell?'

Hugh, who had been helping Mrs Booth off with her coat, turned so that only Sylvia could see him and mouthed, 'The philistines are upon us,' and added aloud, 'One for the road?'

'I won't have another drink, thank you. I was just going,' Sylvia said loudly. 'How do you do, Mrs Booth?'

Mrs Booth offered a nervous hand and then glanced up at her husband to check that she hadn't done the wrong thing.

There were sounds of barking from the kitchen. 'Fetch down Miss Blackwood's coat while you're up there, Hugh,' Jeanette Bell commanded. 'I'd better see to the dog.'

'I wonder if I could use your bathroom?' Sylvia asked.

'It's upstairs. Hugh will show you.'

'You found my note? I was afraid I wouldn't be able to grab a chance to do this,' Hugh said, holding her close. 'I've been circling you all evening like a buzzard after its prey.'

'I'm not sure I know what a buzzard is like but I think I'd rather you weren't one.'

'Not a buzzard then.' He held her out again, surveying her. 'You look like a young larch tree in that dress. Oh, this is more like it,' pulling her to him again. 'Sylvia, darling girl . . .'

'I'd better let you go before the philistines come rampaging upstairs,' he said a little later.

'Wasn't that a bit dangerous of you down there?' She smoothed the bedspread. 'Isn't this?'

'You make me want to be dangerous. By the way, thanks for the mistletoe. I take it that was you.'

For the first time in their acquaintance Sylvia felt a blow of annoyance.

'What are you talking about?'

'I'm sorry.' He looked confused. 'We found a bunch of mistletoe on our doorstep. Rather vaingloriously, I supposed it had come from you. Sorry if I'm being an ass.'

'Good heavens, I wouldn't dream of doing such a ridiculous thing.' It was as if he didn't, after all, know her.

'I'm sorry,' he said again, and looked dejected. 'When can I see you?'

'Isn't it more when you can see me?'

'Tomorrow? At the foundry? Five thirty? I can use Plush for cover.'

'OK.'

'Only OK? Are you annoyed with me about the mistletoe? I'm sorry, I was imagining kissing you under it, Sylvia.'

And hadn't she, in truth, been doing the same? 'Of course I want to see you, Hugh. As soon as soon.'

Coming downstairs to the hall, conscious of his body behind hers, Sylvia was grateful that his wife was not there to see her out. She heard her in the next room, talking to Mr Booth. Her boss was saying, 'She's very young and inexperienced still, plenty to learn, but I'm gradually training her.'

Dee was waiting for her in her dressing gown. 'Come on then, spill the beans, tell me what it was like. There's some left-overs in the oven if you've room.'

After the strain of the party and the encounter with Hugh, Sylvia suddenly felt famished. 'D'you know, Dee, I could eat a horse.'

'The end of my shepherd's pie'll have to do. I'll heat up the peas.'

In the kitchen Sylvia tried to find tactful words. 'It wasn't much fun, Dee, pretend grand.' She felt slightly disloyal to Hugh saying this.

'What was Lady Muck wearing?'

Sylvia strove to be generous to her lover's wife and only partly failed. 'She looked a bit like a dressed-down Alma Cogan.'

'Mutton dressed as lamb, more like. Who else was there?'

'Well,' Sylvia said carefully, 'quite a few of the WI, some I'd met before, the vicar, whom I quite liked.'

'He's not too bad,' Dee agreed. 'He's fond of his drink.'

'He was kind about Mrs Bird. I liked him for that.'

'It's his job, isn't it? Christian charity. How about Himself? Did he show up?'

'Mr Booth? He came as I was leaving.'

'Alone?'

'No, actually.'

Dee banged down the saucepan of peas on the draining board. 'Damn and blast his bloody eyes.'

'If it's any comfort, Dee, his wife seemed a sad creature.' She had felt sorry for meek-looking Mrs Booth.

But one of Dee's qualities was a surprising sense of fair play. 'I bet he bullies the life out of her, poor cow.'

'What do you want with a bully, Dee?'

'At my age anything in trousers is a bonus.'

'Not if he's a bully, surely.'

'There's worse things than bullies,' Dee said gloomily.

'What, for example?'

'Bloody child-molesters, like Cyril. Do you want ketchup with the shepherd's pie?'

19

The approach of Christmas was a matter that Sylvia had mentally tried to avoid, which meant it was always simmering below the surface of her thoughts. Her father would be eager for her return and she could hardly bear the thought of the assumed bravado with which he would greet another dereliction. But to contemplate being out of reach of Hugh . . .

They had met, the day after the drinks party, at the foundry but Marigold had chosen to accompany her father and the encounter was tantalisingly guarded. At one point Hugh had touched her hand and Marigold had turned, and for a horrifying moment had seemed to notice the swift gesture of intimate exchange, but had then chatted cheerfully with her, so it seemed the girl had noticed nothing.

Then for a whole long week there had been no sight or word.

Mrs Bird popped into the library with a package which

proved to be a calendar with colour photographs of the countryside and quotations to mark each month. Sylvia, who had opened the parcel in order to judge what level of gift she might be expected to give in return, read, under a photo of some ponies huddled together on a snowy Dartmoor, *January brings the snow, makes our feet and fingers glow*.

Sylvia had calculated that she had fifteen shillings and sixpence to spare for Christmas presents. This money had to include her fare home. She spent the Saturday afternoon wandering round the town in search of suitable cheap gifts. She settled on a box of Coty's Black Rose bath salts for Dee, for Mrs Bird a set of coasters depicting the sights of London and for the twins, hair slides. June and Ray were to have a tin of biscuits with a pair of Scottie dogs on the lid and two packets of runner-bean seeds. Sam, she knew, craved the latest *Beano* annual and by tradition she always gave her father a book. This left only her mother – a perennial problem – and Hugh.

The former was the easier problem to solve. In the end, she selected a pale blue scarf to match her mother's eyes. This left her time to consider the most incalculable purchase because perhaps Hugh would buy her nothing at all and then any gift from her would simply look foolish.

Pondering this, she ran into him in the High Street.

They swapped stilted politenesses. 'Oh, hello there.'

'Hello.'

'You doing your Christmas shopping?'

'I've almost done it all.'

'I was wondering,' Hugh said after a few more stiff exchanges, 'if you might lend me a hand with Marigold's present. I'd like to buy her a book,' he said more loudly, so that Mrs 'Packard', who was passing, could hear, 'and I could do with your literary expertise.'

Trying not to sound eager, Sylvia said, 'I have to look for a couple of books myself.'

'Perhaps I could give you a lift to Salisbury in return for your advice about Marigold?'

'Phew,' he pronounced later as they were on the road to Salisbury in the grey Hillman. 'That was well improvised.'

In the bookshop Sylvia hesitated between *Churchill's Wartime Speeches* and *The Bridge over the River Kwai* for her father.

'Which do you think?' she asked Hugh.

'I'd go for Churchill, personally, but then I'm biased. That voice was one of my lifelines as a POW.'

'Dad's too. He doesn't talk much about the war but I have the chess set he inherited from a Czech pilot who was shot down.'

'I was with some Czechs in one of the camps. One taught me a bit of the language.'

'Really?'

'We taught each other a lot in the camps. Most of what I know about Shakespeare comes from the plays a chap called Michael Langham put on there. He's a theatre director now. I put on a couple of Gilbert and Sullivans myself. We all chipped in, pooling what we knew. It helped to pass the time.'

He stood, apparently pondering, turning in his hands the Churchill book. Long-fingered hands. 'It was an education, in more ways than one.'

Fearful of crossing some shadow line, she changed the subject. 'Might Marigold be ready for Jane Austen?'

'I'm sorry to have to tell you I'm a Jane Austen ignoramus.'

'So long as you don't call her "the divine Jane", like the vicar.'

They settled on Churchill and *Pride and Prejudice* and Sylvia bought a new children's book for the twins that she had read good reports of in the trade magazine.

Hugh squeezed her arm. 'Now, lunch.'

'What about your wife? Shouldn't you get back?'

'She has a friend staying, a frightful woman who can't stand me. Frankly, the feeling's mutual. Jeanette will be only too glad to have me out of the house. Where shall we go? Not the George this time.'

They found an Italian restaurant near the cathedral, hung about with fishing nets in which plastic vines bearing purple plastic grapes and Chianti bottles were improbably entwined. They ate veal escalope and drank wine and for afters Hugh ordered zabaglione.

'This is delicious,' Sylvia said, 'but it's making me tipsy. What's in it?'

'So long as it makes you tipsy you don't need to know.'

Over coffee, he produced from his pocket a small box. 'This reminded me of you in your green dress.'

'Oh, but I haven't –'

'Don't. I would have to conceal anything you gave me. You can wear this and say your mother gave it to you.'

'Hardly my mother,' Sylvia said, pinning to her blouse a beaten-silver brooch in the shape of a slender leaf. 'She's never given me anything half as lovely.'

'Lovely people should have lovely things.'

'Hugh,' Sylvia said, 'what's going to happen? I mean . . .' But she herself didn't really know what she meant.

'About you and me?'

'I'm sorry. I shouldn't ask.'

He stretched across the table to squeeze her hand. 'It'll all be Sir Garnet Wolseley.'

For a moment she was irritated. 'Who's he when he's at home?'

He laughed and said, 'A famous general in the Crimean War. It means, trust me, it will all work out OK.'

Sylvia couldn't help reflecting that the Crimean War was not the most reassuring parallel for a love affair, but she kept the thought to herself.

Back in East Mole, Mrs 'Packard' was saying to Mrs Brent, 'I saw her go off with him in his car. Bold as brass.'

Mrs Brent looked grave. 'She seemed a respectable enough girl when she came to speak to us at the WI.'

Mrs 'Packard' had noted Sylvia avoiding her at the Bells' party. 'It's the quiet ones you have to watch, in my experience.'

20

Although it snowed before Christmas the fall was the faint-hearted kind, which turns to slush before it even settles, and a blow to the East Mole children's hopes of snowmen and snowball fights. Sylvia's hopes for a possible impediment to her journey to Ruislip were also dashed. But her conscience smote her at her father's joy at having her home again. Even her mother seemed glad to see her.

Climbing between the cold sheets of her childhood bed, Sylvia remembered how she had yearned for any sign of her mother's pleasure in her presence, saving up to buy her little gifts, helping with the household chores in order to win her approval. And now it had come too late.

Was it love or laziness that had made her father give up his life for her mother's version of it? Or pity for his wife's straitened vision, the pity that she now felt, in turn, for her father? Impossible not to think of Hugh and Jeanette Bell. Would Marigold, in the years to come, be reflecting on Hugh like this? It was horrible, this pity she felt for her father. He should have had a son, she thought, sliding out of bed to find a cardigan. I should have had a brother too.

On Christmas Eve, by tradition, the Blackwells attended Midnight Mass. Standing in the crowded church, Sylvia's mind was flooded with thoughts of Hugh. 'The first Hugh Bell, the angels did say,' her mind carolled, so clearly it seemed that the whole congregation must hear it. The days during which there was no chance of seeing him stretched unendurably before her.

Christmas Day was not as bad as she had feared. The Queen's Christmas address was to be televised for only the second time and Sylvia's father had capitulated to his wife's desire to keep up with the Joneses and bought a TV on Hire Purchase. The example of the Hedges had been used in this campaign. 'But theirs was one June's dad got off a customer and renovated,' he had protested. But the Joneses won the day and Sylvia and her parents squashed up together on the sofa to witness the miracle of a crowned monarch brought into their sitting room.

'Very dignified,' was Sylvia's mother's verdict.

'She's a chip off the old block,' her father decided. 'You were quite right, Old Girl, making me get this.'

Sylvia's choice of presents went down well too – her father delivered extracts from Churchill's speeches and her mother actually wore her scarf. Her parents' gift to her was a bulky package.

'What is it?' Sylvia was flummoxed.

'It's a Teasmade,' her mother said. 'So you won't have to risk your neck going down those dreadful stairs in the mornings.'

'Your mother ordered it specially,' her father said proudly.

And Sylvia, who almost above all things enjoyed standing in the mornings watching the birds through number 5's window while the kettle boiled, felt her eyes prick with tears. Her mother had tried to think about her. Do you have to remove yourself, then, to be wanted? she wondered. If so, then maybe it was as well that she was at a distance from Hugh.

The library was closed till the New Year but Sylvia had made an excuse for getting back to East Mole earlier. She was greeted by exuberant twins.

'SYLVIA! SYLVIA! We LOVE the Grinch.'

'Oh, good. I am glad.'

'He stole Christmas, the Grinchy did,' Jem said with satisfaction. 'Will you read it us? Please, please, Sylvia, PLEASE.'

'Let me settle back in first.'

Sam, not far behind his sisters, said, 'I made you a thank-you present.'

'That's very kind, Sam.'

'We made you one too,' Pam said, 'but it got thrown out.'

Sylvia had hardly finished unpacking when Sam came to the door. He handed her a length of hollowed-out wood. 'It's from the plum tree that got hit in the storm.'

'It's beautiful.' Sylvia examined the carvings of leaves spiralling round the wood. 'Who taught you to do this?'

'My grandpa. I've got some of his tools.'

She propped the carved branch on the kitchen windowsill. 'I can put leaves and feathers and things in it. Thank you, Sam, I shall treasure this.'

'What's that?' Sam was looking at the Teasmade.

'A machine for making tea automatically. It wakes you up in the mornings so you don't need to get up and put on the kettle.'

'Is that why it's called a Teasmade?' Sam said, reading the packaging. ''Cos the tea's made in it?'

'D'you know, I'd not thought of that.'

'Can we try it?'

'You'll have to read the instructions. I can't make head nor tail of them.'

Sam filled the Teasmade with water and set the alarm to go off while he helped Sylvia make up and light a fire. He stood on the hearth rug, saying nothing for so long that finally Sylvia asked, 'Is there something you want to say, Sam?'

He muttered but all she could hear was '. . . old Gingernut-case'.

Sylvia had worked out the mystery of the surprise appearance of mistletoe at the Bells'. 'Sam, did you by chance rob Mr Collins' apple tree to give Marigold the mistletoe?' Sam assumed his blank stare and she said, 'I'm not cross. I'd just like to know.'

'Did she say?'

'No. But I did hear that some mistletoe had turned up on their doorstep.'

'It wasn't for kissing.' Sam looked fierce. 'It was a dare. She dared me to it. Only I slipped coming down and the branch broke off.'

'Ah.'

'The thing is . . .' Sam started, and stopped again.

'Yes?'

'Dad was asking and I didn't want him thinking I was lying so I kind of said it was for you.'

'Why for me?'

'Dad wouldn't mind if I done it for you.'

'"Did" it for me, Sam, not "done".'

She saw his grey eyes begin to fill and felt contrite. Only sadists enjoy the sight of the proud being set down. 'Sam, listen, that's the Teasmade going off. Let's sample the tea over a chocolate Digestive and you tell me exactly what it is you've said I said that you could do.'

Afterwards, Sylvia saw the row over Mr Collins' apple tree as the harbinger of all the troubles that followed.

It began with her being kept waiting in the late-afternoon chill on his doorstep. When at last she heard his slippers shuffling to the front door he opened it a mere crack.

'Mr Collins, may I come in?'

Her neighbour fumbled with a chain and stood with his back pressed against the wall, as if she were the carrier of some infectious disease.

Number 4's door opened straight into a living room. The room was sparsely furnished with a couple of utility armchairs. No pictures, only a framed photograph on the mantelpiece beneath which one bar of an electric fire gave off a feeble heat.

Sylvia stood uncertainly in the middle of the in-hospitable room. 'It's about your apple tree I've come, Mr Collins.'

'Yes?'

'I may have unintentionally misled you.'

'Indeed?'

With the first rush of resolution ebbing away, Sylvia

floundered a little. 'It seems that I may, that I unintentionally gave Sam Hedges the idea that I would like the branch of your tree that overhangs my path removed.'

'I see.'

'Yes,' Sylvia went on, trying to collect her story. 'I left Sam a note requesting him to tidy the garden, especially round the path, because my landlord, that is to say my landlady's husband, Mr Bird –'

'I know who Jim Bird is.'

'Yes, well, he, Mr Bird, had told me, while Sam was with me, that that branch of your tree which overhangs . . .'

'Which overhung!'

'Yes, of course, which overhung your garden, was by rights mine, as their tenant, the Birds' tenant, to remove, since, technically . . .'

'So it was you?' Mr Collins asked. His pale eyes stared.

'Not as such,' Sylvia said. She was overtaken by a strong desire to laugh.

'I see.' Mr Collins' little rosebud mouth was set. 'The boy denied it – most vehemently. And his parents too.'

'Yes,' Sylvia said, hoping she sounded suitably placating. 'I know. His parents didn't know, they weren't aware. Sam was alarmed that he had unintentionally done the wrong thing and as I was away and he couldn't –'

'But I asked you about it, Miss Blackwell. I asked you most specifically *before* you went away. I have the date in my diary.'

'Yes,' Sylvia said, foraging rather desperately for inspiration. 'You did and I'm sorry. But at that point Sam hadn't had a chance, *we* hadn't had a chance, I should say, to speak and –'

'Miss Blackwell,' her neighbour interrupted. 'You are a public servant. A public servant whom I had a hand in appointing. This behaviour is really most unusual.'

He scratched his freckled scalp and a cloud of dandruff settled on the shoulders of his jersey: an old school jumper shrunk in the wash, moth-eaten and too tight across his little paunch. Distressed by this vision of elderly inadequacy, Sylvia averted her gaze and found it directed at a solitary Christmas card on Mr Collins' ugly sideboard. Although she had delivered cards to the Hedges and to all her East Mole acquaintance, she had not even considered sending her neighbour a card.

Looking at the crude picture of the baby Jesus in his crib being worshipped by a couple of shepherds and a snooty-looking Heavenly Host above, she said, 'I'm most awfully sorry, Mr Collins. I'd like to make it up to you.' June's gift to her had been a tin of mince pies. 'Could I maybe invite you to tea?'

As if divining her thoughts, he brushed his shoulder irritably. 'That won't be necessary.'

'It would be nice if we could be friends.' And at that moment she truly believed this was possible.

But her neighbour closed his eyes, as if such a notion were peculiarly abhorrent to him. 'I shall have to consider reporting this to your superior at the library.'

Sylvia was suddenly spurred to anger. 'Do, by all means, Mr Collins. But I think you'll find that I was perfectly within my rights over removing that branch.'

Mrs Bird had said so. In this at least she could trust Mrs Bird.

21

Sylvia was not too surprised when the following day she was summoned to speak to Mr Booth.

'He wants you in his office,' Dee told her. 'Something to do with your neighbour.'

Her boss was sitting behind his desk, apparently sorting through some papers, when she tapped at the open door.

'Sit down, please, Miss Blackwell. This morning I received a complaint from one of your neighbours.'

'Oh?'

'Mr Collins,' her boss continued. 'Who, I am sure I need not remind you, is the Chair of the Library Committee. He informs me that there has been an issue over his property.'

It crossed Sylvia's mind to say: What the hell's it got to do with you? 'It's about his apple tree, I expect, Mr Booth.'

'He suggests that you are responsible for damaging it.'

'No.'

'You deny that?'

'Yes.'

Mr Booth looked at the open page of a spiral notebook and read out in a pompous voice, '"I became aware that a large section of the tree had been torn down."' He cleared his throat. 'I am quoting Mr Collins' own words.'

'Yes?'

Mr Booth continued to read from his notes. '"Suspecting that Miss Blackwell might know the perpetrator, I approached her and she denied any knowledge of how the damage had come to occur. Subsequently –"'

This was too much. '"Subsequently,"' Sylvia interrupted, 'I told him that I was inadvertently responsible.' Mr Booth began to speak but Sylvia pressed on. 'My neighbour's son removed a branch which overhung the garden path of the property I am renting. Legally, it seems, one can remove vegetation that overhangs one's property. My landlady spoke to the Council about it.'

There was a silence, during which each weighed up their opponent. Then Mr Booth said, 'Mr Collins has of course checked his rights.' He coughed and began to read aloud again. '"It is a requirement that the owner of the said shrub, bush or tree is first invited to remove any extraneous growth himself."'

Sylvia's apparently placid disposition was proving to conceal a temperament that became cold and resolute under fire.

'You see, Mr Booth,' she said sweetly, 'the branch was a hazard.'

'A hazard?'

'A health hazard. Sam was quite correct. I did have it in

mind to remove the branch. He merely jumped the gun. My landlady's husband, Mr Bird, gave his eye a nasty graze on it when he came to help with the garden. I was afraid one of the little Hedges might run into it and hurt themselves and then, you see, I would have been responsible. The tree suffered damage during the storm and the branch was just at the children's eye level – I heard of someone once' – she began to enjoy herself – 'who ran into a branch, a perfectly innocent-seeming branch, and went stone-blind.'

Mr Booth's hyper-thyroidish eyes blinked.

'I, naturally, apologised to Mr Collins,' Sylvia continued, confident that the moral high ground was now hers, 'the moment I worked out what had occurred to cause all this confusion. And I invited him to tea. An olive branch' – here she had a flash of inspiration – 'to offset the apple branch, you see. Sadly, he was otherwise engaged.'

She left the office feeling, as she put it to Hugh, like Daniel leaving the lions' den. Except that Hugh, save in her mind, wasn't there.

She had seen nothing of him. Not even a letter, which, over their lunch in Salisbury, he had hinted he might send to soften his absence over Christmas.

This is madness, she said to herself. I'm involved with a married man. What a cliché.

To distract herself she tried to revive her plans for the school.

'How about a Roman Britain project?' she suggested to Sam. 'There's plenty of Roman remains round here.'

Sam's interest in reading had receded with the departure of Marigold to her new school. He had painstakingly ploughed through *A Tale of Two Cities* and had come faithfully to the library in the hope, Sylvia was sure, of discussing it with Marigold. But neither Marigold nor her father made an appearance. Sylvia didn't know whether to be worried or angry and veered crazily between both states of mind.

After two bleak weeks Sam didn't even fake an excuse for accompanying her to the library. He mooched along the towpath, morosely kicking stones and audibly swearing when he missed his mark. Sylvia had developed a rare spot on her forehead and had picked at it so that it resembled a Hindu bindi and was now trying to pretend to herself that she didn't care what she looked like or who saw it.

They were both therefore surprised to find Marigold sitting on the library steps. 'Hi there, slowcoaches!' she yelled.

A change had come over Marigold. Her Edwardian-style girl's frock had been replaced by a pair of tight blue jeans. Her copper-coloured hair was scraped up in a ponytail, she wore a sloppy mohair jumper and over her shoulder an army haversack.

'Hello, Marigold,' Sylvia said. 'You look as if you've run away from home.'

Marigold sighed. 'No such luck.'

'What you doing here?' Sam tried to sound indifferent.

'Waiting for you, fathead. I came to see if you fancied going into Salisbury.'

Sam assumed his super-casual tone. 'Yeah, don't mind if I do.'

'Righto,' Marigold said. 'Let's go, Daddy-O.'

*

'I found the Bell girl in here cool as a cucumber without so much as a by-your-leave when I arrived,' Dee said. She had taken to coming in on a Saturday, which Sylvia guessed had something to do with her affair with Mr Booth. 'She claimed she was waiting for you. I packed her off outside. Little minx.'

'I think it was Sam she was waiting for,' Sylvia said.

Dee assumed a disapproving expression. 'I didn't so much as look at a boy till I was well gone fifteen.'

Sylvia, who rather doubted this, said, 'She's probably just a bit in want of companionship.' She made no mention of Hugh's concerns about Marigold's lack of friends.

Dee's expression became knowing. 'I wouldn't be so sure. They start young these days. I read in the *Express* that they reckon it was the war.'

It was a dull morning. Few children came to change their books and those who did chose mostly books Sylvia disliked. By a quarter past twelve she was in a thoroughly bad temper. The spot on her forehead hurt and seemed to have spread and a malicious ladder had appeared in her stocking.

'Damn, that's my last matching pair.'

'Do you want to borrow my nail varnish?' Dee asked.

Sylvia was bent over, applying nail varnish to her stocking, when from behind her she heard, 'I was wondering if by chance you've seen my errant daughter.'

She spun round, tipping nail varnish down her skirt. 'Oh, bloody, *bloody* hell!'

'Hey,' Hugh said, grabbing her arm. 'Are you all right?'

Sylvia looked swiftly round. Dee had disappeared and they were alone.

'Not really.'

'What's up?'

'Oh, nothing. Just life.'

'You're too young to say, "Just life."'

She had turned her face away so he would not see her spot and she couldn't judge his expression. 'I said it, didn't I?'

'Sylvia, are you by any chance cross because you haven't seen me?'

'I'm not a child. I know you have many claims on your time.' She sensed he was scrutinising her averted face.

'Well, I'm *very* cross that I've not seen you. So there.'

'Dr Bell is looking for Marigold,' Sylvia said as Dee swung in through the doors. 'I was telling him you saw her here earlier.'

'I thought you said you saw her outside.'

'Oh yes, I was forgetting. She's gone into Salisbury with Sam. I'm sorry, Dee, I seem to have spilt your varnish.'

Dee gave Sylvia an old-fashioned look and said, 'All right if we lock up now, only I've got to get on?'

'You go, Dee. I'll see to it.'

'If you're sure, then I'll be off.'

When Dee had gone Hugh said, 'I've missed you like hell and, by the way, that spot isn't so very terrible.'

'I never have them usually.'

'Of course not.' He brushed a hand over her hair. 'But I rather like it that you're still really a teenager. Listen, I've been unable to get away because my partner, Dr Monk in the surgery, is ill so I've had to work double time. And Jeanette's been in a pother over Marigold . . .'

'I thought you'd gone off me,' she said, trying not to show the uprush of tears.

'More likely you'll go off an old buffer like me.'

Reconciled for the moment, they stood holding hands beneath the plaster gaze of Mr Gladstone.

'Look,' Hugh said, 'this dodging about and hiding in corners is no good at all. I was wondering, I mean, you must say if you'd rather not, but there's a weekend conference for GPs about managing a practice in the NHS coming up next month which I can legitimately say I have to attend. I was thinking that maybe you might like to come too, if only for an evening dinner, or . . .'

'Where is it?'

'London. They put us up in a not half-bad hotel and I could always get you a room there if . . . I mean, there's no need to decide now. You can think about it.'

It required no thought. 'I'd love to come, if you're sure it'll be all right.'

'Oh, it'll be all right, all right,' Hugh said, kissing her.

22

The prospect of the forthcoming trip to London with Hugh was disrupting Sylvia's days and had overtaken her nights. Her sleep was undermined by waves of anxiety, the fear that some catastrophe – another storm, a life-threatening illness in Marigold, a general strike – would upend the whole enterprise, and a conviction that the whole affair was hopeless. She swung like a madwoman between planning a trousseau complete with silk underwear and mentally composing a brave note to Hugh hinting at self-denying reasons for her leaving East Mole. Somehow, this left no room for any feelings of guilt over his wife.

Sylvia had not liked to probe Sam about his trip with Marigold to Salisbury but from his few remarks she gathered it had gone well. They had apparently found a coffee bar with a juke box, where Marigold had produced money to play the latest hits. Marigold, it seemed, was now a committed follower of Cliff Richard and The Drifters.

'Who are they, Sam?'

Sam looked scornful. '"Move It"'s been in the charts since last summer.'

Since the Salisbury outing Sam had become almost ostentatiously helpful at the library. In an effort to salvage some sanity, Sylvia had attempted to float her Roman Britain project.

'I can't seem to get your colleague Sue interested,' she had complained to Gwen one evening at the Troubadour.

'Sue's a bit of a shrinking violet.'

Sylvia had met Sue Bunce and had grown sceptical of her supposed fragility. 'To be honest, Gwen, I wouldn't say that was the first image that comes to mind.'

Nevertheless, she had ordered in all the Rosemary Sutcliffs.

'What's this about?' Sam asked, holding out a copy of *The Silver Branch*.

'It's part of a trilogy about Roman Britain. The hero's a Roman doctor,' Sylvia began, and the demon that compels us to voice the names of those we are smitten with made her add, 'Like Marigold's father.'

Sam shared this malaise. 'Marigold says her dad might take her and me to Bath to see the Roman baths. There's a Wimpy Bar she says he'll take us to.'

Marigold's visits to the library had resumed. Nowadays she arrived unaccompanied and she and Sam spoke in lowered voices and guffawed together in corners so that Sylvia had to banish them to preserve the quiet.

She was proud of her library. Her early hard work had borne fruit and the East Mole children and their parents now came regularly and eagerly to change their books. At times she experienced surges of overwhelming love for her little customers, prospecting the shelves for new finds, or sitting spread-legged on the floor, absorbed in exploring the varied kingdoms to which the books she had chosen for them had opened doors. Enthused by the affair with Hugh, she had set up a Poetry Corner, where poems she had Roneod on the copy machine were posted up, and started a Story Club for the under-fives.

Although she missed Hugh's visits to the library, there was London to look forward to and she was glad on the whole not to have to meet him with Dee around. Dee was sharp-eyed and continued to make the odd allusion to Sylvia's 'love life'; Sylvia was banking on the affair with Mr Booth guaranteeing her colleague's discretion.

While Mr Booth had recovered a veneer of politeness and made no further outright mention of the unpleasantness with Mr Collins, he referred from time to time in vaguely threatening tones to the Library Committee. Sylvia was conscious that her boss's dislike of her had grown incrementally with her popularity. There was nothing he could say about the Poetry Corner but she suspected he was looking for reasons to close down the Story Club, which Mad Mary had taken to attending and where mothers left their children so they could get in their shopping unencumbered. So when one morning he met her in the hall with a grave face and pronounced solemnly, 'Miss Blackwell, a word,' she followed him to his office guessing that he had contrived some new angle of attack with which to try to close down this enterprise.

But it was not the Story Club that he had summoned her to speak about.

'I am afraid, Miss Blackwell, there has been a very serious incident. A theft has occurred.'

'Oh dear, what has been taken, Mr Booth?'

Mr Booth's brow contracted. 'I am sorry to have to tell you that the Restricted Access cupboard has been rifled.'

'Heavens! What has gone?'

Mr Booth looked fleetingly discomposed. 'I am not at liberty to reveal that at present. Suffice to say that one of our most artistic acquisitions has been removed.'

'How?'

'That, Miss Blackwell, is exactly what I wanted to ask you.'

His hard-boiled eyes stared at her and Sylvia, to her intense annoyance, began to blush. Damn this wretched habit of hers! 'Honestly, Mr Booth, I don't know anything about it.'

Her boss marched her back along the corridor to the Children's Library. Dee was already there, inspecting the Restricted Access cupboard.

'We put it here in the corner to be well out of the kids' way. It was locked when I last checked and you have the only key, Mr Booth.'

Mr Booth shot her a warning look. 'It would appear,' he pronounced, 'that the Restricted Access collection has been entered by other means.'

Whoever had penetrated the cupboard had done so skilfully. It had been prised open with some care and then, with the use of chewing gum, stuck shut in order to give an impression that nothing had been tampered with.

'How did you discover it?' Sylvia asked.

Dee looked at the floor and Mr Booth said, 'I asked

Mrs Harris to check it, as a precaution, to make sure that all was well, and the theft became apparent.'

'Has much been taken?' Sylvia asked.

'Just the one book.'

Sylvia looked at Dee, who looked quickly back down at the floor. 'I suppose the book is replaceable?'

Her boss flushed. 'It was published in Paris, a special edition. It is unlikely that we can readily avail ourselves of another copy.'

Dee winked at Sylvia. Dee, she surmised, had used her renewed position with Mr Booth to ask if she could view the contents of the cupboard.

Mr Booth had rung the police to report the theft but when a policeman turned up he hurried out of the room, saying, 'Back to work now, you two.'

'He doesn't want you hearing what was taken,' Dee said once he was out of earshot.

'What was taken?'

'*Tropic of Cancer* by Henry Miller. Blue as an Eskimo's arse in winter, by all accounts. I don't blame whoever took it but I wish they'd had the decency to let me have a dekko first.'

'Who do you think it was, Dee?'

'Himself has no need. He has the key.'

'And I'm assuming so do you now, so to speak?'

'It's how he discovered it,' Dee said rather smugly. 'I was on at him to let me have a look. He's quite proud of his power there, you know, so after quite a lot of buttering him up he agreed and that's when we found that someone else with an equally dirty mind had got in beforehand.'

'Oh Lord,' Sylvia suddenly realised, 'if it can't be him or you then I'm bound to be the chief suspect.'

'It wasn't you, by any chance?' Dee asked.

'Of course not!'

'I did wonder.'

'Dee!' Sylvia was hurt.

'Don't get your knickers in a twist. Curiosity's perfectly normal. If you want my opinion, shutting books away like that just fires your imagination; only makes you want to read them more.'

This was the start of a fuss that was to become the chief talking point of East Mole for many weeks. But at the time Sylvia had more personal matters on her mind. As the day for her visit to London approached, she seemed less and less able to function normally. She borrowed Misty and Melanie from the Hedges and marched them restlessly up and down the towpath. A couple of times she encountered Lizzie's cousin Ned fixing the windows in the lock-keeper's cottage.

He greeted her with, 'See you're keeping fit.'

'I like walking.'

'You must, in this weather.' The weather had turned foul and the towpath was a slurry of mud. 'The wind's coming through these windows like a hound from hell.'

The second time he saw her he invited her in for a drink.

'You all right then?' he enquired, handing her a whisky and ginger.

Sylvia was stricken with the fear that her demeanour must be giving something away. 'Yes, I'm fine, thank you, Ned.'

'Funny old place, East Mole,' he opined.

'I like it.'

'There's no accounting for tastes.' Ned got up to tip more coal on the fire.

'I came from a London suburb that was dull as ditch-water. I like . . .' What was it that she liked . . .? 'I like the countryside, the birds and the flowers, and the people too. I've made good friends here.' She schooled herself not to blush as, inevitably, her mind summoned Hugh. 'Gwen Williams, the teacher at the school, and my neighbours the Hedges and their children and you, Ned, and your cousin Lizzie and, well, all the children who come to the library. I –' She wanted to say 'love them' but was too shy. 'I like them a lot. Don't you then?'

'Like them or East Mole? I was born here, remember. The kids are all right but there's some evil tongues around. Nice as pie to your face, those old biddies, but behind your back . . .' He grimaced.

Suddenly apprehensive, Sylvia said, 'You make it all sound rather sinister.'

'Don't mind me. Anyway, you have to make the best of things.'

'I suppose you do,' Sylvia agreed. For a moment she juggled with the idea of confiding about Hugh.

'You're all right,' Ned said. 'Auntie Thelma likes you. She can't speak well enough of you since you helped our Liz. Her word goes a long way round here.'

Sylvia abandoned any idea of confiding. For all he appeared so trustworthy, Ned was Mrs Bird's great-nephew and she was beginning to know enough to recognize that whoever else she might trust it was not quite safe to trust Mrs Bird.

*

It had been agreed between Hugh and Sylvia that she would come to London to meet him on the Saturday afternoon when she had finished work.

'I'll be tied up for most of the day, worse luck,' Hugh had said. He had sounded nervous and among Sylvia's anxieties was the apprehension that he was now regretting his invitation. She was old enough to have learned that the things we most look forward to often turn out to be disappointing, just as the things we dread are usually, in practice, less awful than we suppose. Reminding herself of this bleak truth, she tried to concentrate her efforts on fearing the weekend but, boarding the train in Swindon, she felt weak with a deluge of excitement.

Hugh had given her money for a taxi – 'I can't take this,' she had protested but he was adamant: 'I don't want you getting lost in London. It's for my peace of mind.' And she had to admit she was glad of it because by the time she alighted at Paddington her legs had begun to shake so much she wasn't sure she could have managed the Tube.

The hotel, a tall white stuccoed house with a man in green uniform and gold braid standing guard at the entrance, was near the museums in South Kensington. She was shown to a room on an upper floor with a single bed and grimy windows that overlooked a noisy street.

Sylvia unpacked her case, put on the coral-coloured frock she had worn at the Elgar concert, took it off again, studied herself in her underwear in the looking glass, changed first the bra and then the knickers and put back on the skirt and blouse she had travelled in. For some reason this made her feel more secure.

Hugh had said he wouldn't be free until six so she spent an hour in the Natural History Museum, pretending to look at dusty-feathered birds with dead eyes and their plundered eggs and the stuffed elephants standing lofty and imperious in the great central hall. Then it was time to meet Hugh.

He met her by the entrance to South Kensington Tube station.

'Hello there.'

'Hello.'

'Journey here OK?'

'Fine, thanks.'

'No difficulties with the taxi or anything?'

'No, it was fine, thanks.'

'Your room all right at the hotel?'

'Yes, thank you, it's very nice.'

'Sorry the weather isn't better for you.'

This was dire. She followed him round the corner to an Italian café.

'I wasn't sure where but if this isn't . . .?'

'No, honestly, this looks fine.'

They sat opposite each other at a table by a window, which laid them open to the stares of passers-by. Feeling exposed, Sylvia said that she didn't know what to order so Hugh ordered spaghetti Bolognese for them both. They drank red wine out of a raffia-skirted bottle and tried to recapture the will-o'-the-wisp spirit that had led them there.

Hugh examined the dessert menu for longer than the content could warrant while Sylvia tried surreptitiously to wipe away with a wetted napkin a tomato stain she'd dripped on to her skirt.

'Ice cream or fruit salad and cream, though the signs are both may be out of a tin?' he asked abruptly.

Sylvia said, 'Out of a tin's fine and, if you like, I can go home.'

After that it got better.

They walked hand in hand up the road to the park and along to the Albert Memorial.

'Poor old Albert,' Hugh said.

'Why "poor"?'

'Consider his life with that monster of a woman.'

'I thought they were supposed to be madly in love. Weren't they a great love story?'

'That was *her* story! If you ask me, he died to get away from her.'

There was a jazz concert about to start at the Albert Hall.

'Shall we go?' Hugh said.

'I don't know anything about jazz.'

'That don't mean a thing. You don't need to "know" about jazz. But it's up to you, my darling. You say.'

He had called her 'my darling', which was enough for her to want to fall in with any plan. They bought tickets and sat, Hugh with his arm around her, high, high up at the back of the hall. Far below them men in striped waistcoats and narrow ties played saxes and trumpets and clarinets. One of the band, with a neat beard and a bowler hat, began an improvised solo on the clarinet.

'That's Acker Bilk,' Hugh whispered. 'Listen.'

She listened. But afterwards she could recall nothing but the effect of the music which was to take her somehow bodiless up into the great grandiose dome where her mind seemed to loosen and drift deliciously away from her.

Walking back after the concert, in answer to his question, she said, 'I can't say whether I "liked" it but it was – it was different and strange and I liked that.'

'Funny child.'

Not entirely relishing this, Sylvia tried to sound adult. 'I wish I knew more about music. How do you know so much?'

'I don't really "know" all that much. But I find it consoling.'

'Like me with books?'

'Music is my private prescription for my moods. I have a feeling you don't have moods.' He pulled her closer to him so that her hipbone knocked against his. 'A pair of walking skellingtons, we are.'

But she wanted to hear more of his moods. 'Surely everyone has moods, don't they?'

'It's a matter of degree. I'm willing to bet my stethoscope I'm a whole lot moodier than you.'

'A stethoscope's not much to bet.'

'That's what you think. They're darned expensive. But OK, my blood-pressure unit too.'

As they arrived at the hotel door he said, 'Listen, darling Sylvia, I honestly don't mind how you answer this but you must say if you want to go straight up to your own room now.'

'Did you really "not mind" how I answered your question last night?' she asked the following morning. She would have bet she hadn't slept a wink but had awoken with him leaning on one elbow, gazing down at her.

He bent and kissed her forehead. 'What do you think?'

'I certainly hope you would have minded.'

'Thank God for your honesty. If you had been coy, I'd have kicked you out of bed here and now.'

'I don't believe that.'

'You're right. I'd have considered that ungentlemanly. But I'd probably have kicked you out of my mind, which, I can tell you, is far worse.'

Sylvia sat up. 'That's rather frightening.'

'What is? Here.' He lit two cigarettes and put one in her mouth.

'The thought that I might get kicked out of your mind suddenly.'

He laughed and said, 'I don't see it looming.'

'Isn't that what happened to Jeanette?'

'Oh God, do we have to bring Jeanette in?'

He got out of bed and put on pyjama trousers.

'Sorry.' He was in his dressing gown by the door. 'Where are you going?' She was genuinely frightened now.

'To urinate. It's not considered good form to walk stark naked down an English hotel corridor.'

When he came back she was sitting on the end of the bed wrapped in the sheet.

'Why are you wrapped up like a mummy?'

'I haven't got a dressing gown.'

'Now you're being sly.'

'And you are being bloody unfair!' To her horror, tears were spilling out of her eyes and she turned away, trying hopelessly to hide them.

'Oh, darling Sylvia, I'm sorry. I'm a brute. Come here.'

A little later, unlocking her naked body from his, she said, 'That was only the third time I've made love.'

'Who were the first and second? Not that I'm jealous.'

'You were, idiot!' It was safe to call him that now. 'Last night. I've never, I mean you were, you *are* the first.'

'Oh, Christ. I *am* an idiot. A blithering idiot. I should have known. Did I hurt you? You should have said. Sylvia?'

'I didn't want to. And no, you didn't.'

'Did you think I'd think less of you if you told me? God, I'm so sorry. Darling girl, are you sure I didn't hurt you?'

'No, honestly, you didn't. It was, it was fine.'

'Only "fine"?'

'More than fine. Especially, well' – here she became embarrassed – 'the second time. I didn't say because, because I thought you might change your mind.'

'I doubt if I'd've been able to. Come here.'

Later still she said, 'Would you really not have been jealous if, I mean if there had been someone else before?'

'What do you think?'

'I really don't know. You've had people before.' She was careful now not to mention Jeanette by name.

'That's different.'

'Why? Why is it different?'

This time it was he who sat up. 'I don't know. It's tradition, I suppose. The man is allowed to be experienced and the woman –'

'Isn't allowed to be?' she interrupted.

'I didn't make the rules.'

They seemed to have been parachuted back into the terrifying no-man's-land of the restaurant the previous evening.

Why did I come? Sylvia thought. I don't know him. I don't know who he is.

After a few minutes he said, 'Look, I'd better dress. I should probably make a token appearance at the conference. There's a bathroom down the hall.'

She began fumblingly to pick up her discarded clothes and, without looking up, he said, 'Borrow my dressing gown, if you like,' and went on putting on his socks.

In the bathroom, while the taps were running, she sat on the bath mat and cried. Then she lay in a few inches of lukewarm water in the stained bath until someone rattled the bathroom-door handle and a stranger's voice called crossly, 'Can you hurry up in there?'

Hugh was dressed when she got back to the room. Not looking at her, he said, 'Do you want any breakfast because they don't serve it here?'

She pulled on her clothes hastily, her body still clammy. 'Shall I go and pack my things?'

'Yes, better had.'

Outside, the sky above them was white and minatory. They walked side by side lugging cases and scrupulously avoiding each other's body, to a coffee bar by the Tube, where a waitress with a beehive hairdo and pale lipstick waved them to a booth.

'I'm glad you don't look like that,' Hugh said.

Thinking of Jeanette Bell's Alma Cogan outfit, Sylvia said, 'How do you like women to look?'

'I don't know about "women". I liked you in your flamingo dress. Where is it, by the way?'

'It's in my case. I brought it with me but then I didn't feel like wearing it.'

He laughed and said, 'Daft apeth!' and quite suddenly everything was all right again.

Hugh said that if she could bear to wait he would be finished by one o'clock and then they had the afternoon.

By the time they met in Trafalgar Square, the day had brightened along with their mood and they clambered up to sit by the lions and eat hot dogs bought from a hawker.

'I've never had one of these before,' she told him.

'It's the Yankees,' he said. 'They like to think they won the war for us and now they feel they have licence to take over our culture. Marigold has become the latest victim. She nagged us into getting her a gramophone of her own and now we have to suffer all this ghastly rock and roll.'

It was his first mention of his daughter since they had met in London and some instinct in Sylvia kept her from making a response.

He seemed preoccupied and for a moment she feared the black hole was opening up between them again but as he jumped her down from the high platform he said, 'This sounds crazy but you wouldn't put your flamingo dress on for me? I'd like to remember you here, as a flamingo among the lions.'

And because it seemed that they had, after all, found each other again she went to the public lavatory at the corner of the square to change.

When she emerged up the steps he grabbed her by the

waist and whirled her round so that her skirt billowed out and a passing sailor wolf-whistled.

'There, all the boys in town want you,' he said, setting her down. 'Aren't I the lucky one? What now? The National or the Portrait Gallery?'

'I've never been to either.'

'Then you must say.'

Unable to choose, Sylvia did a schoolgirl 'Ip dip dip' and it came out for the National Portrait Gallery.

Arm in arm, comfortable together now, they discussed the portraits and argued about which of the subjects they would choose to invite for dinner. Hugh chose Handel. 'He's terribly ugly,' Sylvia objected.

'I didn't know looks were a criterion. His music is divine.'

'All right, you can sit next to him.' She chose Richard III.

'Why on earth? He was a monster.'

'He wasn't,' Sylvia said. 'That was all Tudor propaganda.' She was delighted to find a subject about which she knew more than him.

Hugh decreed that they should take a taxi to the station so they could hold hands. As he was helping her alight from the cab at Paddington, a voice said, 'Evening, Bell,' and a man in pinstripes hurried ahead of them into the station.

'Damn,' Hugh said. 'That was Geoffrey Wynston-Jones.'

'Who's he?'

'A neighbour. He's usually drives into town in his company car, which he's inordinately proud of. Why the bloody hell has he turned up here, today of all days?'

'Oh, help,' Sylvia said. 'I remember that name. It's Mr "Packard".'

She explained about Mrs Packard and the WI. 'I think she's got it in for me. I ducked her attempts to corral me for a soiree.'

'Ah, yes, that's her. I've had to suffer one of those.'

They discussed damage limitation on the train home.

'I can say you're a colleague,' Hugh said. 'He can't have caught more than a glimpse of you and you're in your flamingo disguise.'

'Not much I'm not. It's mostly covered by my coat.'

'He's too busy thinking about his own image to be very perceptive,' Hugh said. 'I shall make sure to tell Jeanette I gave a colleague a lift to Paddington.' And Sylvia, who held her tongue, was rewarded with 'Look, I'm sorry I snapped about her. She's my Achilles heel, if you know what I mean?'

'Not really.'

'The thing is, Jeanette was never enough "in" my mind to be kicked out of it. It was, well, I've told you, it was circumstance and then, after the war and all we'd been through, coming home and her waiting for me, or so I thought, and me being too bloody feeble to put things right and, oh, I suppose I feel guilty about that, and then Marigold.'

Of course, she thought, there will always be Marigold.

'And about Jeanette,' Hugh said. 'Her too. I feel guilty about her. She is who she is. She can't help it.'

'No.'

'And she's not a bad mother. She does her best.'

'Yes.'

'Damn these platitudes. Why in God's name am I defending her?'

'You're loyal,' Sylvia said. 'It's right to be loyal.' She was thinking of her father as she said it.

23

Hugh's wife had been much on Sylvia's mind so it was a jolt when the following afternoon Jeanette Bell walked through the library doors. Sylvia was sorting out the shelves at the back of the room and it was Dee at the desk. She greeted Jeanette Bell with a less than cordial 'Afternoon.'

'Actually, Mrs Harris, it was Miss Blackwell I was hoping to speak to.'

Dee turned an enquiring face to Sylvia, who, heart thumping, hurried forward. 'Mrs Bell?'

'I am sorry to trouble you, Miss Blackwell, but I wondered, has Marigold been here?'

Relief made Sylvia gush. 'I'm sorry, I'm afraid not, Mrs Bell, but wouldn't she be at school today?'

Jeanette Bell frowned. 'It appears she didn't arrive there this morning. I've been at the hairdresser's and have only just received a telephone call from the school.'

'Dear, dear.' Dee was looking thrilled. 'What can have happened? Maybe she felt unwell and went to the doctor's.'

Jeanette Bell's frown deepened. 'Obviously, I have checked with my husband.' Turning her back on Dee, she addressed Sylvia. 'I wouldn't have heard at all – the school would have simply assumed she was ill – but today is her violin lesson and the teacher comes in specially so if Marigold isn't going to be there we always . . .' She trailed off and looked so bothered that Sylvia felt stricken. She's human, she thought. I mustn't make her into a monster.

As if in response to this unspoken sentiment, Jeanette Bell's frown softened. 'I wondered if maybe she might be here or with your neighbour's son.'

'Sam?'

'Yes.'

'He'll be at school too. But I can ring his mother if you're worried.'

There was no reply from the Hedges' phone. Sylvia promised to ask June about Marigold once she got home but shortly after four Ray also arrived unexpectedly at the library with the twins.

'Hello, Sylvia,' the girls chorused, hoping to be corrected by their father. When no correction was forthcoming they pointedly asked, 'Can we look at the books, please, SYLVIA?' and ran over to the bookshelves without waiting for permission.

Ray said, 'You haven't seen my son by any chance?'

'Sam? No. Why?'

'He was supposed to collect these two from the school caretaker and wait for me to take them on to the dentist's. I suppose he forgot, the ninny.'

Sylvia began to feel uneasy. 'I've not seen him, Ray, but if he happens along I'll tell him you were here.'

When Ray had rounded up the twins and shooed them through the door Dee said, 'They'll be truanting, the pair of them, the saucy monkeys.'

The thought had been occurring to Sylvia. 'Oh Lord, do you think so, Dee?'

'It's the girl leading him on. Girls do that. I've seen it time and time again. Sam'll be off somewhere with Miss Bell, you see if I'm right.'

Hugh had promised Sylvia that he would try to meet her after work at the foundry. She waited in the cold, smoking and reflecting on what Dee had said. It was true, Sam was captivated by Marigold and perhaps it did suit Marigold, who seemed to have trouble making friends with her school peers, to have Sam as an acolyte.

Hugh didn't appear at the foundry. She lingered there awhile in hope so it was late when she passed number 3 and Ray called out to her to come in.

From the kitchen the twins could be heard in the bathroom arguing with June about how best to clean their teeth.

'Come on, girls. It's way past your bedtime.'

'The dentist man said at least five minutes we had to brush and it's not nearly that much time yet.'

Sylvia asked, 'What is it, Ray?'

'It's the boy. He's gone missing.'

Sam had not returned home and a call to his teacher, Sue Bunce, revealed that he had not turned up for school that day.

'It seems Marigold has gone missing too. The doctor and his missis have been round here,' Ray said, his wide friendly face crumpled with concern. 'They rang the police station and the police are coming round.' No one had seen either child since early that same morning.

Ray's account, especially his report of the visit by Hugh and Jeanette Bell, was disturbing. Sylvia was, in turn, visited by a horrible feeling that whatever had happened to the children she was to blame. 'I'm sure they'll be OK, Ray. Sam's sensible.' Or was.

'I'll tan his backside if this turns out to be one of his daft bloody jokes.'

June appeared, looking harassed. 'I can't settle the twins. They know something's up. Can you go and shut them up, Ray?'

While Ray was attempting to quieten the twins June put Sylvia more in the picture. According to Marigold's mother, Marigold's new patent shoes and mohair sweater were gone from her room. June had thought at first that Sam had taken nothing but she'd just discovered his long trousers and best shirt were missing from the wash.

'Looks like they might have run away together or something. Mrs Bell made it plain that she's of the view that it's all Samuel's doing.'

Recalling Dee's observation, Sylvia said, 'I can't see why Marigold wouldn't be at least equally to blame for whatever it is they've got up to.'

'Probably six of one and half a dozen of the other,' June agreed. 'Anyway, who cares, so long as they both come back safe and sound.'

The police had come and gone when, around midnight, Sylvia, anxiously awake, heard the sound of a car draw up. She got up and looked out of the cottage door to see Hugh escorting a shadowy Sam through the Hedges' garden

218

gate. A pale face that she took to be Marigold's was pressed to the window of the Hillman.

She got the gist of the miscreants' adventure from June the following morning. Marigold had acquired a couple of tickets for a studio recording of Cliff Richard and his band and the two children had gone off to London to be part of the screaming crowd of fans. Afterwards, they had hung around in London, doing no one knew quite what, before catching a train home. Marigold had rung her father from Swindon station to beg a lift.

Sylvia relayed this later to Dee. 'They don't know how Marigold got hold of tickets. It seems she had the money for the rail fares.'

'It'll be one of those teenage comics she reads. I've seen her stuffing them into her bag. That and too much pocket money. I told you she'd be behind it all.'

'June says Marigold's parents are blaming it all on Sam.'

'Doesn't surprise me. They'll believe their precious lambkin can do no wrong. I could tell them a thing or two.'

'What?' Sylvia felt alarmed.

Dee's reply was not reassuring. 'I'm keeping my counsel for the time being.'

The truant officer came round to give Sam a talking-to and it was decreed that he was to be kept in at school for all breaks until the end of term. How Marigold was being punished – if at all – was not known.

Sam was curt with Sylvia when she tried to make overtures but when after a day or so she offered to walk to school with him he grudgingly accepted. She was sorry for her young friend but also eager to discover what he and Marigold had got up to. In the Bells, she and Sam had common cause.

'It must have been fun,' she suggested, recalling her own flight to London with Marigold's father.

Sam looked suspicious. 'What?'

'Bunking off to London.'

'S'pose.'

'Sam, I'm not going to tell on you. Honestly.'

Sam judiciously aimed a stone at the lock-keeper's house. 'It was OK.'

'I hope it was better than OK, given all the trouble it has got you into.'

Ned came out of the house and waved at them. 'Hello there, Sam, Sylvia.'

He beamed across the canal at them and Sam's mood softened.

'We went to the 2i's, the coffee bar where Tommy Steele started. Cliff played there.'

'Was Cliff Richard there?'

'He doesn't play there now.' Sam sounded superior. 'But we got his autograph after the recording. Well, I didn't.'

'Marigold did?'

'I got one of the Drifters, that's his backing group. I'm going to learn guitar.' His clear grey eyes were alight with new possibilities.

'How did you know all about this, the concert and the coffee bar?'

'The 2i's was on *Six-Five Special*. We saw it on TV when Marigold was round ours. And Marigold's in Cliff's fan club. She entered the draw in *Valentine* – that's a magazine – and she won two tickets and she asked me to go with her.'

It was a shame, really, Sylvia couldn't help thinking, that the adventure had caused so much trouble. 'It was very enterprising of you both. I wouldn't have dared be so bold at your age,' she volunteered, and was glad she had because Sam looked grateful. 'How's Marigold?' she asked, but he said wistfully that he didn't know.

It wasn't until the following Saturday that Sylvia heard again from Hugh. He arrived as the library was closing, carrying some books in a string bag.

Dee, who was about to go home, suddenly found something that required her urgent attention so Sylvia's conversation with Hugh was reserved.

'Marigold has been grounded so I'm deputised to return these.'

'There's more than three books there,' Dee said, pointedly looking at the pile he had placed on the desk.

'I know. I'm very sorry. We found these in her bedroom. It looks as if, well, I'm sorry to say, it looks rather as if she's been taking more books than she is officially allowed.'

Sylvia examined the books. 'These are from the Adults' Library.' She laid out *Married Love* by Marie Stopes and *The Second Sex* by Simone de Beauvoir and a new book by Ian Fleming.

'That *Dr No*'s only just come in. I shelved it myself,' Dee said. 'Look, no date stamps.' She picked up the Marie Stopes. 'This is about, you know . . .'

'Yes,' Hugh said shortly. 'I of course know that it's about contraception.'

'How old is your daughter, Dr Bell?'

Sylvia had become aware that Dee's favourable opinion

of Hugh, occasioned by her fall, had been dwindling as her disapproval of his daughter had grown.

'Dee, Dr Bell has returned the books. I believe a fine is in order but, as they've been returned . . .'

'You'd better not let Mr Booth hear about this, that's all I can say.'

'Thank you, Dee. I'll sort it out.'

'Right,' Dee said. 'If I'm not wanted, I'll be getting along.'

'Christ,' Hugh said, when Dee had finally left. 'How do you cope, working with her – old battleaxe?'

'She's all right, really.'

'Jeanette calls her the nosy parker. Look, I'm sorry about the books. Youthful curiosity, I'm afraid.'

'It's having the Adult section in here,' Sylvia said. She wanted to let Marigold off the hook. 'Hugh, the Hedges are in a bit of a state over all the business with her and Sam.'

'I know. I'm sorry about that too. I've no doubt Marigold led him on. As I say, she's been grounded for the rest of term and her pocket money's been stopped. It's that wretched Clifford what's-his-name they seem so mad about.'

'Cliff, not Clifford,' Sylvia said. 'Cliff Richard. But I think it's Marigold rather than Cliff who Sam is really "mad about". He'll be missing her.'

'I can understand that,' Hugh said. 'Just how private is it here?'

'Dee will have gone. And Mr Booth goes with her these days.'

'I see. So we have the library to ourselves.'

*

222

Afterwards, Sylvia was never quite sure how much Mr Booth had seen when, some time later, he swung in suddenly through the doors.

'Oh, Mr Booth.' Sylvia was pulling discreetly at her skirt. 'Dr Bell was wondering if his daughter could maybe join the Adults' Library –'

'She's very advanced in her reading,' Hugh intervened. 'She's rather outstripped all that Miss Blackwell has on offer in the Children's section.' Sylvia glanced at him sideways; only his shirt looked slightly rumpled.

'Really?' Mr Booth raised his eyes to the upper shelves, where the volumes of Dickens were ranged.

'She's read most of Dickens,' Sylvia explained. 'I told Dr Bell I would consult you but I thought you'd gone home.'

The hard-boiled gaze ran over her body. 'I shall give it due consideration. If you have a moment, please, Miss Blackwell.'

He hurried out and Hugh said, 'Phew, that was close. But worth it. I shall never look at a Dickens the same again. We can use it as code – *Our Mutual Friend*.'

'More like *Hard Times*,' Sylvia said. 'I have to go and be talked at.'

She skipped along the corridor, careless, after the interlude with Hugh, of whatever new wet blanket Mr Booth was about to produce.

He was sitting at his desk, playing, as usual, with his papers.

'Ah, Miss Blackwell. I have been in communication with the Library Committee, which is of the view that the resultant costs arising from devastations of the storm require that we take the necessary steps to obviate any unnecessary expense.'

This took a moment to untangle. 'You mean there's a problem over the cost of the repairs?'

'There are, shall we say, pressing financial imperatives. I must impress upon you, Miss Blackwell' – Mr Booth cleared his throat – 'that the Library Committee is obliged to make fundamental economies. I am sure' – he smiled, showing a set of alarming teeth – 'you would not want anything to threaten the continuance of your position here.'

His glance seemed to settle around her midriff and, nervous now, she readjusted her blouse. 'I'm not quite sure what you mean, Mr Booth.'

Her boss dispensed with the smile. 'In the current climate it is a not altogether impossible eventuality that the Committee may decide to curtail your hours.'

'I don't believe he's sorry one bit,' Sylvia said. She had gone round to the Hedges' in search of sympathy and was drinking tea and eating custard creams in their kitchen. 'I don't believe he's ever wanted me here at all.'

'How's he getting on with Mrs Harris these days?'

Sylvia had been reticent about Dee when June had made veiled enquiries. Now she said cautiously, 'They seem to be friendly enough.'

'She's not paid, is she?'

'You mean he might suggest her in place of me?'

June was putting a hotpot into the oven. She paused with the dish in her hands. 'I wouldn't put it past him.'

'Dee wouldn't stand for it.'

June raised her eyebrows. 'I wouldn't bank on that.'

'It's Mr Collins,' Sylvia decided. 'It's him, not the Committee as a whole, I'm sure of it.'

She didn't say as much to June but she had been regretting introducing Sam to *Treasure Island*.

24

Sylvia met Mrs Bird with her basket in the High Street.

'I hear there's been trouble with the Hedges boy.'

'I think that's all blown over, Mrs Bird.'

Mrs Bird's sharp little features became shrewd. 'Not so far as the doctor's wife goes. You'd think the boy had deflowered her blessed daughter, the way she's carrying on. What happened there, do you know?'

Hoping to deflect this line of enquiry, Sylvia asked after Lizzie.

'Funny you should mention her. She's been on about some play she's in she wants to tell you about. I'll bring her round to you.'

Lizzie had remained a regular at the library. Sylvia had encountered her reading the poems she had set out in the Poetry Corner and they had discussed *The Way through the Woods*, one of Sylvia's girlhood favourites. Lizzie had volunteered that she liked the otters and became surprisingly eloquent on the subject of the ghostly lords and ladies who rode through the shadow woods of the past. But her shyness had resurfaced and Sylvia hadn't had the time to recover their former intimacy with any real conversation. But there was no resisting Mrs Bird and the girl might be a distraction for Sam. Nothing of Marigold had been seen since the London escapade. And since their felicitous encounter in the library Sylvia had seen nothing of Marigold's father either. Once again, she and Sam were comrades in the trials of love.

The following Saturday as Sylvia began to close up the library Lizzie approached her to say she had been told to wait there for her grandmother. 'I'm sorry, Miss.'

'No, that's fine, Lizzie. Shall I stamp your books?'

Lizzie was reading the Anne of Green Gables saga. 'I hope she marries Gilbert. She does, doesn't she, Miss, only she's gone and got engaged to someone else?'

Recalling their shared dislike of uncertainty, Sylvia reassured. 'She does in the end, Lizzie. And it's still Sylvia.'

Mrs Bird arrived just before one, pushing a basketful of shopping. 'There you are! There was a queue as long as the Devil's spoon at the butcher's and then they were out of tongue. All right if Lizzie goes back with you? My husband'll fetch her this afternoon.' She hurried off again before Sylvia could suggest an alternative plan.

Sylvia and Lizzie walked back to Field Row discussing how hiccups were necessary in the lives of the lovers of romantic fiction. 'We're doing *Northanger Abbey* at school this term, Miss.'

'What d'you think of it?'

'I like it but I think that Catherine Morland's dim.'

'I think Jane Austen's laughing at her a little, don't you?'

Lizzie considered this. 'I'm going to read *Pride and Prejudice* next.'

The book she and Hugh had bought together for Marigold. Sylvia hadn't heard how it had gone down. 'It sounds as if you're enjoying school, Lizzie.'

'Oh, it's smashing. And I'm in *A Midsummer Night's Dream*.'

'Yes, you said. Mustardseed.'

But Lizzie had been elevated and along with the fairy in Titania's retinue she was now also playing the part of one of the mechanicals.

'It's the one plays the wall. I can't remember his name but I have to do this.' Lizzie stuck out her hand and parted her fingers, making play of a chink.

'I'm pretty sure that's Snout,' Sylvia said. 'We can look it up when we get home.'

Over lunch Lizzie became quite loquacious.

'I don't like it when the lovers laugh at Bottom and the others when they do their play, do you, Miss? I remember you said how Shakespeare liked him.'

'I'm sure he does, Lizzie. I reckon the laugh's on the grandees.'

'That means the posh ones, doesn't it, Miss?'

For all her newfound confidence, Lizzie became agitated when Sylvia proposed they call round at the Hedges'. 'Sam'll have forgotten me.'

'Don't be daft, Lizzie. Sam will be glad to see you.'

'It was nice, wasn't it, Miss, doing the Comprehensions and when we watched the foxes. It was fun.' The appeal in her blue eyes behind the round wire specs was touching.

Oh, Sylvia thought, why must love be so harrowing?

Sam didn't seem at all glad to see them when they went round to number 3. June called him from his bedroom and when he finally emerged he just said, ''lo,' and stood in the doorway, looking blank.

Lizzie stared at her shoes and June said, 'Why don't you take Lizzie into your room, Sam, and show her your Hornby set?'

'She's seen it.'

Lizzie hung her head further.

'Your Meccano then. I'm sure she'd like to see the funicular.'

Sam gave an audible sigh and tilted his head at Lizzie, who followed him wordlessly out of the kitchen.

June sat down, sighing in turn. 'I don't know what to do with him. He's been like that since the blimming London caper. My mum says not worry, it's his hormones, but he's too young for it to be that.'

No one is too young for love, Sylvia thought. She said, not really believing it, 'He probably feels guilty about scaring you. Guilt makes people behave badly. I expect, underneath, he's very sorry.'

'You could have fooled me,' June said. 'I reckon it's that Bell girl. She's changed him.'

For all her own reservations, Sylvia felt prompted to defend the girl. 'Marigold's very bright and she's been good company for Sam.'

'To be honest, I'm relieved her parents have put us out of bounds. Ray says she gives him ideas.'

'Have the Bells really made you out of bounds?'

'From what I hear, she's forbidden to come round here.'

'I dare say it will all blow over soon,' Sylvia said, not quite believing this either.

She was pleased to see that when, later, Lizzie emerged from Sam's room Sam seemed more cheerful. He waved Lizzie goodbye in quite a friendly manner when her grandfather arrived for her in his van.

'It was Thelma Bird who told me about us being banned by the Bells,' June said when Mr Bird and Lizzie had driven off. 'There's some woman friends with the doctor's wife who claims she's telling all kinds of taradiddles about Sam.'

'No one will believe them,' Sylvia said, devoutly hoping that this was indeed the case.

A couple of weeks later, Mrs Bird in her feathered hat called at the library, pushing the wheeled basket.

'Miss Blackwell. May I have a word?'

Her landlady's usually expressive features looked oddly set and Sylvia suddenly had a premonition. 'Is everything all right, Mrs Bird?'

Mrs Bird bent laboriously over her basket and took out a brown-paper bag. She handed it to Sylvia. 'Take a look at this.'

The brown bag contained a book. *Tropic of Cancer* by Henry Miller.

'Is that your idea of a book suitable for children?'

'No,' Sylvia said cautiously, her mind working fast.

'Look inside. East Mole Library. It says it there in black and white.'

'Yes,' Sylvia said. 'I see that. But this book isn't from the Children's Library.'

'Then explain to me how our Lizzie got her hands on it.'

This was certainly a conundrum. 'I can't imagine, Mrs Bird.'

'She got it from here, right enough. She told us as much.'

'What else did she say?' Sylvia had begun to feel scared.

Mrs Bird became opaque. 'She's not told us. Just that.'

'Well, all I can say is that I'm awfully sorry. With all the reorganisation it must have somehow found its way into the Children's section. We have been in a tremendous muddle since the storm.'

'It's obscene.' Mrs Bird pronounced these words in a voice that so startled a toddler who had just tottered into the library holding his mother's hand that the little boy began to cry.

Sylvia, who felt like joining the child in his tears, said, 'I wonder if I could maybe have a word with Lizzie so we can get to the bottom of this.'

Mrs Bird, her feathers nodding dangerously, had swollen into an angry turkey. 'That girl is not setting foot in this place till we've had some answers. The book's got words in it, words that no decent human being, never mind a child, should have to set eyes on. I had to ask my husband what some of them meant and, I tell you, that man didn't want to have to face me explaining them. Call this literature? It's disgusting.'

'Look, Billy, *Teddybear Coalman*,' the mother said to the toddler. 'A book about a clever teddy.'

Mrs Bird raised her voice. 'It's obscene,' she denounced again.

231

The toddler's tears renewed and his mother, looking reproachfully at Sylvia, hurried him out of the library.

The beastly woman's enjoying this, Sylvia thought. She felt sick. The book was unquestionably the one that had been taken from the Restricted Access cupboard and she was sure now who had been responsible for the theft.

'I can only say I'm terribly sorry, Mrs Bird. I will of course look into this.'

'I shall be having words with your boss, don't you worry.'

Sylvia began to protest but Mrs Bird grabbed back the book and made to go.

'May I have the book, please, Mrs Bird?'

'Not on your life, young lady. I'm keeping that. It's evidence.'

She swept out, trundling her basket, which cannoned into Dee, who was coming through the door.

'Bloody hell,' Dee said, rubbing her shins. 'What's got her going?'

Sylvia described the essence of Mrs Bird's tirade.

Dee listened, frowning, and then said, 'There no way you'll persuade me Lizzie Smith took that book. That girl wouldn't say boo to a goose.'

'I wish I could speak to her,' Sylvia said for the third time.

'You'd better inform His Lordship before she gets her hooks into him. He's off on one of his trips to the Trustee.'

'What can she be planning to do with the book, d'you imagine, Dee?'

'Search me. Show it to the police? I'd like to see young Tim Farmer reading Henry Miller.' Dee laughed.

'Don't, Dee. It's serious.'

'I don't see how anyone can blame us. Dawn Smith couldn't care less about her daughter and she's too bone idle to make trouble. Thelma Bird's just throwing her weight around.'

'The thing is . . .' Sylvia halted. Dee was basically kind-hearted; she thought she dare risk it. 'The thing is, I'm fairly sure that Lizzie was given the book by Sam.'

'That sounds more likely. When? How?'

'Lizzie was round at the Hedges' a week or so back. Sam's been missing Marigold – you've said yourself how smitten he is – and Lizzie's in awe of him because he helped her through the 11+. I thought seeing her might give him a boost, cheer him up. It did seem to.'

But maybe only because he'd managed to foist a dubious book on poor gullible Lizzie.

Dee was considering. 'It's not him,' she announced emphatically. 'It's the girl. The Bell girl. She'll be behind this, you mark my words.'

Sylvia reflected. 'But then, if I'm right about how Lizzie got hold of it, how did it come to be with Sam?'

Dee shrugged. 'Any number of reasons. To impress him. Or she could have given it him to hide from her parents. Look at all those books her father brought in the other week she'd got hidden in her room. Highly unsuitable. I tried to say so at the time.' Dee assumed the expression of the prophet without honour.

'Marigold *is* a very advanced reader.'

'I've not read any Henry Miller myself,' Dee said. 'But if you want my opinion, it was never for literary reasons that that book was nicked.'

233

From what Sylvia pieced together later Lizzie held out for a whole evening before finally capitulating under the onslaught of her family's grilling. Hysterical weeping accompanied the confession that was finally squeezed out of her that she had been given the book by Sam Hedges. Lizzie was reported to be 'a bundle of nerves' and 'in a shocking state' after reading it, though in Sylvia's view that was more likely to be a result of the inquisition to which she had been subjected. The worst fallout was on the Hedges and Sam.

Predicting that it was only a matter of time before Lizzie would break, Sylvia had tried to warn Sam on the evening of Mrs Bird's dramatic appearance. Sam had abandoned his regular place on her gate so she found an excuse to ask his help in moving some books on to a bookshelf that June's dad had acquired for her.

'He got it off one of his grand customers who was chucking it out. He says to say you're welcome to it,' June told her. 'Dad's a reader too.'

Sam lugged down the old Swindon boxes from the spare room. He sat watching as she began to unpack the books.

'Is this the book that Father William poem you read us comes from?'

He had picked up her old copy of *Through the Looking-Glass* and Sylvia said, 'No, that's the one about chess – you might like to read it.' Sam put down the book hastily. 'How *is* the chess? I keep meaning to ask.'

'I don't play any more.'

'That's a pity. My father thinks you're good.' Sam shrugged and, not wanting to continue under false pretences, Sylvia said, 'I don't know if you've heard, Sam, but Lizzie's in trouble.'

'No. What?' The alarm in his grey eyes looked genuine.

'She's been found with the book that was taken from the library. From the locked cupboard in the library.'

His face very red, Sam said, 'What book?'

Sylvia was on the point of saying, 'I think you know,' but checked herself. How easy it was to join the ranks of persecutors. Instead she said, 'From what I gather from her grandmother Lizzie has said nothing so far. But she's bound in the end to say where it came from.'

There was a silence.

'How about a cup of cocoa?' Sylvia suggested.

They sat drinking cocoa in the room that Sam and his grandfather had decorated for her. This isn't right, Sylvia thought. He's a sweet, rather innocent boy. And brave. This is all bloody Mr Booth and bloody, bloody Marigold.

For a while she let him sit, honouring his need for silence. Finally she said, 'Look, Sam, I don't suppose whoever took the book meant to steal it and, probably, whoever it was meant to give it back. The trouble is it has been reported as theft. And I can't believe that it was Lizzie who took it.'

More silence.

'And Lizzie's family are making a tremendous hoo-ha because the book's –'

Mumbling, Sam said, 'Yeah, I know, full of dirty words.'

'Did you read it?' Sylvia was curious.

'We looked at some of it.'

'We?'

A slight hesitation. 'Me and Lizzie.'

'Only you and Lizzie?'

'Yeah.'

'Sam –'

Tight-lipped, he said, 'I took it. Now you know.'

'And no one –'

'No one else.' So he was going to be noble.

'Sam, it's important not to tell tales but this is going to cause an enormous fuss and –'

'There wasn't anyone else, I told you – *I took it!*' he shouted. And '*Sorry!*' he shouted again.

'How? How did you take it?'

'When I was at the library one day with you.'

'I don't think you could have done. I'd have seen you. And how did you get the cupboard open? The lock was pretty stout.'

'I've got tools.'

That was true enough. She had the little plum-wood vase with the jay's feather in it to prove it.

'Sorry, Sam, I still don't buy it. Why would you want to take that book?'

He shrugged. 'Don't know.'

'Exactly. You're not that interested in literature. And although you might be curious about, I don't know, a book that had been hidden from you, breaking and entering isn't your style.'

But she could see that his resolve had hardened under pressure, the sign of a martyr's temperament as much as a fanatic's; indeed, she thought, the two are much alike.

'There wasn't anyone else,' he insisted. 'I didn't mean to get Lizzie into trouble.'

'It's you that's in trouble, Sam, not Lizzie. Why on earth did you show the book to her? That was plain daft.'

Sam shrugged again and said, 'I couldn't think of anything else to do with her when you brought her round.'

So it was all her fault. 'But why did she take it home with her?'

Sam shrugged again.

'Was it because you don't like her as much as she likes you that you gave it her?' The kind of sop that will often cause more trouble in the end for the kind of heart.

But if Sam grasped the truth of this psychological insight he didn't bother to say so.

25

In the days and weeks after the recovery of *Tropic of Cancer* the book was the focus of excited debate in East Mole. If Henry Miller's agent had set the whole affair up as a publicity stunt, Sylvia reflected bitterly, he could hardly have done better by his author. Next to adulation, notoriety must surely be what a writer most craves.

Mrs Bird, true to her word, had delivered the book to the police station, where, despite Dee's predictions, it had been retained. It was rumoured that the book was being sent to London to the Official Censor for his judgement.

Mr Booth had applied unsuccessfully for its return. 'It's a work of literature,' the desk sergeant reported him as saying. This, when widely repeated, only fuelled the indignation of the main body of local opinion, which had an inherent mistrust of anything intellectual. The local Conservative MP, when appealed to by Mrs Bird, had agreed to write to the Library Committee and Mrs Bird, who had been heard to vow that she'd 'cut her own throat rather than vote Tory', declared that Mr Ducannon was 'a gentleman' and would be getting her support at the next election. She quoted the MP, who had allegedly said that it was 'the influence of left-wing socialism' and that the book was banned in America. 'Where they are still God-fearing,' Mrs Bird occasionally threw in.

The Reverend Austin was more charitable. 'To be frank,' he remarked to a fellow cleric who had heard of the scandal, 'I am rather surprised at Booth. I had him down as more of a *Peyton Place* man.'

Dee was in her element and relishing the fuss. The renewal of her affair with Mr Booth had lessened none of her contempt for him. 'Ashley wouldn't know literature if it stripped to the buff and danced a can-can in front of his eyes.'

'What I don't understand,' Sylvia said, 'is why on earth he got the book in the first place. It's hardly choice reading for East Mole.'

'It was a chap he met at the Birmingham conference – remember, the one I told you about? He said it was pretty ripe. He couldn't house it in his library, even in the Restricted Access, because his boss would know and he'd smuggled it back from Paris. This chap claimed it was a masterpiece of modern writing, blah, blah, and passed it on to His Lordship. If you ask me, he only had it in the Restricted Access to hide it from his wife.'

Sylvia said that if she lived to be ninety she would not want to read a single word of Henry Miller. She was too angry at what his book had done to the Hedges. Most especially at what it had done to Sam.

Lizzie, once she had confessed, had been taken into the bosom of her family with all the fervour meted out to those who have suffered a wrong. Poor Sam, by contrast, was being outlawed.

June and Ray had been summoned to bring their son to the police station, where he was interviewed by an officer from the Juvenile Bureau, who extracted from him a sulky assurance that he had 'meant to put the book back'. Sam was read the riot act and told that any further instance of delinquency would result in a court appearance. His parents were advised that in view of his former good character he was being let off with 'a warning'.

'As if that's any comfort. There's never been a stain on our family's character,' a distraught June said to her husband as they left the police station with a sullen Sam.

Ray, if anything, was taking all this harder than June.

'Spare the rod and spoil the child,' he said to Sylvia when she called round to ask how things had gone with the police.

'I can't believe that beating Sam would have helped, Ray.'

'My dad hit us regular as kids and it didn't do us any harm. I've been too soft with Samuel.'

Sylvia was aghast to learn that Ray had been as good as his word.

'Sam's been lammed,' Pam told her solemnly. It was a Sunday and the twins had called round to play.

'It's 'cos he didn't tell the truth,' Jem said.

'No, it's 'cos he stole,' Pam corrected her.

'I don't believe he stole anything,' Sylvia told them.

'He did, too. Our dad lammed him for it.'

'To be honest, I think it hurt Ray more than Samuel,'

June said later. Sylvia felt too implicated to express her concern but she could tell that June was troubled by this rare demonstration of paternal authority in the usually pacific Ray. 'I was hoping that policeman would have frightened the living daylights out of him. He did me. But Sam hasn't taken a blind bit of notice. You tell me you have your doubts but he insists it was him. And if it wasn't him, then all I can say is he's lying and they've been brought up to tell the truth.'

There had been worrying talk of Sam being expelled from school. Sylvia heard this from Gwen and it had left her sick at heart. Sylvia had pointed out that Sam had not committed any theft from the school. Nevertheless, Gwen said, she thought that the policy was expulsion for any criminal activity. The Easter holidays had begun and Sam and his parents were left in limbo.

Lizzie, who had been forbidden to see Sam or visit the library, ambushed Sylvia on her way home one Saturday lunchtime.

'Will you give this to Sam for me, Miss?'

'Lizzie, are you all right?'

'I didn't mean to tell, Miss. They made me. They said the school would expel me for a thief if I didn't say I hadn't done it.'

The girl was a pathetic sight. Her mousy hair was parted in two greasy clumps, her pink wire-rimmed glasses had come to grief and were stuck with sticking plaster, her blue eyes were bleared from weeping and a glistening snail-track of snot was running from her nose on to the grubby Chilprufe vest visible beneath the cut-down frock she was dressed in.

Sylvia took the sad little bundle in her arms. 'Lizzie, no one could expect you to take it on yourself. You simply told the truth.'

'Sam'll hate me.'

'He won't, Lizzie.'

'I'll never see him again.'

Sam screwed up the note when Sylvia presented it to him and threw it on the ground without reading it.

'It's not Lizzie's fault, Sam. She's almost as miserable as you.'

'Who said I was miserable?'

'All right, upset.'

'I'm not upset.'

'Have it your own way. But Lizzie and I are upset for you.'

He went off, ostentatiously whistling 'Colonel Bogey'. Sylvia retrieved the screwed-up note.

Dear Sam

I couldn't help it. They made me. I am very, very sorry.

Your loving freind
Lizzie Smith

By her name she had drawn in red crayon a small bleeding heart.

All this while nothing was seen or heard of Marigold, or her father. Sylvia had come to the conclusion that Dee's analysis made sense. Marigold, with her precocious taste in reading and bounding self-confidence, was far more likely to be the architect of an act of such daring. She had simply dumped the evidence on Sam. And it was love that was impelling him now to shoulder the blame.

She swung insanely between fury at Hugh and a helpless desire to excuse him. Perhaps he didn't know of the *Tropic of Cancer* debacle? Improbable given that it was the talking point of the town. He had acknowledged that Marigold was the likely force behind the London escapade but maybe, as Dee suggested, the thought that his beloved daughter had a part in a theft was for him a step too far. Marigold might have been forbidden to visit the library but her father had been there on her behalf and there had been that dangerous, ecstatic reunion. His failure to make contact pained and puzzled her. Why had he made no effort to see her?

'I hate him,' screamed a savage voice in her head. 'I hate him, damn him, damn his bloody eyes.' But the super-subtle voice in her heart whispered, 'You don't. You adore him.'

She lay awake at night agonising: should she loiter in the vicinity of his house in the hope of catching him? But the fear that Jeanette Bell might see her was too great and what if he refused to talk to her? Should she write? But a letter could be ignored or read by prying eyes and, for the moment, at least, she wanted to cause no trouble.

One night, unable yet again to sleep, she got up and went outside.

It was a not-quite-full moon, whether on the wax or the wane she was unable to tell; but in her present mood it seemed to her a counterpoint to the young crescent moon which on the evening of *The Dream of Gerontius* had flung her into Hugh Bell's arms. 'Seeing that I seem to have become a lunatic,' she said, 'tell me, O Moon, what should I do?'

The following day, she walked after work to Dr Monk's surgery.

With the advent of the National Health, the problem of doctors' fees no longer arose but Sylvia had been bred to consider good health a virtue. Illness was costly and her mother's genteel penny-pinching had encouraged in her daughter a disinclination to fuss. So she had had no thought since arriving in East Mole of seeking a doctor's advice.

She was therefore unsure of the proper form when she knocked at the door of the large Edwardian house, fronted in summer by dusty laburnums, where the two GPs shared a surgery. All she was sure of was that this was Dr Monk's afternoon off and that therefore only Hugh would be available.

Doctors' receptionists in most general practices were the harassed wives of the GPs, who were expected to take phone calls, arrange home visits and assess the level of urgency when a patient presented with symptoms. But the practice receptionist here was Mrs Eames, of whom Sylvia had heard those worrying reports from Dee.

She was admitted into the tiled hall by the housekeeper in a flowered overall, who gestured towards the waiting room.

'There's a queue. If it isn't urgent, I'd advise coming tomorrow, when Dr M's on.' She moved closer to Sylvia and mouthed into her ear, 'The women all want to see Dr Bell.'

Sylvia tried to look nonchalant and said that she was afraid that it was quite urgent. She went into a room where chairs were placed around an oval dining table on which copies of the *National Geographic*, the *Lady*, the *Field* and some very tattered comics were left for the benefit of the waiting patients. There was a copy of *Valentine*, which Sam had mentioned as the source of the tickets for the Cliff Richard recording. For something to occupy her, she took it up to read.

Sylvia was the last of the evening's patients and by the time she was called by Mrs Eames, who appeared and announced, 'I'm getting the doctor's supper so I'll leave you to see your own way out,' her mood of defiance had leaked away and she climbed the stairs to the surgery, feeling shaky.

Hugh was behind a desk, smoking and studying a card. 'Your NHS number's here and your date of birth but there seems to be nothing else.'

'That's because I'm never ill.'

'You are fortunate then.'

Across the desert of the desk they stared at each other. Hugh began to finger his stethoscope. 'I'm assuming then this isn't a medical matter?'

'Not really. No.'

Hugh sat there, then suddenly stubbed out his cigarette, got up and went out, leaving Sylvia wondering if this was a signal for her to go too.

She looked round the room, which showed signs of having been Dr Monk's study. Two pairs of oars were hung cross-wise above the mantelpiece, a tired-looking stuffed hawk sat dully on a tallboy under a glass dome and beside it a Chinese vase full of dried pampas grass. A crewel-work screen half hid the examination couch, above which hung a line of framed certificates confirming Godfrey Monk's success in various medical exams. A full-size yellowing skeleton was lolling in a corner.

'Is that a real human skeleton?' she asked Hugh when he returned.

'It's a standard requirement of our training. How can I help?'

His voice, so far removed from the warm tones of affinity, prompted a redoubling of her resolution. 'I've just been reading *Valentine* in your waiting room. I take it that's Marigold's contribution to the gaiety of nations.'

'My dear girl, I haven't a clue what you're talking about.'

'It's a rubbishy teenage comic full of tripe.'

He raised his eyebrows and made a face of incomprehension.

Furious now, she hissed, 'Jesus Christ, Hugh, haven't you heard what's been going on?'

'Please don't shout. Mrs Eames is just below us.'

'I wasn't shouting. Sam Hedges is being blamed for the theft of a book from the library. *Tropic of Cancer* by Henry Miller. Haven't you heard?'

'I vaguely remember hearing something about the book.'

Now she did raise her voice. 'Not the book. I don't give a damn about the book. Have you heard about Sam? He might be expelled.'

'I'm sorry to hear that.'

246

For a moment there was a glimmer of contrition in his eyes, and Sylvia said more calmly, 'I'm sorry too because he's insisting that he took the book alone and I think – actually, I'm pretty sure – that Marigold was at least involved.'

'Is there any evidence for that?' All contrition had vanished and the eyes that had gazed so lovingly on her body in the Kensington hotel and sparked with such fierce passion beneath the rows of dusty Dickenses were terrifying little blanks.

'Hugh? You can't let this happen to Sam. It will destroy him. And his parents. He's already badly messed up his mock exams.'

It was this that under the silent counsel of the moon had decided her. Or, more truthfully, had given the aching desire to see her lover the added heady shot of righteous indignation. Sam, who was expected to sail through the 11+, had failed all his mocks. Ray had called round to tell her.

'Not the arithmetic, surely, Ray?' Sylvia was appalled.

Ray's large handsome face looked pouchy and pale. 'His report says he only got forty per cent. That's a fail.'

'Have you checked that with the school?'

'To be honest, we don't like to. Not after all that with the twins.'

To add to the Hedges' shame, the twins had been sent home before the Easter holidays for reciting a 'rude rhyme' in the playground. All June would say was, 'I keep worrying that it's the language in that book that put it into their heads.'

And now Hugh, for whom Sylvia would have laid down

247

her life, was looking at her with a face that betrayed no more concern for this tragedy than the hollow skull of the skeleton in the corner.

'I'm sorry but I can't see how my daughter comes into this.'

He took out a fountain pen and wrote something on the card.

'That's my medical card! What are you writing?'

He looked up. 'I've written a diagnosis of dermatitis, in case Monk needs to know why you came.'

'Dermatitis?'

'It's a skin complaint.'

'What?'

'A skin complaint,' he said again, and smiled. A professional doctor's smile.

'Damn you, Hugh,' Sylvia said. 'Damn you and damn your – your fucking family.'

In her furious haste to get out of the room her shoulder brushed against a frond of pampas grass which, toppling the Chinese vase, brought it crashing to the floor.

It was late when Sylvia left the surgery, too angry for tears. Passing the big houses fronted with ugly yellow privet and a pervading aura of complacency, she swore aloud. Field Row and the Hedges, Sam and Lizzie and, yes, Marigold, never mind Hugh, had become her little universe – the first that she could properly call her own.

And it was she, or rather her library, that had been the source of this devastation. It was the library that had brought Sam and Marigold together, had brought her and Hugh together, if it came to that. If she were not a

248

librarian, would Mrs Bird ever have thought of asking her help with Lizzie? Without that, would Lizzie have ever been close to Sam? But Lizzie had at least gained a place at the Grammar School. İt was Sam, her own ally, who had helped and befriended and trusted her, who was the sufferer.

The evenings were beginning to stretch towards light. Not wanting to return to Field Row and the silent reproach of the neighbouring Hedges, Sylvia walked purposelessly and ended up in the High Street. The ABC Café, where she'd eaten before the WI meeting, in the days when she had a picture of herself as an angel of enlightenment, was open and, suddenly famished and in need of physical comfort, she went inside.

There were quite a few local customers eating there and she found a corner table, praying that she wouldn't be recognised. She had ordered when she saw a woman wearing a tweed jacket approaching her table.

Instinctively, Sylvia flinched. Conversation would be intolerable. She dimly recognised the woman's face but couldn't at once place her. Then she saw the cream-coloured whippet at her heels.

'May I?'

Without waiting for permission, the woman sat down. Although she was heavily built she moved with a dignity that suggested deportment training.

The whippet pattered round to Sylvia and pressed her nose into her lap before settling at her feet.

'Sylvia recognises her namesake,' the woman observed. 'Have you ordered?'

'Yes.'

'I don't eat here often but they do good scones. Much better than the tea shop. I don't care for the tea shop. Too dark.'

A waitress in a frilled cap and apron came and took the woman's order. Sylvia politely waited to drink her own tea till this arrived. The woman poured herself a cup and extended a soil-encrusted hand.

'Flee Crake.'

A little reluctantly, Sylvia took the hand. 'I'm Sylvia Blackwell.'

'Yes. The new librarian. I heard about the' – the woman paused, apparently searching for a word – 'shenanigans at the library and had hoped to speak to you so this is fortuitous, though I am not in fact a believer in coincidence.'

'I'm not that new,' Sylvia said. 'I came here last year.'

The woman waved a dismissive hand. 'I gather the theft occurred in your province – the Children's Library.'

'Yes.'

'But it is not a child's book. I have been unable to discover the title.'

'It was *Tropic of Cancer* by Henry Miller.'

Miss – for surely she was a 'Miss' – Crake opened her handbag and took out a spectacle case and a small notebook. Sylvia, who half expected lorgnettes, was amused to see that her glasses were the same round National Heath model as Lizzie's. She folded the wire arms carefully over her ears and opened her notebook.

'The book is not on my current list. Do you recommend it?'

'I haven't read it,' Sylvia said. 'It was in the Restricted

Access cupboard and to read anything there you have to apply to the Head Librarian, Mr Booth.'

Miss Crake had a face which, though pale and rather flat, conveyed authority. 'Such nonsense. All prohibitions inflame resistance. You would imagine people would have grasped that by now.'

Too drained by the encounter with Hugh to do more than indicate assent, Sylvia nodded.

'I gather from the buzz of gossip that the book is avant garde. I am not averse to the avant garde, provided the style is good. I'm told that the boy who took it is a neighbour of yours.'

The reference to Sam reignited Sylvia's anger. 'Sam Hedges. And I don't believe he took it.'

'Ah.' Miss Crake raised an eyebrow. 'I did wonder. I am acquainted with the boy's grandfather. A good man. A genuine autodidact and very skilled at his trade.' She bit into her scone and chewed slowly. 'Do you have any recommendations for books?'

'I'm really only a judge of children's books.'

Miss Crake looked pained. 'Only fools disregard children's literature. Clarity of vision is shed with childhood but one can sometimes recover a glimpse of it in the best children's literature. I re-read Lewis Carroll about once a year.'

'Father William was in an 11+ paper,' Sylvia said.

'Imbeciles. How to put young minds off.'

Sylvia, who had sensed that her companion would be sympathetic, felt gratified. 'The questions the children were being asked – it was as if the examiner didn't at all see the poem's point.'

Miss Crake shook her head. 'The trouble is, few adults retain a true recollection of their childhood. Are you acquainted with *My Friend Mr Leakey*?'

'I'm afraid I don't know him.'

'You misunderstand. It is the title of a book written by a colleague of mine,' Miss Crake explained. 'I shall send you a copy for the library.'

Sylvia reflected. 'A book I can recommend is *Tom's Midnight Garden*. I've just read it myself.'

Miss Crake reopened her notebook. 'What is it about?'

Sylvia considered. 'That's hard to describe without giving the point of the book away. It's about a garden where two children meet.'

'Something of *The Secret Garden*?'

'No,' Sylvia said. 'Not really.' She felt it didn't give too much away to say, 'A clock strikes thirteen and it happens – the children meet, I mean – in a garden which is both in and outside time.'

Miss Crake asked for the author's name and wrote this down in her notebook with a gold propelling pencil. She beckoned over the waitress for her bill. When this was paid she stood up, brushed down her skirt and summoned the whippet, who scrabbled to her feet with an effort, shivered and limped obediently round to her mistress's side.

'Sylvia and I suffer with arthritis. But we are fortunate in having each other to complain to. I shall order your book tomorrow. Goodbye.'

Sylvia walked back along the towpath pondering this encounter. Miss Felicity Crake – who, while awaiting the change from her bill had accounted for her name: 'My parents were Humanists who believed in the possibility of universal happiness' – was the first person she had met in East Mole who seemed to share her own passion for books. Their conversation had lightened her mood. But walking home, the black misery seeped back.

The evening had darkened, it was cold and, without her bicycle lamp to show her the way along the towpath, she was glad of the lights from the lock-keeper's cottage.

As she drew near it the door opened and someone shone a torch across the water.

'Sylvia?'

'Ned?'

'Fancy a hot toddy?'

Intending to refuse, she said, 'Thank you, Ned, I could do with one.'

'Come over then. I've a fire going.'

The little cottage was warm and the cramped sitting room friendly. Sylvia sat down on the sofa and, suddenly squeezed of all emotion, felt as if she might never rise from it again. She accepted a glass of hot whisky and ginger and sat back, welcoming its effect.

'D'you know, Ned, I hardly touched alcohol before coming here. I'm becoming a regular drunk.'

'I doubt that.' Ned's voice was kind and his ugly lumpish face, innocent of any malice, seemed to her suddenly beautiful. Extraordinary to think that he was related in any way to sharp-featured Mrs Bird. As if he had read her mind, he said, 'You don't want to take too much account of Auntie. She loves a to-do but it never lasts.'

'You've heard then?'

'I'm afraid it's everywhere.'

'She's been to the police and Sam's had some nasty official warning. It's upset his family dreadfully.'

'Ah, that I didn't know.'

They sat in silence. Sylvia began to wish she had not accepted his invitation. It seemed impossible now to dig up the energy to leave.

'Young Sam. How's he bearing up?'

'He's pretending he doesn't care.'

Ned grimaced. 'Boys. I did that.'

Sometimes exhaustion of the kind that follows a serious illness has the effect of demolishing inhibition. 'Sam didn't do it, Ned. He's protecting someone.'

'Not our Lizzie?'

'No. Another girl he has a crush on.'

'That'll be the doctor's daughter.' He was looking away from her into the coal fire. 'I seen the two of them together enough times.' Then it was likely he had seen her with Hugh. Sylvia felt herself begin to flush. 'And the two of them scarpered off together, to London, wasn't it?'

'Yes.'

'She not said anything about the book, the girl?'

'She might have done if the police hadn't got involved.'

'I see that.'

She shivered. He got up and walked over to a window and pulled it shut. 'The draught keeps the fire going. You haven't had a chance for a word with the doctor?'

'Yes,' Sylvia said, 'I have,' and burst into tears.

Ned said nothing while she dried her eyes. Then he said, 'The reason I took this job is because of a fondness

I had for someone. I thought there was a fondness back, in return. And perhaps there was and perhaps there wasn't but anyway I never found out.'

Sylvia, sure that no one's tragedy could compare with hers, was nevertheless polite. 'What's happened to your –'

'Dead,' Ned said.

Aghast, she said, 'Oh, heavens. I'm sorry, Ned.' Then, as he said nothing, 'Did you, have you, I mean, got over it?'

'You don't "get over" things,' Ned said. 'You get used to them.'

They sat drinking the hot whisky together until Sylvia felt her head would split open with knocking weariness.

As she began to stagger up to go, he suggested, 'You can stay here if you like. That settee's quite comfortable and there's plenty of blankets.'

'I'd better go.'

'Suit yourself. I wasn't –'

'Oh, no, I didn't think . . .'

They laughed, embarrassed at first and then more easily, and she said, 'D'you know, I will stay, if that's really all right. Thank you, Ned. That is truly kind.'

He bedded her down with a cushion and an eiderdown and a blanket made of coloured knitted squares.

It was the blanket of a childhood story, about a sick child staying at her grandmother's. One she had read to herself before she even went to school. 'I always wanted a blanket like this.'

Ned nodded. 'My mum made it. When she died, I slept under it for years. It still smelled of her.'

He went out, turning off the light, and Sylvia lay there

listening to the small rustling feral sounds along the canal outside. Rats, very probably. And shrews and mice. Far off, she heard the shriek of what she now knew was a barn owl. If only, she thought, you could choose and I had fallen in love with Ned.

26

Over the Easter holidays the Children's Library was almost sinisterly quiet. Mr Booth strode about in a manner that conveyed he was nursing a grievance. Sylvia's suspicion that he might be holding her responsible for the Henry Miller debacle had grown stronger. This was irrational, but when did rationality have anything to do with the human need to blame? Dee was as friendly as ever but her affair with Mr Booth made her, in Sylvia's mind, something of a double agent. With the Hedges, too, she felt uncomfortable. June's face had become drawn and Sylvia felt too guilty about her role in Sam's disgrace to drop in at number 3, as she had been used to doing. Bereft of her lover, her colleague and her companionable neighbours, she took to reading the library journals in search of a new post.

There was also the prospect of the possible expulsion hanging over Sam.

Sylvia tried to talk to Gwen about this one evening. 'All

this is having a dreadful effect on Sam and his family. I can't begin to see how he could have failed his mocks, Gwen.'

Gwen said she had been told by Sue Bunce that Sam had scribbled down strange calculations on the arithmetic paper and written nonsense for his comprehension and verbal reasoning.

'He's on strike,' Sylvia said glumly. 'Though did anyone check the calculations? From what I know about Sam, it might have been some very advanced maths.'

'He could be Sir Isaac Newton but it counts for nothing if he didn't answer the questions set. Can't you talk to him? He adores you.'

'He won't talk to me, Gwen. Believe me, I've tried.'

Gwen said that she and Chris were off camping again if she fancied getting away, to Dorset this time.

But Sylvia didn't dare ask for any more time off. 'Mr Booth keeps dropping hints about problems with funds and the Library Committee. I can't help wondering if he's out to get me sacked.'

'Surely not after all you've done for the kids with the library.'

'That was before all this bother about *Tropic of Cancer*.'

'It's sex,' Gwen said. 'People get into a flap about sex.'

'What was it the Hedges twins said that caused such a rumpus at school, Gwen?'

'It's a hoot. It was that silly rhyme about Buffalo Bill.'

But Sylvia didn't know it.

'You must have had a very sheltered childhood.'

Gwen recited it for her.

'*Buffalo Billy*
Had a ten-foot willy,
And he showed it to the girl next door.
She thought it was a snake,
And she hit it with a rake,
And now it's only five foot four.'

'Oh dear,' Sylvia said, laughing in spite of herself. 'I can see, coming from five-year-olds, that might have caused a stir.'

'It's nothing compared to some of what you hear. They're a pair of monkeys but they didn't have a clue what they were saying.'

Sylvia, who knew the twins better, wasn't so sure.

One afternoon, Sylvia was startled to see Ivy Roberts from the WI, dressed formally in a hat and gloves, come through the library door. She looked nervous.

'Miss Blackwell, I haven't come for books, not that I'm, you know, against them or anything, but since all the, well, really I came to ask you, like I said I would, if you would like to come to tea?'

Sylvia, who would once have hoped to duck this invitation, was grateful. 'Thank you, Ivy. I'd be delighted. When shall I come?'

Ivy said next Saturday would be best and wrote down her address.

On Saturday, Sylvia called at the appointed time at the Roberts' house. Ivy was alone. Her husband, she explained, was at the football.

She showed Sylvia into a room thick with rugs and

furniture. Two budgerigars were visible in a cage by the window. 'The tea's all ready in there. Len's a bit, you know, because of all the fuss about that book – not that I – anyway, I thought best to ask you when he was out.'

'I don't want to cause you any trouble, Ivy.'

'He can be funny but he's – it's about all that I wanted to see you. Do you take sugar?'

'No, thank you.'

'That's why you're so slim. After all the rationing I can't find the willpower to stay off these.' Ivy offered Sylvia a plate of foil-wrapped teacakes. Not wishing to seem impolite, Sylvia took one. 'What I wanted to say,' Ivy continued, 'was that I've heard, I mean, people are suggesting, what with the funds needed over the repairs for the library and the to-do about the book and all that, well, what I wanted to tell you was there's a mood to have the Children's Library shut down.'

Something cruel and sharp pierced Sylvia in the region of her ribcage. 'Shut down? Why?'

'On account of what happened, you know, with the little Hedges boy.'

'But that's nothing to do with the Children's Library,' Sylvia said, indignation rebuffing tears. 'It was a Restricted Access book taken. Nothing to do with the Children's section. It was mere chance, the storm damage, that it was there.'

'It's only what I've heard.' Her hostess blinked and smiled nervously over the teapot.

Sylvia felt a rush of compunction. Ivy was sticking her neck out for her while she, for her part – she felt ashamed of it now – had looked a little down at Ivy.

'Yes, yes, I see.'

Ivy appeared to pluck up more courage. 'The talk is, well, what I've heard people saying is, that it was you who – not that you would encourage him to steal, of course, I don't think anyone believes – but, this is only what is being said, you let him loose in the library, not that, I mean . . .' She faltered to a halt and picked up her teacup. Her age-freckled puffy hand, Sylvia saw, was slightly trembling.

Sylvia, who had unwrapped the teacake, began to twist the foil round her finger. 'Who is it saying all this? Can you tell me, Ivy?'

Ivy replaced her cup carefully. 'I'm not sure I should –'

'I won't say you told me, I promise.'

Her hostess took another sip of tea. She looked towards the front window, as if checking for possible spies, and then appeared to come to a resolution.

'It's Mrs Wynston-Jones and Thelma Bird mostly, though heaven knows there was no love lost between them before all this – they got the talk started. Gloria Wynston-Jones is very in with the doctor's wife and she, the doctor's wife, Mrs Bell, is up in arms against the Hedges after that trouble with her daughter running off with the boy to London – Gloria Wynston-Jones has a lot of influence in the WI and when I heard she'd been on at Mrs Brent, she's, you know, our Chairwoman, anyway, I thought, this isn't fair on Miss Blackwell, who was kind enough to come to speak to us, so I thought you ought to know.'

Sylvia had unconsciously fashioned a tiny chalice out of the foil. She placed it carefully down so that it balanced on the plate by the teacake.

'Thank you, Ivy. I'm very grateful for your telling me. But what do you think? Do you think the library should be closed?'

Ivy, having made her revelation, seemed to have found her fighting form. 'Bunch of old cats, is what I think. Gloria Wynston-Jones won't hardly pass the time of day with me and the doctor's wife is very full of herself. Thinks she's, well, she hasn't much time for the likes of me and Len.' She looked slyly at Sylvia. 'You're not too popular with her either.'

Sylvia's heart lurched. 'Why do you say that?'

Ivy's expression lost its knowingness and became embarrassed. 'From what I've heard, she reckons you're setting your cap at the doctor. Gloria Wynston-Jones will have it that her husband saw you up in London with the doctor. I said to Gloria Wynston-Jones, Miss Blackwell is a decent girl, there's no way she'd behave in that fashion and your husband needs his eyes testing. She didn't like that – more like he was half cut if you ask me, and she knows I know about his habits. Mind you, I always say if a woman can't keep hold of her husband then there's something wrong with her.' Ivy's unremarkable features became emphatic. 'If Len started to stray, I'd be down the street after him with a carving knife.'

'Good for you, Ivy,' Sylvia said. She felt shaky.

'And, I shouldn't say this,' Ivy added, 'but your boss also says he saw something. He should talk! We all know what he gets up to behind his wife's back.'

Leaving Ivy's house, trying to analyse this new influx of poison, Sylvia considered calling on Dee. But Ivy's parting words had raised the spectre of Mr Booth.

Electing to go on an altogether different route, she turned a corner and met Marigold.

The girl stared at her, her face so white it might have been that of a child haunting a Victorian story. Sylvia could see the freckles etched on the pallor of her skin.

'Marigold!'

For a moment it seemed the girl was about to speak but she suddenly turned and bolted.

'Marigold, come back!' Sylvia called after her. 'Oh, please come back.'

Too paralysed to pursue, Sylvia stood there. If she had managed to catch the girl, what would be the good? She would only lie. Everyone, it seemed, lied. Or, worse, twisted the truth. And the truth, she was beginning to see, was no proof against evil. She started home with a heavy heart.

Coming down the track from the towpath, something warm and soft rubbed against her shins and, looking down, she saw the ginger tom. 'Hello, Cat.'

The cat wound itself round her calf.

'Are you the cat who walks by himself?'

Two limpid green eyes stared up at her unblinkingly.

'Oh, Cat,' Sylvia said, enisled in her loneliness. 'It's my birthday tomorrow and I'm going to be twenty-five.' She bent down and stroked its fur and the cat racked out its spine, contentedly purring. 'If only you *were* the cat who walks by himself, Cat, and could talk.'

As she approached Field Row she saw Lizzie. The child was standing at the corner of the lane and as Sylvia drew near she started and then smiled wanly.

'Hello, Miss.'

Sylvia had come to the view that it was a kind of cruelty

263

to correct the girl. She was so clearly happier to continue with formalities.

'Hello, Lizzie. Have you come to see me?' She hoped not. She could hardly bear the thought of having to dig further into her ebbing resources.

Lizzie hesitated. 'I came to give Sam this.' She held out a book.

'That's the book my father gave him.'

'Sam lent it me,' Lizzie said defensively.

'I wasn't accusing you, Lizzie. I'm delighted you are learning chess too.'

'Will you give it him, Miss?'

'You can give it to him, Lizzie.'

'I don't think he wants to see me.'

Sylvia looked at the girl. Her hair was clean and her round doughy face seemed to have acquired shape. She had put on a spurt of growth and her dirty little neck, which no longer bore the gold cross, had lengthened and become slender.

'How about we take it to him together?'

But Lizzie had also acquired a new determination. 'No, you give it him, Miss.'

'No message I should give him?'

'Just give it him, please, Miss.'

When Sylvia called by number 3 the front door was as usual ajar but no one inside replied to her call so she left her father's book on the hall floor. On the doormat of number 5 there was a card-size envelope addressed in her father's handwriting together with a typewritten manila envelope. She opened the card first.

A photograph of some sailing boats with 'Birthday Greetings' printed over a violent orange-and-magenta sky.

Inside, her mother had written, 'A little memory of our many happy times together in Cromer.' Her father had written, 'May a fair wind blow in all your sails.' Enclosed in the card was a postal order for thirty shillings.

The other letter was from the council.

Dear Miss Blackwell,

In the light of the comprehensive repair works required for the library, we have decided to close the Children's section and are consequently rationalising staff.

We hereby give notice that your employment as Children's Librarian for East Mole will cease from 31 July 1959.

Sylvia carefully smoothed out the letter on the kitchen table and went outside.

Well, that was that. She had come to East Mole, taking it as her oyster, and the pearl she'd hoped to find had proved the sharpest grit. The sweaty face of Clive Henderson, her Swindon boss, flashed across her inward eye. She felt almost affection for him now. Perhaps he would have her back? If not at Swindon, no doubt she could find another job before July and Mr Booth would let her go.

'He'll be only too glad to be shot of me,' she said savagely to Boris, who had ambled over, hoping for food.

Boris rotated an ear in an effort to dislodge a late-afternoon fly from the vicinity of one of his liquid brown eyes.

'You know what, Boris, I think I'll retrain as a vet. I prefer animals.'

The donkey stared at her. The fly had returned and he gently flicked his ear again.

'But you're right, Boris. I'd have to have sciences. What do you think, Doris?'

At the sound of her name, the other donkey looked up briefly before resuming her steady cropping of the grass.

The bottle of sherry from her father was in the kitchen, more than half full. She poured most of it into a pint beer glass and went back outside.

Sylvia lay on the grass looking up at the blameless sky. Enough blue there to make a sailor, or a Dutchman – which was it? – a pair of trousers. Bags of pairs of trousers apiece. No clouds to play at being mad with, like Hamlet. He wasn't mad, of course, except maybe at the end when it all got too much for him – she wasn't mad either, a pity because she would quite like to be mad – that must be what he wanted, Hamlet, to go mad to escape – what a relief to let go, drift away from your moorings, talk bibble-babble, strip off your clothes along with your wits and dance naked. Who was it who danced naked before the Ark? King David? Or was it his son, Solomon? No, David's son was Absalom, 'And the king was much moved, and went up to the chamber over the gate, and wept: and as he went, thus he said, O my son Absalom, my son, my son Absalom! would God I had died for thee, O Absalom, my son, my son!' They learned David's lament at school. Solomon was the Queen of Sheba and Comfort me with apples. Sam stole an apple bough for his beloved. My beloved's beloved. Comfort me with apples, comfort me with mistletoe, for I am sick of love . . .

A steam train was puffing clouds of soot into her face. It ran so close by that she could see the fireman bent over, frantically stoking coals. A thin child stood beside him in the cab, placing some flowers in a tin can. But now the train was a barge on the canal and the child, a girl, was standing on deck, ringing a bell and waving at her . . .

Sylvia sat up. A clock was chiming. What time was it? Not yet midnight; there had not been enough chimes. It was dark and cold and her head ached like hell. The grass beside her was damp, her bottom was wet and her skirt and stockings drenched through. It came back. She must have fallen asleep on the lawn, drunk on the sherry. She rolled over on to all fours and groaned, trying to push herself up.

There was a smell of smoke and burning. Surely no one was having a bonfire at this time of night? She pulled herself upright and staggered, stumbling in her stockinged feet, to the fence.

It was not a bonfire. The smoke came from the open window of number 4 next door. Sylvia ran to the front door and as she did so a dark shape darted away and round to the back of the house.

She banged hard on the door, shouting, but getting no reply fled to the Hedges' and knocked wildly.

'Ray. June, wake up, *wake up*. Fire!'

27

The fire engines had left and the twins and Sam had been coaxed back to bed. Sylvia and Ray and June were in the Hedges' kitchen, recovering.

'Thank God they caught it in time.' June tipped an extra spoon of sugar into her tea. 'We were dead lucky being right next door.'

'"Dead"'s the word. Next door might have copped it for good.' Ray shook his head.

Mr Collins had been brought down by ladder in his pyjamas. The fire had done only surface damage. Apart from the sooty legacy of the smoke, very little of number 4 had been destroyed.

'I must say he could have been more grateful to you, Sylvia,' June said. 'If it weren't for your quick thinking . . .'

Sylvia's mind was also on Mr Collins. Before being taken by ambulance from his blackened quarters she had gone to commiserate with her neighbour, who had glared at her with red-rimmed eyes. 'Don't think I don't know who's behind this.'

Sylvia was very afraid that she too knew who was behind the fire. The crouching shape she had spotted in the garden – there was no question in her mind that it was Sam.

Monday was the first day of the summer school term and June and Ray had decreed that the children must attend.

'You don't want to miss any school, Sam, with the exams coming up and the school still not saying what they plan to do with you. And I have to go round to your gran's.'

Sylvia, who had called by number 3 to see how they all were, observed Sam's pallor and offered to escort the children on her way to work.

She waited till the twins had run off ahead to say what was on her mind. 'Sam, this is difficult, but I have to ask, was it you I saw last night in Mr Collins' garden?'

Sam said nothing so, swallowing reluctance, she pressed on. 'Only, if you had anything to do with the fire, that counts as arson and it's extremely serious.'

Sam still said nothing and Sylvia, more frantically, said, 'Don't be a bloody little idiot and go making things worse for yourself.'

The face Sam turned to her was tragic. 'I *never*. I never did nothing.'

'Was it not you then I saw?'

'I was going to knock on his door to tell him. Then you come along.' Distress had sent his grammar to pot.

'But what were you doing there? And why run away like that?'

Tears began to spill down Sam's cheeks. Jem, who had run back to inform the stragglers that they had found a doll's head abandoned on the towpath, looked horrified.

'What's wrong with our brother?'

'Run along, Jem. Sam's just hurt himself.'

Jem ran off, looking scared, and Sylvia put an arm round the boy's thin shoulders. 'What was going on, Sam?'

She could just make out from his mumble, 'Meeting someone.'

'Who?'

'Just someone.'

'Marigold? Was it Marigold?'

Silence.

'Sam, why were you meeting Marigold?'

'*Mind your own business!*' he roared suddenly, so loudly that Ned came out of his cottage.

'Everything all right, there?'

Sylvia waved at him across the water. 'We're all right, thanks, Ned.'

But Ned was already halfway across the lock gates.

'You all right, Sam, old lad?'

Sylvia made a decision. 'Ned, could I leave Sam here with you? I'm going to take the twins to school and tell them there that Sam's not well. There was a fire last night and Sam's had a shock. I'll come back as soon as I can.'

Sam looked terrified but Ned put a brotherly arm across his shoulder and said, 'C'mon, I've got Penguins in my biscuit tin.'

Sylvia delivered two rather subdued twins to the Infants

and then went round to the Junior school. She mounted the stone stairs to Mr Arnold's office.

The headmaster was at his desk and looked up frowning, but his expression cleared when he saw Sylvia.

'I thought you were Miss Buckeridge come to hound me over the hole in the asphalt. Have a seat.'

But Sylvia felt that her message was best delivered standing. 'I've come to tell you that Sam Hedges will be off school today.'

Mr Arnold looked questioning.

'There was a fire in our road last night. I was taking the Hedges children to school and Sam, he's a bit over-wrought, became poorly on the way. I've brought his sisters in.'

'I heard about the fire. Lucky no one was hurt. His parents can send in a note.'

As she was going Mr Arnold said, 'I'm sorry the boy has been in such trouble.'

For a moment she considered raising the question of Sam's expulsion – but the headmaster was perusing a letter so she left him undisturbed.

A smell of bacon met her at the lock-keeper's cottage. Sam was sitting on the draining board in Ned's galley kitchen.

Ned was stirring a frying pan. 'There's fried bread, if you fancy.'

'Thank you, Ned. I'm not terribly hungry.'

'I'll be getting along then. Kettle's on. Make yourself a cuppa.'

Sylvia, with her back to Sam as she took the kettle off the stove, said, 'I told Mr Arnold you weren't well.'

'What d'he say?'

'He said he was sorry.'

Sam gave a cynical laugh. 'Yeah, he's "sorry", I don't think.'

'What he actually said was he's sorry you've been in trouble. I'm sorry too.'

'I never started that fire.'

'Did Marigold have something to do with this? Sam, you must say if she did.'

Sam looked woebegone. Then he slid down from the draining board and rushed out of the room.

Sylvia was cradling her teacup in her hands when Ned came back. 'Sam's run off.'

'Best to let him go.'

'This fire –' she began, but again he surprised her.

'The doctor's girl was here last night.'

'Marigold? Here with you?'

'Not with me. Skulking on the towpath over there. Young Sam came and talked to her.'

'What time was it, Ned? D'you remember?'

'I'd put it just before ten o'clock because I listen to the jazz on the wireless at ten and I was in the kitchen making myself a brew-up just beforehand when I saw the two of them hobnobbing.'

'Only it may be important because the fire can only have just started at ten. I heard the Town Hall clock.'

'I suppose he could have started it before but –'

'But you don't think he did it, do you?'

'He's not that sort of kid, young Sam. The girl now, if you ask me she's got a screw loose.'

Sylvia considered this. 'She's phenomenally bright.'

'Doesn't mean she hasn't got a screw loose. Bright's not everything.'

'I don't suppose you have a phone I could use?'

But he did. It was necessary, he explained, in case of any problem with the lock or the narrowboats. Sylvia rang the library and got Mr Booth. 'I'm sorry, Mr Booth, but I can't come in today. Something has arisen that only I can deal with.' There could be no answer to that.

Mr Booth made uncomprehending noises and put down the phone.

Sylvia walked back towards the foundry. She sat down on the wall where she had sat with Hugh and lit a cigarette and watched the swallows, which, constant creatures, had begun their work of repairing last year's nests in the tall ruins.

All around her nature was at work busily renewing life. The leaves on the willows by the canal were a tender young green and the boughs of a wild cherry, which, thanks to some passing bird, had rooted among the foundry ruins, glimmered an intricate patterning of translucent white. *Loveliest of trees the cherry now/ Is hung with blooms along the bough* . . . There were no wild cherries in Ruislip.

Looking up, there was Hugh.

He was standing on the far side of the gate and his face was frozen and, yes, surely he was frightened.

Sylvia's was a naturally kind heart but the kindest heart is hardened by hurt. Her lover had hurt her, hurt her friends and their son; and it was his wife's influence which had helped to bring about the closure of her library, which she also loved and had worked hard for.

'Hello, Dr Bell.'

Still he stood there, saying nothing.

'At least you don't run away like your daughter.'

'Has she been here?'

'Oh, so you *can* speak?'

But she had silenced him again.

'The last time I saw your daughter she fled, no doubt feeling guilty at having implicated the son of my friends the Hedges – who by the way have lived in East Mole for generations with an unsullied reputation, unlike your family, who are pushy newcomers – in a crime he didn't commit. Two crimes now, quite possibly – I suppose you've heard about the fire?'

He nodded, wordless.

'Your daughter has so beguiled this unfortunate boy that he is valiantly defending her, refusing to give her up to the authorities for punishment, a punishment she richly deserves. Unlike your cowardly daughter, he has acted with nobility – a nobility I cannot agree with but which is none-theless admirable – in taking upon himself the sole blame for a theft for which he is not responsible and as a result of that being landed with a serious police warning which could adversely affect his whole future life. Now it seems he may be shouldering the blame for an act of arson to boot.'

Later she couldn't imagine where the 'to boot' had come from but at the time she was in full spate.

'But this cowardice in your daughter isn't surprising. Obviously, she has learned it from her father, who is also a coward and a seducer and speaks words of utter, utter . . .' But rage and resolution buckled and gave way to helpless weeping.

'Sylvia!' Fuck it, he had got over the gate and got his bloody arms round her.

'Get off me! *Get off!*'

'Sylvia!'

'Get off me or I'll bloody bite you.'

'Christ, Sylvia!'

'I warned you. He was rubbing his hand. 'I hope it bloody well hurt.'

'I hope it's some comfort that it did.'

'It's no comfort.'

'If you could calm down a minute –'

'Don't you *dare* tell me to calm down. That's another form of bullying.'

'Where did this sudden fluency come from?' She, too, was surprised by it. 'Why are you laughing?'

'I assure you, I wasn't laughing.'

'Smiling, then.'

Now she did laugh, but harshly. 'I was thinking what a bloody little fool I've been, with my la-di-dah ways, as Dee would say. Imagining I could transform East Mole. Imagining I was the love of your life.'

'You are.'

'Don't you fucking dare.'

He said nothing and she said, 'Do you know, that day I came to your surgery was the first time I ever said "fuck"? I've been saying it ever since. My mother used to say, "Once you've crossed a line, Sylvia, you can never go back."' She didn't add that her mother was speaking of sexual intercourse.

'Could we sit down? I won't touch you. I only want to talk.'

Too wrung out to resist, she sat down by him on the wall where they had sat months ago, when all that had happened since was waiting in the world's wings to unfold.

'Well?' She was still shuddering with fury.

He took off his glasses and passed a hand across his eyes.

'Sylvia, you're younger than me and you have what I've not got – purity, no, don't laugh. Please. When one is young it's easy to be pure, pure in spirit, I mean, undivided, whole, wholesome. I've been thinking, a lot of growing up is about becoming fragmented, fractured, if you're unlucky, with different parts of yourself not terribly in sync, so the thing you say and mean, truly mean, one day, you don't or can't the next because a different part of you has taken over. Is this too unbearably pompous?'

'I don't know yet.'

'You *are* the love of my life. I've truly never felt about anyone the way I feel about you but –'

This was intolerable. 'You mean how you felt at the surgery?'

'I know. I'm coming to that. Just because I love you doesn't mean I feel nothing for Jeanette. If I met her today for the first time, she'd mean nothing at all to me. Less than nothing, I probably wouldn't like her much, probably not at all – and I'm paying you a kind of awful compliment in saying that because I feel very guilty admitting it. But I've lived with her too long to simply dismiss her. She's not a bad woman, not an especially good one but not a bad one either. Probably with a different man she would be nicer and better, and me being as I am – and you've not seen the half of me – hasn't been exactly a picnic for her. The war, or maybe it wasn't the war, but something changed me, changed in me, I should say. I get the black dog on my shoulder and that can be hell to live with. It's a cliché to say your wife doesn't understand you but I hope you'll forgive my saying that Jeanette doesn't fully understand me. And why should she? There's no requirement in the marriage ceremony for one to be understood. Hers is a very different character from mine but she's no fool and she sensed something was up and she knows me well enough to guess that you would be the sort of girl I'd want, if I had my time and my chance again. But – here's the tricky bit – she trusts me – or did – and it was only a faint unease until recently. Although, apparently, according to her, you and I were very obviously avoiding each other at that God-awful drinks party.'

'She's right about that. We were avoiding each other.'

'Yes, well, Jeanette's no Sigmund Freud but she has the usual woman's intuition and she'd already sensed you were some sort of rival. The business over that bloody book was simply fuel to her fire. Do you think I could have one of your cigarettes? I'm out.'

Silently, she offered him the packet and he took one and lit hers for her, careful not to touch her hand.

'I would like to tell you something, if I may?'

'What?'

'It's this. A week or so ago, in fact the night before you stormed my surgery, Jeanette and I were in Salisbury and went for supper at the George, where you and I ate before *Gerontius*. Remember?'

She could hardly forget.

'I've avoided it since – for sentimental reasons – but we were nearby and she suggested it and I could find no plausible reason to refuse. Jeanette had gone to the Ladies when the manager suddenly appeared with a bundle, which turned out to be the clothes you left behind that evening, and she came back just as he was explaining how "my wife" had rung and left a message with the duty manager and he hadn't known where to send them and here they were . . .'

'What did you say?' She'd forgotten – no, not forgotten, been too distracted to pursue – those clothes.

'I couldn't really deny it. He had plainly recognised me and then your name is sewn into your skirt.'

'My mother used up all my school nametapes on anything she could find when I left home.'

'Yes, well, I expect Jeanette would have rumbled anyway. I told her we'd met by chance in Salisbury and –' He stopped. The mournful look that had always moved her now irritated her.

'What?' she asked angrily.

'What you don't know is that I was actually going alone to that concert. Jeanette was never coming – she can't bear, she doesn't care for classical music. So I told her that it was sheer coincidence that we met and that you were going to the concert independently – which she didn't believe.'

'No,' Sylvia said. 'Naturally, she wouldn't credit me with that degree of taste.'

He looked anguished. 'To be fair . . .'

But she didn't feel like being fair. 'All right, I admit

that I'd never heard of *The Dream of* Bloody *Gerontius* before you delivered me from my slough of ignorance.' He and his wife had ruined that special experience for good.

'Shall I stop?'

'Yes. No. Go on. Tell me the worst.'

He sighed. 'I'm not enjoying this. Understandably, Jeanette wanted to know why had I said nothing before and what about supper with you and how come this collection of your clothes? I think she imagined that we hadn't gone to the concert at all, that we had slept together there and then, that evening. I showed her the programme later but as she pointed out I could have easily bought that to cover my tracks.'

'Does she know we have – what you said – since?' She wasn't sure she could live if Jeanette Bell had details of their night in London.

'She asked, of course, and I denied it. I don't know if she believes me. She's a proud woman and she'll probably convince herself that that's the truth. Incidentally, about seduction, if it's not too much getting my own back, it was your changing into your flamingo plumage that gave me a flicker of hope that you might be just a little interested in me.'

Sylvia had the grace to blush. 'What happened then?'

'She had obviously been going over it all in her mind in the car and when we got home we had a blazing row, which, unfortunately, Marigold overheard. Jeanette threatened to leave with Marigold and to never let me see her again and, for what it's worth – probably not much – I contemplated letting her do just that. We didn't realise that

Marigold had overheard until she confronted us a few days ago. We calmed her down, or thought we had, she'd been acting very oddly already, and we assured her – I'm sorry, but she's my daughter and I really had no option – that there was no plan to separate. Then on Saturday night we found she was missing again.'

'Where was she?'

'She wouldn't tell us but she came home in a pretty dire state.'

Sylvia tried, and failed, to feel sorry for Marigold.

'Sylvia, listen. I would leave Jeanette today, this minute, for you, if it weren't for Marigold. I did say' – he sounded almost distressingly humble – 'that day, that evening, in the car in Salisbury.'

'I can't leave her. There's Marigold,' he had said.

She nodded. 'But why were you like that to me at the surgery?'

'I'm sorry. That was vile of me. I was in a panic. Mrs Eames is a busybody. I've had to take Monk to task over her breaching confidentiality and I was terrified she'd over-hear and report me and then the cat – and believe me, Mrs Eames *is* a cat – would have been truly among the pigeons.'

'You could have made some sign.'

'I know. I know, and I should have done. I'm sorry. It was a shock after the scene with Jeanette, your coming in like that, unannounced. I'd only just clocked it was you from your card and I wasn't prepared for it. I've served, you see, so long in the line of duty.'

She frowned and he said, 'You, meeting you wrenched me away from all that. But one reverts, you see, or maybe

280

you will one day, to an accustomed shape. And then I . . . and Sylvia, you looked so different.'

Inwardly, she brushed away the appeal in his eyes. 'So did you.'

'I don't know if you know this but your face becomes a sort of visor when you narrow your eyes. You were doing it when you were haranguing me just now.'

'*Your* face takes on a public-school smirk.'

'I suppose there's sides of each of us the other won't know.'

Suddenly, the galvanising anger evaporated, leaving her raw and exposed. 'Yes. Yes, I mean, no.'

'I don't mind you having a visor. I'm glad, in fact, because you may have a fight on your hands over the library.'

So he didn't yet know that she'd got the sack. Well, she wasn't going to let him have the satisfaction of knowing. 'I mind your smirk.'

'I don't blame you. You are right, I am a coward. An emotional coward, anyway. It's one of the faults you could probably cure me of.'

'I can't do anything for anyone,' Sylvia said. 'I ruin everything for everyone.'

'That sounds very melodramatic.'

'Look at it: I've messed up your marriage, which was fine, or reasonably fine, before I came along, maybe messed up Sam's chances of getting to Grammar School, which he was a dead cert for before. And I *was* trying to seduce you. That's not what I told myself but I was. I didn't give a fuck about Jeanette, nor, if I'm truthful, a fuck about Marigold.'

'To employ your new word! May I?' He held out his hand and she put hers into it.

'I'm sorry, Hugh.'

'Christ, don't be. That makes me feel even more of a heel. I'm the one who's sorry, in every sense. Listen, I've loved every minute with you and every particle of you – even when you were assaulting me with your peroration. You were magnificent.'

'That sounds patronising.'

'I mean it. It's that purity I was speaking of. I don't have that. I don't know if I ever had it but if I did I lost it along the way. I have a sort of wishy-washy, namby-pamby fudge which I call being reasonable and sensible, and when I'm being particularly dishonest, tolerant. It isn't. It's faint-heartedness and feebleness and spine-lessness. But your mother's right. You can't go back. What's she like, by the way, your mother? You've never said.'

'Conventional. Quite like Jeanette, in fact. Sorry.' They both laughed awkwardly. Sylvia reflected. Very likely her mother *was* like Jeanette; married to a different man, she might have developed differently.

'For someone like you that must have been –'

Dreading his sympathy, she said, 'She's not to blame, my mother, I mean. She's had few opportunities, and by her own lights she has done her best for me. She doesn't understand me well but well enough to sense that I keep a lot from her and that I prefer my father. I've not thought this before but that must have been difficult for her.'

'Difficult for her daughter too?'

Not wanting to admit this, she said, 'Is Jeanette jealous of Marigold?'

'She might be, I haven't thought. It's true that I love my daughter more than my wife.'

'My father does too. I mean, he loves me more than he loves my mother, at least I think he does.'

'I'm glad we have something in common.'

'It sounds incestuous, put like that!'

'Nothing wrong with incest, provided you keep it out of the family. According to Freud, all love is transference.'

'I don't want you for a father!'

'Nor I you for a daughter. The one I have is quite enough.'

They sat and smoked. Far off, a cuckoo called.

'"In April, I open my bill,"' he quoted and when she looked puzzled, 'It's an old rhyme about the cuckoo.'

'What *are* you going to do about Marigold?' Sylvia asked. She was remembering her dream of the steam train and the girl in the cab. 'She met Sam the night of the fire.'

'How do you know?'

'They were seen. Sam's already taken the blame for the book and if he's suspected of this fire and he takes the blame for that too it will go to court and that will mean prison or a Remand Home or . . .' The idea was too horrible to continue with.

Again he passed his hand over his eyes. 'I can only devoutly pray that neither of them had anything to do with it. Look, I'm not avoiding the question but I have to find her first. She's gone off again without telling us, she's been doing this, and I came here to see if I could track her down.'

You will tell me when you've talked to her?'

'When I find her I promise I'll tell you. But to do that I'll have to see you again. Is that all right, Sylvia?'

There was no help for it. 'Yes, it's all right, Hugh.'

28

When Sylvia got back to Field Row a large green car was parked by her house and when she reached the gate she saw Miss Crake sitting by the upturned barrel in her garden.

'I called at the library but your colleague told me you were unwell. I was just leaving you a note.' Her caller indicated a paperback. '*My Friend Mr Leakey*, the book I mentioned.'

Sylvia eyed the book, which had a picture on the jacket of a man in a top hat, a small red dragon and a turbaned angel. 'Mr Booth said that?'

'Not Booth. A woman with a regrettable taste in scent.'

'That's Dee. But I'm not ill, in fact.'

'I am glad to hear it.'

Sylvia read the short biography of the author, J. B. S. Haldane. 'Who is he?'

'A first-class geneticist and one of the world's wittiest and most accomplished men. We worked together.'

'Are you a geneticist?'

'I was. I retired after JB left for India.'

Not knowing what else to say, Sylvia asked, 'Why did he go there?'

'He is Indian, though he was born here, but he left for political reasons. He is a passionate Marxist and he believes India is more politically advanced.'

'Is it?'

'I doubt it but ideologues are impervious to reason. How is the Hedges boy?'

Sylvia sighed. She hoped that it appeared she was sighing over Sam and his plight but in truth it was because she wished Miss Crake would go away. After all the conversations, first with Sam, then Mr Arnold and finally Hugh, she felt worn to a ravelling, with no words left in her. Politely, she said, 'Sam has clammed up and refuses to talk.'

Miss Crake glanced towards the green car. 'A boy appeared briefly when I parked. He had an honest face. I see there has been a fire next door.'

'Yes. Luckily, no one was hurt.'

'You mentioned when we met over this book affair that in your view the Hedges boy was not the one responsible for the theft.'

'I'm sure not.'

Miss Crake appeared to reflect. 'But he insists that he was? Probably for his own reasons, he's making a stand. When someone makes a stand there's nothing to be done except wait for them to get tired and climb down.'

'Maybe,' Sylvia said. 'But the police are involved. And now with this . . .' She nodded towards number 4.

'You fear the boy might be blamed for that too?'

'He's had a feud with the man who lives there.'

'I'm acquainted with Collins,' Miss Crake said. 'What was the feud?'

Sylvia explained about the foxes.

'Collins is a poltroon,' Miss Crake pronounced. She did not seem inclined to go so Sylvia felt obliged to offer tea.

While the kettle boiled she brushed her hair in the bathroom mirror. 'I look demented,' she concluded.

When she came back out with a tea tray Miss Crake was sizing up Boris. 'To whom do these animals belong?'

'A farmer over the way. I've only seen him once or twice.'

'They need attention. This one has mange. Speaking of genetics, the book you recommended.'

'*Tom's Midnight Garden?*'

'I was most interested in the link between the old woman – who was once the girl whom Tom meets in the garden – and the boy himself. It is a quite remarkable example of the pioneering work I had embarked on at UCL.'

Sylvia poured her guest a cup of tea. She was too weary to listen properly but it seemed rude to close her eyes. Resting her gaze on the horizon, she pretended to listen as Miss Crake talked on.

'We could never prove it but my hunch was that with certain people there is a correspondence, an affinity, between the ninety-eight per cent so-called "irrelevant" element of their DNA, which enables a kind of communication commonly referred to as psychic and as a consequence dismissed by materialists. You are spilling your tea, my dear.'

Sylvia jerked herself upright.

'In Philippa Pearce's ingenious book I detect just such an affinity between the DNA of old Mrs Bartholomew and Tom, which is why, when she dreams of her youth as the child Hatty, he can enter her past and become her playmate before he is even born. It is excellently done. I should like to write to the author. Do you have an address?'

This last was declared so loudly that Sylvia came to. 'I'm so sorry, Miss Crake. I'm afraid I wasn't paying attention.'

'You seem distracted, my dear.'

'I suppose I am.'

Her visitor looked hard at her and then turned her gaze on the donkeys cropping grass in the field.

'JB and I were lovers.' She spoke as if to the animals. 'He is a moral man, not that morality is always the best guide for human conduct, but be that as it may he was bad at confrontation so for some time I and his future wife, his second wife that is, were unaware of the other's existence. In the end it was I who had to break off the liaison. He hadn't the heart to do it. Men, weak as water, as my godmother used to say.'

'How did you . . .?' Sylvia asked. For some reason, this hint that Miss Crake was aware of her own love affair was not alarming.

'I don't "know" anything. But East Mole is a small town and a small-minded town and, while I don't care for gossip, I have eyes and ears.'

'Do you know about them closing the Children's Library too?'

'Yes,' Miss Crake said. 'I was informed. The Hedges boy is taking another look at the Wolseley. Thank you for the tea. Goodbye.'

She left and Sylvia heard her a car door bang and the engine start up and she watched the green car back past the row of houses and heard it turn on the sharp bend. The sound of the car faded and there was the silence that Sylvia had craved and found that she no longer wanted.

The Town Hall clock was striking three when she remembered the twins. June was at her mother's, unaware that Sam was not at school to bring them home. The Infants came out at half past three so there was time to get there to meet them.

Near the biscuit factory, in her hurry she almost banged into Dee.

'You all right? His Lordship was on about you not coming in so I said you had been having women's problems. That always shuts them up. But you have, haven't you, in a way?'

Miss Crake's implied inference was one thing; Dee's was another matter. 'I'm afraid I must dash, Dee. I have to collect the Hedges twins.'

'Come round this evening, if you like. I'm in, doing my hair.'

Sylvia reached the school a little after half past three. She asked for the caretaker's office and was directed to a hut off the school yard. The twins were inside, standing on what appeared to be an old ping-pong table. When they saw Sylvia they began to chant, 'This old man, he played one, he played knick-knack on my –' and bumped down, consumed with giggles.

The caretaker, in a brown overall coat, emerged from a cupboard in the corner with a filthy mop and a pail. He appeared to be deaf, or anyway oblivious to the noise. Sylvia jumped each little girl in turn down from the table and thanked him for looking after them.

He muttered something inaudible and when Sylvia asked him to repeat it Pam yelled, 'HE SAYS HE DON'T MIND US!'

'Goodness, I'd mind your making all that racket.'

'He don't mind us,' Pam repeated sulkily.

'He hasn't got no little girls of his own,' Jem confided. 'He thinks we're cute.'

Sylvia gave the caretaker an appraising look. It seemed unlikely that 'cute' was a part of his vocabulary. She wondered if he was really a fit person to look after the twins. But what did she know? She had already made enough mess by seeming to know better about other people's lives.

Perhaps it was her imagination but Sylvia felt that various people they met on their way to the towpath were avoiding her. Several women crossed the road as they approached and Mrs Brent from the WI barely returned her greeting.

It was a comfort to be in the company of the twins. They bounded up the garden path of number 3, yelling, 'Sylvia brung us home!'

Sylvia followed the girls to the kitchen, where June was spreading slices of bread with jam. 'Where's Samuel?'

'Sam's not well,' Pam said.

'Sam was crying,' Jem said. 'He didn't come to school. Sylvia brung us.'

June looked anxious and Sylvia said, 'He was in a state about the fire. I hope you don't mind, June, but it honestly seemed best. I did explain to Mr Arnold. He was very sympathetic and you were at your mother's so we couldn't tell you.'

For the first time in their acquaintance June looked openly displeased with her. 'It wouldn't have hurt to ask us first. Samuel has his 11+ coming up and we don't want any more trouble.'

'I know,' Sylvia said. 'I am sorry, June. But honestly, he was in no fit state.'

'Where's he now?'

There was a sound of crashing gears outside and moments later Sam appeared.

'Samuel, where have you been?'

'Miss Crake's car.' He stood picking his nose reflectively and then announced, 'She says to say she sends her apologies for any inconvenience caused.'

'Miss who? You don't look ill to me.'

'Miss Crake,' Sylvia said. 'She knows your father, June.'

Sam said, 'She drives a Wolseley. I'm going to have a Wolseley one day.'

Although Sylvia felt worn to a thread, she thought she might take Dee up on her invitation to call round. Her colleague might be able to enlighten her about the proposed library closure. Before she went out, she looked up 'poltroon' in her dictionary.

'Utter coward, early sixteenth century, from Fr. *poltron*, It. *poltrone*.' Miss Crake, at least, had the right idea.

Dee answered the door in her housecoat with her hair in pin rollers. 'Sorry to look a fright. I'm redoing my perm.'

She offered Sylvia a drink. 'It's not alcoholic, or hardly.'

Sylvia admired the picture on the bottle but said she'd really prefer tea or coffee.

'Go on, spoil yourself. You look done in.'

Sylvia consented to sample a glass of the bubbly drink. 'It's very sweet, Dee. What's it made of?'

'Pears. His Lordship brings it. I suppose he thinks it'll put me in the right mood.'

'Actually, Dee, it was Mr Booth I wanted to ask you about.'

Her colleague's expression became serious. 'I know what you want to know. All I can say is it wasn't my idea.'

'I'm sure not. But was he behind the decision? I feel he was.'

Dee looked uncomfortable. 'That neighbour of yours seems to have something to do with it. How about some nuts?'

'No, thank you. If this is about the Henry Miller, I can't see why it's the Children's Library being axed. The blasted book was Mr Booth's acquisition, after all.'

Dee went to a cupboard and brought out a packet of salted peanuts. 'There's a feeling going round, though I'm sorry you have to hear it from me, that it was thanks to you that Sam Hedges got to the Restricted Access, and the Bell girl's mother is spreading it about that her daughter is a victim of your negligence. Apparently, they're taking her to a shrink.'

This dovetailed disturbingly with what she had heard from Hugh. 'But hang on, Dee, you said yourself that it was probably Marigold, and not Sam, to blame.'

Dee poured herself another glass of Babycham. 'All I can tell you is that, with the shortfall in the maintenance money, they had to make a choice. Your neighbour has some sort of grudge. And with all the hoo-ha made by Lady Muck and Thelma Bird and their cronies I'm afraid you got the short straw.'

'Not just me. The children too. What's going to happen to all the children's books?'

'The plan is to send them to Swindon. If kids here want a book, they can order it at the Adults' Library and it'll come through the County service, so they say.'

'But they won't, will they? It's seeing the books that makes them want to read. How will they know what books to order? It's crazy. I don't mind for myself' – this wasn't quite the truth – 'it's the children I mind for.'

'I knew you'd feel that way.' Dee sounded contrite. 'Believe me, if I could get him to change his mind, I would. But to his way of thinking, it's you or him – last in, first out – all's fair in love and war.'

'You said that when I first met you,' Sylvia said wretchedly.

29

Although she believed she had schooled herself to expect nothing from her lover, Sylvia was first fretful, then furious and finally fatalistic when, after their meeting in the foundry, she yet again heard nothing from Hugh. Her days now passed in a miasma of miserable seething. A letter in her father's handwriting arrived but, unable to cope with the thought of another dreary report of her parents' daily life, she put it aside to deal with when feeling stronger.

Mr Booth had perfected his air of having been injured. He scarcely spoke to her but the atmosphere in the library was thick with silent recrimination. One day when he was out on one of his meetings with the Trustee, Dee suggested, 'You should write to her – or go and see her yourself.'

'The Trustee? Why?'

'She has to approve what happens here. It's in the Trust deeds. He told me. That's why he's hither and yon, seeing her.'

'How would I find her?'

'She'll be in his address book. I can look in that for you any time. Once he's dropped off I have to shake him awake to get him up and dressed in time to report back to the wife.'

Although Sylvia had assumed an appearance of surprise at Dee's suggestion, she had in fact been contemplating this move herself. A conviction had grown up in her that the mysterious Trustee was none other than her odd acquaintance Miss Crake. It would explain her interest in herself and the doings of the library. So she was prepared for self-congratulation when next morning Dee presented her with a slip of paper.

'There you are. Address and phone number as promised.'

Sylvia took the paper, ready to be confirmed in her own powers of telepathy, and was the more disappointed when the name and address were unknown to her.

'Emily Thorneycroft. Who is she?'

Dee shrugged. 'Some remote connection to the Tillotsons.'

Sylvia was suffering the deflated pride of a false prophet. By rights, Miss Crake should have been the Trustee. If this was a children's book she would be, she thought crossly. 'I can't see why seeing her would do any good.'

'Go and see her and tell her your side of the story. He'll have worked the facts round to save his own skin, or my name's not Diana Harris.'

'Oh, Dee, bless you.' She kissed her colleague's powdered cheek. 'And here was I supposing you were on his side.'

Dee looked astonished. 'What on earth gave you that idea?'

'Well, you and Mr Booth . . .'

'You're my friend,' Dee said. 'And what's happening here is plain unfair. Don't think I don't know what's right just because I indulge in a bit of how's your father.' She opened her handbag, took out her compact and examined her face in the mirror. 'To tell you the truth, I'm thinking of showing him the door. I caught myself the other day almost wishing Cyril were back. Not that I'd have him. Someone saw him the other day wearing a wig. A wig, I ask you!'

Although Sylvia had been wrong about Miss Crake's connection with the library, her new acquaintance was clearly familiar with the locals. Her address was on the note she had been leaving when she had called at number 5. She might know this Emily Thorneycroft.

That afternoon Sylvia biked out of town. If asked, she would have bet on Miss Crake living in some grand old establishment, a version of the green car. Instead, if the address on the paper was to be believed, Miss Crake's residence was a modern and rather ugly bungalow.

Miss Crake opened the door as if Sylvia was expected. 'I'm just listening to a programme about defence. The Yankees have launched another ballistic missile. Very troubling.'

She showed Sylvia into a large room which was in marked contrast to the bungalow's drab exterior. Books lined much of the walls and a vast abstract painting of blues and ochres hung over the fireplace. A cage housing a grey parrot was suspended from the ceiling and on a yellow silk-covered cushion the whippet Sylvia lay in graceful folds.

The whippet cocked a delicate ear as they entered and began to struggle up.

'Don't get up, Sylvia,' Miss Crake said. 'The other Sylvia will excuse you.' She crossed the carpet, stepping over a large tortoise, to turn off the wireless and gather up a svelte black cat.

'Not allowed,' she said to it severely. 'Absolutely not.' She took the cat over to some French windows and put it outside. 'She's in disgrace. I caught her with another baby blackbird this morning. The third this week. She's a murderess of the first order.'

Sylvia sat down on an ample velvet couch covered with many cushions. 'What a beautiful room.'

'I have always preferred,' her hostess said, 'to live in houses that run counter to that which first meets the eye.'

'It's a good idea,' Sylvia said, squirrelling it away for future use.

Another cat, a plump tabby, jumped up beside her.

'Put her down here if she's a nuisance. Can I offer you something? Tea, Tizer, Tio Pepe?'

'Is Tio what-you-said sherry?'

'Very dry.'

'I'm used to sweeter sherry but I'd like to try that, please.'

Her hostess went over to a lacquered cupboard, from which she took a bottle and two green glasses. The tortoise ambled over to Sylvia. The little black eyes gleamed benignly as it began gently to nibble her toes.

'Kick Sibyl away if she's hurting you. I wonder if perhaps she's going senile. She insists on coming inside. And if it's not your toes, it's the carpets.'

Sylvia looked down at a rug which seemed to be of great age; its muted mellow colours glowed in a pattern of fronds.

'Does she imagine those swirls are leaves?'

'Maybe. I hope she isn't dementing. I'm very fond of her.'

'What are your cats called?'

'The murderess is Minnaloushe; the tabby, who has fewer pretentions, is Geraldine. They came to me already named.'

'I thought Minnaloushe was male.'

Her hostess passed her a glass of sherry. 'Minna's original owner had poetic fancies with little or no understanding. A ghastly combination. Very likely that is what set Min off on her life of crime. Did you come for a reason or is this a social call?'

'A reason,' Sylvia admitted and, fearing this sounded impolite, 'I wouldn't have troubled you otherwise.'

'My dear, *you* are no trouble.'

This was reassuring. 'You said that you had heard about the library,' Sylvia began, and then elaborated in case Miss Crake was ignorant of all the details.

Her hostess listened, her head on one side. Her quick dark brown eyes gave an impression of a keenly alert animal. 'I know Emily Thorneycroft. She's talked to me about Booth. He will have her twisted round his little finger.'

'That's what I was afraid of.'

'But this is not to say she cannot be untwisted and twisted round in another direction.'

The black cat was pawing at the French windows and,

possibly forgetting her own strictures, Miss Crake rose to let her in.

'Naughty boy!' the parrot suddenly screamed.

Miss Crake eyed it. 'Be quiet, Victor, or I'll fetch the cloth.' She gathered Minnaloushe on to her lap and the cat crossed her black velvet paws and draped them elegantly, awaiting a passing artist.

'I spoke with the Hedges boy. He's an unusual child with an unusually well-developed political sense, like his grandfather. I share your view that, whatever he has admitted to, he did not commit this absurd theft. But whether he did or not it is scarcely the responsibility of the Children's Librarian or anything that should lead to the closure of the Children's Library.'

'I think Mr Booth wants to be rid of me.'

'That's quite possible, my dear. Like most seducers, he's a misogynist. They always are, don't you find?'

Sylvia thought, perhaps that's what Hugh is. A misogynist. The thought was not a pleasant one. 'I haven't had enough experience to tell.'

'I hope you won't have to learn. Booth cannot abide clever women. All this nonsense about Henry Miller should have been a flash in the pan but he has puffed it up for his own reasons. I got hold of a copy. It's not a bad book, in fact. Somewhat overblown but not at all bad. I would doubt that those children read it but, if they did, it cannot have done them harm.'

'Ah, go on!' the parrot screeched flirtatiously. Miss Crake ignored this.

'I'll have a word with Emily. She's lonely and Booth flatters her. But I'll also have a word with Clem Austin – he's

299

got a shrewd head under the Lamb of God clothing and she and he have some sort of connection.'

Walking her guest back down the garden path, Miss Crake stopped to point out a rose. 'The Holy Rose of Abyssinia.' She bent to smell the pale pink blooms. 'The scent is heavenly. JB gave it to me when he left for India.'

Emboldened by this reference to her hostess's love affair, Sylvia asked, 'Do you mind that he married someone else?' and immediately feared that she'd been impertinent.

Miss Crake appeared unperturbed. 'Sometimes I do. Very much. Sometimes I am relieved. One isn't consistent.'

'I liked his book, I should have said so.'

'I thought you might.' Miss Crake began to pursue her earlier thought. 'People are not consistent. That is a modern delusion. No one in the ancient world made such an absurd assumption. The Persians debated all important matters twice: once drunk and once sober.'

'Which way did they debate first?' Sylvia asked. She could see a benefit from taking either route.

'That I don't recall. It is in Herodotus, who is not reliable, so it may not in fact be true. But the idea holds good. They, or Herodotus, understood that it is a mark of superior wisdom to be able to sustain contrary views.'

Sylvia decided to risk a drink at the Troubadour. Gwen had invited her and she had intended not to go but her visit to Miss Crake had lifted her spirits. The room with its glowing colours, eccentric animal occupants and Miss Crake's courteous manner and calm observations had revived that part of her that had wilted.

Gwen wasn't at the pub when Sylvia arrived there. She ordered a lemonade shandy and was paying for it when the organ that can detect a presence behind one's back told her someone was hovering.

It was Mr Bird and her spirits dipped again at the sight of him. 'Oh, Mr Bird. Good evening.'

But his faded old eyes looked every bit as fearful as she herself felt. 'Miss Blackwell, I'm glad for this opportunity. I've been wanting to say something.'

She could hardly bear to hear it. 'Yes?'

'It's about all that with our Lizzie.'

'Yes, I'm sorry Lizzie was involved.'

He gave no sign of taking her apology in, which in truth was only half sincere, and continued as if she had not spoken. 'The girl's in a right old state. And now this with the library closing. My daughter too. She's hopping mad.'

Confused about who it was he was talking about, Sylvia asked, 'Mrs Smith is?'

'My daughter Dawn. Dawn was thrilled when Lizzie got to the Grammar and we all knew it was all your doing.'

'No, Lizzie –'

But he pressed on, 'And Dawn isn't bothered about that book. It's all words, anyway, isn't it? Words can't harm. It's the wife, gets carried away. I said to her, "Now see what you've done, only gone and got the library closed that got Liz into the Grammar in the first place." She loves your library, Liz, goes there all the time, as you'll know yourself from seeing her there.' He shuffled off, murmuring, 'Just wanted to say.'

Gwen appeared and said, 'I had a bet with myself you

wouldn't come so I didn't rush. I'm really sorry about the library.'

'I'd like to strangle Henry Miller,' Sylvia said. 'With my bare hands.'

Gwen ordered half a pint. 'It's sex, like I said. Gets people going. It's why Chris and I have to be so careful.'

Sylvia, who had occasionally pondered the precise relationship between her friend and Chris, was aware she was being paid a compliment. All of which combined to make her cycle back to number 5 in a more optimistic frame of mind.

Her improved mood continued over the next week. She still heard nothing from Hugh but Sam, at least, seemed to have recovered enough to be preparing for his 11+.

Ned intercepted Sylvia by the lock one evening.

'Liz asked me to give you this to pass on.' He handed her a large envelope addressed to 'Mr Sam Hedges'. 'Poor kid, she's in a right old stew.'

'I know, Ned. You'd never think a book could cause such a to-do.'

'I don't know,' Ned said. 'They burned books, didn't they, the Nazis?' He seemed about to say more and Sylvia waited. 'About Auntie Thelma,' he said eventually. 'I know what she's done and it's not that I'm trying to excuse her. But she's more or less brought up Dawn's family. I don't like to speak ill but Dawn isn't the most careful mother, she brought up five before Lizzie and it takes its toll. It's Auntie Thelma who sees they're all right. Liz would never have got to the Grammar if Auntie Thelma hadn't taken a hand. To be honest, I think she

302

had a fright over that book. She was worried it might get back to the school and they would take it out on Liz, maybe even expel her, and she's done well by herself there.'

Sylvia was visited by an image of Mrs Bird in her feathered hat, off to buy Lizzie's new school clothes. Bustling determined Mrs Bird was a force to be reckoned with. But she had spirit. And she had a kind of largesse, partial but admirable in its way.

'The thing is,' Ned went on, 'Auntie Thelma's proud of Liz. She's bright herself but she didn't have any education. She respects education. That's why she took to you.'

It was true, Sylvia thought. Mrs Bird had elbowed Lizzie towards the Grammar School and had pressganged her into giving her granddaughter help, help she would never otherwise have had. 'Well,' she said aloud, 'if there's anything I can do, Ned, to heal the rift.'

'The trouble with Auntie,' Ned said, 'is she won't climb down. That's why she and Mum fell out.'

'Why did they, if that's not a rude question?'

Ned laughed. 'Don't ask! It was some argument over how a priest said the Mass!'

Sylvia caught a glimpse of Lizzie's card when she delivered it to Sam – a horseshoe set amongst forget-me-nots on a satin background with 'Good Luck' embossed in gold letters beneath. Costly, for Lizzie's surely slender means. So she was pleased that on this occasion Sam did not throw the card away but folded it up and stuffed it in his trouser pocket.

The first of the 11+ exams was due on a Tuesday morning. On the Monday evening, as Sylvia wheeled her bike past number 3, June came to the door and called out to her.

'What is it, June? What's happened?'

But June was speechless. She led Sylvia dumbly through to the kitchen, where Sam and Ray were sitting in silence at the table. It was obvious that Sam had been crying.

'Ray? What's happened?'

'The police have been to question Samuel about next door's fire. He's made allegations.'

'Who, Mr Collins?'

'Claims he has fair reason to believe it was Sam started the fire.'

'What reason?'

'He says Sam threatened him.' June's eyes were dark with fear.

Sam, his face slimed with snot, cried piteously, 'I only tipped him the Black Spot.'

Ray looked bewildered and Sylvia said, 'The Black Spot is in *Treasure Island*, the book I loaned Sam. But he can't take something from a child's book as a real threat. That's ridiculous.'

'Seems he can. He's produced what Sam wrote to go with it. And he's got chapter and verse, date, time, everything, of the twins telling you Sam was planning revenge. They'll ask you about it, I reckon, the police.'

'Jesus,' Sylvia said. 'The bastard.'

'Me and June's got to go down to the police station tomorrow with him for questioning and we wondered if you'd mind the twins.'

'Of course I will,' Sylvia said. 'But tomorrow's Sam's first exam.'

'We told them that. They said after would be all right.'

'Oh, Sam,' Sylvia said. She put her arm round the boy's stooped shoulders. 'I am so, *so* sorry.'

'I never done it,' Sam said. His terrified face looked pitifully young. 'I never. Honest I didn't, Dad.'

30

Sylvia had left Dee in charge and intercepted the twins on their way to the caretaker's office. They pranced back with her to the library, occasionally pulling down their knickers and showing off their bottoms.

'Don't do that, Twins.'

'We like it.'

'Other people don't want to see your bottoms.'

'Mr Jones does.' Mr Jones was the caretaker.

'I'm sure he doesn't.'

Jem weighed in in support of her sister. 'He does too.'

'Well, I don't,' Sylvia said. 'Bare bottoms are not permitted in the library.'

If the twins had absorbed any of the anxiety which had overwhelmed the Hedges household, they were expressing it with a heightened energy. In the library hallway they cannoned into Mr Booth. Sylvia almost hoped they would show him their bottoms but instead they ignored him and looked only slightly disconcerted when he barked at them, 'Little blighters – watch it!'

'He's rude, that man,' Pam opined, when Mr Booth had marched away, mouthing semi-audible obscenities.

'Yes,' Sylvia agreed.

The twins looked surprised at this validation from an adult. They scampered down the corridor to the Children's Library and tried to push open the doors. 'They is stuck.'

'Hang on,' Sylvia called, coming after them.

But the swing doors had a bar bolted across them, fastened with a padlock.

'Can't we go in?' Jem asked.

'Apparently not.'

'Why?'

'I don't know. We'll go home and do something nice.'

'But I want TO READ,' Pam roared.

Her sister began to roar too and Sylvia, losing patience, snapped, 'Shut up, Twins. This is no fun for me either,' at which they stopped howling and took her hands.

'Never mind, Sylvia. We will look after you.'

'Thank you, Twins. It would be nice to be looked after.'

Back at number 5 she made them marmalade sandwiches, her heart pounding with rage. The gross insult of it – barring of the doors to what had been her own small, surely harmless, version of Paradise.

The twins rushed about the garden, swung violently on the gate and fed the donkeys their crusts.

'We don't never eat these,' Pam explained.

When they grew tired of this Sylvia, hoping her seething fury was not too apparent, showed them how to make animals out of vegetables. Pam produced a crocodile from a raw carrot and Jem carved a donkey from a potato.

'What are they called, your pets, Twins?'

'My crocodile is called Susan.'

'Very good. What's your donkey called, Jem?'

Jem considered. 'My donkey is called Monkey.'

'That's very original.'

'What's "original"?' Pam wanted to know.

'It means unusual, special.'

'Is Susan special?'

'Susan isn't special,' Jem declared. 'There's loads of Susans.'

Pam gave thought. 'My crocodile is called Susan Violet Rose Semolina.'

The Town Hall clock had chimed six when Sylvia heard the other Hedges return.

'Come along, Twins. Mummy and Daddy are home and it's almost bedtime.'

'We want to sleep with you.'

'I haven't got room.'

'You have,' Jem said. 'You can sleep in the little room and we can sleep in the big bed.'

'Sorry, Twins. That's not on.'

But the sight of the wan exhausted faces of the older Hedges prompted her to offer, 'I can have the girls for the night, if you like. They seem keen to stay.'

June began to say, 'No we couldn't –'

But Ray interrupted her. 'That's a very kind thought, if you're sure.'

The twins decided that they should sleep with Sylvia in her bed, along with Monkey and Susan Violet Rose Semolina. They wriggled and gave off squeaky farts and their soft-seeming little feet kicked and poked her throughout most of the night. In spite of this, she was grateful. The children's warm animal bodies provided a comfort that only one other presence could have supplied.

She shepherded the little girls to school in the morning. Sam didn't accompany them. He refused to get out of bed. Sylvia considered going to speak to Mr Arnold but she was unsure what she could say. She had not heard how the questioning at the police station had gone and her offer to talk to Sam had been politely refused by his parents.

'We can't make him,' June said. 'He says he's failed anyway, so what's the use?'

It wasn't one of Dee's days so Sylvia had no chance to discover from her colleague what had occasioned the barring of the doors. But recent events had brought on a new militancy. She felt almost buoyant on her way to tackle Mr Booth.

Mr Booth shuffled some papers out of sight when, without knocking, she entered.

'Mr Booth, when I came back to the library yesterday afternoon the Children's Library door was barred. Why?'

Mr Booth lowered his eyes and addressed the desk. 'I was under the impression you'd left for the day.'

'I was away for fifteen minutes at most to collect my

neighbours' children from school. Dee was aware that I would be returning.'

'Mrs Harris had to leave. I have been asked to implement various security measures.'

'I think you might have warned me.'

'The Committee is of the view that in the light of various acts of delinquency we are obliged to put greater security in place. And Miss Blackwell, I had planned to say nothing of this in view of your imminent departure, but you force my hand.' His eyes glimmered with unguarded aggression. 'I might as well tell you that it is your own intimacy with these delinquents that has resulted in these measures having to be effected. There was another example of it only yesterday afternoon.'

'You are not suggesting that a pair of five-year-old girls are delinquents, Mr Booth?'

For a moment she wondered if he was about to strike her. My God, he hates me, she thought. He truly hates me.

Mr Booth apparently collected himself. 'A decision has been made that until you leave the council's employment you should not be left alone in charge of the library.' He appeared to address this to a calendar on the wall behind her. Sylvia had observed the calendar, which was open at April 1956 with a picture of some gaudy daffodils.

'Decided by who, whom? And why? In case I tear up all the books?'

Mr Booth's eyelids rolled down over his marble eyes. 'The Committee has made its recommendation.'

Too angry to call on Dee, too apprehensive to go home to hear the Hedges' story, Sylvia suddenly badly wanted her father. She dug in her bag for her purse but it didn't contain enough coins for a trunk call.

She wandered on aimlessly and came to the Anglican church, an ugly building surrounded by a flint-encrusted wall enclosing spotted laurels and brooding pink hawthorn.

She had never been in the church nor been tempted to enter it but with a tinge of irony speculated, Maybe God will help? Nothing else seemed likely to now.

To her annoyance, the Reverend Austin was inside, talking to a woman whom Sylvia recognised as Mrs 'Packard'. She ducked away but the vicar saw her and called out, 'Be with you in a sec.'

Mrs 'Packard' hurried out of the church and Sylvia waited reluctantly. She had no desire to commune.

'Splendid to see you,' the vicar said. 'I've been hoping for a chat.'

'Oh?' The last thing she needed was uplift.

'I had a natter with Flee Crake the other night. I was abreast, via the WI grapevine, of what has been happening but she was able to enlighten me further. Clever woman.'

'Yes.'

'I'm fairly thick with Emily Thorneycroft – we both like to go to bed with a Trollope.' Sylvia said nothing to this and he said a little reproachfully, 'It's a joke.'

'Oh. Oh yes, I see.'

'Between ourselves, and not to betray too much of a confidence, it sounds as if Emily has been given a somewhat distorted account of events by your boss.'

'He hates me, Mr Booth,' Sylvia said, with a spear-thrust of anger. 'Why does he hate me?'

The vicar sat down and patted the pew beside him, indicating that she should sit too. 'I'm not sure one needs a reason to hate but I can suggest a few in his case.'

'What? I've done nothing but try to build up the library.'

'Ah yes, but that in itself is reason enough. You are a reproach, my dear. A perpetual reproach. He has done little or nothing for the library and then you come down like the Assyrian on the fold and start to work your magic. It showed him up as what he fears he is, inadequate. Add to that the fact that you are young, clever, vital, attractive and everyone likes you. The East Mole youngsters are devoted to you, you must see that.'

'Nobody likes me,' Sylvia protested. 'I'm a pariah.'

If the vicar found this faintly amusing, he kept quiet about it. 'My dear, nobody hates you,' he said gently. 'If Booth seems to hate you, it's because he hates himself. He's a not very clever, not very attractive, let's face it, vain man who parades himself as something he is not and is married to a woman he despises – quite wrongly, Helen Booth is worth ten of him – all of which conspires to make him feel he is a failure. And nobody likes him. Not even Mrs Harris, I suspect. You don't like him either. I don't suppose you ever did, even before all this.'

This, though true, was not for the moment to be admitted.

'What about my landlady, Mrs Bird? She hates me.'

'If anything, Mrs Bird loves you for giving her this chance to be centre stage. She's an energetic woman without the scope wide enough in East Mole to match her capabilities. She should have been Minister of Transport or something, rather than that blithering idiot they have at present.'

Although reluctant to accept any reduction in her unpopularity, Sylvia could see the truth of this.

'And there's Mrs "Packard"?'

'Who?'

'I mean Mrs Wynston-Jones, who was here just now. She hates me too.'

'She probably feels slighted. I dare say she hoped you would be her friend.' Sylvia made a face. 'Ally then. She saw you couldn't care less about her, and in fact preferred little Ivy Roberts, who in Gloria's view is a very poor fish. Her nose is out of joint, that's all. You can put it right.'

'I don't want to.'

'That's fine but then you must take the consequences. Listen, my dear, you are old enough to be aware that most dislike is envy – you have attracted envy. You are bound to. Call it the shadow side of your gifts. It's your fate.'

'Do you believe in fate? I didn't think Christians did.'

The vicar rotated a stiff shoulder. 'I wonder at times how much of a Christian I am.'

'But you believe in God?'

'Sometimes. Mostly I do. Maybe even on some days a touch more than some of my colleagues. And I'm too cowardly, or lazy, to abandon my faith. But I don't believe in a God who has bad moods and tantrums and punishes people. Nor one who puts things right for us. I presume that is what you came in here for.'

She blushed. 'I suppose so, yes.'

'People do. And then they are disappointed when Divine Justice appears not to be on their side. I'm with

313

the Humanists on this. It's human beings who put right human error. Or don't, more often, I'm sorry to say.'

'Thank you,' Sylvia said, 'for the pep talk.'

'I deserve that. But listen, you hang on. The mills of God grind slowly, and all that, but the yeast of collective decency also takes time to rise.' She got up to go and he added, 'It's worth remembering that not everything that happens is about oneself. It seems so when you're young but most of what seems to be aimed at us is really to do with other people and their own inadequacies.'

The news from the Hedges when Sylvia finally heard it was dismal. Sam had been subjected to lengthy questioning. A sheet of paper had been produced on which he had drawn a large black spot and made threats to Mr Collins.

'What kind of threats?' Sylvia asked.

'All nonsense about how he was going to get him, pay him back. The worst thing was a picture he'd drawn underneath of a hangman's noose with, well, you can imagine.'

'Did Sam admit it was his?'

June shook her head in despair and Ray said, 'Mr Collins had it through the letterbox and it's Sam's handwriting and signed.'

'It's that warning he had over that book.' For the first time, June sounded openly reproachful. 'That's why they're on at him over this, because he's got a record. I said what it would lead to.'

'Not a record, surely?' Sylvia attempted.

'As good as, once you're in the system.' June was no longer willing to be reassured by one so ignorant of the ways of the world. 'They'll want to question you.'

'Yes.' She had been called by the police at the library. 'I said I'd go to the police station tomorrow after work.'

The interview at the station was not as testing as Sylvia had feared. She was posed polite questions by a detective sergeant about the time of the fire and how she had become aware of it.

'You were outside?'

Sylvia had mentally rehearsed this interview. It was in nobody's interests to reveal that she had been drunkenly asleep on her lawn.

'I stepped outside for a breath of air.' This was what people in this kind of situation usually said in books.

'And that was ten o' clock?'

'The Town Hall clock was striking ten. You can hear it from Field Row.' This was God's truth but it sounded so like something in a detective story that even in her own mind it had taken on the quality of fiction.

The sergeant put down his notebook in order to disclose that his auntie had once lived in Field Row, number 2, and he'd heard the clock himself from there many times.

'Then you'll see, Sergeant, why I had an accurate idea of the time.'

'And the fire had hardly got going when you spotted it?'

'I thought it was a bonfire!' They laughed, united in amusement at her simple foolishness. 'Then I saw it was in Mr Collins' house. I tried to wake him up but he was fast asleep. So I knocked up my other neighbours, the Hedges.'

The sergeant's tone became circumspect. 'Did you see

anyone about at all when you went round to number 4? Think carefully now.'

But she didn't have to think carefully. She had already prepared her answer. 'There was no one but me.'

'You're sure?'

'Absolutely, Sergeant.'

'Because if this comes to court you may be called as a witness.'

Sylvia had also practised an accommodating smile. 'I am anxious to help the police get to the bottom of this in any way I can.'

'Now, another thing.' The sergeant consulted his notes. 'Mr Collins claims he heard the little Hedges girls tell you how their brother was planning to start a fire.'

'Good Lord, no!'

'They never said that?'

'Absolutely not. I would most certainly have remembered.' This deviation by Mr Collins from the truth allowed for some extra emphasis.

But the sergeant wasn't born yesterday. 'Or said anything like it?'

'Like that Sam planned to start a fire?'

'Like that he was planning some sort of revenge on your neighbour. I gather there was some to-do about some foxes.'

This seemed a judicious moment for assuming the thoughtful look she had practised. Sylvia appeared to think deeply and then allowed her expression to brighten. 'You know, Sergeant, I think what Mr Collins must have heard was the twins telling me that Sam planned to get his own back on his friend Michael O'Malley.'

'Why would he want to do that?'

'It's a long story.'

The sergeant, accustomed to hearing long stories from guilty parties, settled down to be suspicious.

'Go on, please, if you will, Miss Blackwell.'

'Sam palled up with a girl in the year above him at school, Lizzie Smith, Mrs Bird's granddaughter, you know?'

'I know the Smiths.'

'Apparently, there's some childish habit the boys have of dragging their pals into the girls' toilets. There was some sort of horseplay around Sam's friendship with Lizzie which led to him suffering this indignity and he spoke of one of those childish revenges kids get up to – I'm sure you know the kind of thing? – which the little girls found funny.'

The mention of toilets had mysteriously provided validity to Sylvia's account. The sergeant was grinning. 'Afraid we did much the same in my day. Kids don't change.'

'I introduced Sam to *Treasure Island* – you'll know the book by Robert Louis Stevenson?'

Hearing of the famous book for the first time, the police sergeant nodded.

'There is a scene where an old pirate, well, you'll remember this yourself, Sergeant, tips the Black Spot to a' – she hesitated – 'to a colleague, I suppose you'd call him. Sam was very taken by this and for a while went about tipping the Black Spot to all and sundry, his school friends, me, Mr Collins. It didn't mean anything.'

'Kids' games?'

'I'm sorry if it has confused Mr Collins but then he has

had a nasty fright with the fire and I dare say it's muddled him. I'm afraid it is I, or rather Robert Louis Stevenson, who is to blame. The awful thing is, Sergeant' – here she became confiding – 'as the Children's Librarian, I was feeling rather pleased with myself that the book made such an impact. It's a classic, as you know.'

'Well, thank you for your time, Miss Blackwell. I'll have to watch out for the Black Spot in future.'

Sylvia risked a mild flirt. 'Not from me, Sergeant, anyway.'

Although Sylvia was hopeful that this performance would have dented Mr Collins' allegations, they were not immediately dismissed. A report was being prepared by the fire department. Nothing could be determined until that had been concluded. It was all too possible that June's fears would be confirmed and that, with Sam's previous brush with the police, blame would once again fall on him.

The Hedges remained locked in a state of terror about their son's future. Sam's once-incontestable place at the Grammar School was now an irrelevance: he had point-blank refused to take the remaining two 11+ exams. He was not openly rude to Sylvia but he avoided her. She spent much time with the twins, who attached themselves like leeches to her legs whenever they saw her, begging to be allowed to spend the night.

And very gladly she would have had them to stay, for her nights were made insufferable with anguished thoughts of Hugh.

There had been more silence from him and no news of Marigold. Lizzie, whose mother, in defiance of her own mother, had relaxed the veto on the library, came often to borrow books. Her taste was moving on apace.

'Do you like his books, Lizzie?' Lizzie was returning T. H. White's *The Ill-made Knight*.

'I feel sad for King Arthur. But he loves them both, doesn't he, Miss? Guinevere and Lancelot.'

One afternoon Lizzie shyly produced an announcement about the forthcoming Grammar School production of *A Midsummer Night's Dream*.

'You said you'd come, Miss.'

'I will certainly, Lizzie.'

'Do you think Sam would like to see the play?'

'I'll ask him.'

Sam, when this suggestion was put to him, said, 'Who wants to see a load of poncey fairies?'

'Did you ask Sam?' Lizzie's face as she returned *The Witch in the Wood* was eager.

'He promised to come if he could,' Sylvia said. Among her so-called gifts listed by the Reverend Austin, she appeared to have acquired a talent for lying.

The days passed, heavy with nebulous foreboding. She read more library publications in search of jobs and applied for a position in York, which had the merit of being, of the available posts, at the greatest distance from East Mole. Surprised to be offered an interview, Sylvia decided she might as well stay the night with her parents en route – she had to change trains in London and they, or her father at least, had been haunting the edges of her conscience.

It was then that she remembered her father's letter which she had in her irritation set aside.

'Ray, I'm so sorry to knock you up so late but I need to use your phone.'

'*I'm afraid the tests show it is cancer,*' she had read when she opened the letter. '*It was a shock but Mummy is being a trooper and holding up bravely. I'm sure she would like to hear from you when you can spare a moment to write.*'

31

Sylvia had rung Dee from the Hedges' to explain the situation and asked her to inform Mr Booth.

'Don't worry, I'll settle his hash. You concentrate on your mum, bless her heart.'

Her father's assertion that her mother was bearing her mortal illness like a trooper was, as Sylvia had suspected, wishful embroidery. The oncologist had been frank, and her father had decided, and when consulted Sylvia agreed with him, that it was best his wife remain as ignorant of the prognosis as she had been of the diagnosis. As far as Hilda Blackwell was aware, she had a pain which went right through to her back and clogged up her insides, for which, under the National Health, she was receiving home treatment.

'She's on morphine,' Sylvia's father told her. 'Nurse Godling has given her an enema. She comes morning and evening like clockwork. She's a little gem.'

Almost most painful for Sylvia was the degree to which

her father was affected by this calamity. For years his daughter had nursed the notion that secretly her father would be glad to be free of his wife and she was appalled at the extremity of his sorrow.

'I don't know what I'll do without her,' he sobbed when he met Sylvia at Paddington. He had bought a second-hand Austin shortly before her mother's condition had been diagnosed, in which they had planned, he told her, driving with lethal slowness through Shepherd's Bush, to take trips into the countryside.

'She had a fancy to see Box Hill after that book you gave her she liked so much.'

This too was a revelation. Sylvia had given her mother a copy of *Emma* one birthday and would have sworn her mother had never opened it.

She stayed for ten days, reading her mother *The Wind in the Willows*, another surprising preference on her mother's part, and trying to buoy up her father's spirits. Occasionally, she wounded herself by imagining how her mother would have welcomed a doctor for a son-in-law.

'When I've finished at East Mole I'll come back here and help with Mother,' she promised.

Her unselfish father's ready acceptance of this offer told her more than anything the depth of his grief. And there was her own grief to contend with. She scarcely knew her mother – and now the chance for gaining that knowledge was to be cruelly axed. Too late, she caught a harsh sense of her mother's probable inner loneliness, married to a man with a larger understanding and with a daughter who she had perhaps believed despised her.

Did she, she wondered, despise her mother? The

honest answer was yes. The thought was bitter to her for she had also as a child loved her mother passionately and craved her affection. 'Hell and damnation,' Sylvia said to herself, alighting from the train at Swindon. 'Why does everything come too bloody late?'

In the gap of time she had been away, East Mole and its doings had grown more remote to her. The larger anxiety over her parents had dwarfed, if not obliterated, her worry over Sam and the Hedges. Only the pain over Hugh seemed to have amalgamated with and been sharpened by the pain of her mother's approaching death.

The first sign that something had shifted in the collective mood of the town struck her when she alighted from the bus from Swindon and found herself face to face with Mrs Brent.

Mrs Brent seemed eager to offer condolences. 'I heard about your mother. I lost mine only last year so I know how you're feeling. Not a day passes that I don't miss her. Not that yours has gone yet, of course, unless . . .'

Sylvia said that, happily, her mother was still in the land of the living. At Field Row, as she passed number 3, June met her, smiling.

'They had the report back and they reckon it was the electrics started the fire. Nothing to do with Sam.'

'That's wonderful news, June. My God, what a relief!'

'You can say that again. My only wish now is that next door doesn't show his face here in a hurry or I'll be hard put not to slap it.'

'Sam must be relieved.'

'He's sulking still but he'll get over it.'

'He must be feeling sore about the exams. I was

thinking, June. I am sure Mr Arnold would write and explain the situation to the examiners –'

She halted, sensing June draw back. 'Samuel's all set to be an electrician like his grandfather. It's a good job and Dad'll help him through the apprenticeship. You can go on to the technical from the Secondary Modern so we think it's maybe the best place for him after all and no harm done.'

'Of course. We need good electricians.'

June collected her manners. 'I'm sorry, I didn't ask about your mum.'

Sylvia explained the situation. 'It's right you should go to be with your dad till the end. But you'll come back when . . . You heard about the library?'

But she hadn't. June accompanied her to number 5 and while Sylvia unpacked brought her up to date.

A change of opinion had been slowly forming in East Mole which had culminated in an unscheduled visit to the Library Committee from Emily Thorneycroft, the Trustee. There the Tillotson sisters' letter of wishes, atta-ched to the will and with if not legal clear moral status, had been read out. The letter included a list of books that were being left by the sisters, prefaced by a sentence that read: 'The following shall become part of that part of the library that is to be set up in perpetuity for the greater good of the children of East Mole, this being our especial wish and reason for our legacy.'

'So the Children's Library is spared?'

Oh Lord, Sylvia thought, recalling the books she and Dee had cheerfully weeded out. I bet the list included *The Joys of Obedience.*

324

'Your Mr Booth had more or less bullied them into making the savings through axing your part of the library and, with Mr Collins off at his sister's convalescing, Dad was able to put in a word with some of the Library Committee. To be honest, they were sick to death of our neighbour. So now there's a move to sell off the Assembly Rooms to pay for the repairs. They're a bit of a white elephant and the vicar has promised the WI can meet any time in the church hall.'

'I wonder how Mr Booth is taking all this?'

If Mr Booth was embarrassed by this change of policy, he showed no sign of it when Sylvia returned the next morning to work. On the contrary, he seemed almost friendly. 'I hope there is better news about your mother, Miss Blackwell.'

'Much better, thank you, Mr Booth.' She was damned if she was going to suffer any counterfeit condolences from him.

There was no restraining bar on the swing doors and no Dee in the library. Everything was in apple-pie order. Sylvia surveyed the room filled with the books she had brought so lovingly to the shelves.

'But you don't have to leave now, do you?' Dee said when she came in later. 'The grounds they gave you have all gone.'

But there were other grounds less capable of reversal.

'I've already given notice to Mrs Bird.'

Sylvia had called at Mrs Bird's when the letter of dismissal from the Council had come, apologising, hypocritically in the circumstances, for ending the tenancy.

'I'm sorry, Mrs Bird. I had hoped to stay at number 5 for some years.'

Although Mrs Bird's face registered that she was receiving this apology as only her due, she seemed unusually distrait. The spruce attire with which she habitually confronted the world was somewhat awry: her blouse had come adrift from her skirt and her lipstick was badly blotched. But her attacking spirit was as vigorous as ever. 'I've had enquiries from prospective tenants already,' she lied. 'I'll come round to do the inventory when you set a final day for going.'

This sudden introduction of an inventory for the cluttered effects at number 5 was inspired. Surely Mrs Bird had missed her vocation.

'She'll be more than glad to have you stay,' Dee said. 'That place is a licence to grow mushrooms. The rent she's been charging you is a joke.'

'You know, Dee, I think I've shot my bolt here,' Sylvia said.

A few nights later she went alone to the Grammar School's *A Midsummer Night's Dream* and was pleasantly surprised: the girls spoke the poetry comprehendingly, there were very few stumbles over lines, and the scenery, constructed and painted by the girls in their Art classes, showed an aesthetic awareness of the play's themes. The only real disaster was when an over-ambitious arrival by Puck, bearing the little purple love flower, led to his declaring his speech to Oberon with his wings caught in the branches of some hawthorn which had been imported to add authenticity.

Thanks to an accident on the hockey field, which had led to the girl who was cast as Peter Quince breaking her leg, Lizzie had been further elevated to play his part and delivered the lines with authority. Her face, shiny with make-up remover and pink with success, was beaming when Sylvia found her, after the cast had taken several bows, in the dressing room.

'You were the absolute tops, Lizzie. I am looking forward to seeing your name in lights in the West End.'

'I only had a week to learn the lines.' Lizzie looked understandably pleased with herself. 'We're doing *Twelfth Night* next year. I'm going to audition for Viola.'

'That's one of my favourites. I always wanted to play Viola.'

'She's a twin,' Lizzie explained.

'Yes.'

'I'm going to have twins one day.'

'I hope you do, Lizzie. I always wanted to be a twin myself.'

Lizzie's parents were there and hurried to greet Sylvia.

'She'd never have got here without you helping,' Dawn Smith said. She looked awkward. 'I'm sorry about Mum.'

'Dawn's had words with her mother over you,' her husband explained. He and his father-in-law had discussed their respective wives in the bar of the Troubadour and agreed that, within reason, they liked a woman who knew her own mind.

Lizzie connived to get Sylvia by herself on the pretext of showing her the school library. 'Did Sam come?'

'He sent his apologies. I'll be sure to tell him how good you were, Lizzie.'

As if that will help, she reflected, walking home under a sky spangled with indifferent stars. She stopped when she came to the foundry and looked up into the unfathomed reaches of the night sky.

'You're not even really there, are you?' she said, addressing the long-gone relics of light, emblems of all human delusion.

When she pushed open the gate of number 5 a black shape loomed out of the darkness.

'Christ!'

'Sylvia.'

'God, Hugh?'

'I didn't mean to frighten you.'

'Well, you bloody well succeeded.'

Jeanette was with Marigold in London, he explained. He had walked to Field Row, through the dark to be sure that no one would see him, hoping to find Sylvia at home. He'd waited there on the chance of her return.

'There's no chance Jeanette will suddenly come home and find you missing?'

'Nothing is certain but it's unlikely.'

'You can come in but I'm not going to bed with you.'

'No. No bed. That's not why I've come.'

'Why then? Why have you come, Hugh?' she asked, showing him into the cold sitting room.

'I only want to talk.' Silently, she indicated the sofa but he stood there. 'I hope you've a corkscrew. I've brought a bottle of Chianti.'

'Why? To get me drunk?'

'I don't know, Sylvia. I just . . .'

'I don't want a drink, Hugh.'

'I think I do. Would you mind?'

'What time is it?'

'Hold on, I'll look.' He stretched across the bed over

328

her body to where he had left his watch and she smelled the distinctive slight must of his armpits. 'Hang on, I can't find my specs.'

'Do you know, I've shared this bed with two other people. No, four. Four other people beside you.'

'You don't mean that?'

'I do.'

'To take revenge on me?'

'Got you!' She was laughing uncontrollably until laughter collapsed into delirious weeping. 'It was only the Twins and Monkey and Susan Semolina,' she sobbed.

'Who?'

'Carrot and potato people.'

'Sylvia, Sylvia, darling, come here.'

Towards dawn she said, 'You should go,' to be the one to say it first.

'Not yet. Let me hold you a little longer.'

Then, all too soon, it was he who said, 'I should really go or I'll be seen.'

'I know.'

'And –'

'I know. I know. Shut up.'

'It's –'

'I know, Hugh. It's Marigold. I do understand.'

'I had no idea she'd take the possibility of us breaking up so hard.'

'It is what the child experts supposedly say.'

'It's why she and Jeanette are in London. To see a so-called "expert".'

'I'm sorry.' Was she sorry? Some of her was.

'It was the fire that convinced me. I told him, the

expert, I had to tell him, I could hardly leave that out, and he clearly took that very seriously.'

Sylvia sat up. 'Hang on, the report said –'

'I know what it said. Listen, only you can ever know this. Please?'

'OK,' Sylvia said, unsure what she was about to let herself in for.

He felt across her again for his cigarettes. As he lit them, she saw by the light of the match flare his face, vulnerable without his glasses.

'When I pressed her, after your diatribe at the foundry – no, listen, I know it was deserved – she hinted to me obliquely that she had started it. I couldn't get out of her why she should have done such a mad thing and then she clammed up and I couldn't get anything out of her. I know a chap in the Fire Department, he was a POW like me and there's honour among POWs. The report was ambiguous. It could have been the electrics, they were definitely dodgy, but there was still a possibility that it could have been human malice. And you have to believe me about this, it wasn't only Marigold I was concerned for. It was what you said about Sam. Of course I was concerned for him. I couldn't betray Marigold but I didn't want him perceived as a likely suspect. I knew what all that stupid trouble over that bloody book had meant to you, so I intimated to my friend that, given there was no major harm done, if there was any ambiguity, he might slant the report in the direction of the failed electrics. I'm afraid I used Sam as my reason but what I did tell him, I hope you'll give me credit for this, was that the reason I was asking was because Sam had nobly taken the blame for a silly joke of my daughter's that had backfired. He has teenage children himself so he understands . . .'

'Christ, Hugh.'

'But, you see, I had to tell the child therapist Jeanette has rustled up for Marigold. That was what I came to say tonight. To explain why I might have seemed to be behaving like a bastard all this time but it wasn't because I didn't care – and we got distracted . . .'

'I accept my part in the distraction.'

'Was it worth it, Sylvia? Not just tonight, I mean all of it? It has been for me. Even, God help me, with what it seems to have done to my daughter.'

Was it? At the moment it was worth anything, everything. Tomorrow she would have to see.

'Hugh.'

'Yes, darling. I'm calling you "darling" while I still can.'

'Yes. Did you read that book I recommended?'

'I Capture the Fortress?'

'*I Capture the Castle*.'

'Sorry, "castle". I told you how much I liked it. The girl made me think of you.'

'Did you read it to the end? I don't mind if you didn't.'

In the greenish dawn light she could see his face clearly. He had found his glasses but he took them off again and rubbed his eyes. 'Yes, I read it to the end.'

'The very end?'

'Yes. Why?'

'I suddenly wanted to ask.'

Sylvia sat alone in the bed trying to make sense of her sorrow. Hugh had dressed and gone. Gone for good. Finally, she put on a dressing gown and went downstairs and stood in the chilly kitchen, looking out. Hedge sparrows, chaffinches, wrens, blue tits, coal tits, maybe a linnet, were flitting and threading through the brambles once tamed by Mr Bird, now with nature's incremental stealth fighting back. The guerrilla war waged by the universe against all human effort. She was glad that humankind so far still seemed to be the losers.

The little plum-tree vase was on the windowsill; in it the jay feather she had found by the canal in the days when she stood at the gates of Paradise. She took the feather and went outside and laid it gently by the stump of the plum tree, unsure what she was doing or why.

Beneath her dressing gown she was naked. She opened it and let it fall from her shoulders and stood for a moment facing the rim of crimson sliding up over the hills. The grass was wet and cold to her bare feet and she stepped over the dressing gown and went inside to put on the kettle for tea.

32

Sylvia left number 5 without Mrs Bird appearing there to do the inventory. There was next to nothing that she took that she had not brought with her when she first came. Only Sam's plum-tree vase, the silver leaf brooch and a package she had found outside her front door when she came back from her last day at the library. Even her books she had decided to leave behind. 'My legacy to the children,' she said to Dee, who had promised to buy book plates to inscribe with her name so she would be remembered.

'That's kind of you, Dee, but I shouldn't think anyone will remember me.'

'I shall,' Dee said staunchly.

This exchange took place at the end of an evening during which many gin and tonics were drunk and promises to stay in touch, each aware that neither would do so, were exchanged. Sylvia did not ask about Mr Booth, who had shaken her hand quite heartily and wished her 'all the best' in her new employment.

Her farewells to her other East Mole friends and acquaintances had been few. Only with Ned had it seemed heartfelt. He had squeezed her shoulder and told her to look after herself. Their friendship had been too genuine for either to pretend that they were likely to remain close.

Ivy had sent a card with 'Good luck in your new job' signed 'Best wishes from Ivy and Len'. The vicar had surprised her by dropping by the library with a book, *Wild Flowers of the Chalklands*. Inside was a note which read, 'Consider the lilies of the field . . .' and under it a further note advising her that the 'lilies of the field' were thought by scholars to be wild anemones.

Gwen, it transpired, was moving from East Mole anyway. Chris had decided to leave her job as games mistress and become an air stewardess. 'She was born restless,' Gwen explained. 'And it'll give us more freedom.' She was applying for jobs near Heathrow so she and Chris could live together. 'It's only a step and a hop from Ruislip on the bus. Chris says to tell you you'll be welcome any time.'

The most painful farewell was to the Hedges, who had withdrawn from their old open neighbourliness. Ray shook her hand and June kissed her cheek but Sylvia was aware they were glad for her to go. Sam gave her a scant ''Bye' for which he was not corrected by his parents. Only the twins expressed real regret.

'WE'LL MISS YOU, SYLVIA!' they roared as the taxi reversed past them while they tore alongside trying to race it, bashing against the windows the farewell flags they had mounted on garden canes.

'*I'll miss you too, Twins!*' she shouted back, and for

minutes after the taxi rounded the corner she could still hear their wild young sanity-saving laughter.

Miss Crake promised to meet her in London to take her to the Old Vic, where 'a friend', a Miss Robson, was playing in a well-reviewed production of Ibsen's *Ghosts*, so that was a connection that would not dissolve. She offered to drive Sylvia to the station in the Wolseley and nodded when Sylvia declined the offer, as if aware of her need to leave in solitude.

As the taxi passed the bus stop Sylvia recalled the day Hugh had picked her up in the grey Hillman, and their supper at the inn and *The Dream of Gerontius*, and the time she had mentally composed her brave letter resigning from the affair which had not even started.

The package at the door had contained a recording of some Schubert songs. One song was marked with an asterisk on the record sleeve. By it she read, 'The text of the lied is a German translation of the poem "Who is Sylvia?" from Act 4, Scene 2 of the play *The Two Gentlemen of Verona* by William Shakespeare.' Some time, no doubt, she would play it; but it was the memory of the song he had twice sung to her by the canal that brought harsh tears.

> *I found my love where the gaslight falls,*
> *Dreamed a dream by the old canal . . .*

A dream, certainly. Not *The Dream of Gerontius*; more like *A Midsummer Night's Dream*, in which – and with no one to share this with she rather revelled in the wounding cleverness of her own wit – she had once again played the ass, picked up and then dropped by superior beings from another world.

Even without her mother's illness, her father's need for her, the sense of the Hedges' dereliction, she would have had to go. Hugh had lied to her. She knew this as surely as she had ever known anything. He had not bothered to read, or not all through, *I Capture the Castle*, with its bittersweet ending, where a girl's love in the end comes to nothing.

It was not only the glint of fear in his eyes when she had asked him, the truth had exuded from his pores; but the harder truth was this: she had known it from the first. Had he said, 'I'm sorry, darling, I lied to impress you,' or 'to please you,' or 'I'm sorry, it's not really my kind of thing but I didn't want to say,' or almost anything; but for him to have lied then, for some reason – in time she would work out the reason – this was intolerable to her. One day, possibly, this fact – for, incontrovertibly, it was a fact, however unprovable – would maybe make all that had happened between them better for her. But that was one day; and now she had to dig deep in her courage and return to Ruislip to stand by her father and help to see her mother, who had brought her into the world, out of the world and then find the resolution to find a new – or another – world for herself to try to live in.

PART TWO

'What's so special about this place we're going to?' Alexander asked.

It was the start of the holidays and he and his sister Imogen were packing for a journey.

'It's an old library,' his sister said. 'Granny used it when she was young.'

The idea of a library bored Alex. 'Are we staying there?'

'We're meeting Granny at a hotel. You love hotels. It's got a pool and a spa and everything.'

'Has it got TV? Barcelona's playing.'

'Of course it's got TV. There'll be one in your room, plus there'll be Wi-Fi so you can take your iPad.'

On the drive down the M4 the children's mother explained, 'When Granny was a girl she lived for a time in East Mole –'

'East Mole? What a weird name.'

'It's not "weird", Alex. There was a move to close the Children's Library and Granny was all mixed up with it somehow. Now it's threatened with closure again so she's agreed to speak at an event which they hope might help to keep the library open.'

'I don't see why we need libraries,' Alex said. 'You can get anything you want off the internet.'

His sister, who was of an age to enjoy going against a popular tide, sighed audibly and their mother said, 'Yes, but how do you know what to look for? That's why libraries are so important. Without the library, Granny might not have become a writer herself.'

The children's grandmother was an author of children's books, famed not only for the words but also for the illustrations which she drew herself.

'My friends at school don't believe me when I say she's my grandmother.' Imogen had just completed her first year at secondary school and was having 'issues' with friends.

'I'm sure Granny would write a special message in one of her books for you to prove it,' her mother suggested. 'Now shut up, you two, please. It's the proms with Barenboim conducting and I want to listen.'

The hotel, boasting historic credentials as an old coaching inn, had been made over in a slick contemporary style and now offered a swimming pool, a gym, a beauty spa and a games room. Alex went off with his father to play snooker and Imogen and her mother put on fluffy white dressing gowns to sample the pool. On their way back to their rooms they met Lucy Pattern's mother in the hotel lobby.

'Granny!' Imogen rushed to her grandmother, who hugged her.

'Darling girl, you look like a mermaid but with lovely long legs instead of a tail.'

Imogen, who was thirteen and self-conscious about her appearance, looked pleased. 'We've been swimming. Will you come too tomorrow?'

'I haven't brought a bathing costume.'

'You could borrow Mum's.'

'An old bat like me in your mother's costume?'

'You're not old, Granny.'

'Darling, I'm seventy. At seventy you have to behave decorously.'

'You're welcome to borrow mine, Mum,' her daughter Lucy said. 'We're still about the same size.'

The family met for dinner in the hotel restaurant.

Alex grabbed the menu from his father. 'What's here we can eat?'

'Hey, don't grab, old son. There's plenty here for you.'

'Like?'

'Like pizza or pasta, for instance.'

'Boring. We always have them.'

'When Granny was little,' his mother said, 'she was lucky to get spam fritters, let alone pizza.'

'What's spam?'

'A kind of revolting pink meat that came in a tin.'

Alex said, 'Yuk!' and his grandmother said, 'I quite liked spam, in fact, and don't use me to preach with, Luce. We had other advantages.'

'Like?' Alex was willing to be broad-minded.

'Like being able to play out with no one supervising us. Like green fields and clear streams and very little pollution.'

'That's not quite true,' the children's father put in. 'The

341

London smog was shocking in the fifties. If you read the stats, plenty died of emphysema.'

His mother-in-law was aware that her daughter's husband found her flights of fancy irritating and did her best not to mind. 'You're quite right, Jamie, I'm romanticising. It's the effect of coming back here.'

'Have you written your talk for tomorrow, Granny?' Imogen wanted to know.

'I'm not a great fan of written talks, duck. I'll do as I usually do, wait and see how the spirit moves me.'

'Granny's a medium,' Alex said. He made as if to rock the table.

Imogen pointedly ignored her brother. Grandmothers should not have favourites; but if the children's grandmother had a favourite, it might have been Imogen. 'Are you looking forward to it, Granny? What are you going to wear?'

'I was hoping you'd help me choose, darling. As to whether I'm looking forward to it, to tell you the truth I'm a bit frightened.'

'Why? You're always doing talks.'

'It's different when it's your home town.'

'They'll love you, Granny. You're a star.'

'Maybe. A prophet is generally without honour in his own country.'

Imogen decided that her grandmother should wear a cream linen shift, her amber beads and heels.

'Must I wear those, duck? I'd much rather wear my comfortable plimsolls.'

'Not "plimsolls", Granny. Trainers or sneakers, and not for this, they're not appropriate. When will Gil and Iz be here?'

Gil was Imogen's uncle, her mother's younger brother. His only child, Isaac, was a special friend of Imogen's whom she didn't see enough of as Gil worked in Brussels.

'Their plane should have landed, so fairly soon, I imagine.'

There was a reception party awaiting them at the library. The children's grandmother was welcomed enthusiastically. She presented the Head Librarian with a book.

'How kind of you. One of your own?'

'No, in fact, it's a copy of a book that I failed to return to the library before we moved away. It's rather been on my conscience.'

The librarian laughingly said she was sure the library could spare their famous guest one book and indicated a large display of the books she had herself written that were to be sold as her contribution to the Library Fund.

Her family were ushered to the hall, where Gil and Isaac were already seated.

After a while a middle-aged woman looking nervous in a navy suit appeared and began to speak.

'Can't hear!' a voice shouted from the back.

A young man, hung about with items conveying technical competence, leapt on to the platform and adjusted the mic. The woman introduced herself as the Deputy Mayor. She went on to declare how fortunate they were to have a famous local author come to speak in support of the library and how proud East Mole was to welcome her back to the town.

'She's Tory,' Lucy whispered to her husband. 'It's entirely thanks to them that there are these fucking awful cuts.'

The children's grandmother appeared to polite applause. She spoke, without notes, of her childhood and the books she had borrowed from the library and what an impression they had made on her imagination and how they had influenced her subsequent career. She spoke fluently with none of the shyness that Imogen, who knew her best, was aware was a truer manifestation of her nature. 'You don't ever sound shy, Granny,' she had said once and her grandmother had replied, 'I've acquired a patina of poise, darling, but at work underneath there's a mole ready to bring it all crashing down. I'm constantly amazed that I'm not found out.'

'But what is there to find out, Granny? You're a humungous success.'

'There's always something to be found out, darling.'

Towards the end of her speech her grandmother stopped and appeared to collect her thoughts.

'As you can tell, I am a passionate, a *passionate*, supporter of libraries, especially for children who might otherwise have no access to the resources of children's literature. Children are the citizens of the future and what they are fed and nourished on will form the destiny of our world and the destiny of our beleaguered planet. We have a duty, a moral duty, to ensure that not only the stomachs of our children are fed but also their imaginations. We do not' – here she paused and swept a glance around her audience – 'we emphatically do not want to find that we have reached such a state of dearth in our society that we must provide food banks for the imagination as well as, as we so regrettably have to do today, for the physical body. Up and down the country there are local libraries, granaries of rich supplies, potential feasts of nourishment, often gifted, as this library was, by benefactors for the good of children, their children and the future of our children's children and our children's future children's children, which it is sheer wickedness to waste and destroy.'

She paused again to survey her audience. 'Doing dramatic timing,' her daughter whispered.

'But we also need guardians of this wealth, to ensure that it reaches those who may not know they are hungry. My own life was transformed by one young woman who worked in this library, Miss Sylvia Blackwell, who, single-handed, helped me to enter worlds and find the words to describe them that I should never otherwise have found. Our librarians are the unsung heroes who have served and protected the very best in our civilisation – a civilisation that is now under threat.' She allowed her gaze to linger for a moment on the Deputy Mayor, who was sitting in the front row. Then she raised her eyes back to her audience.

'I hope you will join with me in ensuring that we safeguard our librarians and their domains as they once safeguarded these precious domains of my own East Mole childhood.'

'Mum talked a blinder,' Lucy observed to her brother as they trooped out.

In the hallway a long queue of adults and children had already formed, ready to buy books to be signed by the famous author. The offspring of the author and their offspring went outside.

'It's pretty hideous,' Jamie commented of the library building.

'I quite like that mock-Goth,' Gil said. 'It's quaint.'

'You must have come here as kids?' his brother-in-law suggested.

'We didn't, in fact. Mum's parents moved to Oxford. We visited her parents there.'

'What were they like?'

'Not much like Mum,' Gil said. 'But you know Mum, she's loyal.'

'Thank God that's over anyway,' his mother said when she had finished signing and pictures had been taken of her and posted on Instagram and Twitter.

'You had plenty of admirers.'

'Yes, the children are always a treat.'

'Is all this very different, Mum?' her son asked.

'What's most different is that.' She nodded towards a Moslem family carrying off copies of her latest books. 'I think we had one Indian family when I lived here. And looking back, they had a pretty ropy time of it. The rest of us were thoroughly, and I fear unconsciously, white. Imogen, Dragon child, am I allowed to take off these hellishly uncomfortable shoes?'

Imogen had consented to her grandmother's plea to be allowed to return to the hotel to change. 'I want to go and explore my past,' she explained.

It was tacitly understood that she preferred only her grandchildren to accompany her on this venture. Alex wanted to play snooker so it was Imogen and Isaac who walked with their grandmother along the towpath by the canal.

'A lock,' Imogen said delightedly. 'I love locks, I don't know why.'

'It's the two water levels.' Isaac had been examining them. 'Like it's magic. But totally explicable.'

Their grandmother was looking at the little cottage by the lock, girt about with geraniums and petunias.

'Was that here in your day, Granny?'

But she seemed lost in thought and didn't answer.

The towpath began to run alongside a building site protected by a high fence where yellow notices warned of guard dogs.

'That was a foundry,' their grandmother said. 'It was a ruin even in my day. We used to play there, though we weren't supposed to after a boy drowned.'

They skirted the wire fence and turned on to a tar-macked road.

'This was a muddy track when I was little. There were so many flowers then.'

Finally they came to a terraced row of redbrick houses.

'This has been smartened up no end.' Their grandmother sounded disappointed.

The three of them walked round to the road that fronted the terrace and their grandmother stopped by one of the houses. 'Why are we here, Granny?'

A bird feeder was hanging by the fence and a woman was engaged in refilling it with seeds. A slight woman in her sixties with a sharp intelligent face. 'Can I help?'

'I –' their grandmother began and halted. 'Pam?' she asked.

The other woman blinked. 'No, Jem.'

'Do you remember me?'

347

'I know who you are,' the woman said. 'I recognise your face. I would have come to hear you today but my husband is ill. My grandchildren were there, though. They love your books.'

'No,' the children's grandmother said. 'You don't know me. Or rather you do but you don't recognise me.'

'And you are?' the woman said.

'Guess.'

The woman stared at her. After a minute she said, 'Well, I'm blowed. I see it now. Bloody hell. Of all things and all those years. Bloody hell. But you've changed your name.'

'Pattern's my married name. I took my husband's name because my own was, well . . . The first name's the same.'

'I can't get over it,' the other woman said. 'Of course, we were only titchers when you left. To be honest, I don't remember your surname then.'

'It was Smith,' Elizabeth Pattern said. 'I was Lizzie Smith.'

'It was amazing,' Imogen told the rest of the family. She, her brother and her cousin and their three parents were dining back at the hotel. Their grandmother had stayed behind to eat with her childhood friend Jemima O'Malley.

'She was one of twins,' Imogen explained. 'And she, this twin we met, married a schoolfriend of her brother's, her brother's the one Granny says helped her pass the 11+.

Granny was hopeless at maths and their brother helped her. The librarian she talked about lived next door but one. That's why Granny wanted to go back there.'

'Sounds like she had the hots for the brother,' Alex volunteered.

'Don't be disgusting, Alex. You can't see Granny having the hots.'

'She did cry when she was talking about him,' Iz supplied.

'They were both crying,' Imogen said.

Her uncle put in, 'Mum's quite cagey about all that period in her life. Does she ever talk to you about it, Luce?'

'Not much. The main thing I've gleaned, but you know this anyway, was that we are named after the people in the children's books that her librarian introduced her to.'

'Who's Dad named for?' Iz asked.

Lucy laughed. 'Don't you know? Not a book or books that would suit you, Iz. It's Gilbert, from *Anne of Green Gables*. I'm Lucy from Narnia.'

'Narnia!' Alex said. 'Narnia's Christian.'

'Until you know more about Christianity, old son,' his father elected to advise, 'you should maybe keep your opinions to yourself.'

Alex made a face and his mother chipped in. '*The Lion, the Witch and the Wardrobe*'s not too bad. It's only later in the series that it gets proselytising.'

'It's very badly written,' Gil said. 'I had to stop reading it to Iz when he was little.'

'Didn't matter,' Iz said. 'Granny read it to me and Im

349

when we were staying with her. I didn't know that's why you're Lucy, Aunt.'

Lucy and her nephew grinned at each other. Lucy had never permitted 'aunt'.

'It goes to show,' Gil said, 'how much those childhood books affected her.'

'She was crying,' Imogen said again. 'She hardly ever cries.'

'What I remember most about you, Michael,' the woman who had been Lizzie Smith was recollecting, 'is that you had the cane.'

'I don't remember that. Are you sure?'

They were eating supper in the kitchen of what had been number 3, now a bright open-plan incorporating what had been the old sitting room and a new staircase.

'I remember watching *The Flower Pot Men* with you on a sofa over there.' Elizabeth nodded towards a Welsh dresser decorated with pottery. 'Bill and Ben. You loved them.'

'It was Pam who really loved them,' Jem said. 'She liked Little Weed. She drove our parents round the bend going, "*Weed, weed.*" I was keener on Sooty and Sweep.' She raised her voice to a squeak. 'God, we were terrors. I don't know how our poor parents survived.'

'They loved you to bits,' Elizabeth said.

'Drove them nuts, more like,' Michael said. He beamed at his wife.

Pam, Jem explained, lived in Canada, where she had four children and eight grandchildren. 'She married a farmer who came over here to study and took her back with him. They've done well.'

'We've only the three grandchildren so we're considered inferior breeders,' Michael said. 'She keeps on at our kids to produce a few more. But there's only so much I can do these days.'

He'd been diagnosed with a heart problem, he explained, and it was a slight twinge of angina that had prevented their going to hear the talk at the library.

'But this is much nicer,' Elizabeth said. 'I can't believe that after all this time you're still here.'

'Dad never moved out,' Jem said. 'We were on at him to move into town when Mum died but he wouldn't leave. We bought number 4, next door, when it came up for sale, partly to be near him, and when Dad died we bought number 3 from our old landlord's son and extended sideways.'

'We were lucky,' Michael said. 'We got it before the insane rise in house prices. I'd hate to say what it would cost now.'

Number 4 was where the fire was, Elizabeth thought.

Jem had lost none of her childhood vitality. She began pulling out drawers and standing on chairs to ferret in cupboards until finally she located a collection of old photo albums.

'I knew I'd got them somewhere. That's you, isn't it? From recollection, Sam took it with your Brownie camera and you gave him the picture.'

Even at this distance in time she felt it was not tactful

to confide that their mother had had to fish the snapshot out of the wastepaper basket.

'God, I was plain.' Elizabeth was embarrassed to have been the child with the badly cut hair and round glasses squinting self-consciously at the camera. In the smudgy little black-and-white photograph two donkeys were visible behind the gate on the top of which she was insecurely perched.

'That was Miss Blackwell's gate. And the donkeys. I was frightened of them.' She had been somewhat frightened of the twins, too, as it happened.

'Remember how she liked us to call her by her first name. Mum didn't approve but she didn't know how to tell her.'

'I was too shy to, anyway,' Elizabeth said. 'I felt awkward calling her Sylvia.'

'Here's Sam,' Jem said. 'And that girl he was so crazy about.'

Elizabeth Pattern, former Children's Laureate and author of many acclaimed books, felt her whole system jolt with something resembling pain at the sight of the blurred image of the boy she had not seen for almost sixty years. Small and dark, recognisably at least to her now of Jewish lineage, he stood with the defiant expression she recalled so well, screwing up his eyes against an invisible sun. By him, against the gate on which she had just observed her own young self, lolled a girl with long hair and long legs. The girl was looking into the camera with what to Elizabeth Pattern still seemed an unconscionable sense of superiority.

'Marigold,' she said. 'Whatever happened to her?'

'A little madam, that one,' Michael observed. 'I blame her for Sam missing the Grammar. We all got into the Grammar in our class bar Sam and he was the brightest of us by a mile.'

'By a country mile,' his wife said. 'They tested his IQ and it was over 150.'

Elizabeth was tasting again the anguish she had experienced when Sam, having failed the 11+, refused to speak to her, crossing the road to avoid her faltering attempts at approach. Even then she had been conscious he was avoiding her because she had succeeded where he had failed. He had coached her to pass the exam to the school he should by rights have walked into as one of the lords of creation. Instead, he had gone ignominiously to the Secondary Modern with boys who, released from any obligation to respect him, jeered and beat him up. Sam had fought back savagely. Even before she and her family had left East Mole he had acquired a reputation for delinquency. And it was she who had betrayed him first, over that book which had led to all that awfulness that had then led to their separation – even now she pushed away the full recollection of the sore place in her past. If he had only known how she would have cut out her own tongue rather than give him away; but her grandmother, with her sharp intuition, had plucked out the secret from her best attempts at silence.

'Don't try to tell me that this was your doing, young lady. I know fine well who took that book. You keep that up and the school hears you'll be out on your ear and it'll be the biscuit factory, or worse, for you.'

But it wasn't Sam who took the book. It was Marigold. She had always been sure it was Marigold.

'What about you, Jem? Where did you go after primary school?'

'We were among the first lot to go to the Comprehensives, Pam and I. It suited us and it was best after what had happened to Sam. We did OK there after they split us up. Mind you, we kicked off like hell about being parted. My God, the ructions we were capable of. We used to make up stories about the poor old caretaker who gave us Rolos. What was his name, Mick?'

'Mr Jones. Poor bloke. Looking back, I'd say he was on the spectrum.'

'We could have got him arrested with our silly talk,' Jem said. 'He would have been these days. God, we were awful.'

'They can still make ructions, those two.' Her husband smiled fondly. 'Thank God for the Atlantic. If it weren't for that I'd have run a mile.'

'He loves saying that,' his wife said equably.

'What did – or does – Pam do?'

'A speech therapist working mostly with stammerers. She still does a bit part-time, though kids don't stammer like they used to, have you noticed? I trained as an actress but mostly I only got bit parts in bad telly so I retrained as a landscape gardener. His idea.' She nodded towards her husband.

'And you, Micky? Sorry, Michael? What did you . . .?'

'I'm still Micky to my friends. I ended up a headmaster at the school.'

'The primary?'

'The local Comprehensive, the one she went to. No cane by then, thank God. Plenty of other things I could

354

have done without, though. These days it's mostly admin. I was glad to retire.'

'He's brainy,' his wife said. 'He got to Birmingham. A first in Chemistry. He could have stayed on there but he had a vocation, more's the pity.'

Her husband accepted this rebuke as his due. 'It was a good school, our primary. All the A stream did well, but none of us was brainy like Sam.'

'And Sam?' Elizabeth felt finally able to ask.

'He's done all right. He's in Australia, Melbourne.'

Somewhere in Elizabeth Pattern's chest something contracted. Cautiously she said, 'Funnily enough, I shall be in Melbourne in October, on a tour for my latest book. Maybe we could hook up?' In her confusion she reached for a phrase she would never otherwise have used. 'That is if you think he wouldn't mind.'

Elizabeth Pattern, on her fourth book tour in Australia, remained astonished that the country's reputation was still for a boorishness which seemed to her these days more characteristic of the UK. The Melbourne hotel was exceptionally comfortable. On Sunday she was flying to Perth for the last stage of the tour but now she had a couple of days of free time. There was a concert she might go to and the art galleries – Melbourne had a fine collection of paintings – and there was Sam.

She had emailed him after hearing from Jem, with whom she had checked that he was happy for her to contact him, and they had corresponded with a civility that made no acknowledgement of any difficulty in the past. With a casual politeness she had suggested meeting, and with, she suspected, an equal caution he had agreed.

'*I am not really free until the Friday,*' she had written. '*On Sunday eve I fly on to Perth but any time before then it would be very good to see you and catch up.*'

She read this anodyne message through and then deleted the last three words.

It was she who recognised him at the restaurant where he had suggested they meet. He would have walked past her.

'Sam.'

'Lizzie? I didn't . . .'

'I'm told I've changed.'

'We all have.'

'I knew you at once.' Slight still, grey hair but brindled with traces of the original black, sunburned face with a ring of white showing just below his collar, but then he'd always been brown-skinned. Even his hands she recognised, skilful hands. The gold band on his ring finger was of course new.

He guided her through the menu, though by this time she was familiar with Antipodean fish. But she let him make recommendations uninterrupted while they found a common ground.

'I had no idea you were you, if you know what I mean?' A faint Australian timbre to his voice. 'My grandchildren are crazy about your books. I've even read some to them.'

'I'd gladly give you a signed copy or two if they'd like them?'

'They'd be over the moon. I still can't . . .'

'I know. I feel the same.'

'No, it's that you're different.'

He meant, she guessed, that she had turned out better-looking than he would have predicted but to spare him embarrassment she pretended to misunderstand. 'I always wanted to write from the day Miss Blackwell sent me off into Narnia.'

'I never got those books. I was always more one for the non-fiction until lately. Now I belong to a book group and we read all sorts. Here, this is a fine Kiwi wine.'

He filled her glass and she said, 'In America if you down two glasses they think you're an alcoholic and here if you don't consume at least a bottle over lunch you're a wimp.'

He laughed. Good teeth still. 'Sole reason for coming here.'

'That can't be the only reason.'

'No.'

Backing off, she relayed information about her children and her grandchildren.

'I remember your grandmother,' he said when she had run out of newsworthy relatives.

'Don't remind me!'

'She was something else.'

'It was because of her we left East Mole.'

'I thought it was because your dad got work at Cowley.'

'Only after my mother said we had to leave. She had a massive row with my grandmother which led to a major rift and I only saw my grandmother again just before she died. She wasn't at all as I remembered her. Dementing and rather pathetic. I have a feeling that she never got over our going.'

And it was she who'd been the cause of that. Crying her eyes out over the proposed library closure, finally succeeding in turning her mother against her grandmother. 'It was Miss Blackwell that got me into the Grammar, Mum. They can't close the library. It isn't fair.' Even her mild grandfather had rebuked his wife. 'My God, the worm's finally turned,' her mother had said.

'Your grandmother gave me the biggest dressing-down I'd ever had in my life. Over that book. Remember?'

'*Tropic of Cancer*? Of course. It was my fault you got into such trouble.'

'That's water under the bridge.'

'I've spent the best part of the last sixty years feeling guilty about it.' Lightly as she said it now, it was true.

He frowned. 'There was no call for that, Lizzie.'

'Wasn't that, I mean, didn't that set everything else off for you?'

'On the primrose path of dalliance?' She flushed, conscious that she might seem patronising, but he only grinned and said, 'It did for a while. But I got back on to the strait and narrow. As you see – no visible bones broken.'

'And the invisible ones?' she felt able to risk.

As if in answer Sam set aside the bones from the fish he had expertly filleted. 'How about coming back to my place? I've an excellent dessert wine, better than they'll have here.'

'If that's all right, I'd love to.'

'I wouldn't ask if it wasn't.'

'Sorry.' She was bespectacled Lizzie Smith with the greasy hair again and he was the boy she had worshipped and adored.

Setting out from the restaurant, she observed he was limping slightly and slowed her pace. 'My hip,' he explained. 'Over-enthusiastic running when I was younger.' It was odd, like trying to focus stiff binocular lenses, reconciling the bright spark of a boy whose image she had carried so clearly within her all those years and the elderly if still youthful-looking man she was strolling beside.

On the way to his apartment he told how he had come to the university as a postgraduate to research into cell formation and then sidestepped into genetics.

'So you went to university –'

'In spite of the Secondary Mod? Yep, in the end.' Again she flushed, detecting a taint of bitterness.

They had reached his apartment and he was showing her into a light uncluttered room.

'I can offer you apricot tart. Baked by my own hand. Or cheese.'

'Tart, please, if it's home-made. I'm impressed.'

'You'd better try it first before the compliments.'

They chatted idly, both too wary to plunge too rapidly back into the past. It was he who reverted to their earlier conversation. 'It was mainly thanks to Sylvia – or through her, I should say – I finally made it to university. Do remember a grand old lady called Flee Crake?'

'She was rather out of my league.'

'She wasn't grand, really. Actually very down to earth. She took me up when Sylvia left. She was a geneticist, a pretty high-powered one in her day and she got me interested in the subject and now that's what I work on, have worked on since I came out here.'

She hoped it didn't seem mere politeness when she asked, wanting to know, 'What aspect of DNA?'

'The short answer is that what was thought extraneous, the so-called junk DNA, turns out to be a treasure trove of resource which may allow for what's known as hypercommunication of information. There are some well-attested examples of people intuiting stuff they haven't consciously acquired, but it might work between people too. Is this boring you?'

'No,' She said. 'No, please go on.'

'The funny thing is, Flee had read a book that Sylvia put her on to which seemed to illustrate this theory which she'd proposed and everyone then thought sheer moonshine.'

'What was the book?'

'It's a children's book. You probably know it.'

He went into another room and came back and handed her a hardback, still with its jacket. 'Flee gave me this copy, though I took ages to read it because I considered it beneath me. In fact, when I came to look, I remembered that Sylvia had already tried to interest me in it, but I thought it looked "girlie".'

Elizabeth had recognised the cover. '*Tom's Midnight Garden*. My *very* favourite children's book.'

'Mine too now, bar yours of course.'

'Oh, come on! I'm not even second fiddle to Philippa Pearce. This is excellent tart, by the way.'

'My grandchildren cook with me when they're here.' It was strange to hear he was a grandparent – which was daft because of course she was a grandmother herself. But time and its local inhabitants stand still in memory. She glanced at his left hand and he said, 'Their grandmother and I parted way back.'

'Was she, is she, I mean, Australian?'

'English. Cathy and I came out here when I got the Melbourne job. She hated it at first, until she fell in love with a visiting anthropologist. She lives in Brisbane now. We manage a fairly civilised relationship.' He topped up her glass. 'And you?'

'Two children, a girl then a boy. Three grandchildren. The children's father and I divorced.'

'It's a sign of our times. No one divorced back then, did they? I don't know of any divorces among the folk we knew.' He turned the book round in his hands, apparently studying the picture of the boy on the cover. 'Except the Bells.'

'The doctor and his wife?'

'Marigold's parents. You remember her?'

How could she forget Marigold? 'What happened to her? Do you know?'

'She went off the rails, a whole lot worse than even I did.'

'That, I would never have predicted.' Fearful of betraying a curiosity which after all this time felt a little humiliating, she asked tentatively, 'How?'

'She had some sort of breakdown when her parents split up. But she was always a bit unstable, at least I would say so now.'

'Oh?'

'I ought to have guessed there was something awry when she got me to nick those keys.'

'Which keys?'

'Oh,' he said. 'It's a long story. More tart?'

'Yes, please,' she said, not in truth wanting more but wanting to please.

Frowning, he began to brush crumbs from the coffee table. Then he said, 'One time we were round at Sylvia's she got me to pinch the library keys from her bag. Then she insisted we go into town and get them copied. I went along with it out of bravado but I felt terrible because Sylvia had been, well, you know how she was.'

A lifesaver, for me anyway, she thought, but said, 'How did you get the keys copied?'

'Cato's, the hardware shop in the High Street, remember? Nobody bothered what we were doing with them, but children were more trusted then, weren't they? We did all kinds of things which would be frowned on nowadays.'

'I did half the washing and ironing for our family.' She didn't add that if she hadn't seen to it no one would have done.

'Marigold's plan was for us to break into the library one evening, just as a kind of dare, I think. When we finally did break in we found that cupboard, whatever it was called, full of supposedly "naughty" books.' And, well, you remember the rest.'

So I was right, Lizzie Smith inwardly exulted. I *knew* it. I knew it was Marigold.

The adult Elizabeth Pattern said, 'It was called Restricted Access. I wonder when that went out?'

'In the sixties, I would guess. Did you ever read *Tropic of Cancer*, really read it, not skip through the obscenities like we did that time?'

'I never did. Did you?'

'No. It was too . . .'

Too painful, she thought.

'Too dense,' he finally came up with. 'I might suggest it to my book club now. That would make them sit up.' He smiled ruefully. 'I thought Marigold was the bee's knees. But she turned out to be more like the bee's arse and I landed up being stung.'

'But you got over it?'

'Oh yes, in the end.'

He hasn't, she thought, not entirely. 'My cousin Ned — remember him? — used to say that you don't get over things, you get used to them.'

'What happened to Ned? I liked him.'

'Yes, he's a duck. I always thought he had a thing for Sylvia. I used to hope they'd marry so I could go and live with them.'

'I assume they didn't.'

'He was, is, I should say, gay. Remember the boy who drowned in the canal?'

'Do I? Our parents were always on about it.'

'He was Ned's secret, his great love. They had some sort of bust-up and this young man, he was only nineteen, went off and drowned. Ned blamed himself. He never knew if it was because of him that his friend drowned.'

'God, all the things that were going on under the surface then.'

'Yes,' she agreed. Herself too ashamed to let on that her mother was a slut who rarely washed her clothes. Ned keeping his sexuality under wraps, petrified of the effect the truth might have on the family. 'They, we, our family were Catholics,' she reminded him.

'I'd forgotten you were Catholic. But you say "were" . . .?'

'Oh, you cured me of that! You were so scathing about it I threw away my cross. I thought I'd be ostracised at school.' But she had still gone to the Catholic church to pray for him. Kneeling by the blue plaster statue of Our Lady begging her to make right what she, Lizzie, had made so wrong.

'I'm sorry, Lizzie. What a little varmint I was.'

'Oh, look, it's all so long ago.'

A silence fell. A bad fairy's passing over, Elizabeth said to herself and to change the subject gestured at a painting. 'You've some good pictures.'

'Painting's one of the many things I've acquired a taste for over here. That's one of a series called *Dream Life* by a young Aboriginal artist.'

'It's impressive.'

She got up to inspect it more closely and he got up too so that she smelled the warm, slightly vanillaish scent of his skin.

'Didn't I come to see you as a fairy in *A Midsummer Night's Dream*?'

'Mustardseed. I was Peter Quince too. Peter Quince was my star turn. But you didn't come.'

'I did. I swear I did.'

He was looking at her too intently so she went to sit down again. 'You didn't, I assure you. I was devastated.'

'Oh Christ, Lizzie. How do we know really what went on or what the hell happened to us then?'

She started to say, *We are such stuff as dreams are made on*, but stopped herself. He, their meeting, was worth better than to be treated to an overdone quotation.

'I don't know, Sam,' she said instead. 'It changes,

doesn't it? What happened back then, in the past, changes all the time.'

At the appointed hour the following morning a young man with a neat ponytail delivered a tray of coffee to Elizabeth's hotel room. She drank the coffee, reading her emails.

Soaking her limbs in the deep bath, she rang her publicist.

'Christine, good morning. I wanted to ask, is there any chance of changing the flight to Perth?'

Christine was on to it. 'Let me pull up your schedule. Sure. No probs. You're not down to speak at the Lane Bookshop till Wednesday. I was just giving you space to adjust to another time change.'

'I'm enjoying Melbourne. I'd really prefer a day or so more here.'

The efficient Christine emailed in less than ten minutes to say that they were rebooked on a Tuesday-evening flight.

In answer to an email from Sam, Elizabeth wrote: *Great seeing you too. Another dinner this eve would be lovely. E* x.

After some thought she deleted the x.

He replied at once: *7 o'clock tonight at mine OK for you? S.*

For their first reunion she had dressed formally, in a linen frock and heels. This time she went in jeans and trainers and was gratified when he answered the door in bare feet.

'I'm cooking Thai. There's wine in the fridge, if you'd like to pour us both a glass. My hands are covered in garlic.'

The brief passage of time between their meetings had eased them both into a degree of confidence. Over dinner Sam told her more about his research and she listened, not always understanding but drawn by his evident passion.

'But my own arcane interest aside,' he concluded, 'I'm more and more of the view that most behaviour is nature rather than nurture. My son is the dead spit of me, not just in looks, in behaviour – bolshie, arrogant, in other words a right pain in the arse.'

'Bright like his father too, though, I bet?'

'Bright enough. But the girls are also bright and they take after their mother. Mild as milk, and they were all brought up much the same.' She began to protest but he held up a staying hand. 'And before you say that's all to do with sexual stereotyping, I have a granddaughter who, character-wise, is a dead ringer for her grandfather. I call her Minnie the Minx. Her mother's a classicist and her name's Minerva.' He shook his head. 'These modern names!'

She laughed at the imperious hand. 'And I imagine she's your favourite.'

'You were always perceptive, Lizzie.' He began to clear the plates. 'Shall we have a pause before the next course? What my son refers to as an inter-course break?'

Pleased at this second-hand intimacy, she asked, 'Would you mind if I smoked?'

'Not at all. I smoke. I was concealing it from you.'

'I don't tell the grandchildren, they'd tick me off like anything. I only indulge myself when I feel like a treat.'

'I'm honoured to be classed an occasion for a treat. Shall we go on to the balcony?'

Outside, the Melbourne cityscape was graced by the lingering light of the evening sun. It lightly gilded the tops of the trees, already in full leaf, lining the long streets below. At home, Elizabeth thought, the leaves would be in the sere, yellowing, ready to drop.

'Do you remember playing conkers, Sam? Children never play conkers now. I doubt they even notice them when they fall and for us the first conkers caused such an intense excitement. I still get a twinge of joy when I see that polished mahogany gleam.'

'I love them too. I miss them here.'

'And sticklebacks. I was thinking the other day, no one talks about sticklebacks. Do you remember, you had some in a jar and tried to make me drink them? You said, as they were fish, they would be good for my brain.'

'Did I? I'd forgotten that. I'm sorry. Another occasion for apology. I remember putting one down Micky O'Malley's neck, little tike that I was.'

'And he married Jem.'

'Poor sod.' She stubbed out her cigarette and he said, 'Shall we go inside?'

Inside, it seemed to her that enough bridges had been crossed and they stood now on some shared plain.

'Sam, what happened to Marigold? You didn't say the other night.'

'I don't know that much. We never spoke again after . . . Let me get the next course.'

Over cake and cheese he told her. 'She and her mother moved away. There must have been a divorce because we heard her mother married again. Her father never did, as far as I know.'

'Did he stay on as a GP?'

'He joined forces with another GP when Dr Monk died but I got the impression that he didn't see much of Marigold after her mother remarried. She sort of ticked over at that rather snotty private school in Salisbury that she disliked . . .'

'St Catherine's. We played them at hockey. Well, I didn't, I was hopeless at games, but our school did.'

'I got all this from Mum, by the way, who once she got over her prejudice became very concerned about Marigold – that was very Mum; the only person she never forgave was poor old Collins next door, who in retrospect I see was a sad old bugger.'

Perhaps because she had been less hurt by his querulous neighbour, Elizabeth was more unwilling to forego her dislike of him. 'I'm not sure about "sad". He did kill the fox cubs' mother.'

'That's true. To be fair to Marigold, she genuinely minded that.' She began silently to bridle at this – wasn't it she and he who had found the dead vixen together? – and he must have sensed her objecting as he added, 'Not as much as you did, of course.'

'He was vicious,' she insisted, prepared to forgive Sam but not Mr Collins.

But Sam had long since left Mr Collins behind. 'According to Mum, Marigold went to some provincial university,

I forget which, not Oxbridge anyway, which is what you'd have predicted. But she crashed out after only a year and for a time she was in a psychiatric hospital. I tracked her down on the internet, quite recently. She's running some kind of yoga retreat in Wales. I guess yoga's how she got herself right again.'

How are the mighty fallen, Elizabeth thought. 'That's awful.'

'My daughter teaches yoga!'

'Sorry, I didn't . . . I only meant that she was so brainy.' Too clever by half, she recalled Ned saying once. 'Did she marry, did your mother say?'

'Not that Mum ever mentioned. I've never wanted to get in touch with her. It seemed too sad.'

It was sad. Elizabeth felt compunction. 'All these years, I've been jealous of her.'

'Why? You of all people. You're the big success, Elizabeth Pattern.'

'You've not done so badly, Sam Hedges.'

He looked at her, assessing her tone, then grinned. He's still prickly, she thought. There's the sliver of a chip there still.

'That was my grandfather's doing. He took me on as an apprentice and being with him saved my bacon. Flee Crake had a lot of time for him. It was really him and her who saw me through. Sylvia had been marvellous, of course.'

'Is she still alive, d'you know? I wish I'd thought to get in touch.'

'She died a couple of years back. She would have been

proud of you becoming a writer. But she would have known, surely?'

'She might not have done. My name is different.' My stupid diffidence, she thought. She would have been proud but I was too ashamed. 'Did you ever see her again?'

'Once just before I moved out here. She came to stay with Flee. They kept in touch.'

'What was she like?'

'Much the same. Funny, warm, very left-wing. She'd married a decent-sounding bloke, an expert on John Clare, who taught at Manchester University. She was Chief Librarian there when she retired.'

'So it came all right for her too in the end?'

'As much as it does for anyone, I guess.'

He walked her back to the hotel, where they kissed decorously, each on each cheek.

'Shall I see you again?' he asked. 'You're off, aren't you, tomorrow?'

'As a matter of fact, I misread my schedule. It turns out I'm not leaving till Tuesday, after all.'

'Oh, well, do you fancy, or maybe you've had enough . . .?'

'No, no, it's been fun.' Better than fun. 'It's interesting catching up.'

'Tomorrow, then? Or . . .'

'Yes, OK, tomorrow, if you'd like?'

'Only if you'd like . . .'

'Yes, yes, I would like. Really.' She began to push the hotel doors but she stopped and turned back. He was still there, watching her, with the face of the boy she remembered visible still beneath time's changes. 'There's no one else,' she said. 'No one, I mean, who I can talk about the past with like this.'

This time he rang her on the hotel phone. 'I can take you out to a spectacular place on the beach to eat or I can cook for us at home. Your call.'

'I don't mind.'

'You're not allowed to say that here. They won't have it. You have to choose.'

'OK, if you insist, then truly I'd rather eat in. I spend all my time on tour eating in restaurants.'

'That's the right choice. I shall prepare a feast.'

She had taken more care with her appearance and was amused to see that he had too. They were a little shy with each other – the growth of intimacy had brought wariness in its train and, it would seem, a concomitant need for alcohol. By unspoken agreement, neither brought up the past until the second bottle of wine. It was Elizabeth who broke their tacit pact.

'What did happen about that fire, Sam? Was it a cover-up? Was it Marigold?'

'I've been thinking about that too since our conversation last evening. I never worked it out myself. The report from the fire department did find something amiss with Collins' electrics which could easily have set off a fire. But Marigold gave me the distinct impression that she had started it. She sent me a note saying to meet her by the

371

lock. She wanted to hear that I hadn't "betrayed" her, as she put it, over that book and I was pleased as Punch' – he laughed, cynical for a moment about the innocent he had been – 'to be able to assure her that I hadn't and wouldn't. I saw myself as a sort of knight in shining armour who had saved her unsullied reputation by taking the blame on his own shoulders.'

'You were in love with her,' his guest interjected sharply.

He appeared faintly surprised. 'In love? I don't know. Captivated maybe. Can you be in love at eleven?'

I could, the woman who had been Lizzie Smith thought.

Aloud she said, 'Myself, I think children know more or at least better about love than adults. It's part of the magic for them. Look at *Tom's Midnight Garden*.'

He appeared to reflect on this. 'But Tom and Mrs Bartholomew aren't in love when they meet again in so-called real time.'

'They were as children, though.' This, after all, was her own ground. 'The love changes, as the time changes, but the book tells you clear as a bell that it survives because it was real.'

'I guess what got me,' he apologised, 'is how their affinity trumps time. The echoes in their DNA, as I see it, that lead to their meeting in her dreams.'

But she was still on her own line. 'Yes, but isn't that affinity the being-in-love that transcends time?'

'In that case' – he had found his position – 'I wasn't in love with Marigold. There was no affinity. I believed there was, or maybe wanted to, but there wasn't. Not really.'

'No,' she agreed, maybe almost ready at last to let it go.

'I suppose what it was' – she considered – 'what it was was that you were spellbound.'

He shrugged and for a moment she thought she had lost him but he only said, 'Yes, perhaps that was it. That night of the fire, when I met her she was in a very odd state and I was, frankly, frightened. She laughed, and this I'll never forget, she said, "Anyway, I've paid old Ginger-nut out for you over the foxes." I felt guilty at having been the unwitting cause of the fire, or thinking I was. I still don't know the truth of it.'

'The trouble is,' Elizabeth said, 'everything makes you feel guilty when you're a child, whether it's your fault or not.' Maybe more so when it's not.

'You know, I haven't thought about all this for years but I was thinking last night, I wonder if Marigold knew herself whether or not she started that fire.'

Elizabeth reflected. A memory was mistily rising: Marigold stopping her as she came out of her house and addressing her with a sudden matiness. 'Be a pal, Liz, and take this book back to Sam for me. Only he's out of bounds for me still, worse luck.'

'I think I may have been the unwitting messenger who delivered that note for you to meet that night. Was it in a book on chess?'

'I think it was. I'd forgotten that.' He laughed uneasily. 'I was so keen to impress Marigold with my prowess at chess. I don't think she was interested. Not at all, I suspect.'

'And there I was, *longing* for you to teach me.'

'I'm sorry, Lizzie. You'd have been a much better subject than Marigold.'

'I doubt it. I never had that sort of mind. Do you still play?'

'I do now. I didn't during the years of the protracted tantrum. It was Cathy, my wife, who got me playing again. The Minx is pretty ace at chess.'

Elizabeth, not quite attending though no stranger to grandparental pride, said, 'I'll tell you something I've never told anyone.'

He looked alarmed and she said, 'It's nothing serious, really.'

'Go on then.'

'I did steal a book.'

'From the library?'

'Mmm.'

She had had to screw her courage to the sticking point – feeling so to blame for all that had happened – but still she had gone to the library to say goodbye to Miss Blackwell. And the other woman, Mrs Harris, had been there in her place. She hadn't liked Mrs Harris, who laughed too much and wasn't really kind. Certainly not kind like Miss Blackwell.

Mrs Harris had been looking through a pile of books and when she had asked about Miss Blackwell's leaving Mrs Harris had said, 'Sorry, you've missed her,' in a tone which made you think she wasn't sorry a bit.

Then Mrs Harris had said, 'Miss Blackwell's left us her books. I'm trying to sort them now,' meaning she should go away and stop bothering her, and when Mrs Harris wasn't looking she had slipped one of the books from the pile into her school satchel – was that right? Yes, by then Nan had bought her the satchel.

'What was the book?' Sam asked.

'It was *Through the Looking-Glass*. Miss Blackwell's – Sylvia's,' she corrected herself, 'copy. She left her books to the library and I nicked it.'

'Lizzie Smith! I didn't know you had it in you.'

'I've got it still.'

'So you were a thief, after all.'

'I suppose I was.' She almost preened herself. 'Do you remember "Old Father William" on that old 11+ paper we did together?'

But he shook his head. 'I think I probably suppressed everything to do with the 11+.'

In the silence they each roamed the criss-crossing, overgrown paths of their childhood. Into Elizabeth's mind came lines from the poem that she had read long ago in the Poetry Corner of East Mole Library: *They shut the road through the woods/ Seventy years ago . . .*

'You know,' she said, looking around his room with its clean contemporary colours, the books and pots and carvings and jumble of pleasing paraphernalia, 'I am where I am because I got help from you and Sylvia, and you got help from your grandfather and Flee Crake –'

'And my wife,' he interrupted. 'She put up with a lot.'

But for the moment she wasn't interested in his ex. 'What I was thinking is that no one helped Marigold, not really.'

Reluctantly, for it is truly a task for the angels to surrender a grudge long held, she acknowledged that the brilliant copper-haired long-legged Marigold had been deprived in a way that by the grace of human kindness she and Sam had escaped.

'I would have helped her,' Sam said. 'I thought I had, covering up for her over the book. But that probably made her worse. Who knows?'

'If it's anyone's fault it's her parents',' Elizabeth suggested. 'Though according to you it was all down to her genes. But their marriage breaking down – breaking up? which is it? I never know – anyway, it can't have helped.'

'She told me once that her father was going to leave her mother and marry Sylvia.'

'But that wasn't true?'

'Wishful thinking, I guess. She told me she hated her own mother and she had this notion, I see now it was a child's fantasy, that Sylvia was going to be her mother in her real mother's place. She was full of how the three of them, she and her father and Sylvia, were all going to live together. She was so sure of it that I believed her. I was slightly envious.'

'We all believed her. It was that burning confidence she had. You know, it's a shame. If her parents did break up, as you say, Sylvia and Dr Bell might have made a match.'

'Sylvia asked me about him when I saw her in London,' Sam remembered.

'And?'

'I told her the Bells had split up and that Marigold had, you know, not exactly prospered. She seemed sad.'

'There you are'

'But she would have felt sad. She minded about us all, Sylvia.'

'I still think she and Dr Bell . . .' Elizabeth could see them in her mind's eye, the slight fair-haired woman with the grey-green eyes with the tall man in horn-rimmed specs, almost as if it was a memory she had forgotten or laid aside. In one of her books they would have found each other, finally, sometime, somewhere.

'We don't know, do we?' Sam said.

As with the other evenings, they had each settled on one of the pair of sofas which faced each other in his bright living room. Now, released by the growth of their new acquaintance, he succumbed to the late hour and the bottles of wine, flopping back full length along the sofa. 'You know what I think, Lizzie Smith? In the end, we don't know much.'

'I know that I'm a bit drunk, Sam Hedges.' For all that, she remained upright, spine erect, holding her core tight, as dictated by her granddaughter.

He smiled at her across the gap. 'Did *you* know that, according to Herodotus, the Persians debated all important decisions twice: once drunk and once sober? Flee Crake told me that once when I had the mother of all hangovers.'

'Which way round did they do it?'

'She never told me that.'

'I've not drunk so much since . . .' But she couldn't recall when she had last felt like this: out of herself but in herself – not deranged, or estranged but – she searched for a word for it – yes, rearranged. Maybe that's what the Persians had in mind. 'I doubt I'll be sober much before morning.'

There was a fractional pause while the ambiguous world of chance, which is a mingle of genes and character and circumstance and sometimes a rare flash of good luck, hovered about them, offering and withdrawing and offering again evanescent possibilities, alluring, perilous, disturbing, awaiting their cue to become a living element in their long interrupted tangled history.

Sam pulled himself up and sat, not quite looking at her. 'We could defer any debate until the morning, that is if you'd like, perhaps, maybe to stay . . .?'

Author's Note

The years I have spent as a novelist have taught me that there is no knowing how people will take one's books. And I truly believe that a book is finally made by its readers. Books should not be 'about' anything but if this book expresses any special interest it is the interest I acquired as a child in reading. *The Librarian* grew out of my experience as a young girl with a superb local library and a remarkable Children's Librarian, Miss Blackwell, whose surname I have stolen (I never knew her first name) for my protagonist. It is to Miss Blackwell that I owe many of the books and characters that have informed not only my writing life but probably my whole take on life, what seems to me to matter most, how I brought up my children and how I like to be now with my grandchildren. Several of the books I met through Miss Blackwell, and which appear in this book, became favourites of my two sons, one of whom, Rupert Kingfisher, is himself now a children's writer. These in turn have become favourites of their children, which goes to show how a book can spread influence through the generations. My eldest grandchild, Rowan, one of the dedicatees of this book, already writes her own stories which are fed from this source.

I have listed below those books that appear in *The Librarian*, many of which I first found in the Children's Library of my youth. The book that features most significantly in this story, however, is *Tom's Midnight Garden* by Philippa Pearce, which after reading her first book, *The Minnow on the Say* (one of Miss Blackwell's recommendations) I bought for myself with the birthday present of a ten-shilling book token when it first came out in 1958. It is still in my view one of the greatest children's books of all time. The following year, I bought *The Lantern Bearers*, the last in the great trilogy on Roman Britain by Rosemary Sutcliff, the first two volumes of which, *The Eagle of the Ninth* and *The Silver Branch*, were also Miss Blackwell recommendations, and *Warrior Scarlet*, which remains my favourite Sutcliff (though the competition is steep).

My Cumbrian uncle's father was a local schoolmaster and knew Beatrix Potter when she had removed to Cumbria and become better known as Mrs Heelis, champion sheep-farmer. It was on his editions of her books that before I started school I learned to read. I am for ever in Beatrix Potter's debt for so enhancing my vocabulary at a very young age and for her salutary example in the use of cadence.

My Friend Mr Leakey was written by the brilliant and eccentric Marxist geneticist J. B. S. Haldane, known to my parents through their membership of the Communist Party. His author's autobiography for this, his only children's, book is a model of how these things ought to read. I've included that too after the list below.

T. H. White, author of *The Once and Future King* quartet, taught my father English at school (in between bouts of drunkenness – Tim White's, not my father's). He gave my father the copy of *The Ill-made Knight* which my mother was reading the night before my birth and which I like to fancy thus somehow got into my system. Sadly, the copy was destroyed later in a fire at Barlaston Hall in Staffordshire, where my father was warden for the WEA trade-union college and where we lived for the first few years of my life.

It was through T. H. White that I met another author who has been a lifelong favourite of mine, Sylvia Townsend Warner, whose Christian name I have borrowed for my protagonist. While researching her matchless biography of Tim White, she came to interview my father, as one of his former pupils. By that time I had read her first novel, *Lolly Willowes*, and amused its author, who was as warm, witty and sharp as her books, by telling her that as a child – I was all of fourteen – I had wanted to grow up to be a witch. (She paid me the compliment of saying that I seemed to her 'promising material'.)

There are also books I borrowed from the library which don't feature in *The Librarian* and which I still think of with nostalgic fondness. I raced through the Sadler's Wells ballet books, for example, which were tosh, but engrossing tosh for a would-be ballerina, and two books I borrowed over and over again but never owned, *The Rock Pool* and *Mossy Green Theatre*. The latter, like *Mr Leakey*, is out of print and should be republished by an enterprising publisher to enchant new young readers.

One last word: Miss Blackwell had a fierce dislike of Enid Blyton and I have given this prejudice to her namesake. I mention this as people often imagine that a character's views reflect those of the author, just as they imagine that what a character does is what the author has done or might do. And I suppose that this may sometimes be the case. My editor, for example, was concerned that the views expressed by Dee in this book about her husband's sexual exploits might be misread as my own views and cause some outrage. I reassured her that my readers would have a sufficient grasp of my interest in human blind spots and the very different moral climate of the fifties not to make that mistake. And by the same token, I don't share Miss Blackwell's or Sylvia's opinion of Enid Blyton. While her books are not lastingly important to me, as a child I enjoyed them and I still think that her Famous Five books in particular are good in their own way. It was a great spur to my enthusiasm that my atheist Socialist parents, otherwise unusually tolerant, refused to have Enid Blyton in the house and, as a consequence, I was obliged to read the Famous Five round at a friend's, where I was also allowed Chocolate Spread sandwiches made with sliced white bread. My parents also outlawed the *Beano* and the *Dandy* on the, I now suspect, spurious grounds that the printers of these comics were forbidden to be unionised – happily, I was able to read those in wet playtimes at school. This had the interesting effect that for many years sliced white bread, Enid Blyton, Dennis the Menace and God formed an unholy alliance in my subconscious, one that I naturally wanted to be part of. I have lost my taste for sliced white bread and chocolate spread but I still have time for Enid Blyton, who got children to read who might not have done so otherwise and for that alone she deserves praise. But in any case, tastes differ, thank goodness, and not even the best children's librarian is, or should be expected to be, perfect.

Recommended reading from East Mole Library:

E. Nesbit, *The Story of the Treasure Seekers* and collected children's works

Tove Jansson, *Comet in Moominland* and all the Finn Family Moomintroll books

Ernest Thompson Seton, *The Trail of the Sandhill Stag*

Robert Louis Stevenson, *Treasure Island*

Beatrix Potter, collected works

Gwynedd Rae, Mary Plain books

Rudyard Kipling, *Just So Stories, Puck of Pook's Hill*

Mark Twain, *Huckleberry Finn*

George MacDonald, *The Princess and Curdie, At the Back of the North Wind*

Erich Kästner, *Emil and the Detectives*

Eric Linklater, *The Wind on the Moon*

Munro Leaf, *The Story of Ferdinand*

Andrew Lang, The Blue, Brown, Olive and Lilac Fairy Books

Arthur Ransome, *Swallows and Amazons* and following series

Mary Norton, *The Borrowers, The Borrowers Afield*

P. L. Travers, *Mary Poppins, Mary Poppins Comes Back, Mary Poppins Opens the Door*

Norman Lindsay, *The Magic Pudding*

Norman Hunter, *The Incredible Adventures of Professor Branestawm*

Leila Berg, *Trust Chunky, Little Pete Stories*

Philippa Pearce, *The Minnow on the Say, Tom's Midnight Garden*

Susan Coolidge, *What Katy Did*, *What Katy Did at School*, *What Katy Did Next*

C. S. Lewis, the collected Narnia

Jack London, *White Fang*

Noel Streatfeild, *Ballet Shoes*, *White Boots*

T. H. White, *The Once and Future King*

Lewis Carroll, *Alice's Adventures in Wonderland*, *Through the Looking-Glass, and What Alice Found There*

Geoffrey Trease, *Cue for Treason*

Charles Dickens, *A Tale of Two Cities*

Dodie Smith, *I Capture the Castle*

Dr Seuss, *How the Grinch Stole Christmas*

L. M. Montgomery, Anne of Green Gables series

J. B. S. Haldane, *My Friend Mr Leakey*

PROFESSOR HALDANE has been used for experiments since he was about three years old, when his father started taking blood out of him. Some of the things that have happened to him are nearly as queer as the things that happen in this book. For example, during the war he was working on how to get out of sunken submarines, and some of the work was done in air that had been squeezed up so tight that he could not even move his hand through it very easily. He thinks a lot of the magicians in old days were only doing, or trying to do, what scientists and engineers do now, and that science can be more exciting than magic ever was.

He is 55 years old, and a communist. Besides experiments to find out how he works, his scientific work has mainly been about heredity. He hasn't felt like writing stories for children since about 1933, when Hitler got power in Germany, and the world became a nastier place. But he hopes the world will get nicer again now that we have won the war; and then perhaps he will feel like writing more stories. The nearest things to a dragon that he has in his house are two she-newts called Flosshilde and Berenice. His cat is white and deaf, but she can turn somersaults. He is bald, weighs about 15 stone and is fond of swimming.

THE CLEANER OF CHARTRES
SALLEY VICKERS

A compelling story of darkness and light, of traumatic loss and second chances, *The Cleaner of Chartres* tells of the mysterious and elusive Agnes Morel whose little acts of kindness around a rural French cathedral touch the lives of others with consequences both good and ill. But when her tragic past is exposed, Agnes must face up to the truth of her origins.

'A lovely book . . . wise at heart and filled with colourful characters'

Joanne Harris

'Vickers sees with a clear eye and writes with a light hand and she knows how the world works. She's a presence worth cherishing'

Philip Pullman

'Subtle and ultimately joyous'

Sunday Times

THE BOY WHO COULD SEE DEATH
SALLEY VICKERS

In this collection of stories Salley Vickers, master of the uncanny and the unexpected, explores bereavement and betrayal, closely guarded secrets, unforeseen endings and decidedly odd beginnings. From the woman who finds solace in a haunted graveyard to the artist obsessed by a wolf roaming loose in a park, the crown prince who becomes a great playwright to the refugee whose history lies hidden in an old sofa, we enter lives in which ordinary surfaces conceal dark and often disturbing depths.

'Tremendous, unsettling, brilliantly creepy'

Independent

'Brilliantly realized, pricelessly entertaining'

Observer

'Compelling and often startling'

Daily Express

COUSINS

SALLEY VICKERS

Will Tye and his cousin Cele are kindred spirits who have grown up together. But their very closeness keeps them at a troubled distance until the night that Will recklessly embarks on a misadventure with devastating consequences.

It's a tragedy that engulfs three generations of the Tye family, laying bare dangerous secrets that stretch as far back as the Second World War. It also opens up new wounds, leaving the Tye family with agonizing questions about retribution for the days, months and years to come.

Yet for Will and Cele it cements a bond like no other - a bond that will only be finally broken by an act of exceptional courage and self sacrifice, one which imperils them both but leads at last to a tentative resolution.

'Wonderful. Vickers spins a spellbinding account of a family in distress'

Elizabeth Strout

'Vickers lays bare the inner workings of one family, possibly every family, with an often disconcerting clarity'

The Times

'A fascinating exploration of family love'

Guardian

GRANDMOTHERS
SALLEY VICKERS

This heartwarming new novel by Salley Vickers, publishing in autumn 2019, follows four grandmothers - Blanche, who can't seem to stop stealing things from the local pharmacy; Minna, who just wants a quiet life in her shepherd's hut, though the local children have other ideas; Cherry, who's adjusting to life in a care home; and Nan, whose favourite occupation is researching funerals - whose lives and grandchildren become unexpectedly entangled.

'Vickers writes of relationships with undaunted clarity'

Adam Phillips

'No one can dig down into the shrouded recesses of the human heart quite as forensically as Vickers'

Sunday Times

He just wanted a decent book to read ...

Not too much to ask, is it? It was in 1935 when Allen Lane, Managing Director of Bodley Head Publishers, stood on a platform at Exeter railway station looking for something good to read on his journey back to London. His choice was limited to popular magazines and poor-quality paperbacks – the same choice faced every day by the vast majority of readers, few of whom could afford hardbacks. Lane's disappointment and subsequent anger at the range of books generally available led him to found a company – and change the world.

'We believed in the existence in this country of a vast reading public for intelligent books at a low price, and staked everything on it'
Sir Allen Lane, 1902–1970, founder of Penguin Books

The quality paperback had arrived – and not just in bookshops. Lane was adamant that his Penguins should appear in chain stores and tobacconists, and should cost no more than a packet of cigarettes.

Reading habits (and cigarette prices) have changed since 1935, but Penguin still believes in publishing the best books for everybody to enjoy. We still believe that good design costs no more than bad design, and we still believe that quality books published passionately and responsibly make the world a better place.

So wherever you see the little bird – whether it's on a piece of prize-winning literary fiction or a celebrity autobiography, political tour de force or historical masterpiece, a serial-killer thriller, reference book, world classic or a piece of pure escapism – you can bet that it represents the very best that the genre has to offer.

Whatever you like to read – trust Penguin.